A FALLEN GOD

A FALLEN GOD

MICHAEL J CHAPLIN

The Book Guild Ltd

First published in Great Britain in 2024 by
The Book Guild Ltd
Unit E2 Airfield Business Park,
Harrison Road, Market Harborough,
Leicestershire. LE16 7UL
Tel: 0116 2792299
www.bookguild.co.uk
Email: info@bookguild.co.uk
Twitter: @bookguild

Cover art: A FALLEN GOD © Patricia Betaudier Chaplin

This work is entirely fictitious and bears no resemblance to any persons living or dead.

Typeset in 11pt Minion Pro

Printed and bound in the UK by TJ Books LTD, Padstow, Cornwall

ISBN 978 1915853 493

British Library Cataloguing in Publication Data.
A catalogue record for this book is available from the British Library.

I dedicate this book to my beloved wife, Patricia Betaudier Chaplin, with whom I have shared over fifty years of my life; the person who more than anyone or anything inspired me to write this novel, and who I feel on every page visibly or invisibly keeping the story alive with her unbounded spirit...

PART 1

PART I

1

THE SHAWL

Brittany, AD 1209

When he first saw her earlier that morning, it was as if a particle of sun had fallen through the grey sky that was covering the village square.

He was standing bent over the railing of the church porch, looking down at her. She was on her hands and knees, arranging her shawls on a blanket spread out over the cobblestones to display her wares. But it was her feline body moving under her red silk dress that Marc was looking at when she twisted around to stare up at him.

In later years, Marc was often to reflect that maybe something in their eyes had joined in recognition at that moment, that some awareness had awakened in both of them long enough so that they could peer at one another, as if into a mirror, and then had fallen asleep again.

And yet the young man who was staring down at her from the church porch did not notice or feel any of this, so taken as he was by her striking beauty, by the golden streaks of curls in her bushy brown hair, her mouth half open exposing the gap between two of her front teeth, and by the look of surprise in her black eyes.

And now, as they were riding across the moor in the direction of the cliffs where his ancestors had built a fortress, he could not stop talking.

It was as he was telling her about his father's kingdom and its relationship with the church that he mentioned Eudice, 'the Star'.

'Who is this Eudice?' she asked, her interest suddenly awakened by the name. 'And why did they call him "the Star"?'

'It was because of the appearance of a star with a long tail of fire trailing behind it in the sky, just at the time when he started preaching in the forest,' Marc answered.

'Was he a heretic?' she asked.

'No, Eudice was not a heretic. He was the chief of a band of brigands who lived in the forest of Brocieland some sixty years ago. To some he was a saint, to some he was a villain.'

'Why a villain?'

'Because he also called himself "The Messiah of The Final Days" and rechristened his followers with the names of angels and apostles. They would raid monasteries and churches and live off their bounty, some of which they would redistribute to the poor and needy and thus recruit new members to their ranks. This so-called rebellion against the Church soon spread beyond the forests of the Languedoc and Aquitaine. Their success was due in part to the tolerance of the princes, lords and monarchs who were themselves discontented with the Gregorian reform that gave the clergy greater independence from their secular power.'

'What became of him?' she asked.

'He was caught, arrested, declared insane and imprisoned, where he died a few years later.'

Marc was now looking at her inquisitively. 'So who are you running away from?'

'What makes you think that I am running away?' she answered defensively.

'Because when I asked you your name, when we were bargaining over the price of the shawl, you didn't seem to want to answer. I got the feeling then that you must be trying to escape from someone.'

She stared at the vast stretch of emptiness before them. Far away she could see a structure sticking up out of the ground, breaking the flat monotony of the moor.

'Is that your fortress?'

'Yes.'

Beyond it, a long line of vapour floated over the horizon.

'My name is Isolt. I was hoping I could sell enough shawls in the market this morning to pay for my passage on a boat for Ireland. But I only sold three shawls, and that wasn't nearly enough.

'But you're right,' she added after a moment's silence. 'I am running away from someone.'

'Who? Your husband?' Marc asked.

'No, I'm not married.'

'Then who?' Marc insisted.

'Oh, I don't know. My father,' she said impatiently, and then, in a softer tone, she added, 'Or at least that's what he claims to be.'

'And your mother?' Marc asked.

'She died giving birth to me. But then again, I only have my father's word for that as well.'

It was Marc's turn to stare at the cloud floating over the horizon far ahead of them beyond the moor. The sun was turning red and it seemed to have ignited a vision, a dream that he could have her all to himself out there in his fortress. The awakening of this dream made him feel bold, as if he could escape from who he really was.

'So tell me more about this man who claims to be your father,' he said.

'No,' she answered firmly. 'I don't want to.'

'Well, at least tell me why you are running away from him,' Marc insisted.

'I think he wants to kill me.'

Isolt pulled her mount to a halt. Marc stopped his horse as well and turned to look back at her.

'Do you know why I'm out here on this moor, following you to your fortress?' she asked.

'Tell me,' Marc said.

'It's because you threw this shawl over my shoulders after buying it. You said that some of my beauty would fall onto it like drops of rain, showering it with a special kind of charm that would entice people to buy one just like it. I can't say that it actually worked as you said it would, but your words showered me with a charm of your own, and that's why I'm here on the moor with you.'

'I was spellbound by your beauty,' Marc said.

'Well, if you really want me to follow you back to your fortress, there is one thing you must promise me, and that is to never speak about my father and not to mention his name ever again.'

'But I don't even know his name!' Marc protested.

'Good,' she said, 'all the better. So are you going to do this for me?'

Marc could feel a sharp pain moving up his spine from having to twist around with his arms and legs, fighting to hold his horse still so as not to lose sight of her as she talked, the intensity of her black eyes holding him in thrall. And all at once the pain ceased to cause him any discomfort as it became part of the whole picture, of who he was to her and of who she was to him, as if evoked in a fresco on a church wall. And you could not extract the pain from a picture that seemed more like a vision now.

2

THE HUNT

Three years had passed since Jean of Brittany's departure for Jerusalem. But, as the vicissitudes of fate would have it, what would come to be known as the Fourth Crusade never did lead him to the holy city.

Boniface de Montferrat, under the orders of Pope Innocent III, had been placed at the head of this army of knights and foot soldiers to reconquer Jerusalem. On the journey he had decided to ally himself with the Doge of Venice and sail, instead, towards the Adriatic Coast and the town of Zara. When they had captured and plundered all its riches, encouraged by the success of this brutal act of vandalism they then moved eastwards through what was left of the Byzantine Empire. Finally reaching Constantinople, they partially burnt down and sacked the great city before moving on to Nicaea, where they set up a new Latin Empire of the East.

News of these events took months to reach Brittany. However, from what could be read in the letters that Jean sent to his father, the king, he was now a very rich and powerful man who held a high position in the army of this new empire. This news pleased his father but did nothing to soothe his worries about the situation in his own kingdom, for every year that passed seemed to rob the king of strength, and resourceful as he was he knew only too well that the little reserves he had left could not last for very long. In the last letter the king had written to Jean, he implored him to return home, explaining that the time had come for him to find a wife from the region's nobility that would help strengthen the kingdom he would soon inherit.

Over a year had gone by since the king sent the letter and no answer had yet come back. Deeply troubled, he kept telling himself that his son must be on his way back. Often he would climb to the top of the Eastern Tower and wait for him. Gasping for breath as he scaled the last steps of the spiral staircase, he would lean over the wall and stare out over the ploughed fields, meadows and woods, hoping at last to see a man on a horse riding towards the castle.

On a few occasions he'd had such a vision and felt his heart swell with excitement, forgetting how tired and out of breath he was in anticipation of the rejoicing that would surely follow. But joy turned to deep disappointment as the approaching rider turned out not to be his son.

It was after another such disappointment that the king, turning away from the eastern wall in disgust, walked across to the other rampart and stared out to the west, beyond the market town of Corsan to where the moor began, reaching right out to the tip of the peninsula where his other son, Marc, lived, where the cliffs dropped down into the ocean, where the sun set and called forth the night. That other son who had secretly married a Saracen and lived with her in his remote fortress. The son who had no right to get married because of his horse-like ears, because of the danger that this shameful curse might be carried down into the next generation of their bloodline.

It was perhaps because he felt increasingly old and tired and missed the support and comfort of his son Jean that the king began to have certain regrets about Marc. After all, he could hardly be blamed for having such strangely shaped ears. If there was a fault to be placed anywhere then it would not be on his son's shoulders, but on those of his great-great-grandfather, who, as legend had it, had once burnt down a whole village with all its inhabitants boarded into their houses during one of his raids along the Cornish coast.

For this unspeakable deed a local witch had cast a spell on him, declaring that one of his descendants would enter this world with a very unusual birthmark, and that when all the members of his tribe would swear allegiance to him, after he had been given the crown and sceptre consecrating him as chief of their tribe, the kingdom that they had created for themselves would be taken away from them for ever.

But how could he explain all this to his son now? It was all too late, he thought, as he stared at the hill obscuring Corsan and the moor beyond it, at the far edge of which was the fortress where Marc lived. A strange feeling overcame him, a feeling as though his life was gradually reaching its end. It was as if he were standing at the helm of a ship that was slowly being blown away, out over the moor and beyond, over that great expanse of water that stretched from below the cliffs to a distant horizon where the sun would set and he would fall into the abyss and never return.

'I could make peace with him,' he whispered to himself, as if to exorcise the terrible sense of death that had invaded his heart. It wasn't too late for that. So why didn't he try?

It wasn't only Marc that he wished to see, he realised, but he was also curious to meet his wife, this strange Saracen. She apparently had not been frightened off by his ears since she had given birth to his daughter and had agreed to become his wife, despite knowing full well that they could never move into the castle as he had signed away his right to succeed his father on the throne of their kingdom, which would be passed down to his younger brother, Jean.

She must have known this, the king thought, because Marc would have told her. His son was too much of a coward to trick her into his bed. He hadn't the stomach for this kind of boldness. He even suspected that he might secretly be a Christian, like all the other cowards that adhered to that religion.

Yes, he would be interested in meeting this Saracen, who he had heard was quite beautiful, on top of everything else that was whispered about her…

*

It was a beautiful sunny day. Marc sat by the bedroom window, reading his favourite book and occasionally allowing himself to be distracted by the voices in the courtyard below. Isolt sat on a bench under the linden tree, keeping an eye on Kore, who was two years old now and sitting nearby playing with a cat. Once she managed to catch the creature's tail so that it hissed at her and her mother called out, telling her to stop bothering it.

Gauvin was unloading the wood he had gathered in the cart and was stacking it up against the wall near the door leading into the stables. The old knight had once fought alongside Marc's father and was now living with his wife, Brangien, in the fortress.

'Come, Maman, come…' Kore beckoned to her mother, wanting her to help catch the cat so that she could stroke it.

'I'm busy,' Isolt replied. She had a pile of pea pods beside her on the bench, and she was emptying out the peas into a bowl.

Marc could hear a slight whisper of impatience or frustration in her voice, but it was immediately smothered in love, tenderness and joy.

He closed the book and placed it down on the windowsill. For some reason Isolt disliked him reading this book, St Augustine's *City of God*. If she caught him sitting somewhere, absorbed in it, she would always make fun of him.

'What can you possibly get out of reading that book?' she once asked. 'What does it give you that's so special? Can it give you more pleasure than I can?'

No, Marc thought, this book was certainly no match for her, but perhaps this was why he needed to search in such books, stolen from his father's library in the castle, which was stacked with them, all stolen in raids on other castles long ago by ancestors who, like his father, by all accounts could not even read.

So perhaps he, Marc, who could read, needed to search in books like this one for something he could make his own, something to hold up against the raw brutality of his ancestors – and the fiery beauty of his wife.

For his ancestors and his wife had both come into this world endowed with natural gifts, while he, to stand out from the rest of the mob, had been born with a pair of furry ears. Perhaps in more ancient times these might have been considered something special that placed him apart from his fellow men – a sign pointing to some special, exceptional destiny – but not in the sad world he lived in today. No, they were something he had to hide under his thick mop of curly hair, for any feature that was considered bestial, less than human, was diabolical and automatically associated with evil in the minds of the good Christians who had taken over the world.

Sharpo, their dog, was barking down in the courtyard. Marc stood up and leant out of the window. Someone was tying up a horse to the iron rod sunk into a large stone resting just beyond the open doors.

'There's a man from the castle who wants to see you,' Isolt shouted up to his window a few minutes later.

'This is for you, sir,' the young man said when Marc walked out into the courtyard. 'It's a letter from the king. I'm to wait here and carry back your answer.'

Marc unrolled the parchment and immediately recognised his friend Forsin the midget's handwriting. He began to read. When he had finished, he rolled up the parchment and stared blankly into space for a moment.

'Well, what does it say?' Isolt asked.

Marc turned to the messenger. 'Can you wait here for a moment? I have to talk to my wife.' He took Isolt by the hand and walked her over to the far side of the courtyard, by the stables. He moved up close to her and leant against the wall.

'He's inviting us to the castle,' he said, almost in a whisper.

Isolt looked at him, her eyes wide open with surprise. 'Well, it's certainly taken years for that to happen,' she said. 'I wonder what's got into him?'

'I don't know,' Marc answered. 'I'm not even sure if we should go.'

'Oh, don't be so silly! Of course we should go.'

'He's organised a hunt and he's invited all the lords, ladies and knights in the kingdom to set up camp at the castle next Friday,' Marc said apprehensively.

'Of course we must go,' Isolt repeated. 'Come on! Do it for me.'

For a moment he just stood looking at her, listening to the distant sound of the waves breaking on the rocks beneath the cliff beyond the fortress wall. It was the sound that had accompanied their daily life out there on the moor, sometimes louder, sometimes softer, depending on the whims of the wind. And suddenly the thought of ever losing her became unbearable, she who had so enriched his life that if she were ever to leave him she would take the sound of those waves with her, and the fortress and the moor would become as empty as a shell washed up onto the shore below.

'What's wrong?' she asked.

'Of course we are going!' he replied.

Isolt smiled and her whole face lit up. 'You're wonderful!' she said. 'I love you!'

*

A horse-drawn cart made its way past the brightly coloured tents pitched near the moat that circled the castle. Horses were grazing on the grass between the tents, and dogs barking their false alarms. Footmen, young knights and soldiers went about their business, building fires, brushing horses, polishing boots, or just standing and chatting in small groups.

Marc looked up and saw the high tower looming above them as they approached the gate. He rode with the reins in his hands, Isolt beside him wearing a brown hat, her long, streaked curls falling loosely onto her shoulders. Kore and Brangien were behind them on a mattress.

Isolt smiled, her shining face lighting up the forbidding greyness of the arched entrance as they rode over the drawbridge.

It was clear that the crowd had been waiting for them as the gathered guests lowered their voices or stopped talking altogether. The king was busy with a favoured group while the queen, at his side, patiently listened to their conversation. She looked up to see Marc, Isolt and Kore approaching, and nudged her husband.

'Ah, Marc!' the king exclaimed, opening his arms. Marc stepped up to him and they embraced before the king stepped back to look at his son, holding him by the shoulders with his outstretched arms. Marc could tell that his father was looking for something familiar, something of his own in his son that would feed him with hope for the future. But there was clearly nothing new, nothing that shone through into his soul as he stared at him. The frustration was felt on both sides, something deep and unexplored that neither of them wanted to touch. So the king looked past his son, to the woman who was standing waiting.

'And this is your lovely wife,' he said, as something seemed to harden in his eyes as he let go of Marc's shoulders. 'I understand now why you have kept her locked away at the far tip of the moor for these past three years. Such a fine-looking lady would not be safe here at the castle with all the ruffians we have running loose. I'd have to go to war against my neighbours just to keep all our young men away from her!'

There was a loud outburst of laughter in the hall. The queen left the king's side and walked over to Isolt. 'Don't pay any attention to him, my dear,' she said. 'He is just getting his own back on his son for having stayed away for so long.'

She leant towards their daughter, whom Isolt was holding in her arms, and stroked her forehead. 'And this beautiful girl must be Kore? What a charming little lady. Do you think she will let me hold her in my arms for a moment?'

'Do you want to let the queen carry you?' Isolt asked her daughter.

'You can call me Isa,' the queen said to Kore. 'Isabelle is rather long-winded for a little girl like you. Do you want to let me hold you for a while?'

As the queen stretched out, Kore reached towards her and let herself be taken in her grandmother's arms. 'Come!' the queen said to Isolt. 'Let's go and show her to some of my friends.'

Marc found himself standing alone beside his father, who was now staring at him with an impatient look of barely suppressed anger. Marc recognised the look. He's already regretting having invited me here, he thought.

It was Ganelon, Marc's uncle and one of the lords who had been talking with the king, who broke the silence. 'So tell us, Marc. How do you fill your days out there on the moor?'

'Well, now I have a wife and daughter to look after,' Marc said. 'And when I am not busy with them, I spend a lot of my time reading.'

'Reading!' Ganelon exclaimed with evident surprise. 'What on earth for?'

'To learn,' Marc said.

'The best way to learn is to get off your arse and do something,' exclaimed the king. 'Not to sit down and read about it.' He looked away from Marc and resumed the conversation he'd been having with his companions before his son's arrival had interrupted it.

Marc found himself staring across at the group of people who had closed around Isolt, his mother and Kore, and hesitated over whether or not to join them. He had quietly slipped away from his father and was standing alone in the middle of the hall, feeling a little lost and rather ridiculous.

'So, is any of this familiar? Or had you completely forgotten what it looked like?'

Marc looked down and saw his old friend Forsin, the dwarf who oversaw the administration of the castle, gazing up at him.

'Thank God you're here!' exclaimed Marc. 'Where have you been hiding?'

'Some of us have to work, you know,' Forsin said with a smile.

'Well, I'm glad you're here. You're the only bit of furniture I do recognise, to tell you the truth.'

'And did the king give you a good hiding for staying away for so long?' Forsin asked.

'He tried.'

'I see that a lot of good-looking young men have gathered around your wife. I'd be careful, if I were you.'

Marc laughed. 'My father tried to scare me with the same kind of warning. So what do you think has got into him? Why did he suddenly decide to invite us?'

Forsin shrugged. 'I don't know. I suppose that with your brother being away in Constantinople he's feeling lonely and misses having a son at his side.'

'Don't be silly,' Marc said. 'I'm hardly the one to take my brother's place in his heart. We've only talked for a minute and he's already started getting angry with me. I mean, just look at him.'

They turned to look towards the king. Though he was talking to the group of men surrounding him, he was staring in their direction with a frown on his face.

'You have to understand him; he's getting old and I think that he's really beginning to feel his age,' Forsin said. Marc could feel the warmth and respect in his voice as he spoke.

There were more people now slowly filling all the chairs lined up at the tables along both sides of the hall, with a lot of polite pushing and shoving as each noble family made sure that there were enough chairs for all their clan. Those already in their places were laughing and talking loudly, as if trying to draw attention not only to themselves but to the fact that they were comfortably seated at the top of the hall, near to the king and his family.

What a ridiculous comedy, Marc thought, pleased that he was no longer part of it. He already regretted that he had let Isolt persuade him to accept his father's invitation. They were happy out there on the moor and did not need to be part of this!

But no sooner had he thought this than he heard a voice that seemed to be speaking distinctly to him. 'If you are in love with being in love,' it said, 'then you had better shut yourself away with her in the fortress. But if you think you can really love her, then you can only do this out here in the world amongst your fellow men.'

Suddenly he felt that the people who belonged to this noisy crowd were no different from him, or from Isolt; that for a moment his love for her had descended to the common denominator that brought them all together, had spread its wings to include all of them in his heart, and he realised that it was this that had produced the strange light that seemed to be shining in the hall.

What was happening to him?

He realised that Isolt was beside him, asking him to follow her.

'I have just put Kore to bed. Brangien is looking after her.' She took Marc's hand and pulled him across to the other end of the hall, where two men and their lady friends were waiting.

Donoalin and Godoine were both knights who had owned no land, and so had become professional soldiers who sold their services to the king. Marie and Solene, their lady friends, were both from Port Saint Marie. Isolt had met them in the great hall and they had invited her and Marc to join their company for the feast.

Marc immediately took a liking to both men and their easy-going, carefree attitude to life. As for Marie and Solene, they were pretty, funny and very friendly. At some point in the evening, Isolt asked Solene and Marie if they were going to take part in the hunt. The two girls laughed, saying they had no horses of their own and that their bodies were already very sore from riding behind Donoalin and Godoine for half a day. Donoalin looked at Isolt and asked her if she intended to take part.

'Yes, of course!' she replied.

She had already told Marc of her intention and he had kept quiet, knowing that if he tried to stop her it would only make her even more determined and defiant.

'What about Kore?' was all he could say in weak protestation.

'I'm sure Brangien won't mind looking after her. She is only too eager to spend time with her,' Isolt said.

'And we'd be very pleased to lend a hand if she needs any help,' Marie added.

'Well!' Donoalin exclaimed. 'I have been on quite a few hunts since I've been here but I have never seen a lady ride in any of them. This should be fun. I can't wait to see everyone's faces tomorrow morning when you join us on your horse.'

Marie asked Isolt how well she could ride. As she replied that she had ridden a horse up and down Italy and right across Europe, her four companions sat staring at her as if she were a strange, unknown creature that had been blown into the castle by the wind.

Marc looked at his wife as she talked to her new friends. The great dining hall echoed with the roars and guffaws of the guests enjoying the good food and ale, all of whom were clearly looking forward to the next day. He could see that she was happy too, and that was all he wanted, really – to make her happy.

Anyway, once they were lying in bed together what would he care about tomorrow?

Later that night, Marc lay open-eyed, staring at the half moon as it slowly made its way across the patch of sky outside the window. He could hear Isolt's soft, regular breathing as she lay sleeping beside him. She was his world, the one he clung to, because only she could give any sense to his life. She was the light that cast the dark shadows out of his heart.

And yet there had been that voice that he had heard speak to him as he stood under the threshold leading into the dining hall, staring at all these guests who made up the world that had banished him from the castle. The voice that told him that, unless he was able to include them in the love he felt for Isolt, he would remain merely infatuated with love itself, with the sensation it brought into his life, but he would not be able to love Isolt, to truly love her in the way she needed to be loved. For her love extended beyond him into the world around him, and if he could not do the same it would be as if he were trying to extract her from that world. Then the love she felt for him would no longer feel like a doorway leading her deeper into the world, but would become more like a wall shutting her away from the world. And then she would feel that he was trying to suffocate her.

This voice must surely have come from the spirit of St Augustine, talking to him through the pages of the book stolen from his father's library, which had itself been pillaged in turn from another castle by one of his ancestors; this voice, this spirit, that could at last speak out and say what it had to say to the first of this long lineage of illiterate brigands who could actually read the book, and had managed, with its words, if only for a brief moment, to light up the dining hall with the power of their truth.

Was this an omen of what was about to fall on them all and shatter their kingdom? Marc wondered, but as sleep drew a thick blanket over his thoughts, fears and desires, the fear left him.

*

When Isolt appeared in the morning, she had her hair tied up in a bun and tucked under her brown hat. She was wearing a long jacket that hung down from her shoulders to the top of her thighs, with tight pantaloons and boots.

'Is that Isolt?' Godoine asked in disbelief as she rode over the drawbridge and headed towards the gathering of noblemen on their horses and the barking dogs.

'Yes, that's her,' Marc said with deep resignation, as if he rather wished it weren't. He had seen that outfit in her room, though he had never seen her wear it. She had told him that her father had bought it for her because he said it was sometimes useful for a woman to be able to disguise herself as a man. She had laughed and said that, ironically, it had come in quite useful for she had worn it when she crossed through forests and wild stretches of land on her own, on her way up through Italy and France while she was escaping from him.

Feeling uncomfortable and embarrassed, as Marc watched his wife riding up to him he realised that this was one of those moments when she was way beyond the reach of reason and already totally beyond his control. He knew that these moments were always linked in some way to that mysterious and obscure figure he was never allowed to talk about – her father.

'Ah, what a sight!' the king exclaimed. 'Finally we have a woman bold enough to dress up in our garb and join us in our most uncouth of sports; other than waging war on each other, of course. And she is going to ride at her husband's side, who I know has no taste in his heart for this kind of activity. Maybe you will succeed, my dear, where I have failed, in teaching him how to behave like a nobleman.'

'He is kind and gentle, which I would certainly count amongst the qualities of nobility,' she replied. 'As for me, sire, I would like to thank you for accepting me in your party this morning.'

'Well, I didn't really have any choice in the matter, since you are already here amongst us, uninvited,' said the king. 'But if you wish to thank me, at least wait until the hunt is over, for your heart may not be of the same disposition by then.'

Isolt was about to say something, but Marc reached over and squeezed her arm. She turned round and looked at him with rage burning in her eyes.

'What?' she asked.

'Don't answer him!' Marc said between his teeth.

When the party was complete, they started out towards the Moroi forest, led by the pack of howling dogs, and as they rode Isolt asked Marc why he had stopped her from responding to his father.

'You don't know what he's really like,' Marc replied. 'It's best to let him have the last word.'

'But why does he always try to humiliate you?' she asked.

'My ears,' Marc answered. 'You may not have noticed yesterday, but the first thing he looked at when he saw Kore was her ears. He wanted to make sure the curse I carried has not been passed on to her.'

'You never told me that your ears were from a curse,' said Isolt, surprised. 'You mean somebody actually cast a spell on you? Is that what you're saying?'

Marc hesitated for a moment before replying. 'Yes, it has to be a curse. How else would I have been given such ears?'

'Do you know the reason?'

'No,' Marc answered, but he could see that Isolt knew he was lying, that he didn't want to talk about it.

'Do you think your father does?'

'If he does, he's not about to tell anyone. Anyway, it's not going to change anything. I don't know why I bothered coming on this trip,' said Marc, suddenly angry.

As Isolt stared at him, Marc could see her frustration.

'Sometimes I really don't understand you,' she said. 'Your ears are not your own doing. You can't let him blame you for something like that. It's not right. And yet you don't seem to want to stand up for yourself in front of him.'

Marc did not answer. It was as if a distance had placed itself between them, and the spell of complicity that had brought them together had suddenly been broken. For the first time he thought that for them to really love each other, perhaps they would really have to be out here amongst their fellow men. A place where division, misunderstanding and confusion were so much part of the daily diet that they were taken for granted, and it was love, true love, that was the exception, something close to a miracle. But he could not contemplate even the slightest suggestion that they might be drifting apart without triggering a terrible feeling of panic and alarm that shook the very foundations on which his existence was based.

'Why are you holding on to the reins of your horse as if you were hanging off the top of a cliff?' Isolt asked with a smile, and just that smile was enough to change night into day inside him.

'I don't know,' Marc answered with an embarrassed laugh.

Soon they had reached the edge of the forest and as they entered the shade under the cover of its foliage the dogs fell silent and began turning in all directions, their noses to the ground. They advanced in this manner, deeper into the forest, followed by the party of men – and Isolt – on their horses. All of a sudden one of the dogs picked up a scent and began to yelp and rush forward. The other dogs, barking in unison, rushed after it. The hunters stirred their horses into a gallop and followed the pack.

For the rest of the morning they pounded through the forest, stopping every now and then when the dogs lost the scent. Then they would surge forward once more, ducking under branches as they followed the dogs chasing after an as yet invisible creature fleeing before them.

At first Isolt was engrossed in the excitement of it all, the danger as the horses ran close up against each other, dodging between the trees, the high-pitched baying of the dogs leading them deeper and deeper into the forest. But by the morning's end she was beginning to feel quite dizzy with exhaustion.

Fortunately for her she was not the only one to feel this way. The creature they had been pursuing, after running ahead of them all this time, must have sensed that its reserves of strength were reaching their end and decided that enough was enough. It was time to stop running, to turn and face the enemy and to fight with whatever resources it had left.

They turned out not to be negligible, for their quarry revealed itself as a wild boar of considerable size whose tusks, as

sharp as daggers, had already torn open the stomach of one of
the dogs, who now lay dying beside it.

The other dogs wisely kept their distance, advancing and
retreating as they barked at the beast, displaying their canines
but not daring to risk making use of them. Behind the dogs
were the riders on their horses, now also surrounding the
defiant creature. The cornered animal looked up at them,
panting heavily. Despite its ferocious appearance it was probably
terrified, realising by now that it would not leave the small patch
of ground it was defending alive.

'Marc!' the king shouted as he removed his sword from its
sheath and tossed it, handle first, to his son. Marc was forced
to make a clean catch for fear that it might otherwise hit Isolt,
sitting on her horse beside him.

'Get down and finish him off!' the king ordered.

The king's sword in his hand, Marc sat motionless in his
saddle, hesitating.

'Go on!' the king bellowed. 'Show that wife of yours that she
may have married a man after all.'

Marc looked at his father. The king's face was red with
exhaustion and rage. He too was panting, trying to catch his
breath. As ferocious and dangerous as the creature before him,
perhaps he, too, could feel death waiting not so far away.

Maybe it was because he had no wish to see his father die
there and then, on his horse, or maybe it was out of fear of what
the king might do to him if he disobeyed. Whatever the reason,
Marc jumped down from his saddle and stood, sword in hand,
staring at the boar.

'What are you doing, Marc?' Isolt cried out.

'He's trying to show you he's a man,' the king shouted back at
her. 'So shut up and let him get on with it.'

'Don't do it!' Isolt shouted, but Marc ignored her and took
a step forward, raising the blade and pointing it at the boar. In

response the trapped animal let out a deep, hollow roar. Isolt screamed, jumped from her horse and ran towards Marc just as the boar leapt forward and charged at him. He tried to stop the beast by stabbing it in the chest as it rushed at him, but the blade struck something hard, perhaps its collarbone, and did nothing to stop its onslaught. Marc was thrown to the ground, the boar nearly toppling over as it stiffened its legs in an effort to stop, turn and come charging back again.

Isolt was bending over Marc, pulling on his arm and screaming at him to get back to his feet. The dogs had crowded back around the boar, barking furiously but still keeping safely out of reach.

The wild beast came charging back towards Marc and Isolt, but someone else had jumped down from their horse and now stepped into the animal's path, thrusting his sword just behind its shoulder and straight into its heart. The boar jumped into the air and fell onto its side, kicking out its hind legs a few times in a desperate effort to get back up. Then its whole body stiffened and its neck twisted as it lifted its head to stare up, with its small, sparkling eyes, at the man in the blue tunic who was still holding on to the sword stuck into its side.

As its muscles relaxed, the beast's head came to rest on the forest floor. It coughed once or twice as blood streamed out of its mouth onto the rotting leaves. All movement seemed to leave the creature as it lay there, suddenly very still.

The dogs had stopped barking and were now cautiously approaching the carcass to get a whiff of its odour up close, until the man in blue stamped his foot and frightened them back as he extracted his sword from the dead animal.

Marc had risen to his feet and stood at Isolt's side. They both looked at the newcomer as he turned to face them. He was young, perhaps even younger than them, with dark, curly hair and bright blue eyes that shone out from beneath his heavy brow and high forehead. There was something quiet about his face that added to the mystery of why he was suddenly there amongst them.

The king was first to speak. 'Who are you, sir, who have appeared out of nowhere so opportunely to save my son and his wife from a most embarrassing situation?'

The man in the blue tunic looked up at him. 'You must be King Cedric of Brittany?' he said.

'Yes, I am. And who might you be?' the king replied.

'Tristan,' the man answered. 'I am a friend of your son Jean.'

'And what are you doing wandering through the forest?'

'I was on my way to your castle last night,' said Tristan, 'and as it was getting late I decided to sleep in the forest. Then I heard the dogs this morning and decided to follow the sound of their barking, feeling that it might lead me to you. I carry with me a letter from your son.'

'What?' shouted the king. 'You have come all the way here from Constantinople?'

'Yes, sire. I am on my way to Ireland.'

'And you have that letter with you?' the king asked, his face lighting up with joy.

Tristan nodded.

'Then hand it to my son Marc, whose life you have just saved. He can read it out loud to us. And he can return my sword first, for it has not been of much use in his hands.'

Marc felt himself about to turn around and throw the sword at his father, but something stopped him just in time. Instead he controlled his anger and, walking over, handed the sword up to the king. Without looking at him, he turned and took the rolled-up parchment from the man who had saved his life.

'Thank you for coming to our rescue,' he said.

Tristan laughed. 'Is that woman dressed as a man really your wife?'

'Yes,' Marc answered. 'Her name is Isolt.'

Tristan laughed again. 'Excuse me, my lord,' he began, 'I don't mean any disrespect. But it was a very strange sight, seeing her from the back, bent over you and screaming in such a high-pitched voice and all the noble lords on their horses all around you, with the dogs barking like a chorus. I actually thought it was some kind of pantomime that was taking place, until I saw the boar and realised that you were in real danger.'

There was a loud burst of laughter from the men, but Isolt was not amused. This fellow may have just saved them from certain injury but had now succeeded in making her feel ridiculous, dressed up, as she was, like a man. She wanted to take off her hat, untie her bun and shake her hair loose, so that it fell down over her shoulders, to show him who she really was. This irritated her even more because she realised that he had managed to awake her vanity with his stupid pleasantry.

'Perhaps, Marc, you will now read us what Jean has written in his letter,' the king said.

Marc broke the seal, unrolled the parchment and began to read.

Dear Father,

Please find it in your heart to forgive me for keeping you so long without any news. I have been travelling far and wide across this empire, setting up garrisons everywhere to consolidate its frontiers that are under constant threat from attack by the Turks.

You asked me in your last letter when I intended to return home. Before I give you an answer, please let me greet you first with some good news. I am now married to a beautiful woman. Her name is Claudia. She is the daughter of Count Alberta Ferranzia Dondolo, brother of the Doge of Venice, who has appointed him as the man in charge of this empire. His wealth can no longer be counted, and in a year's time I shall be sailing back to Brittany with Claudia in a ship full of treasures that will bring new wealth to our kingdom.

My heart can hardly wait for the day when I shall see you and Mother again.

Your loving son,

Jean.

When Marc had finished reading, there was a moment of stillness in the forest as everyone waited for the king to speak. Isolt looked at Tristan, who was standing by the dead boar with his bloodied sword in his hand. He was staring down at the beast, his eyes hidden under his heavy brow. She noticed a vein sticking out on his forearm, where it ran down from his sleeve to the wrist that gripped the handle of his sword. When she looked up, she saw that he was now watching her, and she was caught for an instant in the blue glare of his eyes.

'Did you hear that?' the king shouted. 'My son has picked himself a wife. And this one's got a father! He is the ruler of a whole empire out there in the East.'

Marc looked up at his own father with hatred in his eyes. He wanted to throw the parchment at him and tell him to learn to read, so that next time he received a letter from his beloved son he could read it himself. Instead, he simply rolled up the parchment, turned, walked over to Tristan and handed it back.

The king, however, was not finished. He was clearly angry at not having his favoured son there with him, the one who reflected back at him the image of himself that he wanted to see, flattered him even. Instead he had to make do with this other son, the one who had just read his brother's letter, who could only reflect something he did not want to recognise or acknowledge as belonging to him, like some intruder in the dark waters of a pond whose reflection he would see when he peered down expecting to see himself. This anger was boiling over inside him and it seemed he had to let some of it out.

'So tell me, Tristan,' he said. 'Is this wife of his as beautiful as Jean proclaims her to be in his letter? Has she grace? Does she know how to behave in court? I ask this because we are really in sorry need of such a woman to grace the walls of our castle with her presence.'

Tristan stared up at the king. There was a look of pure innocence in his eyes as he answered. 'I must confess that I have no experience of how to behave in court myself, having spent most of my time in this world on battlefields. I would, therefore, be a poor judge of how well or not a person behaves there. But, as for her beauty, yes, she certainly has that. For beauty does not need an experienced eye to recognise it. It proclaims itself to all who wish to see it.' Tristan paused for a moment and looked towards Isolt. 'Take, for example, your other daughter-in-law. The one who is right here with us today. Is she not beautiful, despite her attempt to hide that beauty from us?'

The king stared at Tristan, taken aback for a moment by his impudence and naïve honesty. Then, as if catching himself, he burst out laughing. 'Perhaps it is her husband who wishes her to hide that beauty from the eyes of other men.'

There was a general outburst of laughter.

Marc calmly took hold of Isolt's hand and pulled her towards her horse before she could say anything. 'Get on the horse,' he said. 'We're leaving.'

Isolt was about to protest, but when she glanced at her husband she saw something in his eyes that she had not seen before. Something less than human, which he seemed to be making a great effort to keep buried inside him. It was not fierce or violent, but he looked as if he was about to fall apart and lose himself to something less coherent and more chaotic, and she felt frightened for him.

So, without saying a word, she climbed into the saddle and waited for Marc to do the same. As they rode away, someone behind them made a comment, which neither of them could make out, and there was another burst of laughter.

*

'Why did you not stand up to your father when he insulted me?' Isolt asked.

They had been travelling for most of the afternoon, and now the sun was setting in a vibrant glow over the moor. Marc was driving the cart with Isolt at his side, and behind them Brangien was sitting with her legs stretched out on the mattress, holding Kore, who was asleep in her arms.

Before they left the castle, Marc had gone with Isolt and Kore to kiss his mother goodbye. They had avoided having to take their leave of his father, whom they had heard return with his party of hunters and the barking dogs. Instead, they had managed to slip away soon afterwards without having to confront the king again.

'I don't think it would be very intelligent to stand up to him,' Marc said.

'It's not a matter of intelligence, it's a matter of showing some pride,' Isolt answered.

'I am proud,' Marc replied. 'I'm proud of you and I'm proud of Kore. And because I've got you both, nothing my father may say can touch me any more. I don't need his kingdom. I don't need his castle or his throne. I've got you, Kore and that fortress up on the cliffs. That place is ours now. It was given to me in exchange for my renunciation of any right to succeed my father on the throne of this kingdom. I'm happy with the exchange, but my father can't understand how I can be content to live out there with you and wish for nothing more. So let him insult me if he wants. I'm happy and he's not. I know that and so does he. I don't have to play his silly game and try to stand up to him.'

Isolt did not answer. As she listened to him she could feel a part of her that seemed to fit perfectly in his description of their life together, and she knew that this part of her was his, that she had given it to him, and that it belonged out there on the moor, to the fortress sticking up at the edge of the cliff, lit up by the drowning sun sinking into the ocean far behind it. But that was only a part of her, she thought.

'Do you understand that?' Marc asked after a moment's silence.

'Yes,' Isolt answered.

Marc looked at her and smiled.

'I asked Donoalin and Godoine to pay us a visit with their two lady friends tomorrow. I persuaded them that it was not such a great detour for them. They can stay the night and leave for Port Saint Marie the following day.'

'When did you arrange all this?' Isolt asked, smiling.

'First thing this morning, just before we departed for the hunt.'

'You did this for me, didn't you?'

'No, not at all,' Marc said. 'I happen to like them. They make for good company. I just thought it would be nice to invite them. Besides, we've got a whole leg of boar we can stick into a stew for them.'

'What?' Isolt exclaimed. 'Who gave you that?'

'I'm afraid I helped myself,' said Marc. 'When you went up to say goodbye to Marie and Solene, I sneaked downstairs to the kitchen to say goodbye to Forsin. The boar's skinned carcass had just been placed on the kitchen table. When I told Forsin how I tried to stab the boar in the chest with my father's sword and was knocked to the ground, he couldn't stop laughing. He tried to stop me from cutting off one of its hind legs, but I told him that I deserved to take some kind of trophy home with me after such a brave exploit.'

Isolt leant over and grabbed Marc's hand. 'I love you, Marc,' she said.

*

The following night, Donoalin, Godoine, Marie and Solene were sitting with Marc and Isolt. The flickering flames of the candelabra in the middle of the table moved their shadows on the walls and lit up their faces. They were eating the fine stew Brangien had cooked for them, and sipping ale. The guests were talking about the feast held at the castle the night before, which Marc and Isolt had missed through their early departure.

Apparently, the king had gone down to the kitchen with Tristan and seen the dead boar lying on the table with one of its hind legs missing. Forsin, not wishing to embarrass the king in front of Tristan, said that Marc, having to leave early on his way back home to the fortress, had taken the share of the beast that the king had so kindly offered him. And the king, not wishing to appear mean-spirited in front of Tristan, had simply said, 'Oh, of course, that's fine.'

The story was told and retold by the small party sitting round the table that night, to their amusement.

'So this man Tristan has made quite an impression on the king?' asked Isolt.

'He most certainly has,' Donoalin answered. 'The king showed him all round the castle and kept him at his side like a guest of honour. He even told him that he was welcome to stay for as long as he wanted. But I think everyone was impressed – the way he appeared out of nowhere just in time to kill that boar. There was something quite unnatural about it.'

'You mean supernatural?' Marie asked.

'Yes, maybe I do,' Donoalin agreed.

'He certainly made an impression on some of the ladies. I saw more than one pair of eyes staring at him,' Solene said mischievously.

'Well, I certainly was not impressed,' Isolt said. 'I'm not saying that I'm not grateful he killed that boar and saved us from certain injury. But I thought his behaviour afterwards was quite obnoxious. I don't like that kind of man.'

'What kind of man?' Marie asked.

All eyes were looking at Isolt and she seemed flustered all of a sudden. Her face was shining in the light thrown by the burning candles.

'I don't know,' she said. 'He just seems so sure of himself.'

'But tell me, Isolt,' Marc went on. 'Why did you jump down off your horse and come rushing after me?'

'I was trying to stop you from doing something you didn't really want to do,' she said, her face still burning in the candlelight.

3

DEATH OF THE FATHER

'Kore is now four years old,' she said to herself. 'Four years old!'

Isolt had quarrelled with Marc and climbed down the cliff to be on her own for a while. These quarrels had become more and more frequent. It would start with a feeling of restlessness, usually at night, of not being able to find a comfortable position to lie down in. Unhappy thoughts would take over her mind, thoughts she did not want that would impose themselves on her and she would toss and turn, trying to break loose from them. And then during the day she would feel fragile and easily irritated, she would get angry with Marc over nothing and often felt on the verge of bursting into tears.

For a moment she just lay there on the rock, feeling confused. She knew it had something to do with all those years she had spent growing up in the convent, feeling trapped in a life, in a body even, that didn't really belong to her.

She felt none of it was real, the nuns, their silly values, their prayers, that it was all a dream and that one day she would wake up and find out who she really was. She thought of the fairy tale that an old nun, considered to be 'not all there' by the other sisters, told her when she was still a little girl. Although she was illiterate, it seemed that she could read what was going on in this little girl's heart, and she wanted to heal her.

The fairy tale was about a young princess who was changed into a frog by a witch, jealous of her beauty. And she remained a frog for many years, trapped in a small pond full of other frogs until, one day, a prince came riding by on his horse. Seeing him, the princess decided that she had suffered enough in her meaningless existence confined to the pond. So, she jumped in front of his horse, hoping that it would tread on her and put an end to her wasted life.

The prince, seeing the frog jump into the road, pulled his horse to a halt so that its hoof only grazed the poor creature. He then jumped down and, seeing the frog sitting motionless on the road, dazed by the collision, picked it up in his hands. He was immediately overcome with a strange feeling of sympathy for the beast, as if it had somehow crossed the great distance that separated their two forms of life, so that the flame that burnt inside them, that animated them both, became for a brief instant a single fire as he brought the frog close up to his lips and kissed it.

The frog disappeared in a puff of smoke and the prince was left holding a beautiful princess close up against him as she stared into his eyes.

Isolt loved this tale, and she clung to it like a precious gift for the remainder of the time she spent in the convent. She held it up as a symbol of hope that gave credence to her dream that one day she would be delivered from the drudgery of her life, imprisoned in that place.

And someone had turned up and delivered her, but that turned out to be a disaster, too painful to think about, the memory of which she had to push back and keep as far away from her heart as she possibly could...

35

'Isolt!'

She could hear her name, carried over the cliff by the wind, falling into the roar of the waves as they crashed against the rocks. It was Marc calling to her. She sighed, thinking that she would have to get up and climb the path that wound its way to the top of the cliff.

There he would be standing waiting for her, and as their eyes met she would smile, and he would be relieved.

She liked Marc. She felt safe with him. She liked it when they had long talks together. She thought that the things he said were very clever and she liked to be close up against him. She liked the feel of his body, that sense of familiarity, and above all else she loved her daughter, their daughter...

And yet, somewhere roaming around her heart, stalking her, was this sense of not really living, of her life not being lived to its full intensity, something she could not talk about with Marc because he was happy with his life just as it was.

But when he had told her the story of the Holy Grail, about a quest to unearth something that had been lost by his ancestors, what he said had touched something in her heart that resonated inside her: that feeling of 'the good' that once shone like a star over their lives, the loss of which had left their kingdoms adrift in a vast wasteland.

But Marc was just talking. It was just one of his fancy ideas. It didn't go any further than that and he was happy to leave it that way, because he couldn't transform it into action, couldn't do something that would make it real.

*

Marc pulled the heavy doors of the fortress towards each other, closed them and locked them together. He then walked through the small side door and locked that behind him too.

Isolt was already sitting on her horse and Kore was in the saddle of Marc's, which Isolt held by its reins. It was Easter Sunday and they were on their way to Port Saint Marie to join the parade that would follow the town priest and a group of monks down the shoreline to a chapel where a special Mass was celebrated every year. It was to be more of a social occasion for them than a religious one, a chance to spend time with their friends.

Far away, Marc could see a small shape moving across the moor. At first he thought it was a deer, but then, squinting, he said, 'I think there's someone out there riding towards us.'

Isolt and Kore turned and looked at the dark shadow moving over the purple and green carpet that stretched far away into the distance.

'Do we have to wait?' Isolt asked impatiently. 'It's going to make us late for the parade.'

'He's definitely heading our way. I think we should,' Marc said.

'Well, let's at least ride towards him and meet him halfway. We can cut back from there towards the road to Port Saint Marie,' Isolt insisted.

Marc hesitated before agreeing.

A quarter of an hour later, as they rode up to the man on his horse, Marc recognised him as the messenger who had brought an invitation from the king a year or two before.

'Good morning, my lord and lady,' the young man said.

'Good morning,' Marc answered. 'What brings you here?'

'The king and queen have requested that you join them at the castle right away,' the messenger said.

'Whatever for?' Marc asked.

'A letter has arrived from the East concerning your brother, Jean.'

'And what has that to do with me?' Marc responded.

'These are not good tidings that are written in the letter, my lord,' the young man replied.

'Well, explain yourself a bit more.'

'I am not supposed to know this, my lord. But Forsin told me to tell you, should you not wish to follow me back to the castle, that the king is bedridden with grief and the queen fears for his life.'

'What on earth has happened to Jean?' Marc asked, suddenly looking worried.

The young man lowered his eyes but did not answer.

'I think you'd better go back with him to the castle,' Isolt said.

'I want to go too!' Kore said, as she sat behind Marc with her arms wrapped around his waist.

'Yes, you will go too, as well as your mother,' Marc said.

'Shouldn't you go on your own, Marc?' Isolt asked.

'No. If I go at all, it will be with both of you. Jean has either got himself into some kind of trouble or has had an accident, or worse.'

'Who is Jean?' Kore asked.

'He's your uncle,' Marc replied.

'Why has he had an accident?' Kore asked.

'We don't know if he's had an accident or not,' Isolt reassured her. 'We will find that out once we get to the castle.'

*

It took them all morning to reach the castle. When they crossed the moat and rode in through the archway, they saw many horses tied together to the pillars that surrounded the courtyard. Isolt was the first to dismount. She helped Kore down from Marc's horse and, as Marc dismounted, Forsin came out of a doorway and rushed towards them. He bowed to Isolt, went up to Kore, kissed her and then looked up at Marc, who could see the big black circles under his eyes and drops of sweat on his forehead.

'What's happened?' Marc asked.

'It's Jean!' Forsin said, as tears appeared in his eyes. 'He's dead!'

'How?' Marc asked.

Forsin let out a sob and then made a gesture with his arm. 'Come down to the kitchen. You can go up the back way to your father's bedroom and avoid the crowd in the hall.'

Once they had crossed the busy kitchen and stood in the dark, empty corridor at the bottom of the stairway, Marc asked again. 'How did he die?'

'He was ambushed by a battalion of Saracens as he was passing through the country on some mission or other. That's all I know,' Forsin said in a whisper. 'Now, you'd better take your wife and daughter up to the king's room. They are waiting for you.'

When they entered the bedroom, Marc saw many familiar faces. There was his cousin Alice and her husband Gerome, who was a captain in the king's army of knights. There was the king's brother, Ganelon, and his wife, Susanne, together with Santerre, the priest, who officiated at the castle. And, of course, there was the queen, surrounded by a group of children of various ages. When she saw Marc, she let go of the hands of two young girls and walked over to him.

Though she was pale and her face was drawn with lines of fatigue, she seemed calm and had lost none of her usual composure. She kissed Kore and Isolt, then turned to Marc.

'Go over and say something to your father,' she urged. 'He is overcome with grief and pain. He refuses to eat anything. And try and get that man Santerre to stand further away from him. Your father never believed in any of that nonsense anyway.'

Marc walked over to the big, heavy oak bed where his father lay under thick woollen blankets. The king's face had grown thin, the bones of his cheeks pushing out sharply under his brittle, pale skin. His eyes were hollow and empty as he stared up at the woven canopy over his bed.

'Hello, Father.' Marc took the king's hand and bent down to kiss it. Cedric looked up at him and Marc saw a flicker of recognition light up his eyes. But the anger, the resentment and the malice did not follow behind it, as it usually did. There were no flames to rise out of the cinders as he stared up at his son's face, and all he could do was smile weakly and hopelessly at him. Marc felt the sudden cold shudder of death pass through him as he looked down at his father.

'I'm sorry,' Marc said. 'I'm sorry!'

As he repeated the words he no longer knew if he was expressing his sorrow for his brother's death or if he was apologising for himself, for being the way he was. But it did not matter, because the flicker of recognition had sunk once again behind the dark, empty pools in his father's eyes to join all the other memories that had huddled together in the unreachable depth of his soul.

'Can you not stand back and recite your prayers at a greater distance from him?' the queen said angrily to the priest as she came over to join Marc at the bedside.

'I don't think it matters,' Marc said to her. 'I think Father has already created that distance himself.'

The queen looked at Marc and he saw the panic rush into her, breaking down her barriers as her face twitched. She stood very still for a moment before regaining her composure, then grabbed Marc by the sleeve. 'Come with me.' She walked him across the room and out through the door. When they got to the hallway, she stopped. 'Do you think he's dying?' she asked.

'He's got no strength left,' replied Marc. 'When he looked at me, there was not the least glimmer of disapproval in his eyes. I think he has lost all interest in life now.'

The queen grabbed hold of Marc and buried her face in his chest. She let out a few sobs that shook her whole body, like the grunts of an angry dog straining against its collar. Marc could feel her fingers digging into his ribs as she gripped his robe.

'Oh God!' she cried out. 'Why have you done this to us? Our son left us to go and fight your battle for you! So why have you done this to us?'

Holding her shoulders, Marc pushed her away from him.

'Please, Mother! This is no time to be weak. You have to take hold of yourself. You have to be strong.'

The queen opened her eyes and looked up at her son. Her manner was more steady and alert as she stared at him.

'You don't know how right you are,' she said. 'This is indeed a time to show great strength. There is more than one vulture perched in that crowd downstairs. They already know about Jean, and if they suspect that the king is dying they will see this moment as their golden chance to give full vent to their ambitions. So we not only have to be strong right now, we also have to be very careful.'

The queen let go of Marc's robe and backed away from him. She stared down at the space on the floor that separated them and then looked back at him. 'Wait for me here. I won't be long.' She opened the door to the bedroom where the king lay dying, entered and closed it behind her.

Marc hesitated. He too wanted to open the door and go back into that room. But before he could do anything, the door opened again and his mother stepped back into the hallway with a large key in her hand. She closed the door behind her and told Marc to follow her.

They went to the end of the hallway and then down some steps, along another hallway to a circular stairway. Halfway up the stairway they reached a small landing. The queen fitted the key into the lock of a low, reinforced door and opened it. Marc followed her into the small room. It was the first time he had ever stepped beyond the door, which he remembered as always being locked. A window looked out onto a field, speckled with freshly sprouted green shoots. Inside the room, shelves were built along one of its walls, stacked with dusty parchments. Behind an iron-barred gate, a niche that looked like a shrine had been dug into the wall facing the shelves. Inside, the king's crown rested upon a stand and his sceptre lay beneath it on a red silk cloth. Several jewel-encrusted chests stood on a table below the shrine. Marc picked one up.

'What's inside these chests?' he asked. 'They are beautiful.'

'Put it down!' his mother said. 'They contain the bones of dead saints. Your grandfather brought them back from one of his expeditions.'

'You mean one of his raids,' Marc replied as he put the chest back on the table.

'Here it is,' the queen exclaimed. She had been searching through the parchments and was now holding one of them, partially unrolled, in her hands. When she finished unrolling it, she seemed to recognise something.

'What are you looking at?' Marc asked.

'Wait!' she said, then gripped the parchment firmly in her two fists and, with a sudden jerk, tore it in half.

'What are you doing?' Marc asked, aghast.

'I'm destroying this document,' she said. 'We must take these two halves down to the kitchen and burn them.'

'Why? What's in the document?'

The queen stared straight into Marc's eyes, the blood rushing through her veins, suddenly bringing the colour back into her face.

'There's your seal and your father's. In it, you renounce your right to the throne in favour of your brother.'

'Why did you tear it up?' Marc shouted angrily. 'That

document also guarantees me ownership of the moor and the fortress. What are you trying to do to me?'

'You will own much more than just the moor and its fortress,' the queen replied. 'You will have the whole kingdom for yourself if you destroy this document.'

Marc looked at his mother, hot with rage. But some foreign element had entered into that rage. He wanted to reject it immediately, but it had already reached through the fire of his anger and awoken an old dream.

'It won't work,' he said. 'Everyone knows that I have renounced my rights to the throne in favour of Jean.'

'And that was very generous of you,' the queen replied. 'But without this document attesting to the fact, there is nothing to prevent you stepping back into your rightful place, now that Jean has been so cruelly taken away from us.'

'I won't do it,' Marc protested. 'I've been very happy living out there with my family on the moor.'

'And do you think that your wife will be willing to spend the rest of her days in that godforsaken place? Have you thought of that?' the queen asked.

Marc hesitated for a moment.

'And anyway,' the queen continued, 'if you don't step up and sit on that throne and wear the crown of this kingdom, what chance do you think you have of holding on to your happiness? If any one of those vultures should get his hands on this crown, he would either have us all murdered or, at the very least, have us banished from this land forever.' The queen stepped forward and took Marc's hand. 'Think very carefully, Marc, before you say anything rash and stupid. If you throw this kingdom to the dogs, it is your own future and that of your family that you are throwing away with it.'

She walked over to the door, about to leave, then turned to Marc once again. 'Are you coming down to the kitchen with me?'

Marc looked away from her and walked over to the table with the relics on it. He looked up through the iron bars into the niche, his eyes resting on the crown, which he had thought inaccessible to him because of his birthmark. It was made of solid gold and had a line of rubies encrusted all around its base.

He only remembered his father wearing it once, at his coronation. Marc had been a child then, sitting beside his brother in the church in Corsan. He remembered the sunlight shining through the stained-glass windows and how the crown had shone once it had been placed on his father's head, as if it were lighting up the whole church.

'What about my ears?' he asked.

'Shut up!' his mother commanded. 'Once that crown is upon your head, no one will dare mention the subject. Just keep them well hidden under your hair. And remember, now that Jean is dead you are the only legitimate heir to the throne. Leave the rest to me. So are you coming or not?'

Marc stared at his mother. Her sudden determination surprised him and unsettled him all at once.

She took a deep breath and exhaled with a sigh. 'This kingdom has never been sanctified by the Church or the so-called King of France, who claims it's just another fiefdom like all the others that are answerable to his regency. A regency that we have never acknowledged or recognised in any form or manner. And he and his predecessors have never tried to impose that regency on us by force, because they know that, if they tried to raise an army against us, they would find that many of their so-called fiefdoms might join us and turn against them as well. And don't forget that your brother has just given his life up in defence of the Christian cause out there in the East. So it is even less likely that the Christian Church would give its blessing to an army raised against us now.

'And you have your father to thank for this. Even though he had no sympathy for the Christian faith, he foresaw that sending his son and heir out East to fight for the Christian cause would help protect us at home. So I'm sure that you understand that if your father passes away we must be ready with a legitimate heir to place on the throne, and can waste no time in doing so. Now, are you coming with me to the kitchen?'

'Yes, I'm coming,' Marc replied, still unable to overcome a sense that he was about to betray himself and Isolt in some way. But there was also that other feeling, the one that had taken possession of him the first time he and Isolt had visited the castle together. The voice that had whispered to him as he stood under the threshold of the great dining hall, staring at all the other guests who, like him, had been invited to take part in the hunt.

The voice had cut through the disgust and repulsion he felt for all those people at his father's court. It had whispered to him: 'If you are in love with being in love, then you had better shut yourself away with Isolt in the fortress. But, if you think you can really love her, then you can only do this out here in the world amongst your fellow men.' The voice had challenged him and, for a moment, he had felt stimulated by its challenge. But he had been unable to pick up the gauntlet, because the events that had taken place during the hunt on the following day had only proven to him how inadequate any attempt he could make would be to overcome the great obstacle of his father, who blocked his way to any participation in the life of the castle.

But all that was two years ago, Marc thought, looking up at his father's crown as it reflected the dim light from the window onto his face. And today, he thought, fate had thrown the gauntlet back at him, and this time it seemed that he had no choice but to pick it up.

But still he hesitated. What about Isolt? he wondered.

Marc opened the door to the bedroom and saw that everyone had left except for Santerre, who was sitting on a chair near the bed reading his bible. Without knowing why, Marc rushed over to the window and looked out. Beyond the walls of the castle, on the other side of the moat near where a small chapel had been built, he saw Isolt and Kore sitting under a tree. Marc ran back across the room and closed the door behind him. He made his way to the back stairs, and rushed down to the kitchen and out into the courtyard over to the drawbridge. Once outside the castle, he followed the moat over to the tree where they were sitting.

'Mama's been crying,' Kore said as Marc rushed over.

Marc looked down at Isolt. The light blue linen dress that she had put on for the Easter parade brought something of the brightness of the morning into the dim evening light under the cover of the oak tree where she was now sitting, as if a piece of that early sky had fallen on her and wrapped itself around her body.

The blond streaks in her hair ran down over her dark face like flames that had escaped from the burning hurt in her eyes as she stared up at him. He felt that pain stab into his heart. So this was what it was like to 'love' out here in the world, and not to be just 'in love' with love.

'What's the matter?' Marc asked.

'That uncle of yours is an awful man,' Isolt said.

'What did he do?'

'When you left and didn't come back, he walked up to me and said I had no business being in that room without you and asked me to leave. Why did you leave us there for so long?' Isolt sobbed. 'How could you just go like that and say nothing? Don't we matter to you any more?'

'Of course you do!' Marc answered. 'But my father is dying and my mother is worried.'

After a moment's silence, Isolt spoke again, but this time in a softer voice. 'I can imagine she must be. Her son has been killed and now her husband is dying. How much harder can things get for her?' Isolt looked up at Marc and the expression on her face changed.

'If the king dies, who is going to take over? Your mother?' she asked.

'No, she can't,' Marc replied. 'She is not linked by blood to the royal lineage.'

'When are we going to go home?' Kore asked.

'I don't know, sweetheart,' Marc replied, and he knelt to stroke her cheek. 'Your grandfather is not well. We might have to stay here for a few days.'

'Is he going to die?' Kore asked.

'I don't know.'

'What were you talking about with your mother?' Isolt asked Marc.

'I told you. She's worried. Worried about the future.'

'And how does that involve you?'

'It's not just me. It will involve all three of us.'

'But you have nothing to do with the kingdom any more,' Isolt protested.

'I don't,' Marc replied. 'But I'm still the king's son. And whoever climbs up onto that throne after my father's death will not want me around.'

'But you've already relinquished your right to the throne,' Isolt said.

'In favour of my brother, Jean, who is now dead,' Marc replied. 'And even if that could bar me from the throne, there would still be our children. They could legitimately claim their right to succession and would be a threat to whoever stepped up in my place.'

Isolt stared at him with the eyes of a wild, hunted beast. 'Let's run away from here now!' she said.

'Where would we go?'

'Anywhere! We could sail on a boat over to Ireland.'

'And how would we feed ourselves once we got there?'

'I don't know. I could sell things in the markets. I was pretty good at that.'

'We don't have anything to sell,' Marc protested. 'I barely have enough to pay our fare.'

'Then go into the castle and find some precious objects and pack them into your saddlebag,' said Isolt. 'We can sell them.'

Her words came out in a rush, as if something buried deep inside her, something she had managed to keep hidden in the darkness of her soul, had finally seized its chance to jump out in her voice, using the intensity of its pitch to manifest itself.

'Isolt, do you know what you are asking me to do? Not only to steal things but to leave my dying father and my mother when they most need me, and to run away like a scared rabbit.'

Isolt's eyes remained unchanged. 'Don't pretend to me that you care about your parents, or that they care about you,' she said. 'In the five years I have known you, this is only the second time you have visited them and they never once came to see us. You're just frightened to get up and leave, that's all.'

'I can't get up and leave. It wouldn't be right, or fair to you or Kore. What possible life would be awaiting us if I just got up and left? A life of hardship and misery. When we first met, I promised to look after you and to protect you. Well, that's what I'm going to do, and I won't achieve that if I run away.'

For a moment they stood and stared at each other. Isolt looked away at the castle and then back at Marc. It seemed to her that something was being repeated. She remembered making that same gesture five years before, when they stood outside the market town and he had asked her to go back to the fortress with him. She had looked away from him and stared at the walls of the town, and then looked back at him. This memory gave her a strange feeling. The hard look in her eyes softened as she stared at him.

'Very well,' she said. 'Do what you have to do and I'll follow you. But don't disappear again without telling me where you're going, or why!'

As they walked back along the moat, Marc looked up at the high wall towering above them. For hundreds of years, a series of kings had battled to hold on to this peninsula at the far tip of Europe, this kingdom like a defiant finger pointing to the distant horizon where the sky fell into the sea, and beyond which the known world disappeared into the dark abyss.

Their history was a long story of butchery and bravery, of treason and honour, of cowardice and heroism. He could feel all that looming over him as they walked, hand in hand, in the shadow of the castle. But another feeling swelled his heart. To his surprise, he began to think that not only was there a place for him behind those stones, but that he could perhaps bring about something new, something that might mean a real change for this land. Had any of those kings ever really loved? he asked himself.

*

Marc had sunk into a deep sleep, and it took some time for him to realise that someone was shaking his shoulder. Finally, he opened his eyes and looked up. For a moment he did not know where he was, though the face staring down at him seemed vaguely familiar in the dim candlelight above him.

'Sir, your mother wants to see you,' a voice said in a whisper, and he realised he was lying in his old bedroom in the castle.

He reached over and felt the warm hips of the body lying next to him. Isolt had her back turned to him and, on her other side, Kore lay huddled up against her mother.

'I'm coming,' Marc whispered. He rose, found his smock on the floor by his bed, pulled it over his nightshirt and closed the door gently behind him. In the hallway, he recognised that it was

Germaine, the cook, who had awakened him. She stood facing him in her nightdress, a candle in her hand.

'What's happened?' Marc asked.

'The king is dead,' she said.

He followed her to the royal bedroom, where he embraced his mother, who was waiting, in tears, just inside the doorway, and then he walked over to the bed where his father lay.

In the candlelit room, the old man seemed to be looking up at the canopy above his bed. It was the same empty stare Marc had seen on his face in the afternoon, except that the silence behind his eyes was now complete. Something had gone. Something that had been there all those years, behind the bravura, the shouts and the cries, the fits of temper, the sudden outbursts of violence, the cruelty, the laughter and the kindness.

All had left their mark on his face and, as he stared up silently, the signs were still there somewhere. But what had lain behind, what had pushed it all into motion, was gone, and one could feel its absence in the silence and stillness left in its wake.

Marc bent down and kissed his father. Then, with his thumb and index finger, he gently moved the old man's eyelids down over his eyes.

*

For the three days that followed the king's death, his body lay in an open coffin in the hall of the castle, and all those who wished to pay their respects to him were welcome to do so. There had been a procession of people, of noble blood right down to the common beggars from all parts of the kingdom, entering and leaving the castle.

And throughout those three days, there were many more people gathered together in the castle courtyard and outside its walls, talking in low voices and sometimes in whispers.

'I find it rather sordid the way they all stand around whispering to each other,' Isolt remarked, as she stood by the bedroom window looking down into the courtyard. 'I would love to know what they are saying.'

'I should think it is mostly about who is going to be their next king,' Marc said.

'I thought word had already gone out that it's going to be you?'

'Yes, it has,' Marc said as he got up from the bed where he had been lying, deep in thought. He looked at Isolt for a moment and then, with a worried frown on his face, began to pace up and down the room. 'But it hasn't happened yet. Even once I've been crowned by the Bishop of Rennes and he has given me his blessing...'

'Has he agreed to do that?' Isolt interrupted.

'We should get the answer by tonight,' Marc replied. 'But it seems almost certain that he will. Even if there was no love lost between my father and the Church, and even though there will be no high-ranking official to conduct my father's funeral, my brother did nonetheless lose his life while defending the Church's cause, and he was himself blessed by the bishop before his departure on the crusade. That should count in our favour. But even with his blessing, I will still have to go through the ordeal of having all the gathered nobility swear their allegiance to me, one by one.'

'When will this happen?' Isolt asked, her eyes wide open in excitement.

'Later in the day, after the coronation is over,' Marc answered.

'And I will be witness to all this?'

Marc stopped pacing and turned to Isolt with an uneasy look on his face.

'No,' he said. 'It would be safer if you and Kore went back with Gauvin and Brangien to the fortress after the funeral.'

'Why? What would we risk if we stayed here?' Isolt asked.

'There have been rumours.'

'What rumours?' Isolt asked.

Marc looked embarrassed. 'I had not been aware of this,' he replied, 'but for a long time the word has been going around that I have married a Saracen.'

'A Saracen!' Isolt repeated with astonishment.

'Yes, a Saracen,' Marc said. 'Obviously, because of your dark skin, people make assumptions. And, as everything depends at the moment on my receiving the bishop's blessing…'

'You would rather not have me around when he arrives,' Isolt said, finishing Marc's sentence for him. There were tears in her eyes as she stared at him. 'So that's it!' she said. 'I've become an embarrassment to you.'

Marc walked over and took hold of her shoulders. 'Can't you see the tight spot we are all in at the moment? If I am not given this crown, we are finished anyway. And there are a few people who will jump on any excuse they can find to stop me. But our one great strength will be the bishop's blessing at my coronation, for whoever wishes to contest it will then be going against the Church.'

'So if anybody wants to stop you, he will have to stop the bishop from giving you his blessing?' Isolt asked.

Marc looked at Isolt and hesitated for a moment before shaking his head and replying. 'What you have to understand is that our new pope, Innocent III, is young and ambitious. He wants to unite all the warring factions within Christendom. He wants to channel all the energy and violence that is tearing it apart into a single united force that will serve a noble cause. That cause will be the reconquering of territories that were once under the tutelage of the Catholic Church and have now fallen into the hands of barbarians, the most obvious of which are the Saracens.

'Now it is pretty clear that, if he is willing to have one of his bishops bless my coronation, it will legitimise my right to rule this kingdom, and this is entirely due to the part my brother played in helping to set up a new Latin empire in the East. He thinks that this gesture, this sign of gratitude on the part of the Church, will not go unnoticed and will encourage other lords, princes and barons throughout Europe to depart for Jerusalem and join the crusade that is being fought there. And this is why he is willing to overlook the rumour that has obviously reached his ears, that I have married a woman who resembles a Saracen. Nonetheless, I'd prefer you not to be there at the coronation while the bishop gives me his blessing.

'I know this must sound very silly and hypocritical to you, but I promise you that, once I have been sworn in as king of this land, I will ride with you throughout the whole kingdom to show you off as its new queen, and a very beautiful queen you will be indeed, for I will spare no expense in making sure that you have the finest wardrobe to take along with you on this journey.'

Marc looked at Isolt hopefully, but the expression on her face, the look in her eyes, had not changed. She was in one of those moods that brought forth something so much deeper than anything he could say to her, that could not be moved or shifted by the kind of empty promises he had just made to her, for it demanded a level of sincerity he was unable to find in himself.

And yet, as he held on to her shoulders, he could see clearly that she was the only thing he really cared about, her and Kore. But he knew she wanted something more than that. Of course she wanted someone who cared about her and her daughter, but that someone had to be strong in himself, in who he was, so that he could help bring her closer to who she was. And in her eyes he seemed to be moving in the opposite direction, away from doing that.

'So what's the point of the swearing-in ceremony?' she asked.

'It goes back to way before we converted to Christianity,' explained Marc, letting go of her shoulders. 'Of course, anyone from the nobility of this kingdom could still refuse to swear allegiance to me. But, since our conversion, it has become more of a ritual, a formality, than anything else. The only thing that really counts now is the bishop's blessing.'

Isolt was staring at him, her eyes squinting slightly as if she was having trouble seeing him.

'All right,' she said. 'I will play along with you because I love you. You are a good man but I can't help feeling sorry for you. It's a shame you did not have the courage to run away with Kore and me to Ireland. We could have tried to make a life for ourselves over there. We could have, but it's too late now. You didn't trust me enough, did you? You preferred to stay here and become king. Well, what do you think that's going to do to you?'

*

Early in the morning on the day after the funeral, Marc, Isolt and Kore stepped out into the castle courtyard. Gauvin had finished loading up the cart with supplies and was sitting up front with Brangien at his side.

'Do you want to sit up on the cart, or do you want to ride on the horse with me?' Isolt asked Kore.

'I'll sit on the cart,' the little girl replied.

After kissing Kore goodbye, Marc picked her up and handed her to Brangien, who lifted her over onto the space between herself and her husband. Isolt climbed up onto her horse that was held by Philippe, Gauvin's son, who had come back from Jerusalem and was now part of the king's guards.

Marc walked over to Isolt and reached up for her hand.

'So, Donoalin and Marie will be waiting for you at the fortress and I will see you in a few days.'

'Yes, of course,' Isolt said. 'We'll be fine.'

Marc held on to her hand. 'Do you still love me?' he asked.

'Yes, of course,' she said again, with a slight tone of impatience.

'Do you realise that the next time you see me I shall be king?' Marc asked self- mockingly.

Isolt pulled her hand loose from his grip and bent down towards him. She combed her fingers through his hair and touched his ear.

'Make sure that the next time I see you you're still yourself,' she whispered.

The drawbridge came to rest with a groan on the other side of the moat.

'I'm going to miss you both,' Marc said.

'Then you'd better hurry up and come to fetch us back,' Isolt replied.

'I will, as soon as I'm done here.'

Then, with a gentle kick of her heels, Isolt ushered her horse forward towards the drawbridge.

Philippe followed behind her, then the cart with Kore, Brangien and Gauvin. First the hoofs and then the wheels of the cart echoed off the drawbridge and up into the early morning air.

Marc walked out onto the drawbridge and watched them move down along the road that cut through the fields of green winter wheat. Suddenly he felt the presence of someone beside him. He looked round and saw that it was Forsin.

A cooing wood pigeon on a nearby tree had joined in with the blackbirds and the finches to serenade the rising sun. Their songs gradually drowned out the sound of the hoofs as Marc and his friend watched the small company of travellers grow smaller until finally they disappeared over the hill towards the moor.

'It's a shame,' Forsin said.

'Don't you start!' Marc said, looking down at him.

'All I was going to say was that it's a shame they won't be here to witness your coronation.'

Marc thought of the fortress up on the cliffs, and of Isolt, and the warmth of her breath, how it had breathed life into that lonely place, filling it with her stories, her dreams, and then with Kore, and he realised that the wonderful years they had spent there together had now come to an end.

Suddenly the clamour of singing birds welcoming back the spring seemed loud and brash, jeering and sarcastic, like the voice he heard speaking out from somewhere inside him.

'Can your love step outside those protective walls and survive in the harsh cacophony of this agitated world?' it asked.

4

THE CHALLENGE

The two baskets of damp clothes they had brought back from the stream were resting on the ground. They had spent all morning rubbing the clothes with black soap and then rinsing them out. Now they were hanging them up on a set of washing lines just outside the fortress walls. The wind had dropped and it had turned into a fine, spring day.

'Soon you won't have to do this any more,' Marie said to Isolt.

'Well, if that's so I can't say that I'll miss doing it much,' Isolt answered, then paused with one hand resting upon the line. 'I would hate to have to count the days I spent washing clothes in the convent when I was a girl.'

Marie had bent down to pick a white blouse from the basket and now stood staring at Isolt. 'It must have been hard growing up without knowing who your parents were,' she said.

'I used to make up all sorts of stories about my parents,' replied Isolt. 'It was always very dramatic because they had to die in the end. It was the only way I could justify being left in the convent.'

'And what about the nuns? What did they tell you?'

'Not much. Just that a man had brought me there, not long after I was born, and had left me in their care. I think that, once a year, or sometimes every two years, someone would bring money to the nuns to pay for my board, but I was never allowed to see him. I'm not even sure if it was always the same person, but that didn't stop me from making up all sorts of stories about this person as well.'

'And in any of those stories, did you ever see yourself as a queen?' Marie asked, laughing.

Isolt spread her hands out with her palms turned up. 'Do these look like hands that could belong to a queen?'

Marie had already noticed that Isolt had large hands and that the skin of her palms had been thickened by hard work.

'Maybe not, if I just look at your hands,' she answered. 'But it's the way you hold yourself. The way your eyes look straight into people. The way you move. You can feel real strength behind it and I think it makes you beautiful and noble.' Marie stared intently at Isolt for a moment. 'It's strange,' she continued, 'but sometimes, when I look at you, I get the impression that you have been touched by some kind of special grace. It's hard to explain, but I really feel that sometimes.'

A distant cry reached them. The two women looked across the moor and saw a group of men riding their horses towards the fortress. Isolt squinted and stared at them for a moment.

'My God! It's him! He's come back to fetch me!' she cried and bent down to pick up a red garment from one of the baskets. Waving it over her head she shouted out Marc's name as one of the horsemen broke away from the other four and rushed forward at a gallop.

*

The table downstairs in the dining hall was laid with a large bowl and several platters. Apart from the soup that Brangien had prepared there were four hares, roasted on a spit outside. One of the guards escorting Marc had shot them with his bow as they travelled over the moor.

It was after dark when Marc and Isolt came down for dinner, accompanied by Kore, who had gone to join them in their room earlier on. The three of them sat down at the table with Gauvin, Brangien, Philippe, Godoine, Marie, Donoalin, Solene and the four guards.

'Well, sire,' began Godoine; 'is this now how we must address you?'

Marc hesitated for a moment and looked at Isolt.

'You'd better tell them the whole story, Marc,' she said, and he saw then that what had been lost between them had somehow miraculously returned. He could see it in her eyes as she spoke to him and it flushed away any doubts he had been nurturing about the future.

'Well,' Marc said, taking a deep breath, 'you may go on calling me by my name for the time being. The coronation did take place, and the bishop did give me his blessing. It was afterwards, though, that things turned sour, when the bishop was already on his way home and we held the meeting with all the nobility of the realm. The ceremony began and each of the lords in turn took an oath, swearing their allegiance to me as their king. But when it came to Nordstram's turn, he would not stand up. When asked why, he said he had no intention of taking the oath.'

'What?' Godoine shouted. 'That old bear refused to take the oath? How dare he!'

'Well,' Marc continued, 'as is the custom, I then stood up and asked him to voice his grievance. He, in turn, stood up and said that, since I had left the castle and had lived for many years on the moor and had cut myself off from the affairs of the court, and since I had married a foreign woman without a title who had the appearance of a Saracen, and as neither the king nor the queen were present at our wedding, I had lost all legitimate right to be sitting on my father's throne. And, to top it all, he said that I had signed a document ceding that right to my brother and could not reclaim it now that he was dead.'

'And what was your answer to him?' Marie asked.

'I answered that this was not the opinion of the Bishop of Rennes, since he had just given his blessing to my coronation.'

'Well answered!' Marie shouted. 'And what did he have to say to that?'

'He proved himself to be quite clever in his answer,' Marc replied. 'He said that he was not challenging the legitimacy of the coronation, but that he was simply going to exercise his right not to take the oath of allegiance to me as his new king until his grievance with me had been settled according to the ancient laws of this kingdom. And since the cause of his grievance was the manner in which I had conducted my life prior to the time of my coronation, which conduct he had now openly criticised in public, the only way to settle this grievance would be to fight it out with him in a duel.'

'What?' Godoine exclaimed. 'But this is madness! There is no one in this kingdom that can defeat him man to man. That is well known. He would destroy you if you accepted his challenge.'

'I'm afraid I have no choice.' Marc sighed. 'He has been very clever. He has insulted me and my wife in public and, if I do not take up his challenge and save my honour, I am obviously not worthy to wear the crown of this kingdom. I will never have the full support of all the people, let alone the nobility. I will never be seen as their true king, but only as somebody placed on the throne by the Church. I have no choice; I must take up the challenge.'

Isolt was staring at Marc and, as he finished talking, she felt something tighten inside her chest. It was more than just fear, for there was something exciting and invigorating in what he had just said. She felt that something unsuspected was revealing itself in him, something she liked, and it made her wish she were lying on the bed upstairs again, with him on top of her.

'You are not telling me that you have accepted to fight a duel with him!' Donoalin was saying.

'Yes I have,' Marc answered. 'And it has been decided that I shall have three months to prepare myself.'

'But you cannot learn in three months what he has acquired through twenty years of hard practice. The man is an animal, a wild beast! He will cut you to pieces!' Donoalin protested.

'Don't exaggerate,' Marc said. 'I have been coached in the use of a sword and I am strong and sturdy, plus I have youth on my side. If I train hard I have every chance of teaching him a lesson.'

Marie and Donoalin looked at each other with dismay. The four guards looked down into their plates, not wanting to be drawn into the debate. Brangien was looking at Isolt, who was staring at Marc.

The only person who went on eating was Gauvin. He seemed to have barely registered what had been said at the table, as if it were just everyday conversation. He had fought in many campaigns; he had spilt his share of blood and knew what it was like to feel a sword cut through his flesh. He had followed his king, fought at his side and served him loyally for most of his life; but now that his king was dead, so too was any interest in the affairs of the kingdom.

As silence filled the room, Isolt felt a sudden twinge of doubt and looked away from Marc. She saw Gauvin gazing out across the table at nothing in particular and found the serenity in his stare reassuring. She did not want to let go of that new feeling Marc had awoken inside her. 'Why don't we worry about the outcome of this duel tomorrow and enjoy our meal and each other's company right now?' she said, and raised her mug of ale. 'Let us start by drinking a toast to Marc, to his foolhardy courage, and hope that it has not gone unnoticed by God, or whatever forces rule over our fate. May they be favourable to him in his trials, for he is a good man.'

In a sudden change of mood, everyone joined Isolt and raised their mugs. Even Gauvin joined in, before guzzling the remaining ale to wash down a hunk of wild game.

*

Marc felt someone shaking him. He opened his eyes. It was dark and he couldn't see anything, but he vaguely remembered he was back in the fortress. 'Who is it?' he asked.

'It's me, Isolt. I've had an awful dream.'

Marc lifted himself onto his elbow, searched with his hand for her face and then stroked her cheek. 'What was so bad about it?' he asked.

'I dreamt that you were fighting a duel against this man Nordstram. He had knocked your sword out of your hand, and all you had was your shield. He was charging you, striking blows at you from all sides, and you were having more and more trouble fending them off, and he was about to kill you. It was horrible. I don't think that you should fight this duel, Marc. I think that Marie and Godoine were right. It's absolute madness.'

There was a long silence. Marc could feel the movement of her body as she took in deep breaths and then released the air from her chest with long, whispering sighs.

'There is something I have never told anyone,' he said. 'It happened long ago, when my brother and I were just little boys. There is an apple tree in the orchard behind the stables in the castle, where two birds came to build their nest. They were beautiful birds and they would sing a very melodic song. The female bird laid her eggs and my father would often wander round to the back of the stables and watch her sit on her eggs, attended to by her companion who would bring her food.

'My father would talk about these birds when we sat having our meals. When the eggs hatched, he placed a chair near the tree so that he could sit and watch the two parent birds feed their chicks, and he even took my brother and me with him sometimes. To this day I don't really understand why a violent man like my father, such a ruthless hunter and fierce soldier, had suddenly taken an interest in these two birds and their nestlings.'

Marc paused, stroking Isolt's arm absent-mindedly. 'Perhaps even he needed to find some light in the great tragedy that the spectacle of life seemed to offer up to him; needed to find something beautiful and tender that would, like a star, shine out of the darkness caused by all the turmoil, the greed, the plotting and conspiracies that dominate this heartless world.

'Anyway, one morning, as we were playing outside, chasing each other, my brother and I found ourselves panting under the apple tree in the orchard where we had stopped to get our breath back. Staring up at the nest, I suggested to my brother that we go to the stables and fetch the ladder. We could rest it against the branch of the tree so that we could climb up and get a closer look at the chicks in the nest.

'We did this, but once up there, the parent birds appeared and began to fly over our heads, going from one branch to the other and screeching loudly. My brother, who had an impetuous nature, grabbed a chick from the nest and threw it at one of the parents. I joined in the game and suddenly the nest was empty and all the chicks were scattered in the grass under the tree. Realising what we had done, we climbed down the ladder, ran out of the orchard and went to play somewhere else.

'That very same day, in the afternoon, my father came rushing into the castle, just as my brother was on his way down the stairs. My father, seeing him, stopped and stood at the bottom. Raising his arm, he opened his hand, exposing a dead chick in the cup of his palm. He bellowed at my brother, asking him if he was responsible for such work. My brother, halfway down the stairs, stopped and stared into the open palm. He squinted for a moment, then nodded his head.

'My father couldn't see me, but I could see him. I was on the first floor and was crouching down, looking at them through the poles of the balustrade. "And where was your brother when this happened?" my father asked. To my great surprise and relief, my brother shrugged his shoulders. "So you dragged that ladder out of the stables and lifted it against the tree all by yourself?" my father asked. My brother nodded his head once more.

'My father rushed up the stairs and grabbed my brother by the arm. He dragged him down to the landing and out across the courtyard to the stables, where he pulled off his smock and horsewhipped him. I was still crouching behind the balustrade on the first floor and I could hear his screams.

'That's the sort of person my brother was. Years later, when it was explained to me that, because of my ears, it would be best if I relinquished the throne in favour of my brother, I had no grief and put up no arguments. Deep down in my heart, however, I knew that it had nothing to do with my ears, but that what I was really doing was paying back a long overdue debt that I owed him.

'But in the years that followed that incident in the orchard, when we continued to grow up together, our relationship had changed. I might still have been his older brother, but I knew now that he was a better person than I was, and this knowledge stuck to me. I couldn't forget it, however hard I tried.'

Marc looked directly at Isolt, stroking her hair.

'And it was only when I met you that things seemed to change,' he continued. 'Because you accepted me, because you let me into your heart, it seemed to me that I had at last managed to escape from this feeling I had been carrying inside me. I felt that, at last, I had become somebody worthwhile, because of you, because you felt that way about me.

'So you see why I have to fight that duel; because I know that, if I don't, I will go back to being the person I was before I met you, and I couldn't bear that now. It would kill me. If I have to die, I want to die as the person I am now, not as the person I once was.'

*

Nearly a month had gone by since that evening. Isolt, Marc and Kore were now settled in the castle, where Marc had been spending his time trying to perfect himself, day after day, in the art of fighting with a sword.

Kore enjoyed living in her new home, although she did miss Brangien, whom she had grown to love as if she were her grandmother. But she had two cousins, a boy and a girl, who were living at the castle and with whom she spent most of her time.

For Isolt, things were not so simple. As Marie had foreseen, she no longer had any household work to do. With Marc being busy most of the time, and Kore occupied with her cousins, she seemed to be on her own a lot.

She wished she could spend more time with Marc, especially at the meetings he held with the lords and knights, presided over by his mother, Isabelle, who was temporarily in charge of the realm until Marc had settled his difference with Nordstram.

She did not like the way Marc's mother would take up so much of his time and keep him away from her, and she wished that he would stand up for her more and insist on including her in the affairs of the castle.

So Isolt would often spend time sitting in her bedroom with her embroidery. Through the open window she could hear the sound of Marc's sword as it clashed against the blade of his fighting partner, accompanied by the shouted instructions from the knight who was coaching him.

Sometimes she would get up, walk over to the window and look down into the courtyard. There she would see Marc, either backing away and blocking a succession of blows or rushing forward with a series of attacks of his own, which were all skilfully parried by his partner.

She could not tell from these displays what his chances would be in a real fight against such an experienced swordsman as Nordstram, but what was plain to see was that Marc was giving everything he had to these practice sessions, pushing himself with all his force, energy and will until he was on the verge of collapsing from fatigue.

She fully realised the danger and uncertainty that was hanging over them. However, as she watched Marc throw himself with such abandon into preparing himself for this fatal challenge, she seemed to lose all sense of fear and, instead, feel a rush of excitement spill into her heart as if a voice was whispering to her, 'You are the cause of all this. You have awakened this passion in his soul.'

But at other moments, when Marc was attending meetings from which she was excluded, her mood would switch. She would lose the feeling and become a lost child again, pushed into situations she could not control, and the sudden feeling of loneliness killed her resolve.

One particular night they lay together in bed, after a long day during most of which Marc had been away. She asked: 'So, what was the discussion this afternoon?'

'Oh, it's just my mother,' Marc said. 'She's still trying to find a way to avoid this duel. She wants Ganelon, my uncle, to give back some land that was taken away from Nordstram's family generations ago. She thinks that he would then drop his grievance and take the oath. But Ganelon will never give that land away. He has every reason to want to hold on to it. So my mother tried to negotiate with him, saying that, since I lacked experience, he should be made my chief adviser for the coming years. She was clearly insinuating that she and my uncle would be ruling the kingdom for some time to come.'

'But that's outrageous!' Isolt exclaimed. 'I, for one, could never live here with those two running our lives. I would just leave. I'm sorry, but I would simply have to go!'

'Don't get so angry,' Marc said. 'For one thing, my uncle has no intention of giving up that land. He obviously has plans of his own. He doesn't think I stand a chance against Nordstram and envisages me being cut up into several pieces by the end of our duel. After that, all he will have to do is sit on the throne in my place. So why should he go along with my mother and try to stop our fight?'

Isolt reached over and grabbed Marc's hands. 'But that's awful,' she said. 'Now you're really frightening me.'

Marc lifted himself up onto one elbow and leant over her.

'Don't be frightened; they are all old and tired – my mother, my uncle, and Nordstram. I've got you on my side. The desire that drives them is drowned in fear and suspicion. I am fighting for love, for you and for Kore. And that's why I must fight this duel. Because only then will you have your place here, once I have defeated Nordstram. Only then will people see that I am their king and you their queen. And that's why I will win this duel, because I have something real to fight for.'

Isolt's eyes stared up at him through the darkness of the room, like two pearls glowing at the bottom of the sea. He felt her hand stroke his face, her fingers comb through his hair and her thumb rub over his ear. Her other arm had wrapped itself around his back and was pulling him towards her.

'Come and lie on top of me,' she said.

*

Another month and a half went by, and in two weeks it would
be the summer solstice. The day that had been set for the duel.

Not a day had gone by which Marc had not spent practising
his sword-fighting skills. He could now feel that real progress
had been achieved and all those hours of effort and sweat had
not been in vain.

One day, after another long session of hard practice, he
walked over to a bench on the shaded side of the courtyard so
that he could sit and rest, sheltered from the hot afternoon sun.
Forsin, who had been watching, was waiting for him there.

'So, what did you think?' Marc asked as he sat down.

'It's pretty impressive,' Forsin answered. 'Your partners seem
to be having more and more trouble parrying your blows, and
finding an opening through which they could strike back at you.
You have come a long way since the days when even I would have
given myself a good chance at cutting you open like a feathered
goose, had we for any reason fought a duel against each other.'
Forsin burst out laughing.

'Very funny, very funny,' Marc said. 'It's easy to see that I'm
the one who is going to be risking my life in two weeks' time,
and not you. And I'm not surprised to hear you talk in terms
of cutting open a feathered goose, because the nearest thing to
a sword you have ever held in your hand has been a kitchen
knife. I'm a little surprised, though, Forsin. Being an old friend,
I thought you'd be a little more concerned at the risks I'm taking
in accepting this challenge.'

Forsin looked at Marc inquisitively. 'Have you not talked to
your mother lately?' he asked.

'No,' Marc answered irritably. 'Her lack of confidence in me
is sapping my morale. I don't want to be a witness to any more of
her attempts to find a way around my having to fight this duel.

As a matter of fact, she seems to be avoiding me at the moment. All the better, though, as I don't wish to talk to her right now.'

Forsin hesitated before replying. There was a strange look of compassion on his face. 'Perhaps you should have a chat with her all the same,' he said.

'Why? What's…?' Marc did not finish his sentence. At the far end of the courtyard, standing in the doorway of the entrance hall, was a man he did not immediately recognise, but knew he had seen somewhere before.

The man descended the steps and started to cross the courtyard.

'I know him,' Marc said.

'Tristan!' Forsin said in a low voice, as the man stepped out of the blazing sun and into the shade.

'Hello, Marc,' he said, stopping a few steps away from their bench.

'Ah, Tristan,' replied Marc, standing up to shake his hand. 'The man who once saved our lives. What a pleasure this is. And what happy twist of fate brings you here?'

'I have come at your mother's invitation,' Tristan answered with a surprised look on his face.

Marc looked over at Forsin, who stared back at him with the same mixture of irony and sympathy as before. 'Perhaps you should have a chat with her all the same,' he repeated.

Marc turned to Tristan. 'I hope you will be staying amongst us long enough that you may be a witness to my demise or change of status,' he said.

'But your mother sent for me so that I may relieve you of the burden of having to fight that duel,' Tristan said.

Just at that moment, the knight who had been practising with Marc came back into the courtyard, carrying his sword and shield. Tristan looked down at the sword and shield lying on the floor by the bench where Marc had been sitting.

'I think there may have been a misunderstanding,' Marc said. 'But please, feel welcome here and treat this castle as your own home. I hope you will forgive my rudeness, but I must take leave of you and shall be back presently. Meanwhile, Forsin here will keep you company.'

'Don't worry yourself about me,' Tristan said. 'Forsin and I are like old friends. I shall see you later at your own pleasure.'

As Marc ran up the stairs, he could feel a torrent of blood rushing into his head. What is it with this man who always seems to show up unannounced, as if falling out of the sky? he asked himself.

As he reached the door of his mother's private chamber, he gave three loud bangs with his knuckles and pushed it open. Isabelle turned from the window where she had been standing, staring down into the courtyard.

'I do wish you would wait for an answer before barging in like a wild boar,' she said in a calm, tired voice. 'Otherwise, what's the point of knocking on the door?'

'You know very well why I'm here,' replied Marc angrily, 'so don't pretend to be surprised by my manners. I want to know why you've invited Tristan here.'

'Oh, him,' she said. 'I was going to talk about it with you, but it's this kind of reaction that has put me off doing so. You get so worked up about everything. It makes any kind of reasoned discussion with you very difficult.'

Marc stared straight into her eyes.

'I'm not having anybody fight this duel in my place,' he said slowly and emphatically.

'You see!' his mother answered. 'You don't want to listen to what anyone else has to say. Anyway, it's not just your decision. The stability of the whole kingdom is at risk.'

'He has no right to fight in my place,' Marc said. 'He is not a member of this kingdom. He comes from Ireland. It's you who have lost all reason for even considering it.'

'You are quite wrong,' his mother answered. 'Tristan was made an honorary knight of this kingdom by your father, for having saved you and your wife's lives. If you had had the politeness to stay on for the feast after the hunt, which your father had invited you to, you would have been aware of this.'

Marc was taken aback for a moment, but then caught hold of himself.

'I will not let him fight in my place,' he repeated.

His mother stared straight back at him. 'That is not your decision,' Isabelle replied. 'You are not king yet. The decision falls upon my shoulders and I cannot put the whole kingdom in danger just to save your pride. I'm sorry.'

Marc stormed out of his mother's chamber, slamming the door behind him. When he reached the stairway, he met Isolt on her way up, accompanied by Kore.

'Oh, Marc, so there you are. I've been looking for you,' she said excitedly. 'You'll never guess who I saw downstairs in the courtyard?'

'He's the man who saved your life!' Kore said before Marc could answer.

'Yes, I know.'

'And Mama's life too,' she added.

'Yes,' Marc said. 'I met him downstairs.'

'Did you talk to him?' Isolt asked.

'A little.'

'Did he tell you why he's here?' Isolt enquired.

'Yes,' Marc answered. 'But he didn't have to.'

'What do you mean?' Isolt asked.

Marc took hold of her shoulders. 'Look, I haven't got time to explain,' he replied, 'but I've got to leave right now for the fortress. I won't be back before tomorrow, but it's very important. Don't worry. Everything is all right. I just have to talk to Gauvin. Otherwise we are going to be in a mess. Do you understand?'

'No,' she said. 'I don't understand.'

Marc squeezed her shoulders. 'Then trust me,' he said.

Isolt looked at him. She didn't understand what was going on, or what he was trying to do. But that didn't matter. 'I trust you,' she said.

*

The two men sat on a bench under the linden tree in the fortress courtyard, drinking ale.

'I don't see why you're telling me all this,' Gauvin said.

'My mother will listen to you. She respects you. If you were to tell her I stand a chance against Nordstram, she will believe you.'

The sun had finally dropped into the ocean beyond the cliffs, and a cool breeze was blowing as the day's fading light surrendered to the oncoming night.

'For me to tell her that, I would first have to believe it myself,' Gauvin said after a moment's silence.

'Why do you think I've ridden all the way out here?' Marc asked. 'It was to take you back with me to the castle so that you can watch me cross swords with some of the knights there. Then you could make up your own mind.'

There was more silence as Gauvin's big, oval face peered into the growing darkness. He liked Marc. Perhaps because he had known his father so well, had known what a tempest of brute force and willpower that man had been, how sure of himself he was; and not without reason, because he was rarely wrong when it really mattered. Yet, none of this seemed to have rubbed off on Marc. He was in every way the opposite of his father, and it was for this reason that Gauvin couldn't help but like him.

'I don't have to ride all that way to make up my mind,' Gauvin said. 'We can settle this right here in the courtyard, tomorrow morning.'

'What? You and I?' Marc asked.

'Yes, you and I,' Gauvin answered.

Marc looked at the old knight, but he couldn't see any expression on his face. While they had been sitting there the sharp outlines of the day had been swallowed by the invading night.

The following morning, when the sun was still low in the sky, Marc stood outside the fortress door, his eyes contemplating the glow of purple vapour rising off the moor.

What is it? Marc asked himself. What is it that you are trying so hard to prove? That you are as much of a man as your brother was? Or is it Isolt? Have those dark eyes convinced you that you will never fully be a man until you have conquered that last piece of her soul that slips through your fingers when you hold her close up against you?

'What's happened? Has your foolhardy courage scampered over the moor like a scared rabbit this morning?' Gauvin asked.

Marc turned around and saw the old man standing in the middle of the courtyard. He was wearing his suit of chain mail. His sword, in its sheath, hung at his side from a belt. In one hand he held his shield and in the other his helmet. He had a cheerful smile on his face and appeared to be in a good mood.

'Have you at least found a sword and a shield in the armoury?' Gauvin asked.

'Yes,' Marc replied. 'They're on the bench. I've even found a helmet that fits me.'

'Well, why don't you get them and show me what you can do?'

This is ridiculous! Marc thought. What can I possibly prove by fighting an old man? He stepped into the courtyard, crossed over to the linden tree and picked up his helmet, which he pulled down over his head. He took the sword and shield and walked over to Gauvin, who stood waiting for him, his helmet now covering his head and his sword in his hand. For a moment, the two men stood facing each other.

'Do you want me to take you out right away?' asked Gauvin finally. 'Or do you want to try a few attacks on me first and I'll just defend?'

The words were enough to irritate Marc and send a flash of anger into his heart. All the accumulated derision he had suffered from his mother and the other lords at those endless meetings now exploded inside him. As if in a dream, he found himself rushing forward and striking a blow with all his might down onto Gauvin's sword in an attempt to knock it out of his hand.

With a minimum of effort, Gauvin stepped to one side, pulled his sword away from the descending blow and raised it up, so that its point pushed against Marc's neck, just under his Adam's apple.

'That's very good,' Gauvin said. 'Don't hold anything back when you attack. But you should never strike in anger, because you're liable to leave yourself open to a counter-attack. Now try something else.'

Marc took a step back and a few deep breaths. He knew it was stupid to have lost control of himself like that. If he'd done that in a real fight, it could have cost him his life.

'Come on!' Gauvin urged. 'Try to do better than you've just done. But remember, don't hold anything back.'

Marc moved forward slowly, his shield held out in front of him and his arm with the sword pulled back, ready to strike. As Marc advanced on him, Gauvin circled around to Marc's left. Marc feigned a few attacks with his sword, and each time Gauvin dodged them by moving away to his left so that Marc, sucked in by the rhythm of this evasion, suddenly sprung far out to his left and thrust his arm forward in a full attack. Gauvin, almost simultaneously, circled to Marc's right and brought his sword down onto his outstretched arm, stopping it in time so that it only lightly cut his skin, just enough for a thin line of blood to surface on his forearm.

'Even with your chain mail jacket on, I could have cut your arm off,' Gauvin boasted. 'So come on, show us a bit more of what you know. Try to put a bit of imagination into it.'

Under his helmet, Marc could feel drops of sweat running off his temples and down the side of his face. He felt as if he had just walked into a nightmare, as if he was now facing the cold reality that had been awaiting him at the end of this madness, this foolhardy adventure that he had pushed himself into. And yet he couldn't believe it, he couldn't believe that this old man could anticipate every one of his moves.

Marc continued to attack. He could feel a fever of contained fury boiling inside him, rushing up to his head and into his limbs. It made him awkward and clumsy as he moved in and struck at Gauvin with his sword. The old man just circled around him once more, countering his attacks as if he knew where they were coming from even before they were launched.

The more this happened, the more Marc's thoughts and body were invaded by his fury. Eventually, no longer conscious of what he was doing, he felt something strike him, pushing him off balance so that he went crashing down onto his back.

'That's enough!' Gauvin said. 'The sun is getting hot and I'm beginning to sweat like a pig under this armour.'

*

When Gauvin stepped back into the courtyard, he found Marc sitting in the shade under the linden tree. His body was bent forward, his elbows resting on his knees, and he was staring at the ground between his boots. Gauvin sat down on the bench beside him. 'How are you feeling?' he asked.

'How do you think?' Marc answered.

'Don't be disheartened,' Gauvin said. 'You're alive and breathing. At least you know what you have to do if you want to stay that way.'

'You mean, let Tristan fight the duel in my place?'

'I think that's obvious,' Gauvin replied. 'If he's fought in the Crusades, then chances are he's got some experience.'

Marc straightened himself up and looked at Gauvin.

'I don't understand how you anticipated every move I made,' he said. 'Back at the castle, I was beginning to get the better of some of the young knights I practised with.'

'That's because they lack experience,' replied Gauvin. 'It's not just how well you handle a sword by practising all the different moves. You learn in time how to sense where a man is placing the weight of his body, so you know where he can strike directly at you, and where he can't without shifting his weight. That's how you can anticipate. You see how his body is aligned, if his breathing is deep or shallow, where he's vulnerable, where he's not, and you move accordingly. But, aside from all that, and most important of all, you have to know why you're there facing your opponent. If there is the slightest doubt about the purity of your motives, then you're in danger.'

Marc was leaning forward again and staring down at his boots. 'And you think that, when we faced off against each other this morning, you had less doubt about the purity of your motives than I?' he asked.

Gauvin looked at Marc, his small eyes peering out of a face that seemed to have been cut out of granite. 'Yes.'

'Why?' asked Marc.

'Because you are trying to prove to me, and yourself, that you are someone you are not. And I was simply trying to knock some sense into you.'

*

That very same morning, Isolt and Kore were once again outside the castle. Isolt had gone to sit under the big oak tree near the chapel with her book while Kore and her cousin, Lorna, were playing in the meadow. They had a pig's bladder that Forsin had washed and blown up for them and they were now throwing it at each other.

Isolt closed her book. She was unable, that morning, to concentrate on what she was reading. For the last few days she had been feeling restless and could not bear to be confined within the castle walls.

If she had not been able to sleep that night, it was because she was worried about Marc. She knew now why he had gone to see Gauvin. He obviously wanted to get him to persuade his mother that he was skilled enough to hold his own in a duel with Nordstram. But that was not why she was worried about him, because it was pretty clear to her that he was not going to fight in that duel at all. His mother had decided otherwise and she had found a way of stopping him. What really worried her was that she had this strange feeling that there was some kind of force that was pulling her away from him, and that she felt weak and vulnerable and unable to resist what was happening to her.

She knew it was unfair to ask him to fight a duel against a man who was sure to defeat him, but when he had seemed ready to take that risk it had awakened something inside her, a feeling for him that was stronger than anything she had felt for him before. But for the last few days, the feeling seemed to have been slipping away from her. And it was all Brangien's fault, she remembered now. Had she not thrown the runes, several days ago, and read them for her as she often did, telling her to expect a visit from someone?

'Who?' Isolt asked.

Brangien would not answer, and the more Isolt asked the more vague and evasive Brangien became. She reluctantly told her that this visitor was a man and not a woman, but insisted that he was of no importance and should be forgotten.

A strange noise interrupted Isolt's thoughts as she sat under the tree. Looking up, she saw that it was the door of the chapel being pushed open from inside.

A man walked out from the shadows and closed the door behind him. Tristan. He stood for a while, very still, and then began walking towards her.

'Good morning,' he said, looking down at her.

'So it was him,' Isolt whispered to herself, and at that moment felt a rushing, unbearable turmoil.

As Isolt had not answered his greetings, Tristan stood and looked up at the sky. It was a beautiful sunny day. He shook his head. 'If the sun has chased the clouds away this morning, I'm sure it was to put all its light on you.'

Isolt asked herself what it was about this man that so disturbed her. Was it because, from their very first encounter, he had decided he could just walk into her life and impose himself upon her? When she had seen him the previous day, just after his arrival, she had already felt a pang of uneasiness about his presence, but now that she had finally made the connection between his arrival and what Brangien had read in the runes, she was overwhelmed by a feeling of panic.

'Locking yourself up in that chapel is not the best way to appreciate our weather,' Isolt said, trying to hold on to her composure.

'I'm sure you are right,' Tristan said with a smile. 'It must be far nicer to sit under that tree. May I come and join you there?'

'Absolutely not!' Isolt answered. 'As an honorary knight of this kingdom, don't you know that I will soon be your queen?'

'Is that really your ambition?' Tristan asked, his face changing its expression as he now stared at her with genuine interest. 'To become a queen?'

She heard his words echo inside her and a shiver reverberated right down through her body. What a very strange question to have asked, she thought. Everybody around her, those who were close to her and those who were not, had all assumed, without the slightest doubt, that this was a great privilege being offered to her. And he, in all innocence, had just asked her if this was really her ambition.

She felt his words reach right into her and touch some part of her that she thought to be beyond the reach of most people – some part of her she even tried to keep hidden from herself. And suddenly she realised that the person she was looking at was no longer the same person. 'And what about you?' she asked. 'What were you doing in the chapel? Were you praying to the virgin mother holding her child in there? They say she has secret powers. Is that how you intend to win this duel you are now supposed to fight?'

'I could have been praying for something else,' he said.

He no longer seemed the boorish lout she had taken him to be. She could hear a longing in his voice, an unspoken passion, something vulnerable hiding behind his uncouth manners. For a moment, they just stared at each other.

'Will you at least tell me what your book is about?' he asked finally.

It was obvious to her now that he, too, had been shaken by something he could see in her.

And as for her... well, it was as if the person who had come with her book to sit under the tree, so her daughter could play with her cousin in the meadow, the mother who was the cornerstone, the support holding up all her decisions and her opinions, the shield that fended off all her doubts and uncertainties and that helped her look straight into the face of life... it was as if that person was no longer clearly there.

As if the peace she had enjoyed for the past few years, away from the storm that had been raging in her heart just before she met Marc – who had rescued her in a way, when she accepted to follow him back to his fortress – it was as if this choice she had made was being challenged now by this man who was looking down at her.

*

And yet Marc had managed to convince himself that he had to fight this man, even though he knew in his heart that, short of a miracle, he was going to be defeated and perhaps even killed. He also realised now that the outcome of the duel had never been his main preoccupation; what really mattered to him was the fact that he was willing to fight. That was what was so important to him, that he was willing to go through with it, whatever his chances were. All along he knew that his real defeat, his only defeat, would be to back out and not fight.

So what had pushed him into this madness in the first place? He did not have to search very far for the answer to this question.

It was her of course, Isolt. Because, by all the laws that limit the world to being what it is, she should never have fallen into his arms, into his bed.

She was too beautiful for that market square where she was selling her shawls, where they first met. Too beautiful for the desolate moor they had crossed on their way to the fortress where he kept her. Too beautiful for him. And it was this truth that he had to fight, that he wanted so badly to defeat, even if it would cost him his life.

And that's why he had jumped at the opportunity to fight this duel. Because he knew that if he could push himself into that arena, and walk up to Nordstram with a sword in his hand, he would find that something inside him that could sustain and put a seal on his fancy that he and Isolt were made for each other.

As Marc rode up to the castle, he saw Isolt sitting under the tree by the chapel, and went over to join her. Kore was still playing with Lorna nearby. When Isolt saw Marc, she began to gather together the remains of their picnic.

'So what happened?' she asked. 'I know why Tristan is here. Is that why you ran off to see Gauvin?'

'I thought that maybe he could offer an impartial judgement on my chances,' Marc answered. He did not get down from his horse, for he felt that it would be easier to face this painful moment if he stayed up in the saddle.

'And what was his judgement?' Isolt asked, staring up at him.

'It was more than just a judgement. We actually fought a duel of our own this morning.'

'What! You and him?' Isolt asked with a surprised smile.

Marc looked down at her and felt very uncomfortable. He realised that there was no place he could sit or stand that would make what he had to tell her sound any better. Whether he told it to her from up here in his saddle, or whether he whispered it to her from a dark hole dug in the ground, it would still be the same sad truth that would come out of his mouth. 'Yes,' replied Marc. 'Me and him.'

'And what happened?'

'Well, he could have cut me up into several pieces had he wanted to.'

'But he's an old man!' Isolt protested. 'You were holding back, weren't you?'

'No, I wasn't,' Marc said. 'I would have cut his arm off if I could have, or stabbed him through the belly, but I never got anywhere near being able to do that. You know how much it means to me to fight this duel!'

'So what are you going to do?' Isolt asked.

Marc saw her big eyes staring up at him expectantly and he knew that somewhere in their depths there was something waiting to judge him, something she made no attempt to conceal. She, at least, was not trying to prove she was something other than what she was, Marc thought, and that something, whatever it was, wanted him to fight, no matter how great the danger. And nothing he could say would change her mind.

'So?' she asked again.

'He made me understand that I haven't got the slightest chance if I fight,' Marc said.

'So you're not going to do it?'

'Even if I still wanted to, I couldn't,' Marc replied. 'It's not my decision. My mother has the final word, and she's already arranged for Tristan to fight in my place.'

'Yes, I know,' Isolt replied. 'Well, never mind. It was a nice dream while it lasted.' She got up and called out to Kore and Lorna, who came running over.

'Papa! Papa!' Kore shouted. 'Can I come up on the horse?'

Isolt lifted her up and, with her mother's help, she climbed onto the saddle behind Marc and held tightly on to his waist.

Seeing that Lorna was looking up at them, Marc asked her if she wanted to come up as well. The little girl nodded, so Isolt lifted her too and Marc sat her in the space in front of the saddle between his arms. He then gently urged the horse forward along the moat, towards the drawbridge. Isolt brushed the dirt off the back of her skirt, picked up the basket of leftovers, and followed behind them.

5

THE DUEL

Early one morning, down through the fields of winter wheat, which, thanks to the fine weather, was already turning to a bright gold, a long procession could be seen making its way to the Moroi forest.

Leading the parade were Marc, Isolt and Isabelle, Marc's mother. Riding just behind them were his uncle, Ganelon, and his wife, Susanne, and behind them was Tristan with two attending knights, followed by all the other lords and knights of the kingdom accompanied by their ladies. Behind them came knights without any fiefs of their own, who manned the fortresses and guarded the castles.

It was a colourful occasion, the lords and ladies all dressed in their finest attire. Even their horses were combed and brushed and had their manes plaited and tied with ribbons. At the very back of this procession were two horse-drawn carts, one of which was driven by Forsin. They were stacked with food and drink, plates, mugs, trays and dishes. Valets and maids sat on the sides of the carts, with more following on foot.

It was the summer solstice and their destination was a patch of flat, bare land in a clearing in the forest, where the duel between Tristan and Nordstram was to take place.

Marc's eyes were vacant. He could see the steam rising up from the fields and smell the scent of the earth as it warmed in the morning sun. He could hear the song of the lark flying high above him, but it all seemed far away and unconnected to him.

He was also aware, like everyone else moving down that road, that this was the day when the fate of the whole kingdom was to be decided. That soon, he, like everybody else, could only watch as the invisible strings that tied all their lives together were pulled and tugged by two men engaged in mortal combat. But, unlike everyone else, the outcome of this battle did not matter to him any more. For what difference would it make, in the long run, who was to be king of this little patch of land lost at the tip of the world? Would it not all be the same in the end? Would they not, once it was all over, go on with their lives? Would their children not marry and have children of their own, and would they not toil and suffer and eventually die just as before?

No, of far greater concern to him was why Isolt was torturing him. Why was she ignoring him? Why was he being made to suffer for events that she knew as well as he did were entirely out of his control? After all, he was not the one who had called Tristan to come and fight this duel for him.

And the worst of it was that she never now missed an opportunity to spend time in Tristan's company. She even went and watched when he trained with the young knights to help them improve their swordplay, whereas she had only watched her husband on one or two occasions from her bedroom window, and then only briefly, before returning to her occupations.

He didn't understand her behaviour. They had had their quarrels and she would sometimes become distant and moody with him, but this time it was different. She was treating him like a complete stranger, as if he were hardly there at all, and giving all her attention to Tristan.

She was like another person! What was she trying to do to him? He wanted to confront her and ask this very question, but he was frightened of hearing the answer. He preferred to think that she was punishing him for being a coward, for fooling her, for making her believe he was going to do something he never really had any intention of doing.

And he tried to comfort himself by thinking that her strange behaviour was for one reason: to punish him. Once she got over her anger, all would return to normal. He had to believe this. He had to believe that she still loved him. Anything else would be too hard to bear.

Unlike Marc's, Isolt's face was full of expression. Her dark eyes were alive and vibrant, and never had she seemed more beautiful. She could feel something growing inside her, the green ripening corn, the scent of the earth, the song of the bird flying overhead; all seemed each in their own way to carry the resonance of this force growing in her heart, which had pushed its way out of the dark shadows of winter and was sinking its roots into her.

And now, on this bright, clear morning, it finally had acquired a face, a shape, and she understood that it was Tristan. He had reawakened something that she could see in his eyes, in his smile, in his quiet self-control and confidence, and in the deep longing hiding behind it. That something, that she had tried to forget and cast aside, which had now returned to claim its rightful place in her life. And all this had started under the tree by the chapel when he had asked her if her ambition was truly to be queen.

Had he really come all this way to fight a duel? Or was it for another reason? To find her, to save her, just as her father had done when he had rescued her from that convent. To save her from what her life had become, to bring her into the light, to awaken her to what life really was.

But with her father she had not been able to learn fast enough, too young and naïve for such a violent change. Whereas now she was a woman, and, though Tristan carried the same charisma as her father once had, he had none of that man's darkness hidden in his heart. She could see this very clearly and was no longer afraid of the passion she could feel burning inside her.

For she knew, and could feel it now without any doubt, that this passion had awakened something inside her – her soul perhaps – and that her life had to serve its demands now, wherever this might take her.

And even though she was afraid of the pain this passion might inflict on the people close to her, on Marc especially, she knew that there was no point trying to resist it, for once your soul has been awakened to itself, there is no force that can hold it back from achieving its mission.

Isabelle was frowning. Once or twice she had turned her head to catch a quick glimpse of Tristan. It was hard to read anything on his face, but there was an aura of calm concentration that floated over him as he sat upright on his horse, his eyes staring straight ahead.

I hope this boy is as good as his reputation, she thought. They say he has never been defeated in a sword fight. But this tale about him has accompanied him over the sea from Ireland. And has not every story from Ireland a supernatural element in it? Who knows what can be believed about the strange things that are supposed to happen in that place? A place where miracles are as frequent as the changing of the seasons…

'Oh, my Lord! Please help me come through this! I am but a poor woman left alone now, without anyone to support me but you, my Lord.'

She had spoken these last words quietly to herself and then looked to see if Marc or Isabelle might have overheard her. She was relieved to see that they were both lost in their own thoughts; she was embarrassed by this sudden outburst of faith, which, even to her own ears, had sounded only half sincere.

The procession moved into the forest, leaving the bright sun behind as they entered under the thick blanket of leaves, where something of the stillness of the night was yet lurking in the filtered light and heavy shadows.

Tristan was staring at Isolt's back. Her blue dress seemed to glow amidst the shadows of the forest, but he did not find this strange because he could no longer look at her without seeing a light shining out of her. Whether it was her eyes, her whole face, her hands... Something shone out of her and he knew what it was. It was the light of destiny.

He knew it because an astrologer he had befriended in Constantinople had told him that there were two forces that ruled the world. One was the force of history; the other was the force of destiny.

History rules you from below. It belongs to this world and keeps you trapped here. But destiny descends on you from the heavens and is connected with the movement of the stars. History pushes you forward from the past, whereas destiny calls to you from the future and pulls you towards it. And such is its power that you can override history should you fall under its spell.

But it was only now that he understood what the astrologer was talking about; up until now, his life in this world had seemed to be continually trapped by a series of circumstances that stood in the way of him ever finding what he was looking for. And what was it that he was looking for? He had thought he knew until the moment he had spotted her sitting under that tree.

When he had walked over to talk to her and she had looked up at him, whatever it was he had been carrying in his heart up until then had dissolved in the glaring light of her dark eyes. And, from that moment on, he knew that his life belonged to those eyes. This was his destiny, and nothing could stand in its way.

It was not long before they reached the clearing in the forest, where the morning sun once again shone directly down on them as they dismounted from their horses. Pickets had been hammered into the ground in a large circle, linked together by ropes with triangular flags tied to them to demarcate the area where the duel was to be fought. A rostrum had been erected at one end of the clearing, while chairs had been placed in several rows to accommodate Marc, Isolt and the rest of the nobility who had come to watch the duel.

Most of the seats had already been filled. Isabelle, Marc, Isolt, Ganelon and Susanne were all sitting in the front row, and a crowd had gathered around the ropes along the periphery of the circle. At the far end, opposite the rostrum, a small party of people surrounded a figure who stood head and shoulders above them.

'Is that Nordstram?' Isolt asked.

'Yes,' Marc answered. Even from that distance, he could not mistake the man's large, grey moustache that sharpened into two points at the side of his mouth like deadly daggers.

'But he's a giant!' said Isolt. 'No wonder nobody wanted to fight him!'

I did, Marc was about to answer. However, he stopped himself in time, realising how pathetic it would have sounded coming from his mouth as he sat up there on the rostrum, ready to watch someone fight in his place.

It had been decided by his mother and the elders that, because of the controversial nature of this duel, there would be no public announcement in the market squares of the towns of when and where the contest was to be fought. But as more and more people appeared from the darkness of the surrounding forest into the clearing, knights were posted around the boundary of the circle to keep the crowd outside.

When this was done, Isabelle turned around to the arbitrators sitting behind her. 'Don't you think we should get this duel started now, while the crowd can still be held back?' Everyone agreed that it would be better not to delay any longer. Isabelle was beginning to suspect that a lot of the people gathered around the ropes belonged to the village attached to Nordstram's castle and the local region. There was already some shouting between them and the people from Corsan, and none of them wished to see this hostility develop any further.

Ganelon walked across to the other side of the arena and talked for a while with Nordstram and his attending knights. He then marched to the middle of the clearing, unwinding the flag from the pole he carried with him, which he then raised above his head.

Marc's mother looked to her right, where Tristan was standing talking to the two knights seconding him. She nudged Marc. 'Tell Tristan to place himself inside the circle. Can't he see that your uncle has raised the flag?'

'Tell him yourself!' Marc replied sharply. 'You're the one who insisted he should fight in my place.'

At that moment Tristan looked up at the rostrum and Isabelle pointed to the spot where he should be standing. But instead of putting his helmet on and stepping in under the rope, he climbed up onto the rostrum, strode over and stopped in front of Isolt.

'You should be standing at your place in the circle,' Isabelle said. 'My brother-in-law is waiting to drop the flag.'

'Yes, my lady,' Tristan answered. Then he turned to look directly at Isolt. 'And you, my lady, would you accord me the honour of receiving from your hand one of the ribbons you have tied in your hair?'

Isolt stared at him. He was smiling at her, his eyes clear and unafraid. His courage and audacity astounded her. She felt herself reach up, untie one of the ribbons that held the strands of her hair from her face and hand it to him. He took it and pushed it through the steel mesh at the tip of the sleeve on his right wrist.

'Could you tie it for me?' he asked, stretching out his arm to her.

Was it because it seemed like everyone in that clearing, whether from afar or nearby, was now looking at them, that she felt as if she was standing on the edge of a cliff? And that, if she took another step in his direction, she would fall and would never climb back?

'I hope you're not going to ask me to go down there and fight this duel for you,' she said.

Tristan looked at her and smiled again. 'No,' he replied. 'But with this ribbon, more of you will be down there with me than you may now think.'

'Are you not being presumptuous?' she asked dryly, only too aware that Marc and his mother could overhear.

'Wait and see,' he said. He turned, walked to the edge of the platform, jumped down and joined the two knights who were waiting with his sword, shield and helmet.

Marc could only sit in his chair and watch, impotent and unable to react. He, too, could not believe the impetuosity of Tristan, walking up there and courting his wife without fear or shame. And he could also see that Isolt was enjoying it, which made him furious. How could she humiliate him like this? Was she really that angry with him for not fighting this duel himself? Had she really wanted him to die for her? Was that it? Did she not realise that this would put her own life, and Kore's, at risk as well?

Across the width of the roped-off arena, with an expectant crowd waiting in near silence, Tristan and Nordstram now stared at each other through the visors of their helmets. Ganelon stood in the middle of the circle with the flag held high above his head. Three crows cawed loudly as they flew off the top of a tree and chased each other to the other side of the clearing.

The flag dropped. Ganelon walked to the edge of the circle and made his way along the ropes, back towards the rostrum, as the two men marched forward with their swords and shields. The whole crowd seemed to be holding its breath as Tristan and Nordstram advanced in a straight line that would lead to a head-on collision somewhere near the centre of the arena.

As they came within striking distance of one another, the difference in size between the two men became sorely apparent. It was Tristan who stepped out of the line of direct collision at the last moment, ducking around to Nordstram's right and attempting a stab into his ribs. But just as impressive as his size was Nordstram's speed, and with a sweeping blow his sword came down in a flash and crashed against Tristan's with such force that the clash echoed, like the clang of a church bell, through the forest, sending the crows flying up over the clearing once again as Tristan's sword fell from his hand and dropped to the ground.

Tristan hesitated for a brief instant as he glanced down at the sword lying at his feet. He looked up at Nordstram, whose weapon was already swinging down onto him, with just enough time to duck under his shield. There was another clang of crashing metal and Tristan felt the power of the blow shaking his whole body as he crouched and searched with his hand for the sword on the floor, but Nordstram had already kicked it out of his reach.

'My God! He's going to kill him!' Isolt cried out. She reached for Marc's hand and squeezed it hard.

Tristan had just enough time to straighten up and balance himself firmly on both legs in order to block the next blow that came swinging at him from the side. Once again, he felt the pain run through his arm, right up to his shoulder as Nordstram hit his shield.

'He's going to kill him!' Isolt repeated in a trembling voice as she still held on firmly to Marc's hand.

Tristan backed away, but Nordstram never allowed him out of reach as he charged forward, striking his shield and nearly knocking him down as he fell back in retreat. They moved in this way until Nordstram had pushed Tristan to the far end of the arena, right up against the rope. Tristan tried to escape by moving to the side, but Nordstram sidestepped with him. He turned the other way, but Nordstram moved with him again, keeping him blocked against the rope.

'Oh dear! Oh dear!' Isabelle sounded as if she was watching her whole life collapse before her eyes. For a moment the two men seemed to be catching their breath as they stood, face to face, staring at each other.

Isolt could not see the expression on Tristan's face under his helmet; even without it he was too far away from her now. Yet had he not been right here, breathing down on her, just a short while ago as she tied the ribbon to his sleeve? It seemed that a great knot was being tightened around her heart and would stop her from breathing were he to be killed in the coming moments.

Why have you been such a fool? her heart cried out to her. Why weren't you as audacious as he was when he walked up onto the rostrum to talk to you? Why didn't you tell him that you loved him! That you did not want to be queen. That you wanted him!

'Go on, Nordstram! Kill the foreign bastard! What are you waiting for?' a voice shouted from the crowd. It seemed to distract the giant knight for a moment, and Tristan seized his chance to spring forward in one great leap and thrust his shield into Nordstram's chest and head. Ducking under the arm that blindly swung its sword at him, he let go of his shield and, as it dropped to the floor, regained his balance and started running, as fast as his legs would carry him, back towards the centre of the circle where his own weapon was lying on the ground.

There was a loud cry from the crowd as they watched Tristan struggle with both hands to remove his helmet as Nordstram marched back towards him. Releasing his head from the armour, Tristan shook it like a dog who had freed itself from its collar. He bent down, placed the helmet on the ground, picked up his sword and stood calmly waiting for Nordstram.

'What's the matter with him? Has he lost his mind?' Marc's mother asked.

'Maybe,' his uncle answered. 'But he has found his sword again.'

When Nordstram was close enough, his sword cut through the air with the same speed and power with which he had struck at Tristan before, but this time the attack failed to push him off balance. Instead, Tristan jumped within inches of the cutting blade as it swung past him, then circled around in the same direction as the weapon's trajectory. Leaping up, he struck a blow with his own sword to the back of Nordstram's helmet. An exclamation of awe and astonishment rose up from the watching crowd, as if from a choir.

Nordstram was clearly furious, perhaps suspecting that Tristan had hoodwinked him into underestimating his abilities and was now trying to make a fool of him. He charged forward, stabbing and swinging his sword in all directions. But Tristan continued to jump, dodge and circle just inches away from its reach, hitting back occasionally with more strikes to the back of the head. The crowd was laughing and jeering in a confused cacophony of shouts and cries.

Finally, boiling over with rage and frustration, Nordstram threw his sword and shield to the ground and then lifted his own helmet from his head before bending down and picking up only the sword. His eyes had the wild look of someone with only one aim in his heart. It was as though he had forgotten everything else in the world and could see only Tristan. It was clear he wanted to kill him.

'All right, you bastard! Let's fight this thing out on equal terms!' he yelled.

He advanced on Tristan once more, but this time with caution, ready to step back. When he got close enough, he feigned a few attacks to try to catch Tristan off balance before striking a real blow at him.

Tristan still circled around him, keeping just outside his reach but gradually drawing his opponent towards him. Finally, he allowed him close enough for Nordstram to attempt a real stab at him, jumping forward and thrusting his arm out with lightning speed. But Tristan knew it was coming and twisted his body so that the blade, like an arrow, brushed past his chest. At the same time he stabbed his own sword deep into Nordstram's shoulder, cutting clean through his chain mail jacket.

Tristan drew his sword back. Blood rushed out of the open wound and Nordstram, stunned and shocked, took a step backwards for the first time since the duel had started. He tried to lift his arm, but Tristan's blade had severed the muscle and he couldn't move it. His hand opened and the sword it had held fell down onto the ground at his feet.

The duel was over. Tristan picked up his shield and helmet and carried them to the rostrum, to cheers and whistles from the crowd. Nordstram, his hand placed over his wounded shoulder, watched him as the blood gushed out between his fingers and ran down in dripping red streaks along his sleeve.

The ropes had been untied in several places and the carts had been parked in front of the platform. Plates of salted ham and millet cakes, as well as mugs of ale drawn from two large barrels, were distributed to the nobility as they stood in groups reliving what they had just witnessed. The duel was being fought and refought many times over as each person expressed his opinion on the why and wherefore of its unfolding.

The largest crowd was the one grouped around Tristan. He stood with a mug of ale in his hand, listening to their congratulatory remarks, answering their questions with jokes and an amused smile. But the real person, the one who had played with his own life and his opponent's, he kept concealed within himself.

Isolt was not part of that group. She stood not far away eating a millet cake, chatting with Marie, Solene and some of their friends.

As for Marc, he was the only person left sitting on the rostrum. Both Isolt and his mother had urged him to come down to join the party below, but he had stubbornly refused. Isabelle had looked at him with despair, wondering how, now that he could finally sit legitimately on his father's throne, such a fragile, stubborn soul could possibly cope with the strains and responsibilities of governing this kingdom. As for Isolt, she had simply told him that if he was going to be miserable, she had no intention of sitting there and being miserable with him. And as he had not answered her, but had simply looked at her with an expression of deep reproach, she had got up and left him there on his own.

'This is a great day for you! Why aren't you down there celebrating with the others?' It was Forsin who was staring up at him now, carrying a plate of ham and a cup of ale. 'Here, have some food at least,' he urged.

Marc looked at him with a feeling of pain tightening his heart. For when he looked at his old friend, was it not in some way as if he were looking into a mirror? Was there not something that they both shared that reflected back at him in Forsin's face?

Something painful and unanswered that Marc thought he had been able to escape, but that had now settled back in his heart and was staring at itself again with deep recognition.

'I don't want any food. I don't feel like eating or drinking,' Marc said, unable to hide his disgust.

Forsin studied him for a moment before replying. 'Where is that smile? Where is that good humour you used to have? These are perhaps the two things you could have brought to this throne that would be truly yours. So why have you lost them?'

For a brief instant Marc felt a ray of hope light up inside him, as he looked at the twinkle in Forsin's eyes. But, before he could catch hold of it, it was drowned in his own darkness. 'You know as well as I do that it was all just bluff,' he said.

'Then keep on bluffing. Don't give up now!' Forsin answered.

But Marc was staring at Isolt. Tristan had left the group surrounding him and gone to the cart to refill his cup. Isolt said something to Marie and Solene and had walked over to join him there.

'It's her, isn't it?' Forsin said.

Without looking away from Isolt, Marc replied, 'If it's her or whatever else, I can't talk about it.'

Forsin looked at Marc with deep sympathy. 'I understand,' he said. He placed the cup of ale and the plate of ham on the chair next to Marc and went back to join the party down below.

'You had us all worried for a while,' Isolt said to Tristan.

'Who's to say that wasn't my intention?' he answered.

'What? You mean you deliberately wanted to give us all a scare?' Isolt asked with amazement.

'Would you like some ale?' Tristan asked her. He looked over the cart to see if there was a spare cup, but could not find one. So he emptied his own cup, filled it up again from the barrel and handed it to her.

'I hope you don't mind drinking out of my cup,' he said.

Isolt shrugged indifferently, took a sip and looked up at him. 'So?' she asked.

'So what?' Tristan replied.

'So, why did you want to scare us?'

'I only wanted to scare you,' he replied. 'I wanted you to be down there with me, and you were there, weren't you? I mean your heart, of course.'

Isolt did not reply.

'You may want to resist it,' he went on, 'but there is nothing you can do about it. It's written up there in the heavens and you know it.'

As he talked she became aware of the strange mixture of strength and innocence in his eyes, that same lack of guile that had once made Marc so attractive. She smiled at Tristan. 'I'd better go and join my friends,' she said.

*

Why did I walk away from him? Why did I let Marc's sorrow drag me away? Isolt wanted to weep.

Tristan was somewhere behind her, lost amongst the long line of people joyously following them back to the castle. Jovial voices called out and answered as they moved out of the forest and started through the open fields, where the late-afternoon sun was still bright and hot.

What stopped me? she asked herself again. What held me back?

As if in answer to her question, a lark flew up out of the ripening wheat and rose high above in the sky, almost vertically, singing his song of love as if carried up there by the passion and sweetness of its melody. Isolt watched and felt a sudden flow of determination rush into her heart from an unknown source.

Does that little bird worry about what is right and what is wrong? she asked herself. Is he not taking a big risk up there, calling attention to himself with his song? Could not a passing hawk hear him and dive down on him? But without that risk, would his song sound so sweet and so pure?

'I must tell him!' she whispered. 'I must live! I must have the courage to be true to who I really am.'

Later that night, in the darkness of their room, Marc sat up on the bed waiting for Isolt, trying to stop the gloomy thoughts that were pushing their way into his heart from taking full possession of him.

Why was Isolt taking so long? What was she doing down there? Had they not all gone to bed? She had spent the whole evening ignoring him and as soon as she had finished eating she'd left the table and gone over to join Tristan and his companions who were sitting by the window. Soon she was taking part in their conversation and then they were all listening to her. She was telling them a story and they were teasing her about something she had said, laughing about it. She then quipped back at them and there was more laughter...

This was too much for Marc. As he looked at her across the room, he could see that she was having fun. How resplendent she looked, sitting over there enjoying herself amongst them, and how far away he felt, sitting in his father's seat, incapable of taking part in her pleasure.

He was jealous. He could feel the fire of his jealousy burning him up from inside. Finally, unable to take any more of his mother's and Ganelon's attempts to draw him out of his stupor with their endless comments on what a great day this was – that at last their kingdom had a king, whose coronation had been blessed by a high-ranking representative of the Church, and how this would ensure its continuity – Marc stood up and left without even excusing himself.

He had gone upstairs to their room and waited for her to come up and join him, so he could have her all to himself at last. But it seemed like half the night had gone by already and she had still not come up those stairs.

What was happening to him? He had the strange feeling that he was slipping back to where he had been, many years ago before he had met her. At the time, living alone in the fortress on the moor, he had never felt himself to be all that miserable; but now, the very thought of being alone again left him with a hollow feeling that was painful beyond anything he could have imagined.

And yet before he'd met her he had been able to fill that hollowness with his dreams and imagination, with his pleasantries, and his derision and disrespect for the world beyond the moor, as if he had found an answer to it all there in his fortress.

But all that was just bluff; he'd admitted as much to Forsin. It had seemed to work for him then because he had never before tasted anything real in his life. But then she came along and brought with her a sense of what it was like to really be alive, something he could never have imagined until she showed up that morning with her shawls in the market square.

Where was she, for God's sake!

Marc got up from the bed, picked up the candlestick, carried it out into the hallway and walked over to the stairway that circled up from the entrance hall. He could see no light down there and stood for a moment, listening, but there was no sound of voices. It seemed as if everyone had gone to bed. So where was Isolt?

The question had formulated itself at first as a simple response to her not seeming to be anywhere he could immediately think of. But the surrounding darkness and silence soon moved in with their own answer, and Marc's heart began to beat thunderously inside his chest, sending blood like hot flames into his head.

Was he running away from the staircase and whatever lay beyond it, or was he just heading back to his room because he wanted to make sure that she was not lying on the bed after all? Or was it because he suspected she might be somewhere outside the castle and he wanted to put on his boots and go out looking for her? He wasn't really sure what he was doing as he entered his room again. He saw that she was not lying on the bed, then walked over to the open window and looked down into the courtyard.

In the light of a half moon he saw two silhouettes in the middle of the courtyard. He recognised Isolt, because the fair streaks in her hair sparkled faintly in the white light of the moon as she moved her head as she talked. He could not hear what she was saying because her voice was very soft, almost a whisper, but he could see by the way she stood up close to the other silhouette, and by the way she moved her arms up and down in big sweeping gestures to emphasise what she was saying, that there was a real intimacy, an intensity, a passion even, passing between them at that moment.

Everything in Marc seemed to freeze as he stood looking down at them. Nothing inside him was able to move. No thought, feeling or breath. And then, as if he were swimming underwater, he pulled away from the window, went over to the chair, placed the candlestick on the floor, sat down and pulled on his boots. Forgetting the candle, he walked out into the dark hallway. Fumbling his way to the stairs, he nearly tripped on the first step as he descended to the entrance hall, which he crossed to the open door and the steps down into the courtyard.

He crossed the yard without looking to see if the two silhouettes were anywhere nearby. By feeling his way through the shadows under the wall, he found the handle of the big wheel that worked the drawbridge, which he unlocked and unwound until the drawbridge came crashing down on the other side of the moat.

It was only after he had crossed the bridge and left the confinement of the castle that he felt he could allow himself to breathe. But the air was hot, like flames in his throat, and the thoughts it ignited inside him heated the blood that rushed through his limbs until it felt like his whole body was on fire.

As he walked down the path that followed the moat, he saw the chapel. He crossed over to its rear wall, sat down in its shadow and rested his back and head against the stone to cool himself.

For a moment he just sat looking up at a star shining dimly in the sky. As long as he fixed on that star he could stop himself from thinking about what he had just witnessed outside his bedroom window. The life that had filled him, in which he could rejoice and which he cherished, was slipping away from him, or perhaps had already abandoned him. But if he kept staring up at that star, perhaps, somehow, he could bring it back.

He remembered that, as an adolescent and even as a young man, he would sometimes wonder why things were the way they were and not otherwise. It seemed that, in his imagination, there were no limits to the way things could be.

So why were there rivers, mountains and trees? Why were there fish, crows, deer and not something else in their place? Why was everything limited to being the way it was? Why did God choose to create this world and not another one? He could never see any reason for it, and would sink into a state of disbelief, feeling there was only futility about everything going on around him.

But before he had those thoughts, when he was still a child, he felt that mountains, rivers, fish and horses all had a light shining out of them that pointed to a hidden significance, and it was this that caused them to shine. His young heart somehow intuited that all these different meanings were intertwined together and that it was this that stopped the world from falling apart.

And when he met Isolt, it was as if the world had regained some of the magic that it had lost as he grew up. And that was why, in spite of the jealousy and possessive feelings he would fall into at times, there was still hidden behind them a deeper feeling that he and Isolt could never part because they were both woven into this carpet of intertwining significances that held the world together.

'So what happened?' Marc shouted out loud, into the night, his voice broken with despair.

He turned at a noise, thinking that perhaps it was an animal walking nearby, and then a voice called out suddenly.

'Marc!' It was Isolt. 'Marc, where are you?'

'I'm here,' he answered.

'Where?' she asked.

'Behind the chapel.'

He heard her steps walking over to him and saw her approaching shape.

'What are you doing here?' she asked, barely visible in the shadow of the wall.

'What were you doing in the courtyard?' he countered.

There was a long silence. Marc stared up at the star that still shone dimly through the white veil cast over the sky by the moon, but it was no longer able to hold back the great wave of despair.

He felt Isolt sit down and lean back against the wall beside him. 'I have to talk to you,' she said.

'I hope it's good news.'

'Marc, I love him.'

'What does that mean?' he asked. The words cut his throat like knives and he started to cough, then managed to say, 'I thought you loved me?'

'It's possible to love two different people at once,' she answered.

'Maybe you can perform that trick. I certainly can't. I can only love you.'

'If you really loved me, then you should have shown it a bit more,' replied Isolt. 'You should have listened to me when I asked you to come with me to Ireland, but you were too interested in becoming king. You didn't really care about me. You expected me to spend the rest of my life in this castle, where no one really likes me, while you went to your meetings with your mother and your uncle, from which I was excluded and where you took your big decisions, full of your own self-importance. The whole thing went to your head, Marc. You even thought you could fight that brute of a giant in a duel and defeat him. Thank God Tristan was there to come to your rescue. He would have killed you! What were you thinking of?'

'You were only too happy to think of me fighting that duel, weren't you?' said Marc. 'And you were deeply disappointed when I backed out of it. Is that not so?'

There was a moment's silence before Isolt replied.

'Yes, I was disappointed,' she said finally. 'Not because I was eager to see you get yourself killed, but because you had me believing that you could do it, that you could go out there and fight this man, and that you were going to do it for us. And yes, I wanted you to fight that duel. I thought that, finally, you were going to stop talking and actually do something, and that this was going to change our life, move it out of the drudgery it had become, into something exciting, something worth living. But then, when you pulled out, I realised that nothing was ever going to change. That life would just go on as before, except that it would be worse, because we would now be living in this castle with your mother and your uncle, and that you would go on talking, talking me into accepting things I didn't want.'

'So what do you want?' Marc asked.

There was another long pause before Isolt replied. 'I've already told Tristan that I love him, that I want him.'

In the silence that followed, Marc felt the pride, honour, self-respect and whatever else he had invented to hold himself in one piece was now burning in the fire of his despair. 'Were you lying in his arms when you told him?' he asked finally.

'No, of course not,' she answered. 'I would never do that without telling you first.'

'And are you telling me now?' he asked. Then, suddenly regretting the question and not wanting to hear her answer, he spoke again. 'What has he got that I haven't got?'

'He makes me feel that I'm alive again. That there's a reason I'm in this world. That I'm going somewhere,' she answered. 'Look, Marc, I'm telling you now. I have to spend some time with him. I want to go away with him tonight. We will take Kore with us and I will leave her at the fortress. She will be all right there, she loves Brangien.'

'You can leave her with me,' Marc said.

'No. You won't have time to look after her. She will be better off with Brangien. I won't be away long. But I need some time to sort things out in my heart.'

'So you're not going to leave me?'

'I didn't say that. But if I decide to leave you, I'll come and tell you first.'

Marc looked up to the star again, but the white veil cast by the moon seemed to have grown brighter and he couldn't see it any more.

'I want to leave while it's still night,' continued Isolt, rising to her feet. 'You can tell your mother that Kore wanted to visit Brangien and that Tristan escorted us there early this morning, so that we could complete the journey before it got too hot.'

'I can't do it. I can't let you leave!' cried Marc.

'I'm afraid you're going to have to,' Isolt replied calmly. 'Whatever respect you want to keep alive in my heart will depend on how you behave now.'

She turned to go and took a few steps away from him. Marc flung himself forward, face down with his whole body stretched out on the ground and two arms extended. He grabbed her ankle with both hands and held on to it. 'Don't leave me!' he said, as a great sob rose up from his belly and escaped from his throat. His whole body was shaking as he repeated, in a voice that had become suddenly high-pitched and broken with tears, 'Don't leave me! I beg you, please don't leave!'

Isolt looked down at him as he lifted his head and arched his neck to stare up at her. His face was pale and white in the light of the moon that now shone directly down on him. Tears ran down his cheeks and his chest jolted as he tried to catch his breath. 'Don't leave me!' he wailed. 'Please... Please don't leave me!'

Isolt knelt down, stroked his cheek, slipped her hand under his hair and felt his ear. It was hot and she could feel the pulse of blood being pumped through it.

'I'm sorry, Marc,' she said gently. 'I have to do it. If I let you stop me I would never forgive myself, or you. Something stronger than me is pulling me to him and I can't pretend it's not happening. I have to find out what it is. I need to spend some time with him. I can't promise you anything except that I'll come back. And after that, we'll see.'

She stood up and took a few steps away from him, leaving him lying face down on the ground, then turned around and looked at him again.

'Despite anything I may have said before, I realise that part of this is my fault. I should never have accepted your offer of shelter when we first met. I should never have gone back to the fortress with you. I remember I tried to warn you about myself. I must have known that one day something like this would happen, but I never realised I was going to hurt you so much. I'm sorry.'

Marc heard her steps grow fainter as she walked away from him until they disappeared into the silence, into the great sea of darkness that was the night.

6

Return of
The Prodigal Wife

Say it's not so, Tristan! Tell me that our leap forward across the highest peaks is not doomed to lead us down again into the valley of fog and mist from which you delivered me. Say it's not so! Tell me that life is possible up there, where the wind blew in our faces and the sun blinded our eyes as we trod dangerously along the edge of that great precipice. Say that is what's true, that is what's real, and not the life of dreariness that I am returning to. Say it's not so! Say that what we lived was not an illusion, not a dream.

Why can't I hear you any more? Why am I clinging so soon to memories and not to the warmth of your hand? Why can't I feel your arm on my shoulder, the cool breath of your laughter on my cheek? Don't tell me that this was just a cruel potion that we both drank that intoxicated our hearts, blinded our reason and sent us on a wild rampage, believing that we had become like gods. That we must now return to our mortality, where, though we think we are still alive, death has already taken hold of our hearts.

Say it's not so! Tell me the fire will not become just a pile of cold ashes. Talk to me, Tristan! I can't hear your voice. Where are you?

*

The wave of heat that had hung over the kingdom for the past month had at last moved on and the sky over the moor was once again covered with heavy grey clouds. A soft, soothing rain fell gently onto the burnt, dried-out heather.

Isolt was on her horse, heading towards the market town and the castle beyond. Kore was sitting behind her. She had picked her daughter up at the fortress where she had been staying with Brangien for the past few weeks. It was a relief to feel those little hands holding on to her waist, and it was also good to feel the raindrops, but there was another woman inside her heart, who had finally shown herself and was about to take possession of her soul, but whom she was now about to betray as she rode on her way back to Marc and to life in the castle. And she could hear that other woman crying in the depths of that soul now.

Isolt reached the castle early in the evening. The first person she met after handing her horse over to the stable boy was Isabelle, who walked out of the entrance hall and down the steps into the courtyard with a basket in her hand, as if she had been expecting her arrival. She kissed Kore and asked her matter-of-factly if she had enjoyed her stay at the fortress. Kore nodded and asked her grandmother if she knew where her father was. Isabelle told her that the last time she had seen him, he was in the kitchen with Forsin, but that he had probably returned to his bedroom. She said she hoped Isolt felt well rested after her time away from the castle; that the whole business of the duel must have been an awful ordeal for her and she quite understood that she would want to go away somewhere and recuperate for a while. She would have liked to do the same thing herself, but unfortunately Marc hadn't enough experience yet to handle the affairs of the kingdom without her help.

'But I don't want to hold you back,' she continued. 'I'm sure you're both eager to go and see him. He must be shut away in his room. I think that he, too, has been deeply affected by the duel and has not quite recovered yet, but I'm sure that seeing you back here again will lift his spirits. So I'll let you go and find him. I'm off to pick some cherries, if I can find any ripe ones, that is.'

When Isolt entered their bedroom, Marc was standing at the open window with his back towards her.

'So you're back,' he said without turning around.

'Papa!' Kore shouted, running across the room to join him.

Marc half turned and picked her up, kissed her, and held her in his arms. They were both staring out of the window now.

'So, how did you spend your time in the fortress?' Marc asked, still holding her in his arms.

'I played with the cat and the chickens and helped Brangien in the kitchen. And sometimes, when Maman and Tristan came to visit us, Tristan let me ride his horse.'

Marc said nothing but just continued staring out of the window with his daughter in his arms, his back turned to his prodigal wife.

Isolt was only too aware that beyond the window, beyond the road that dipped down towards a stream and rose on the other side of the bridge to climb a small hill, a few miles beyond on the other side of Corsan, the same road crossed through fields of wheat and barley until it reached the moor, its vast expanse of wilderness stretching all the way to the cliffs and the beaches further north along the coast, where she had left Tristan.

'And what about you, Papa? What did you do while we were away?'

'Oh, I'm the king now. I have to rule over the kingdom.'

'Is that very difficult?' asked Kore.

'No,' answered Marc. 'I have a lot of people to help me do my job. But I'm sure you had a lot more fun than I did, because it can get a little lonely, even if you have people helping you.' Marc could feel all his anger, bitterness and humiliation rise up suddenly, and these last few words scraped his throat as he pronounced them.

'Kore,' Isolt called out, 'why don't you go and find your cousin? She will be very happy to see that you are back.'

After Kore left the room, closing the door behind her, Marc remained silent with his back turned to his wife, still staring out through the window. Isolt began to unpack the clothes Brangien had washed for her, folding hers into a chest and Kore's into a little pile on the bed.

'I'm sorry,' she said finally to break the heavy silence.

Marc turned around and watched as she knelt by her travel bag. There was hate in his eyes.

'Sorry!' he shouted. 'You're just sorry!'

'I'm sorry this had to happen at such a difficult time,' she said, looking up at him. 'Just when you've been crowned king.'

Marc walked up to her and bent down over her, his chest heaving as he spoke with a trembling voice.

'Do you think I give a damn about being crowned king? Do you think that it's being a king that makes this a difficult time? Don't you see that it's you? You! You! You! Can't you see that? Don't you see what you have done? Don't you see that you have destroyed me? That you have taken everything away from me, everything I ever had?'

And then, releasing all his pent-up anger, pain and outrage into a single kick, he sent his foot crashing into her bag so that it went flying across the room, spilling what remained of her clothes onto the floor as it hit the wall.

He left her there amongst the scattered remains of their lost happiness as he slammed the door behind him.

Isolt sat alone in the room staring at the door.

'This is going to be harder than I thought,' she whispered to herself.

*

That evening, as they lay in bed, Marc turned towards her, propping himself up on his elbow, and ran his fingers through her hair. She took his hand in hers and moved it away from her face.

'Do you regret making love to him?' he asked.

'No. Don't make me say that. I don't regret anything we did. But I am deeply sorry, Marc, that it had to hurt you.'

Marc shook his hand loose from hers and, as a swell of anger rushed into him, felt ready to choke. He sat up and swung his fist into the heavy wooden headboard of the bed. The skin of his knuckles tore and blood dripped down onto his pillow.

'Go on, and you can hit me next time if that makes you feel better,' Isolt said.

'I could have you killed if I wanted to.'

'You can do that, too, if you want,' she said.

Marc sat for a long time looking at the blood forming into small pools over his wounded knuckles. Finally he extinguished the torch and they lay silent in the darkened room.

Isolt lay still beside him. So he wasn't going to throw her out. He wasn't going to kill her. He wasn't even going to hit her. Instead, he had chosen to hurt himself by smashing his fist into the back of the bed. And yet she could feel tears run down along her temples and into the hair at the back of her neck.

But she knew those tears were not for Marc, but for Tristan and herself. For she could feel him, everything she could remember about him, everything that had been so real, that had reached so deeply into her and had transformed her, if only for a short time, had brought her so close to herself, to the person she was meant to be in an ideal world.

*

A month had gone by since Isolt's return to the castle. It was becoming clear to all those who were close to Marc that he had not yet found his footing in the new role that fate had thrust upon him, even though his mother, his uncle and two other lords were there to advise him. The lords had left their own fiefdoms and chosen to make the castle their main place of residence so they could advise the king in all the difficult decisions he had to make. But although he never tried to evade his official duties and always participated in whatever activity required his presence, it was clear that his heart was just not in this new role he had to play.

Of course, no one knew what was really going on in this heart of his. No one knew that, on some days, it was an enormous effort for him to just get out of his bed. The thought of having to be with other people, of having to keep up appearances, of having to pretend that all was well when, in reality, his insides were being devoured by rage, jealousy and a feeling that he was the world's greatest fool, drained him of all his strength. Maybe there was a certain degree of false pride and vanity involved in hiding away his feelings as he did, but there was also a genuine sense of not wanting to disappoint or let down the people around him. Of course, this was not altogether without self-interest; experience had shown him that when your ship has sunk, as his definitely had, you cling to whatever bit of debris you can find that will keep you afloat.

But there was one person who did know what was really going on, and that person was Isolt. She knew, also, that if she could muster up the will and strength in herself – or, more simply, just allow herself to be touched by his pain – she could, more often than not, pull him out of this state. All she had to do was sit on the bed beside him, take his hand, stroke his forehead and slowly allow her presence to fill the emptiness and terror of his solitude. After a while, he would reach up with his arm, feel the side of her body with his hand and then reach up with his other arm and pull her down over him, placing his hand behind her head and pressing her lips against his. A little later, he would have rolled on top of her, would be making love to her, furiously and passionately, and she would lie there, receive it and absorb it, knowing that she was giving life back to him, that she was bringing him back to himself, away from the demons that had invaded his heart.

It was during a hunting trip that she told him she was pregnant. She had set out early one morning with Marc, Donoalin, Godoine and a young knight called Albert. They were in the Moroi forest when the dogs picked up the scent of a stag, which they had been chasing for a while when Isolt pulled her horse to a halt.

The rest of the party continued the chase until they noticed that Isolt was no longer with them. They retraced their tracks and found her sitting on her mount, pale and breathing heavily. Marc asked her what was wrong.

'I don't know,' she answered. 'I feel a bit sick.'

They made their way to a clearing on the bank of the Tavel river, where the riders dismounted, sat in the sun and shared out the dried meat and bread they had brought along with them in silence as they watched the water flow by below them. Their animals had cautiously made their way down to the river's edge to quench their thirst and were now resting too, the dogs lying on the grass in the sun and the horses grazing lazily. When Isolt had finished eating, she stood up suddenly and stretched out her hand for Marc to take hold of.

'Come on!' she said. 'We're going for a walk.'

Marc stood up and took her hand.

'Enjoy your nap while we're gone,' he said to the other knights. 'I don't expect we'll be too long.'

They followed the bank of the river upstream until, some distance away, it flattened out into a large sandy beach, strewn with rocks and boulders. Isolt sat down on the sand. Without letting go of his hand, she pulled him down beside her. She then let herself fall backwards so that she lay flat on her back.

Marc stared at her. She was looking up at him, her parted lips showing the gap between her two front teeth, a faint smile on her face and a mysterious glint in her eyes, caused partially by the sun shining down on her but also by something hidden, buried inside her. 'Come and lie on top of me,' she said.

Later, as they were lying on their backs in the sun, staring up at the sky, Isolt told him. 'Marc, I think I'm pregnant.'

'What?' He raised his head and propped himself on one elbow to look at her.

'I think I'm pregnant.'

'Are you sure?'

Isolt did not look at him as she answered, but kept staring up at the sky. 'It's been this way for a while. I was not sure at first, but now I'm practically certain.'

Marc stood up, walked out into the middle of the river, knelt down and splashed water onto his face. Then he just knelt there in the water, watching the current brush against his knees.

Isolt called over to him. 'Marc, come back!'

He looked back at her as she sat up on the sand. Her hair was untidy and her dress crumpled. She was so beautiful and untamed. How could God and all his angels ever forgive him for being so neglectful of such a gift? And how could he go on living, knowing what he had lost?

'Come back, Marc!' Isolt shouted.

Marc sank his hands into the cold stream and threw his arms up. Water splashed on to him as he cried out with all his might. He got up, dripping water, walked over to the bank and onto the dry sand, and knelt down in front of Isolt. He held both her hands in his and stared into her eyes. He wanted to say something, but no words would come to him.

Isolt hesitated. She was about to say something when a voice shouted out from somewhere downstream and moments later they saw Godoine, Donoalin and Albert running along the bank towards them. The three seemed embarrassed at finding them sitting quietly together on the sand.

'We're sorry to disturb you,' Donoalin said. 'We heard someone cry out and thought maybe you were in trouble.'

Isolt laughed.

'It was just your king splashing water on himself,' she told them.

For the rest of the day Marc seemed overjoyed. He was joking with Isolt, his two friends and the young knight. He was light-hearted and had lost his self-conscious, brooding manner. Isolt watched him. Why can't he be like this all of the time? she thought. Yet Isolt herself did not seem to fully share in Marc's joviality. Although she joined in with the pleasantries, her companions thought she seemed to be holding back a little, that her attention was somewhere else.

That night as they lay in bed, when Marc said goodnight to her she did not answer. He turned towards her and saw the outline of her profile and the faint glow of light in her eyes that were open and looking upwards.

'Marc,' she said finally, 'there is something I should tell you.'

'What?'

'I don't want to hurt you, but I feel I should tell you.'

'Tell me what?'

'Well, I think you're the father, but I can't be sure. I mean, it just could be Tristan.'

'Are you sure?' Marc asked.

'No. That's what I'm trying to tell you. I can't be sure of anything,' she replied.

There was a long silence.

'I just wanted you to know,' she said finally, 'in case it makes a difference to you.'

'No,' Marc said. 'I suppose it had already crossed my mind that Tristan might be the father. But if you can't be sure...'

'No, I can't be sure,' Isolt repeated.

There was another silence in which Marc felt a distant pain, a kind of surrender in which he saw that his expectations, aspirations and dreams were being reduced to something that was more in keeping with who he really was. It hurt, but he knew that he would take with open arms whatever was given to him if it meant her coming back to him.

'And does that make a difference to you?' he asked.

'No. If it makes no difference to you, then it will make none to me. In fact, I could only love you all the more. It would just make our love much deeper.'

'And what about Tristan? Does he know?' Marc asked.

'That I'm pregnant? No, of course not.'

'Do you know where he is?'

'Yes, he's still in Port Saint Marie,' she replied. 'I'm going to send him a letter and tell him he has to forget about me.'

'And what about you? Will you be able to forget about him?'

Isolt looked away and focused her gaze on a star that twinkled far away in the night sky outside their bedroom window.

'Yes, I will try; and you can help me by remembering what I said to you when we first met. I said that I would follow you back to your fortress and spend some time with you there on one condition: that you don't ask me any question about my father ever again, that you refrain from even mentioning him to me. Well, you can help me if you apply the same restraint on yourself with regard to Tristan.'

*

Another month went by. Marc had officially announced the news of his wife's pregnancy. Word spread throughout the kingdom and it seemed for a while that Marc had found a new belief in himself and was even beginning to take a real interest in the affairs of the kingdom. This pleased his mother and the lords and advisers.

But what no one else knew, except for Isolt and himself, of course, was that behind this assertiveness and apparent self-confidence, hidden in its shadow, a dark hole of doubt, despair and anger haunted his dreams and filled his unspoken thoughts, not only persisting but poisoning his life whenever he remembered what had happened between her and Tristan. And it had grown deeper and more insistent now that he knew that Isolt had decided to stay on at his side and resume her life as his wife.

Now that he no longer lived in fear of losing her, his anger and his sense of failure could fully manifest themselves in his heart, and it was this sense of failure and insignificance that pushed him to try harder to assert himself.

Isolt could see all this, she could see that he was not able to sit comfortably inside himself any more. She could see that he was making an enormous effort to seem to be concerned about everybody, about his daily tasks, about her, and was trying to appear to be happy.

He still joked around with Forsin using the friendly sarcasm they always displayed to one another, and there were times she could almost hear the old Marc reappearing in his voice, see the old pride and joy in his eyes again. But they were only fleeting appearances of something he couldn't hold on to for any significant length of time, like ghosts blown into a familiar place only to vanish through its walls, back into the night.

*

For some time now, far away in the south, in a region known as the Languedoc, a heresy had been spreading that threatened to take over the whole region.

This new religion preached by the Cathars was gaining ground, much to the horror of the Christian bishops and priests who were losing their congregations to the heretics, and the consternation of Pope Innocent III, who received their alarming reports back in Rome.

And it was the outrage, the unspeakable blasphemy written down in those reports that finally caused the clergy from all over France and even beyond, as far as the empire of Frederick I in the north, at the Pope's instigation and with his blessing, to call for an army to be raised against the heretics. Their sermons had proved useless in halting the spread of this fire, and so an army of knights, foot soldiers and mercenaries was formed to storm down to the south and put a stop to this scourge with their swords.

Amongst the members of Marc's court, there were three lords, including his uncle Ganelon, who argued strongly in favour of this call to arms. It was not hard to see why, for all three spent most of their days in the king's castle away from their own fiefdoms, performing their duties as sworn advisers to the throne, and were thus not rich men themselves like some of the other lords of the kingdom.

The rumour had spread that when the day came for him to give his blessing to his army upon its departure to the south, the Pope would include in this a remission of the sins of all the participants in the crusade, which would assure them of a place in heaven. There would also be an invitation to take all the spoils and loot they could pillage from the lords and barons under whose protection these Cathars had been encouraged to preach their infamy. As the region they were to invade was rumoured to be prosperous, it was well understood that the three barons would want to seize the chance to increase their wealth.

When the prospect of a crusade was first brought up with great enthusiasm by Ganelon, it was quickly welcomed by the other two. So when he had finished talking and the others had stopped nodding their heads and mumbling their approval to every argument he had given with such righteous passion in favour of the crusade, and when they all, his mother included, turned to Marc seeking to know what his own opinion was on this matter, Marc for once spoke out without any regret or hesitation.

To their astonishment, he said not only that what he had heard about the Cathars, their detachment from the world and its riches, their tolerance and simplicity, appealed to him, but he could also see a more sinister and dangerous motive hidden behind this call to arms.

This assembling of all the lords and knights of France, as well as their neighbours to the north and west, would be united under the spiritual guidance of the Pope, Innocent III. But less visible, hiding in his shadow, there would be Philippe Auguste, King of France, standing in as his secular general. He would be dressed up as the executor of God's will, but would in fact be reconquering lost territories for his throne and reasserting his authority over fiefdoms that had strayed from it. Marc went on to add that if their small kingdom was to join in this crusade and find itself under the general command of Philippe Auguste – and, standing behind him, Innocent III – from that moment onwards, once it was all over and they had come back home, both the Pope and King would feel free to interfere in their affairs with the same authority they had exerted over them during the crusade. And he, as reigning monarch, was certainly not going to be instrumental in his kingdom's loss of a good measure of its autonomy if he could help it.

For a moment everyone sat looking at Marc, wondering what had taken hold of him to make him speak out in this way. It was his mother, perhaps understanding that there were deeper personal reasons motivating this sudden radical stand he was taking, who was first to answer him.

'But, sire,' she said, 'the danger of losing our autonomy can easily be averted if we send a sizeable contingent of our lords and knights from our kingdom, who wish to volunteer to take part in this crusade, but without you as king of this realm taking part in it yourself. In this way, we will have made our contribution to this worthy cause without you personally having at any moment placed yourself under the authority of Philippe Auguste, or the Pope for that matter.'

Marc leapt up from his throne and banged his fist down on the table where they all sat. 'No!' he shouted. 'I will not have any of my lords or knights fighting under Philippe Auguste's command. I do not want either him or the Pope to think that every time they want to go into battle to bring new territories under the yoke of their authority, we must feel obliged to send our men to help satisfy their ambitions. That is what I'm trying to say.'

He walked across the meeting hall and stormed out through the door, leaving his mother, his uncle and the two lords to stare at each other in amazement.

*

Isolt stepped out into the courtyard. She couldn't see Marc anywhere, so she walked over to the stables where the boy was cleaning out the stalls and asked him if Marc had taken a horse out. The boy shook his head.

'No, my lady. But I saw him walk out over the drawbridge just a while back.'

When Isolt crossed the moat she saw Marc sitting under the big linden tree near the chapel, and knew immediately that this had some kind of significance. She had passed Isabelle in the hallway and had asked with surprise if the meeting was already over. Marc's mother had told her that he had stormed out of the room. 'Maybe you should go and talk to him,' she had said dryly. 'I know there are things that are upsetting him that I don't understand, and that you probably know more about than me.' Added to what his mother had just said to her, that he was sitting under the linden tree did not bode favourably.

'Are you all right?' she asked.

'No, I'm not.'

As Marc looked up at her he realised that all the objections to the crusade that he had voiced so strongly, and with such anger, could be narrowed down to a single truth hiding behind these arguments. However convincing they might have sounded, the truth was that he didn't want to leave Isolt behind.

'What's the matter?' she asked.

'Well, Pope Innocent III has been clamouring for another crusade. This time, he wants to march against the Cathars. Have you heard of them? They are also known as the Albigeois.'

'No, I haven't,' Isolt said.

He explained who they were and why he was against participating in a crusade against them for fear that this would compromise the future of their kingdom. She listened and expressed her full support, but what he didn't know was that this was not necessarily because she believed him, or even cared about the future of the kingdom, but simply because she could see, when she looked at him, how fragile he had become.

*

When Marc went to the next meeting two days later he felt calmer, especially about the position he had adopted with regard to the crusade. He had confidence in himself, as if a new strength had entered him and given him hope that he might be able to overcome the wounds eating into his heart.

They were all waiting for him when he entered the meeting hall, and he saw that there was now another member sitting at the table: Santerre, the priest assigned to the castle.

Marc did not waste any time. It was usually his mother who opened the meetings by giving a brief summary of the topics that were to be discussed that day, but before she could open her mouth he apologised to everyone for having stormed out of the room at the last gathering. He had done so because he felt no one was listening to him. He added that he realised that it was a childish thing to do and so would like to start the meeting by listening to their reactions to what he had said and to answer any questions they might want to ask.

It was Ganelon, Marc's uncle, who spoke first in response to Marc's objections. 'My lord,' he said, 'I'm sure I speak for everyone here present when I say what joy it gives us all to hear our king speak with such firmness and conviction. Your words show how deeply you understand the seriousness of this matter before us. But perhaps you will listen now to the words of an older man, who has had much experience in dealing with the affairs of this kingdom. You must realise, my lord, that when you stepped up to take the throne you not only inherited the love and respect of the people of this land for their king, but you also inherited the hatred and envy of our enemies across our borders.

'Now, what would these enemies of ours think, who will see the slightest sign of weakness on our part only as an invitation to come in and pillage our land? What would they think if the leader of all Christendom called on us to join forces with him, march southwards and fight a holy and noble battle against the evil heretics there who are eating their way into our faith, if we refused to answer this call? Do you think they would listen to our arguments, however wise these arguments may sound to us?

'No, they would hear only weakness and timidity hiding behind our words. It wouldn't take them long to join forces against us and use our refusal to fight at their side as an argument to mount a campaign against us. They would call us heretics, invade and take our land away from us.

'I urge you, my lord, to think deeply about this matter, and not to let the natural goodness of your heart divert you away from the cruel realities of this world and the dangers that hang over us. For, if we are to remain free and independent, it will be by showing our enemies that we are always eager to go into battle, and not by showing signs of shyness when it comes to taking up arms for a just cause.'

Ganelon bowed his head and sat down. Marc, his heart heavy, nodded grimly.

Later that afternoon, when he recounted to Isolt what had been said during the morning's meeting, she told him she thought Ganelon had made a strong point in his speech, but that the danger he was talking about could probably be avoided. This could be achieved if Marc were to go to his so-called enemies, the lords and barons across the borders of his kingdom, and persuade them of the danger of losing their own autonomy and independence if they agreed to join an army under the command of Philippe Auguste and, hiding behind him, Innocent III.

*

'Do you think this is going to work?' Isolt asked as she rode beside Marc, encouraged that he had taken her advice.

Much to the consternation of his mother and advisers, and especially of Santerre, who secretly reported back to the Bishop of Rennes, they had begun the journey that would take them to all the fiefdoms that touched the borders of their kingdom. There were four main domains that they intended to visit.

Of course, everyone else in the castle believed that this was a foolhardy adventure. Marc's father, during his reign, along with his brother, Ganelon, his son, Jean, the ferocious Nordstram and several other lords who lived in the kingdom were all viewed by their neighbours across its borders as no better than a band of treacherous brigands who were to be avoided, as any contact with them always meant trouble of one kind or another.

But Marc seemed now to think that he was on some kind of sacred mission, which was all the more surprising to those in his entourage who did not know him well. Up until now he had seemed to them to be a cautious monarch, hesitant and ill at ease whenever he had to make a decision.

But what they did not realise was that the strength and self-assurance he now suddenly displayed was, of course, not his own. It had its source in Isolt.

'Yes, I think it will work. It has to. We have to stop this crusade. The world has to change; we cannot just go on massacring each other over our differing beliefs,' he replied.

*

Their first stop was the smallest fiefdom and the most hostile to the Kingdom of Brittany. The Baron de Sergone was a small, middle-aged man, who was reputed to have a pretty young wife he kept hidden away because of his jealous nature. This, at least, was the story Donoalin told as they headed towards his domain. A messenger had been sent several days before to announce their intended visit, and he had agreed to receive them.

The baron's castle was built in the middle of a large clearing surrounded by forest. They rode past sheep and goats grazing peacefully along the road and then a gathering of pigs tended by a keeper just outside the castle walls.

As they approached, Marc could see a woman bending over a dog, patting and caressing it. When they came nearer, the dog looked up, barked half-heartedly and then lay down on the cobblestones and watched their approach. The woman, who was very young, looked their way before disappearing into the castle.

Marc looked up. The glare of the sun blinded him momentarily and an overwhelming feeling of loss made him stop. This should have been his life, in a castle like this, hidden away from the rest of the world with Isolt, Kore and a dog.

The baron greeted them coldly and invited them to sit down in the reception hall. On the table were bread and slices of dried meat, glasses and a jug of water. He told them to help themselves if they were hungry or thirsty. The baron sat and watched them eat but did not take part in the meal himself. Marc tried to start a conversation with him but each of his questions or comments received only a dry, curt answer that didn't seem to allow any further pursuit of the subject.

Marc waited until everyone had finished eating and then presented his arguments against the proposed crusade. Without any real response from the baron, without any exchange of thoughts or feelings, they got up courteously, said goodbye and went on their way. Marc didn't feel too bad, though. At least he had been able to say his piece, and he hadn't expected much from this first visit, anyway.

But Isolt looked unhappy. She had hoped that the baron's hostility might have been weakened by the fact that they had come all that way to talk to him; at least enough so that there might have been some exchange between them. She also regretted that she had not intervened and taken part in Marc's attempt to convince the baron when it became obvious that he was getting nowhere with him.

*

Their next destination was the largest of the four domains they intended to visit. It was, in fact, bigger and more prosperous than the whole Kingdom of Brittany, to which it had once partly belonged several hundred years ago. It was now governed by the Duke de Vitry, a big hulk of a man who could pin any one of his vast army of knights to the ground in a wrestling match. He had come back a richer man from the Crusades, and had also ruled over a vast domain in England through marriage to the daughter of a now-deceased duke.

They arrived late in the afternoon of the following day. Arnaud de Vitry seemed amused that Marc should come to his castle with his exotic-looking wife to plead his case. As he sat listening to Marc, he squinted as if he were looking at some rare curiosity. It was hard for Marc to argue his case, intimidated as he was by the overwhelming physical presence of this man as they sat in his vast reception hall, with its lush tapestries depicting hunting scenes and fierce battles, yet he needed so badly to make a success of his plea. But because Isolt was also watching him and he needed above all to impress her, Marc was muddling things up as he spoke, repeating himself and failing to get to the point.

De Vitry did not seem to be taking him seriously, and Marc was just about to sink into despair when, to everyone's surprise, Isolt stood up and spoke.

'Marc, I think we should leave. I don't think the Duke de Vitry is in the least bit interested in what you have to say. There is no point in our wasting any more of our time here.'

The duke looked over at Isolt as if he had only just noticed her. And she, as if totally indifferent to the attention now focused on her, took off her bonnet and let her hair fall down over her shoulders, shaking it loose with a sweeping movement then tossing it with her hands so that it swelled out, thick and untamed, like a lion's mane framing her face.

For a brief moment, Arnaud de Vitry let himself sink into the dark pools of her eyes as they stared back at him defiantly. It was as if, in that moment, she had appeared in a tapestry that had been unrolled before him, an image of her that was to remain in his heart for the rest of his life.

Marc too stared at her, as surprised as the duke at her sudden interruption, as if she had suddenly cast a spell into the room. When she shook her long, sparkling hair it fell down over her shoulders, not unlike the shawl he had thrown over her head when he had first met her several years ago.

At this unexpected turn everything changed. Suddenly the duke wanted nothing more than to listen to what they had to say.

'Please, my lady,' he said. 'Please, won't you sit down? Do forgive me if I seemed not to follow your husband's arguments, but I think maybe he is tired from your long journey. So, will you grant me the great honour of being my guests and let me put my whole castle at your disposition? Perhaps over supper we can discuss this matter further and I will, I promise you, give it my full attention.'

And it was true that Arnaud de Vitry did listen attentively to Marc as he argued his case that evening. Often he nodded his head slightly, as if in approval of what was being said. Once or twice he interrupted to express doubt over Marc's interpretation of certain events, but each time this happened Isolt would jump in and counter his objections with further arguments in Marc's favour.

'All this is very well,' said de Vitry at one point, 'but it has been my understanding that Pope Innocent III has already asked Philippe Auguste to take military command of this crusade, and that the King of France has turned him down, using as an excuse his dispute with the Plantagenets in England.'

Isolt responded before Marc could think of an answer.

'This may well be true, my lord,' she said, 'but have you not just said yourself that this was an excuse Philippe Auguste gave to the Pope? I would further suggest that he used this excuse because he wanted anyone who might shy away from his command to be reassured by his refusal and thus be encouraged to join this crusade. And I would further suspect, once this crusade is well on its way, and marching down towards the Languedoc, that Innocent III will ask Philippe Auguste once again to take full military command of it. This time the King of France will give no excuse and will give in to the Pope's request.'

'But, my lady,' de Vitry protested, his face a little flushed at this woman's intelligence and impudence, 'though you are quite right to draw attention to the possible exploitation open to the King of France to extend his power, this does not take away from the fact that the Pope has a real cause to defend. The danger exists on his side, too. These Cathars are challenging our faith, and they are gaining ground every day.'

'You speak, my lord, as if the Cathars were a great army marching upon us with their swords to impose their faith on us by force, whereas in fact that is precisely what Innocent III is asking us to do to them. From all that I have heard, the Cathars merely spread the word of their faith by preaching in the streets and in their makeshift temples. What is Innocent III so afraid of? Perhaps it is that these Cathars can convince by word alone, whereas he needs the sword, the threat of torture and the smell of bodies burning at the stake to carry his word?'

When Arnaud de Vitry looked at her he saw flames from the fire burning in her eyes. Never before had he seen a woman like her! Never had he seen such spirit! Then he looked at Marc, sitting silently beside her, sensed her husband's nervousness at her display of effrontery, and he wondered what she was doing, a woman like her, with this man.

'It's a shame Innocent III does not have you on his side.' He smiled. 'He could send you to preach against the Cathars and would have no need to raise an army to defend his cause!'

From then on the duke simply nodded in agreement to everything Marc said, yet his eyes were barely looking at him. Instead he kept glancing over at Isolt, hoping that she would look up and catch his stare. She could feel him gazing at her but did not look back, for she had no intention of playing his little game.

When Marc had finished talking, the duke drew a deep breath. 'Well, you have certainly managed to trouble my peace of mind and plant a seed of doubt into my heart,' he said.

Isolt now did look up at him. The duke was staring straight back at her, as if the words he had just spoken were meant for her and her alone, but Isolt just stared back at him blankly. He knew, though, that she had caught his intention, and that it had touched her where she felt her deepest pride, and he hoped that she would not resist trying to use the power he had placed into her hands.

'Well, my lord, I hope this seed of doubt will grow in your heart enough to stop you taking up your sword,' Isolt said.

'Have no fear, my lady,' the duke answered. 'I shall let the seed grow in my heart. And, should your arguments blossom there, as your beauty already has, then I will not hesitate to change my mind.'

*

The following morning, as they were getting ready to leave, the duke met them in the vast courtyard. He greeted them cordially and asked if they would not be his guests at the castle for another night, explaining that they could spend the day hunting together.

It was Isolt who turned down his invitation, explaining that she was pregnant and that they still had several days of travelling ahead of them, for they had yet to visit the other two neighbours bordering their kingdom and win them over to their cause. She added that she didn't want to risk losing her child by over-exerting herself.

Arnaud de Vitry appeared shocked and disappointed. He looked for a moment at Marc and Isolt. His big broad face and squinting eyes had turned into a mask behind which his thoughts were battling with each other. He took a deep breath and looked directly at Isolt.

'I don't think you should be tiring yourself at all, my lady. Why don't you return to your castle and let me do the persuading? What you said last night at supper has profoundly changed my mind about the Cathars. I think I can persuade our neighbours to think twice about embarking on this crusade. I know all the lords of the nearby fiefdoms and I think they will listen to me.'

'You would really do that?' Isolt asked.

Arnaud de Vitry smiled at her.

'You have changed my mind,' he said. 'You are an extraordinary woman and your husband is a very lucky man to have you at his side. And yes, I will really do it. I will speak to them and try to persuade them.'

As they rode away from the castle, Isolt fell slightly behind Marc, who was talking to Donoalin and Godoine. He couldn't help being pleased with the outcome of their journey, but the cheerfulness he manifested was also an attempt to put out the flames of jealousy that had been reignited in his heart and were burning him from within.

Isolt heard the laughter and the pleasantries being exchanged in front of her. But it was Marc she heard most of all, and the falseness of his voice irritated her. Why did he have to force everything? She knew that he was jealous and displeased that the duke had so openly flirted with her. She had heard him tossing and turning before he finally fell asleep, and she had seen that beaten dog look he had thrown at her as she smiled at him in the morning. Perhaps that was why his cheerfulness and good humour sounded insincere. It was all a show put on for her benefit, and it made it seem to her as if he had nothing that was truly his own. She felt that she didn't really know him any more, that the only thing that was real about him was his anger and his pain.

The wind was blowing in from the ocean. For most of their journey the sun had been hidden but now, as they covered the last few miles that would take them homewards, it reappeared, lighting up the green landscape of woodlands and hills.

*

On the day after their return a messenger arrived with a letter for Marc. In it, the Duke de Vitry had copied, word for word, the contents of a letter he had sent on the same day to Pope Innocent III. It went thus:

Your Excellency,
*   Much as I share your concern for protecting the integrity*
of our faith against corruption and misinterpretation,

and am aware of the permanent danger these two evils represent as a threat to the whole of Christendom, I cannot, however, join myself to your call for an armed crusade against the Cathars.

These men do not preach with a sword in their hand and are peaceful and gentle in their way of persuasion and sincere in their faith, however misguided it may be. They do not, in my opinion, represent the kind of threat that needs to be countered with brute force and violence, but rather by a more fervent display of faith and conviction in the sermons of our own clergy already preaching in the Languedoc.

Please accept my most respectful regards,
Arnaud de Vitry

Marc ran to the bedroom to show the letter to Isolt, who, still exhausted from their journey, was lying in bed. He barely noticed as she looked up at him that her eyes were red, as if she had been crying. Nor did he notice how pale she was, for all he could think about was the letter which he handed to her.

'Take a look at this!' he said, trying to hold back his excitement.

Isolt pulled herself up in the bed and squinted a little to see through the haze of her tears.

'Who is it from?' she asked.

'Never mind, just read it.'

When she had finished reading, she put the letter down on the sheet covering her lap. As she looked up at Marc again, more tears formed in the corners of her eyes and ran down her cheeks.

'What's the matter?' Marc asked.

Isolt began to sob, her body shaking uncontrollably. Marc sat down on the bed and held her shoulders with his hands.

'What's the matter?' he asked again.

Isolt continued sobbing and Marc could feel the tremors of her body running up his arms. They reached right into the pit of his stomach.

'Please stop crying, Isolt. Please stop crying,' he said.

Gradually she gained control over herself and the sobbing stopped. She sat there silently, her eyes closed, as Marc held on to her with both hands.

'What's the matter, Isolt? Tell me...' he asked after a while.

'I don't know,' she said, her eyes still closed. 'I'm just tired, I suppose. I didn't realise how tiring this journey would be. And I felt sick this morning, and now I'm just feeling weak.' More tears pushed their way through her closed lids and ran down her cheeks. Marc thought she was going to start sobbing again, but she didn't.

'It's all right. I'll be all right. I just didn't think my life would be like this,' she said.

'You must rest. It was madness for you to have embarked on this journey in your condition. But just look at the result! Just look at that letter! We've done it! The Duke de Vitry has told the Pope he's not going to join his crusade. When word of this gets around, all the counts and lords nearby will join forces with him. He is too powerful for the King of France or the Pope to exert real pressure on him, and with the other counts and lords supporting him still more will follow behind them. This is a great defeat for the King of France and the Pope, and it's all thanks to you, Isolt.'

Isolt remained silent.

'Of course it's down to you!' Marc insisted. 'You helped to open my eyes in the first place. You helped me to see what was hiding behind all this talk of a crusade. And you opened the Duke de Vitry's eyes in the same way. If you hadn't spoken out, he would not have written this letter. It's what you said to him that tipped the scales in our favour, and you know it.'

Marc was overjoyed at the letter. Here it is at last! he thought. The gift from my redeemer, come to save me from my humiliation. Not only will it prove to Isolt that we can work together and make our mark on this little kingdom of ours – even be instrumental in its very survival – but it also shows all the lords who doubted my ability to rule that I am not the buffoon they think I am.

His heart encouraged by these thoughts, Marc called a meeting at which he summoned all the lords of his kingdom to be present. Some two weeks later, on the appointed day, he sat on the throne in the great hall, looking down at all fifteen lords belonging to the five fiefdoms that made up the kingdom. Sitting with them were many knights who, having no land of their own, had offered their services to one or another of the lords. By now all of them had heard rumours about the letter the Duke de Vitry had sent to the Pope, and all had noticed the letter Marc held in his hand as he entered the meeting hall. It now rested on the table in front of him as he sat solemnly staring at them.

When the conversation had died down and all sat looking at him expectantly, Marc began to address them.

'My lords, gentlemen, let me first thank you for having answered my invitation and for having left your families and the affairs of your domains to join me here. Let me start by sharing with you my feelings that these are difficult times we are living in. The world around us is rapidly changing. The freedom and independence we have enjoyed for so many generations are now being challenged by forces that are not so hard to understand. The King of France, it seems, would like to take away from us many of our powers of decision and to speak for us all with one voice – his own. At the same time, the Pope, Innocent III, would like to speak for the whole of Christendom, for all its people, and thus hold the reins of their faith in one pair of hands – his own.

'Whatever good these men feel this may bring to the world, it seems it cannot be achieved without the spilling of much blood. Many people will have to die, in their hundreds or even thousands, for the ambition of these two men to be fulfilled.

'For my part, I find myself sitting on a throne which, had not the vicissitudes of fate intervened, would not have been mine. But I am aware that, though we are today but a small kingdom, this throne represents the ways and customs of a people who once dominated the whole world. Yet even then we were never ruled by a single voice, and our faith and beliefs never rested in the hands of a single man. This is not natural to us as a people, and this is why I have called you here today, to share with me in taking a decision that involves the very survival of our kingdom, its freedom and independence.

'It has to do with our response to a call made by Pope Innocent III, for all of us, lords, knights, princes and kings up here in the north, to join in a crusade in his name, to fight our fellow lords and knights in the south who have given support and protection to the Cathar heresy there. Now, the rumour has spread that the Pope will give his blessing, as a just reward for our joining this crusade, to whatever land or booty we may take into our possession, so long as it is taken from whoever has aligned themselves with the Cathars.

'It is my opinion – and I have voiced this to some of you before – that if we allow ourselves to be tempted by this bait of promised riches, we shall end up poorer men in the long run. Some of us may come back from this campaign with small treasures, but all of us will have lost our independence and freedom, for we shall have placed ourselves under the single command of the King of France and surrendered our faith to the whims of the Pope.

'But we are still, all of us, today, free men, and it is as free men that I call on you to consider this matter and decide for yourselves where you stand in response to this call for a bloody crusade. For much blood will be shed, of that we can be sure, and this deserves your deep consideration. I have here a letter from the Duke de Vitry, with whom I had a chance to speak about this matter. In it he encloses a letter he wrote to the Pope in answer to his call for a crusade. Let me now read it to you.'

Marc read the letter to the assembly of lords and knights, who listened solemnly.

'I have myself written to the Pope,' continued Marc, 'explaining that I cannot give a response to his request until I have consulted you all, the lords and their knights whose fiefdoms make up our kingdom. So now it is up to each one of you. I think you know how I feel. I do not wish to see the power of this throne upon which I sit diminished under my rule. I wish to pass it on unchanged to whoever takes it over from me. I want it to remain a symbol of the independence of the spirit of the people of this kingdom. I do not wish to join this crusade against these men in the south. They, too, are fighting for their independence from those two men, the King of France and Pope Innocent III, who would have us now go against them. If we join in this crusade, then we must ask ourselves: when will it be our turn? When will these same two men mount a crusade against us when we wish to express our independence from their newly established authority?'

Marc got up from his throne and stood with his hands resting on the table before him.

'So, now that you have heard me, will you take this stand with me?' he asked. 'If you will, then please rise to your feet.'

There was a rumble of chairs being pushed back as several lords stood up immediately in support of Marc. Then slowly, one by one, more men stood up until, finally, the last four in the assembly, Ganelon, Lussane, Dargan and Nordstram, who had come to the castle for the first time since losing the duel and had his right arm in a sling, were the only ones left sitting in their chairs. These four, now the centre of everyone's attention, seemed to be waiting for something. And that something did not take long to appear, in the form of two men who stood in the doorway of the assembly hall as all heads turned in their direction.

One of the two was none other than Santerre, the castle priest, and the other was Hubert de Lanson, the secretary and protégé of the Bishop of Rennes. He belonged to a rich noble family close to the King of France and it was rumoured that he would be the next bishop. Seeing that everyone had finally noticed him, de Lanson took a step forward into the hall, turned to Marc and spoke in a loud voice so that everyone could hear him.

'Your Highness, please excuse my intrusion here. It is not my custom to join gatherings to which I have not been invited. However, these are grave matters you have been discussing and I carry with me a letter from His Grace, Innocent III, who is at the present time in Rennes, where he is visiting the bishop. Having heard from Santerre, here present, that you had called this meeting, he wished me to read this letter to the assembly so that his voice may be heard as well.'

De Lanson held up the letter for all to see. Making sure he had everyone's attention, he continued.

'I hope you will not mind sharing with all who are here at this assembly what His Grace Innocent III has to say to you in this letter, for it will give them a chance to hear what someone who is deeply concerned with the salvation of all Christian souls has to say about these heretics. So, with your permission, Your Highness, may I proceed to read this letter aloud?'

As Marc hesitated, the bishop's secretary continued without waiting for an answer. 'I'm sure you won't object to the Church voicing its opinion, even though it may be different from your own, for it too has had to fight vigorously to defend its right to spread the truth.'

'It has always been our custom, in all our assemblies,' Marc answered, 'that all who wished to do so could voice their opinions freely, and we shall not deny that right to His Grace Innocent III, even though he is not here to talk to us in person. So please read us his letter.'

He sat back down on the throne, and the assembled lords also returned to their seats as Hubert de Lanson, seeming somewhat apprehensive, took a deep breath as if to gather all his courage and determination, unfolded the parchment and began to read.

To His Highness, King Marc of Brittany.

It has been brought to our attention that you have been recently travelling to the provinces beyond the borders of your kingdom to express there, to the lords who rule over those lands, your fears with regard to the crusade which is being organised to put a stop to the heresy spreading in the Languedoc.

Though you have not found it necessary to address these fears to me personally, from the mouth of a certain person present at one of your stop-offs in the provinces we have been told that you and your wife who accompanied you have expressed very serious doubts over the sincerity of my motives for calling all good Christians and men of honour to take up arms against these heathens. So let me express my own doubts, not to a third party, but to you directly, about your own motives, yours and your wife's, for conspiring to persuade others that these Cathars represent no real danger to our faith.

But perhaps it would be useful to hear first what Bernard de Clairvaux had to say about the Cathars and the nature of the danger they represent. He compares them to the fox who destroys the vineyards as described in the Song of Solomon. From the simple point of view of his moral behaviour, he abuses no one, never oversteps his rights, never exercises any violence. His features are pale from his fasting; he does not eat his bread in idleness and earns his living with the toil of his hands. So where has the fox gone?

Bernard goes on to suggest that, if we persist in searching for him, 'we shall recognise him by his deeds. For the destroyed vine bears witness to the fox's incursion. The women abandon their husbands, the husbands disown their wives to go and join this sect. The clerks and the priests give up their faithful and their church, and we find them all, the beardless and the bearded, amongst these weavers and their women. Is this not the work of the fox?'

De Lanson raised his eyes from the parchment for a moment and looked over at Marc. There was something twisted and perverse in his glance and Marc saw it. He seemed to both be gleefully looking forward to, and at the same time frightened of, what was going to follow. He quickly looked away and began to read once again from the Pope's letter.

This may, of course, seem to you, Your Highness, a very mild condemnation of these foxes, these so-called weavers who practise their art in the Languedoc. Then may I suggest to you that perhaps this tolerance of yours is due to your indulgence towards your own wife, whose behaviour shows little regard for the sanctity of marriage as professed and upheld by our Christian Church, which has been so vociferously criticised by those very same Cathars.

I have been told by the Bishop of Rennes that your

wife was not present at your coronation. We have since then been able to talk to the priest who performed the sacraments that bound you both to each other as husband and wife. He says that your wife told him that she had been abandoned by her father and was raised by nuns in a convent. If it is true that she was raised in the Christian faith, then why was she living with you in your fortress for some time before she was married? And why was she overheard one evening in a tavern boasting to her friends that her father was a famous astrologer in Constantinople who could bring the dying back to their feet using the power of the stars? Does this sound very Christian, when it is well known that the practice of astrology has been strongly condemned by the Church?

But all this happened before your coronation. She was not yet the wife of a king, whose authority and power to rule over the people belonging to the Kingdom of Brittany had been sanctified with the blessing of the Church of Rome, whose representative here, Guillaume, Bishop of Rennes, performed the sacraments on our behalf. Yet once she became Queen of Brittany by virtue of being your wife, not only did the sanctity of this title not improve her composure and bring more grace to her manners, but quite the contrary. She could do no better than trample it in the murk of her immorality by spending two weeks in an abandoned fisherman's hut on a beach near the town of Port Saint Marie with another man, a knight answering to the name of Tristan.

De Lanson stopped reading to catch his breath and look up to see what effect all this was having so far on the lords and knights in the hall. Their silence and stunned expressions clearly bolstered his confidence, and he quickly looked down at his parchment again.

And now we learn that Queen Isolt carries a child in her womb. We hope, Your Highness, you will forgive us for voicing a question that must be on many lips.

Whose child?

It is not our intention to spread malicious rumours in asking this question, but merely to point to the fact that your wife is Queen of Brittany and that the child she carries in her womb is the potential heir to the throne you now occupy. The lineage of this child is not only a concern for all those who govern your kingdom, but is also the concern of the Church of Rome, which must give its recognition and blessing to your successor.

So before returning across your borders to preach in favour of the Cathars, would it not be more appropriate to put some order into your own house?

We therefore recommend that, in order not to risk excommunication by the Church of Rome and losing our recognition of your right to rule Brittany as its king, that you subject your wife to a test to prove that she has not transgressed the holy vows of marriage upheld by Christian law by committing adultery.

We further decree that this test must consist in her publicly swearing under oath, in the presence of appointed members of the clergy and the appropriate holy relics, that she, Isolt, Queen of Brittany, has at no time committed the punishable sin of adultery.

If the queen is willing to submit to this test and no signs befall on her from the heavens to show that she lies, then she will be considered innocent of the charge against her. In such an eventuality, we will then regard your arguments for not joining our Holy Crusade in the light of reason and take them at their face value. In any other circumstances, we can only take them as an attempt

*to undermine the authority of our Christian faith and as
the disguised voice of those heretics we are determined to
combat and crush.*

*Awaiting your answer, and in good faith, we send you
our kindest regards,*
Innocent III.

Hubert de Lanson looked up at Marc. 'I have nothing to add to
this letter,' he said, rolling up the parchment. 'I can only urge
you to think deeply about what it says before jumping into any
decision that might have the gravest of consequences.' With the
parchment neatly rolled up in his hand, the bishop's secretary
stood expectantly, as if waiting for one of the seated lords, some
of whom were now whispering to each other, to stand up and
say something.

'Since this letter was addressed to me personally, I think it is
only right that I should take possession of it,' Marc said, rising
from his throne. The bishop's secretary handed the parchment
to Santerre, who brought it forward and deposited it on the
table, beside which he stood looking embarrassed.

'As you brought him in here, you can show him the way out,'
said Marc angrily, 'and see him on his way.'

The assembly hall fell silent. The lords and knights stared up
at Marc, who looked back at them and shrugged.

'I think this letter only proves the arguments that I put to you
earlier. It shows only too well how the Pope wishes to impose his
will and law upon our kingdom, and to what depths he is willing
to sink in order to do so. I think it should only strengthen our
determination not to be forced under the yoke of his ambitions.
So, let us continue from where we were before this uninvited
interruption.

'All those of you who stand behind me, please rise and show
yourselves to me again!'

There was a silence after he had spoken, followed this time by the sound of only one chair being pushed back as someone stood up to face him. It was Gothram, an older lord who had fought many battles at the side of Marc's father, the late king.

'Sire, perhaps it would be best if Queen Isolt did as the Pope recommends and submits herself to the test of truth. For there have been many rumours with regard to her disappearance from the castle in the company of Tristan, and the two weeks she was absent.'

'But it's all a pack of lies!' Marc could not hide his anger and frustration.

'Then, sire, why not persuade Queen Isolt to submit to the test and lay all these rumours to rest? It's not healthy for our kingdom to have all this talk going on about the queen, Tristan and the child she carries within her.'

Marc stood, lost for words. In each hand he held a rolled-up parchment, one a letter from the Duke de Vitry, the other from the Pope. One of them he had thought carried the seal of a great victory for Isolt and him, while the other turned out to be the instrument of the worst public humiliation he could have imagined.

'This is all a waste of time. A total waste of time!' he cried, and left the assembly hall without uttering another word.

*

Isolt lay in her bed, which she had hardly left in the two weeks since their return from the journey. She looked pale and tired.

'I don't understand!' Marc was saying to her. 'I made my speech, and it was a damned good speech. I felt really inspired, and when I'd finished, there was a minute, it couldn't have been more than a minute, when they all stood up to show their support. I felt as if dust from heaven was being showered down on me. It was as if, for the very first time, I was holding the entire kingdom in my hands.'

Marc sighed. He was sitting on the edge of the bed and raised his eyes to look at her. She stared back, her eyes wide open and expressionless, and he realised that he had once again been telling her of his failure, just as he had done when he had announced to her that he wouldn't be fighting the duel against Nordstram. He felt suddenly very angry. Angry at those eyes that were looking at him and didn't want to say anything, that couldn't lie to him.

'Anyway,' he said, 'I went from that moment of glorious victory to one of abject humiliation as I stood, moments later, exposed before all the lords and knights of my kingdom as the biggest cuckold in the whole of Christendom.'

Marc was staring down at his feet again. After a moment, he looked up. Isolt's eyes were still open and blank, but they were now staring across the room at the wall as tears ran down her cheeks.

'Why did my brother have to die?' Marc exclaimed, feeling he had already let himself go too far and could not hold back any more. 'Why wasn't he the first one to set eyes on you? You could have been queen at his side. Or, if not him, why didn't they crown Tristan? He would have been a real king!'

'Shut up!' Isolt shouted. She threw the covers back, jumped out of the bed and walked to the window. Beyond the castle walls she could see an animal running across a stretch of open field, far away. She thought at first it might be a horse, but as she squinted she could see that it had antlers and must have been a stag. She felt suddenly better. A rush of determination straightened her body, giving it back its suppleness and strength.

'All right!' she said. 'Let them put me through this so-called test of truth.'

'You can't do that,' Marc said. 'You don't realise the powers these men have. I can't allow you to forswear yourself before them. It's too dangerous.'

'What powers?' Isolt exclaimed angrily. 'What powers can these men have, who would drag a poor woman with a child in her womb out of her bed, to display her in public and have her humiliate herself?'

She turned around and stared at Marc. 'But that's what you want. To have me humiliated as well!'

'I never said that!'

'Not in so many words, but I can hear it in your voice. Well, I'm going to show you that I can't be humiliated, and nothing is going to stop me from doing that. So you'd better watch, take good notice and learn something for once!'

7

IN THE FACE OF GOD'S AUTHORITY

Isolt called for Santerre and instructed him to tell the Bishop of Rennes that she was going to organise a great tournament, to be held on the White Moor, an island of dry sand down by the estuary of the Tavre River. In days of old, at the time of King Arthur, it had been a favourite site for jousting tournaments and many a duel had been fought there according to the legends of those times. But that was long ago, and it had been abandoned since then as a place for tournaments because of the difficult access through the Mal Pas swamp that surrounded it.

She would call on all the lords and knights of the kingdom, as well as the dukes and barons from neighbouring fiefdoms, to come and test their skills. They would be asked them to bring their wives along with them, and also their servants, so that they could all pitch their tents there.

On the day following the tournament, after spending the previous day and night at prayer in the castle chapel, she would come to the White Moor and submit herself in front of this large gathering to the test of truth as requested by the Pope. For this trial she would ask the dukes and barons to bring with them their most sacred relics.

She also gave the priest a sealed letter for the bishop in which all she had told him was detailed. He, in turn, was to hand it over to Innocent III.

When the Pope had read her letter he sent word that he was glad to learn that she was willing to publicly humble herself in the face of God's authority, and that he would himself appoint the appropriate officials to oversee this sacred ceremony.

'Has that wife of yours taken complete leave of her senses?' asked Isabelle in disbelief.

Marc dismounted from his horse and stood facing his mother by the stable doorway. He had just returned from the clearing in the Moroi forest, where he had spent some time sitting alone on the rostrum, listening to the squabbling crows and staring at the patch of turf where only weeks before he had watched as another man had fought his battle for him and stolen away his life. He did not know why he had gone back there. Perhaps he just wanted to punish himself.

'No, Mother, I don't think so. She at least has the courage to fight her own battles and not let someone else do it for her,' he replied bitterly.

'Oh, for God's sake, Marc! Try and forget about yourself for a moment and show a bit of common sense. The Pope has fixed a date for this absurd ceremony. It's going to be the second Friday in August. And, as if that wasn't bad enough, she's decided to organise a tournament around this event and is sending out letters inviting just about every noble family in France to come and take part. She's turning this whole shameful business into a great big circus, just to draw attention to herself at any price. We are all going to pay a heavy cost for it. You can be sure of that!'

'Then we're just going to have to pay,' he replied. 'That's all. You were the one who pushed me onto this throne. Now you're going to have to take the consequences along with the rest of us.'

He made to leave, but then turned to face his mother again. 'There is nothing you can do to stop this from happening,' he continued. 'There is not a single person in the kingdom, apart from you maybe, who does not want to see this happen. They all want her to go through with it now, even if it's only for the pleasure of seeing her fail. For the pleasure of seeing her being struck down. They all love her right now, just for offering them this circus, as you call it, this little bit of distraction that will lighten up their lives. And you're not going to stop it from happening.'

Isabelle looked at her son and was about to say something, but stopped herself, realising that anything she could say would be lost on him in his present state. Instead, she merely shrugged and shook her head as she crossed the courtyard and went into the castle. Marc handed his horse over to the stable boy and was about to take the same direction as his mother, but then saw Forsin standing by the steps that led down to the kitchen. He went over to join him there.

'You've been for a ride?' Forsin asked.

'Yes. I just wanted to get out of here for a while.'

'You're the king now, Your Highness. You should not go out riding on your own, if you don't mind my saying so,' Forsin said with a note of irony.

'Yes, well, I curse the day my brother died and forced me to wear the crown that should have been his,' Marc replied bitterly.

'Don't say that!' said Forsin. 'Don't you see, that's what's wrong with you? You don't accept that life moves on and carries the living with it into unexpected places. But never curse that day that made you king. And I say this, even though it doesn't please me to see you wearing a crown you never wanted. Even though that day has caused me to lose my one and only friend as, now that you are king, I can never again speak to you as I used to.'

'It doesn't seem to be stopping you from doing that at the moment!' Marc retorted.

'Only because you refuse to take possession of your rightful place yourself,' Forsin replied.

'If I'd done that, then my rightful place right now would be in a coffin,' Marc said.

'Not the duel again?' Forsin shook his head with exasperation. 'Do you think that being able to defeat every other swordsman in the kingdom is what makes a worthy king?'

'My wife seems to think so. And the only throne I want to sit on is the one hidden somewhere in my wife's heart.'

Forsin shook his head.

'I thought all that was over. That she had forgotten about Tristan. You both seemed happy together. The bishop and his cohorts had no business interfering in your lives.'

'It's not only that.' Marc sighed. 'You don't run away with someone the way she did and just forget all about him afterwards. What do you think is going on in her heart when, at odd moments of the day, I catch her staring absently into space? Or when, at night beside me in the bed, I lie awake listening to her as she breathes gently, lost in her dream? In those moments of absence I can tell it's not in search of me that her heart has wandered, but in search of him.'

*

Of all the letters Isolt sent out, there were two to which she paid particular care and attention. The first was addressed to the Duke de Vitry.

My lord,

Much has happened since our visit to your castle, and it is with great fondness that I think back and remember the warm hospitality and kindness that was shown to us during our brief stay. It seems so distant now from the harshness and turmoil of events that have taken place since then.

As you might already have heard, the Pope, His Grace Innocent III, feeling that, thanks mainly to your courageous stand, his crusade was now slipping away from him like water through his fingers, has found no better way to fight back than to accuse me of being a Cathar in disguise and to try to soil my reputation with lewd insinuations regarding my virtue.

Rather than allow these accusations to become a major distraction from the real issues at stake, I have decided to accept his request that I exonerate myself in the eyes of the Church by submitting to the test of truth in public, however humiliating this might be for my own person, especially in my present condition.

I know that, by agreeing to submit to this test, I am also accepting the Pope's right to interfere in the ruling of our kingdom. But, at the end of the day, I think that this public display of his authority will only expose his overreaching ambitions to ridicule. That is why I hope that as many noblemen as possible will come with their wives and their entourages, from as far away as can be reached, to take part in the tournament that will start on the second Friday of August and will end with my public exoneration on the following day.

But of all those who attend, I count most strongly on your presence, for there is no nobler and more valiant heart than yours in all of Christendom. And, with you *there, I know that the Pope and his henchmen will think twice about abusing me further in this already humiliating ordeal.*

Awaiting hopefully your answer, I send you my best wishes,

Isolt.

P.S. Should you decide to accept my invitation, could you please bring along a sacred relic, if you have one in your possession. It will help to give credence to my oath on the day of my ordeal.

The second letter was not really a letter in the true sense of the word. It was a drawing of a horse, done by Isolt on a scrap of parchment, which she rolled up and tied with a ribbon. She handed it to Jeanne, a young girl who worked at the castle whom she had chosen to be her personal maid, telling her to find Albert and to go with him to Port Saint Marie and to hand over the parchment to Marie, who lived there.

Jeanne left with the document and returned a short while later. She had found Albert, who was waiting by the stables. He had told her that Donoalin had just returned from Port Saint Marie, where he had gone on leave expecting to find Marie there, but he was told by her father that she had gone to Normandy to look after the children of a cousin who had fallen ill. She added that Donoalin was quite upset because Marie's father didn't want to give him any more details of her whereabouts. When he insisted, saying that he wanted to spend his leave with her to help her out, her father just answered that it would be better if he stayed away because her cousin didn't want any company other than her immediate family.

When Isolt heard this she felt that something didn't sound right. Marie and her parents had seemed to be such generous, open people, but she was too caught up in the urgency of her own situation to start worrying about Marie right then.

She told Jeanne that, when they reached Port Saint Marie, they were to ride along the coast to the south of the town for a few miles, where they would find an abandoned hut on the beach. They were to enter the hut and would see a large, flat stone in its far-right corner. They were to lift the stone and place the parchment underneath it and then return to the castle.

When Isolt had sent Jeanne on her way, she sat down on the bed in her room. She could feel the tightness in her throat and a jolt of excitement rushed through her. She had just done what she had promised she would never do again. She had thrown open the door and let all caution blow out with the wind. She was willing to sacrifice everything now.

Jeanne and Albert were gone all day and did not return until late in the evening. Isolt was sitting on the steps in the courtyard when they rode over the drawbridge and dismounted by the stables. It was already dark. She walked over to greet them.

'Did you find the hut?' she asked.

'Yes, we did,' Jeanne answered. 'And we put the parchment under the stone.'

'You didn't see anyone following you there, did you?' Isolt asked.

'No,' replied Jeanne. 'We passed a few people near Market Town and a few more around Port Saint Marie, but no one followed us. There was someone fishing down by the shore though, not far from the hut.'

'A man?' Isolt asked.

Jeanne nodded.

'What did he look like?'

'He looked more like a young man than an old man,' said Jeanne, 'but he wasn't close enough to really tell. He only looked up at us once, and the rest of the time he had his back turned. It must have been his horse that was eating grass just behind the hut.'

'And the horse wasn't tethered?' Isolt asked.

'No. He had a saddle on him and I noticed a red ribbon tied to the strap, just below one of his ears.'

Isolt's heart jumped and she felt it bounce against her chest. It was a pleasant sensation, full of excitement, as if she could smell the ocean and hear the sound of the waves breaking on the shore. 'Good,' she said. 'Thanks to you both for having gone all this way for me. You must be very tired.'

That night she did not sleep well. She tossed and turned and woke up several times thinking it was already morning. Then, when it was time to get up, she told Marc that she needed to rest, to think things over. She would spend the day in her room and he should tell everyone she would resume writing invitations the following day.

Marc simply stared back at her with a passive, resigned look. As far as he was concerned, she was stirring up the kingdom into a ferment where he seemed to be losing all sense of his own equilibrium, yet the more he lost his footing, the more she seemed to gain strength and assurance.

'Do you want me to keep you company?' he asked.

'No. Just go about your business, try to keep an eye on Kore and see that she's all right. I may have to go out for a while later.'

'Where?' he asked.

'Just trust me, Marc. I know what I'm doing,' she said and stared at him.

He look back at her with hatred in his eyes. Far down inside him, he could feel a pain that told him all too clearly what she was doing. But he didn't have the courage to accuse her of anything; she would only hold it against him. Even if everything was going to fall apart he wanted to still be on her side when it all happened. He was willing to hold on to whatever little piece of her she would allow him to have. It had gone beyond lust or physical craving now. He didn't know how she had managed it, but she had taken on such a stature, unshaken by fear or doubt that, whatever she did, whatever she put him through now, he would still feel a deep moral compulsion to remain by her side.

When Marc left the room she got out of bed and dressed. Then she went over to the window, pulling a chair across the room with her, and sat there looking out. Beyond the high walls of the courtyard she could see the road that cut through the cornfields; it climbed to the top of the hill and descended towards the market town where she had first met Marc.

When Jeanne knocked on the door and entered the room, she was still sitting there. Jeanne put a tray with a hot camomile and honey drink and a plate of millet cakes down on the bed; Isolt thanked her and asked her to tell the stable boy to saddle her horse and have him ready. She said she intended to go out for a ride when she had finished eating.

Isolt ate and drank as she sat by the window. When she had finished, she began to pace up and down the room, stopping every now and then to look out of the window once more, and then sat down again on the chair.

It wasn't until late in the morning when, getting up from the bed where she had thrown herself in frustration and impatience, she thought she saw something moving down the road in the distance. As it descended slowly, moving closer, she saw that it was a horse, a saddled horse without a rider.

'Bonne Aventure!' Isolt whispered. She turned away from the window and rushed over to the chair where her boots were waiting. She pulled them on as fast as she could and went rushing along the hall, down the stairs, across the entrance hall and into the courtyard.

As she climbed up onto her horse, Jeanne came running across the courtyard after her. 'My lady!' she shouted. 'Will you be eating downstairs with the king?'

'No, Jeanne. I'll have something in my room when I get back. If anybody asks, I've gone for a ride. That's all,' Isolt replied.

'Yes, my lady. Good luck,' Jeanne called after her as Isolt, holding tightly to the reins, kicked the horse forward towards the drawbridge. Jeanne watched her mistress move away through the fields of golden wheat and shook her head.

'It's madness! It's pure madness. And in her condition!'

Bonne Aventure, Tristan's horse, was waiting on the road near the top of the hill. He reared up on his hind legs and called out in greeting as Isolt rode up to him. After the two horses had licked each other's noses, Isolt reached out and stroked Bonne Aventure's neck. 'Come on, let's go and find Tristan,' she said.

As they came over the top of the hill, Bonne Aventure left the road and cut through a patch of abandoned land overgrown with bracken and wild berry shrubs. They made their way through, cautiously, until Isolt spotted Tristan sitting under an oak tree, fifty feet or so below them.

Isolt dismounted and found herself running down the slope towards Tristan, who caught her in his arms. He felt the soft pressure of her breasts against him and her belly pushing against his as he pulled her towards him, his cheek against hers, his nose buried in her hair, her arms tight around his waist.

She pushed herself away from him and stared at him.

'Are you coming away with me?' Tristan asked.

She shook her head and saw the disappointment in his eyes.

'Then what is it?' he asked.

'Tristan!' she said. She raised her hand and caressed his cheek, and then moved her thumb over his lips. She had not intended to do this and half expected him to push her away. She felt his arms pull her body against him again. As her lips came close to his, she moved her hand away from his mouth and wrapped it around the back of his neck.

After a while she moved her head back and their lips parted. 'I'm pregnant,' she said.

'I know,' Tristan said, still holding on to her. 'The whole kingdom knows.'

'But I'm not sure it's your child.'

As she looked into his eyes she could see nothing move in them. His face remained the same; there was not the slightest change in his expression. He was still the same Tristan, who had made passionate love to her on the beach, who had joked and made her laugh when he could see that she was troubled.

He would never let anything make him depart from himself, let go of who he was. He had the same look in his eyes as when he had asked her, as she sat under the oak tree by the little chapel outside the castle, if her ambition was really to become a queen.

And now that she was a queen, nothing had changed in those eyes, as if nothing had happened, as if they were looking at the same woman he had interrupted and torn away from the book she was trying to read. As if those eyes had never looked away from her. And suddenly she could feel herself being drawn into him all over again, despite all the promises she had made to herself, despite her resolution to forget him, despite what she had said to Marc.

And she felt no scruples about what was happening to her now, as she stared back at him, because she was overwhelmed by the feeling that to walk away from him now would be akin to walking away from herself. She could see it there, written in his eyes.

8

The Mal Pas

Strange sounds could be heard in the Mal Pas swamp early in the morning on that second Friday of August. There, where the reeds stopped growing and the land rose and flattened out onto the White Moor, a small group of cranes were jumping up and down, flapping their wings and rushing at each other, their beaks pointing like lances. From their throats came a dry, hollow sound, like someone blowing into a horn.

On a stump by the road that ran along the riverbank sat a man; he was looking out across the stretch of swampland, overgrown with reeds, that separated him from the White Moor. Dressed in a dirty woollen smock with a large leather belt around his waist, he was laughing and hitting the copper cup held in his hand with a small hammer that was linked to the cup by a chain, the badge that identified him as a leper. The sound of his hammer hitting the cup was not unlike the noise made by the squabbling cranes, and the leper shouted out to them.

'Come on! Don't stop there! Won't one of you shove the

other to the ground with his lance? Didn't King Arthur teach you anything?'

His hair was knotted and uncombed, his cheeks puffed out and swollen as if he had been in a fight. His voice was hoarse and rough and he seemed not to have washed in years. Who could have guessed this was Tristan, so perfect was his disguise?

Isolt had given him two weeks to prepare himself, though even so she had not explained much. She had simply told him to be waiting there, on that stump, on the second Thursday in August. He was to arrive early in the afternoon, and to just sit and wait for the others to show up; all of them, the lords, their caravans and their followers. He was to beg money from them, to deride those that would not give him any, as they attempted to cross the swampy stretch to the White Moor, where they would pitch their tents. The main purpose of this was that he should draw their attention, all of them, to the fact that he had been there, sitting on that stump, all day.

The following morning he was to return to that stump and be sitting there when they began their tournament, to wave and bang on his cup in praise of a knight who had knocked another knight off his horse, so that, once again, he would draw attention to himself. He was also to return there the following day and to be sure to beg charity from the bishop and his attendants when they arrived to cross over onto the White Moor. After that, all he had to do was to wait for her arrival, still pretending to be a poor leper, and to do exactly what she would command him to do.

Tristan knew about the trouble she was in and why she was to come to the White Moor. However, he still had no idea why he had to be on that stump in such an extravagant disguise, nor of the use she would make of him once she arrived. The only thing he knew for sure was that, whatever it was she wanted him to do, he was not going to let her down.

Up until that moment, when she had looked up at him from the book she was reading under the tree outside the chapel, his life had made no sense to him. He'd had a feeling of not really belonging to this world. But, then, he had recognised something unspeakable and unpronounceable in her eyes that made him realise that, all the time he had been travelling far and wide, what he had been looking for was her.

So, whatever she asked him now, if it offered him the possibility of seeing her again, of being close to her, even if he could not touch her or enter into her embrace as he had done two weeks ago like a thief in the night, then he would do it. It would still be a hundred times better than what he had endured alone, without her, on the beach where she had left him a few short months ago, when she had decided to go back and live with Marc again.

The sun had just peeked over the distant hills in the east. There had been violent storms the previous afternoon and so the lords and their ladies, who had come from far and near, had decided not to cross the Mal Pas swamp on that Thursday afternoon. Instead, they waited until the following morning in the hope that the storm would have blown over and that the swamp would be less clogged with water. They had all pitched their tents in a field several miles up the road. As the sun was now rising into what appeared to be a cloudless sky, Tristan expected these noblemen, with their wives and cohorts, to soon appear, riding along the riverbank on their way towards the Mal Pas where he was sitting. They would be in a hurry to cross over onto the White Moor and set up their tents before the beginning of the tournament.

And, sure enough, it was not long before he heard the distant sound of laughter and saw, far away in the distance, four men on horses. From their bearing and attitude he judged that they were young squires who had just been dubbed and given their knight's armour. They brought their horses to a halt close by to the stump.

'Greetings, my lords,' Tristan called out. 'Would you not have between you some coins to throw to a poor leper who, despite his affliction, must still provide for his family?'

'Where is your family?' one of the young knights asked him.

'In the town called Triaval. They have not been afflicted by this scourge. I have only recently been cursed by it myself and must now live separated from my loved ones. So, have pity on me and give me something to soothe my pain.'

The knight pulled his pouch from his belt, opened it and fished out a coin, which he tossed over. Tristan caught it in his hand and examined it.

'Thank you, my lord, but is a penny all I'm to get between all four of you?' Tristan asked.

One of the other knights laughed. 'He's the only one with a pouch,' he said. 'We, too, have to beg our meals and our drinks from him.'

'Then this coin in my cup shall surely bring him luck,' Tristan said.

'Tell me, is this the best place to cross over onto the White Moor?' asked the knight who had tossed him the coin.

'Yes, it's the only safe place to cross,' Tristan answered. 'Anywhere else, your horse might get stuck. People have been known to sink with their horses into the mud and disappear, never to be seen again.'

'Thank you for strengthening our hearts with such words of reassurance, good friend,' said the knight as he steered his horse down into the reeds and spurred him forward across the wet, muddy ground, followed closely by his companions.

'Don't worry, my lord, your generosity will see you across!' Tristan shouted at his back and watched with delight as the horses lifted their hoofs out of the mud, not wishing to move onwards but spurred forward with great difficulty and much shouting by the men on their backs.

When the knights reached the other side of the marsh, they unsaddled their horses, untied their bundles, laid their armour on the ground and sat talking while the horses, having found a pool of clear water near the reeds, were quenching their thirst.

But the excitement was too great and soon the young knights were on their feet, armed with their swords and shields, practising moves in mock battle with each other, watched from a safe distance by the cranes, which had moved further down the bank.

Tristan felt something stab into him as he sat watching them. It had nothing to do with regret or sorrow that, on such an occasion, he would not be there in his finest attire, the knight whom everyone feared, the one everyone dreamt of knocking off his horse in a tournament. That kind of nonsense had no real meaning to him any more. The only thing that could shine light into his heart now was his love for Isolt. A love that sadly could be compared, he thought, as he sat watching those young knights fighting their mock battles, to two flowers that had blossomed suddenly under a hostile winter sky.

However, he did not have time to allow his thoughts to delve too deeply into their plight for he heard noises coming from far up the riverbank. A long parade was heading down the road towards him. As it came closer, he could make out men and women dressed in noble attire, followed by more men on horses. Behind them were horses with bundles strapped on their backs and, behind them, carts and wagons loaded with more bundles and then people, some sitting on carts and some walking.

As the riders at the head of the parade reached where Tristan was sitting on his little mound, they paused to search for a possible passage across to the White Moor. 'Greetings, my lords and ladies!' Tristan shouted over to them. 'Please excuse my impertinence, but I have never seen such fine and beautiful cloth, worn on shoulders with such noble bearing. This must indeed be no ordinary occasion to draw noblemen and women of your calibre and importance away from your occupations, to such a lost and godforsaken place.'

A man of imposing stature in a blue silk jacket and red velvet cape looked over at Tristan with vague amusement in his eyes. He wore a velvet hat with a long feather sticking up from its rim. He was none other than the Duke de Vitry himself.

'Have you not heard, my poor fellow, that on that sandy island beyond the reeds, known as the White Moor, were fought some of the greatest duels of all times?'

Tristan rubbed his head.

'I must admit that I have heard all sorts of rumours of what went on here in times of old. But, for as long as I can remember, this has always been a most lonely and deserted place. Although the odd person does come by from time to time along this road, never before have I seen such a fine company as yours, so beautifully attired and of such noble lineage.'

'We have come to watch our young knights test their skills,' the duke replied. 'To revive an old custom that was once practised here, as I have told you, long ago in the times of King Arthur.'

'Then more will be following behind you?' asked Tristan, beating on his cup with his little hammer as if to emphasise his excitement.

'Yes, you can expect many more,' said the duke. 'Some will be knights come to test their skills. But most will be here to watch your queen, when tomorrow she takes an oath before God and frees herself from charges brought against her by certain members of the clergy.'

Tristan beat his cup even harder.

'This is indeed cause to rejoice,' he said. 'I, who had come here this morning to mourn in solitude the loss of my good health, now find myself in the presence of great men and women come here to witness a great event. Could you not, my lord, crown my good fortune with a gesture that would bless a poor wretched soul such as mine with the memory of a day that will have made a life of suffering worth enduring?'

The duke laughed.

'If I could make such a gesture, I certainly would not hesitate to do so, my dear friend. What is it you want?'

'Your boots, my lord. I have never seen finer footwear. Please excuse my impudence, but I cannot stop thinking what heavenly joy it would be to have my poor sore feet resting inside them. I could then go my way, no longer in pain and disgrace, but forgetful of this wretched life of mine in the memory of a great honour once bestowed on me by a most charitable and noble soul.'

'My boots!' exclaimed the duke. 'You mean you would have me go barefoot in order that your own feet should be covered?'

The lords and ladies in his company broke out in laughter at the duke's sudden loss of composure. The woman who had been riding alongside him then spoke up.

'Come on, my lord. Surely you can afford to offer this man your boots?'

'All right, then,' the duke replied. 'Come over here, my good man. Pull them off my feet, since they now belong to you.'

'Thank you, sire!' said Tristan. He caressed each boot as he gently removed them from the duke's feet. 'I shall let them hang around my neck and not wear them until I have scrubbed my feet.'

'Very well,' said the duke. 'Now, let us cross over to the White Moor and pitch our tents.' As he steered his horse down into the reeds, followed by his company, Tristan shouted after him.

'God bless you, my lord! God bless you!'

He watched them make their way across, the men shouting and cursing and the women letting out occasional screams as their horses leapt forward in bounds to escape the mud, which splashed up in all directions.

There then followed a large group of young knights and squires, riding their lighter mounts and pulling their heavier jousting horses behind them, loaded with their armour. There was laughter and mockery as mud splashed everywhere. One of the knights had fallen off his mount and was now throwing mud at all who passed near him. The lords and ladies who had reached the other side stood watching this circus, some joining in with shouts and laughter, while others were more concerned with brushing down their clothes.

Back on his mound, with his new boots hanging from his neck, Tristan was beating once again on his cup with his little hammer and laughing uproariously.

Then came the turn of the carts and the wagons, all of which had to be helped across with ropes tied to horses pulling them from the dry sand on the White Moor. For the rest of the morning there seemed to be an endless, unbroken line of people, horses and carts. Some of these noble souls and their attendants had left their castles only the day before, while others had been travelling for several days. They formed a long line down the road that followed the river up to where Tristan was sitting on his stump by the Mal Pas crossing. As the morning progressed, the reeds were flattened, ploughed under by the hoofs and the wagon wheels, and the crossing gradually became a large expanse of sticky mud with deep holes and big pools of water.

When Marc, his mother, and the lords and knights of his castle reached the crossing, Tristan simply banged on his cup and asked for charity, careful not to engage any of them in conversation. None of them, except Marc, who had thrown a few coins over to Tristan, seemed to have paid any attention to him, their main preoccupation being the awful state of the passage over to the White Moor.

Eventually, all the tents had been pitched, a good fifty of them at least, one beside the other in two straight lines, facing each other down a broad stretch of sand. It was along this sand that the knights in their armour were to rush at each other on their horses, their lances pointing straight ahead at their oncoming opponent.

A flag was flying in front of each tent, displaying the coat of arms of the lineage to which it belonged, and heavy wooden armchairs were placed by the flags where the lords and their ladies could sit and watch the young knights of their court defend their colours.

However, once the tournament started, everyone began to crowd near the middle of the long run, to be close to the point where the knights on their galloping horses would clash with their lances. Soon, it seemed that all the lords and ladies had abandoned their armchairs and were now standing together in a lively, noisy gathering, which started early in the afternoon and went on until the sun began to sink behind the horizon late in the evening.

A few knights received heavy injuries but by nightfall they were all still breathing and had their wits about them. The great victor of the day was the Duke de Vitry, whose well-trained army of knights, most of whom had acquired real battle experience in the East, won most of the duels in which they participated.

The only two knights in the Kingdom of Brittany who could have dampened this overwhelming show of force were both unable to participate in the event; Nordstram because of the injury to his shoulder incurred in the duel a month and a half beforehand, and Tristan because he had been asked by his mistress to sit and watch the event in disguise from the vantage point of a small mound on the other side of the Mal Pas crossing.

That night there was much singing of war songs, and then of love songs once the ladies and the maidens approached to join in the fun around the big bonfire. There was also a small orchestra of flutes, drums and a lute, much drinking of ale and much dancing. The intoxication of the night, as it drew on, saw the rivalries and old grudges of all those gathered on the White Moor melt away in the exhilaration of the music, the ale and the dancing. All except two men, Tristan and Marc.

Not that Tristan bore a grudge against anyone in particular who was there that night, and certainly not against Marc. Nor did he feel any real rivalry with regard to Marc, such was his conviction that Isolt's heart belonged to him, and him alone, even if her body was bound by law and convention to the man to whom she was married.

No, his grudge was against life as it was lived in this world, against the absurdity of a world whose rules would not bend to the far greater force of love, and which denied two souls who so obviously belonged to each other the legitimacy of loving each other openly. And the sight of the silhouettes moving to a sweet melody in the light of the bonfire across the way only exacerbated this feeling.

As for Marc, he certainly did bear a grudge against Tristan for having stolen the heart of the one person who had ever brought anything real into his life, any real hope, any real belief that there was a place for him in this world. And that grudge extended beyond Tristan to just about everyone on the White Moor that night, just for being there, for taking part in the music, the drinking, the dancing, and for leaving him out there on his own, drowning in his misery and self-pity. He could feel that this resentment, anger and bitterness was consuming him from inside, and wished he could stop it somehow, but felt powerless to do so.

*

Early in the morning, when a glowing light was reaching up from under the horizon far inland, a group of cranes floated down from the sky, like grey ghosts emerging out of the dawn, and landed on the White Moor by the edge of the marsh. They shook their feathers, stretched their wings and then stood, silently, waiting for the sun to rise.

Tristan opened his eyes and saw them and was pleased. He sat up, stretched his arms and back, and then stood up. He looked around him for a while and then walked over to his mound. The birds looked at him suspiciously and started walking slowly, tentatively, a few steps at a time, towards the bonfire, now just a big pile of ashes and charred wood. When they reached it, they began to poke about, their long necks pointing downwards as their sharp beaks skimmed over the ground in search of any bits of food that might have been dropped in the night by the revellers.

Finally, the sun began to rise over the distant hills and climbed up into the sky, casting long shadows everywhere and lifting vapour out of the fields with its first rays of heat.

A fire had been lit outside the Duke de Vitry's tent by his valet. A tripod had been placed over the fire and a large iron pot was now suspended over the flames. Several attendants were sitting around the fire holding cups of hot broth that had been heated in the pot. They were taking cautious sips as they waited for their master and his friends to waken so they could serve them some of the soup as well.

As Tristan watched from across the way, he was tempted to cross over and ask for a measure of the soup to be poured into his cup, but he realised that this might be pushing his luck and could ruin everything for Isolt. She had told him to remain seated on the stump and that is what he intended to do, even if it meant only drinking water from the river for his breakfast.

He heard a faint rumble and the distant echo of voices. He turned and saw something moving far up the road. It was a group of between forty and fifty horsemen escorting a carriage and two closed wagons. Tristan watched them approach, listened to the hoofs and the creaking wheels breaking through the early morning quiet. He recognised the escorting guards as belonging to the Pope's private army. Some held spears, others had crossbows strapped across their backs and others had just their swords and shields, but all of them wore a white cloth vest with a purple cross painted on it over their armour.

When the convoy reached the Mal Pas crossing, the captain called his men to a halt and studied the sorry state of the stretch of mud they would have to negotiate in order to get to the other side.

'You'll need some sturdy ropes and some valiant horses to pull the carriage over from the other side,' Tristan said in a broken voice. He no longer needed to disguise it since it had grown hoarse from all the shouting and taunting of the previous day.

The captain looked at Tristan dubiously, not sure if someone of such a wretched appearance should be listened to. Tristan picked up his cup and hit it once or twice to indicate that he was a leper.

'And what makes you so sure that our own horses cannot pull the carriage across?' the captain asked.

'The wheels will sink too far into the mud,' replied Tristan. 'The harder the horses pull on their harnesses, the deeper they will sink, until they will be unable to move. I was sitting on this very same spot yesterday and saw it happen more than once.'

The captain examined Tristan again, who squinted up at him, his lips parted into a silly smile to reveal the teeth that he had taken care to blacken the day before with soot.

'And where would I find the ropes?' the captain asked.

Tristan pointed to the left. 'Over there, by the tent with the fire burning in front of it. If you ask the valet there, he will surely give them to you, and provide horses as well.'

The captain and two of his men struggled over to the other side and talked to the valet outside the Duke de Vitry's tent. As Tristan looked round at the fine wooden carriage, its door, painted with a golden cross, was pushed open. Two men wearing linen robes the same colour as their pale faces climbed down and stepped out into the early morning sunlight.

One of the men was Santerre, the other Hubert de Lanson, the bishop's secretary. As Tristan had never seen either of them before, he felt free to engage them in conversation and called out, 'Good morning, my lords. I hope neither of you has been exhausted by a long, hard journey?'

Santerre looked at Tristan with disdain and turned away, but the bishop's secretary took a few steps and approached closer to the mound. The priest, seeing this, followed reluctantly behind him.

'No, my good man,' said de Lanson. 'We have only come a short way this morning, for we have spent the night at the Monastery of St Antoine. I hope the advice you gave our captain is sound, as His Holiness, the Bishop of Rennes, is sitting inside this carriage and would be most displeased if it got stuck in the mud.'

'Have no fear, my lord,' Tristan answered. 'With four of the big jousting horses pulling it from the solid ground of the White Moor, your carriage will be across in no time.'

'We shall see,' the bishop's secretary said haughtily. 'And tell me one more thing. Do you know if Queen Isolt is already over there on the White Moor?'

'No, my lord. Not yet, as far as I know,' Tristan answered.

The secretary turned to Santerre. 'That's another who would do well not to displease the bishop by keeping him waiting.'

'Oh, I'm sure she wouldn't do that!' Tristan said. 'I'm sure our queen is as eager as the bishop to see this whole business over with and forgotten.'

'Well, I don't think it will be quite as easy as all that,' he replied, turning to look at Santerre and exchanging a sneering smile that sent a dark cloud over Tristan's heart. He had sensed something menacing and unspoken hidden behind their smiles, and he automatically found himself staring at the wagon that was lined up behind the carriage. It was made of a much thicker, coarser, unpainted wood, and was completely closed up except for a small, steel-barred opening at its front, high up near the roof. The sight of this prison wagon sent a shiver down his spine, and suddenly he lost all desire to talk to the two men any longer.

By the time the carriage had been pulled across the Mal Pas, Marc and his mother, along with several other lords and ladies, had emerged from their tents and were waiting for the bishop to step down onto the sand. Once he had alighted and they had offered greetings, a long discussion began involving Marc and Isabelle, his uncle Ganelon, the bishop and his secretary, and the captain of the guards. Once the two closed wagons had been tugged across the Mal Pas, followed by the bishop's army of guards, a large table was unloaded from the second one and brought over to where they were talking. From the same wagon a beautiful embroidered cloth was unloaded and spread out on the table.

There was a great deal of movement between the tents and the table as all who had brought relics brought them to be displayed for everyone to see. The bishop himself had brought some of the finest treasures belonging to the Cathedral of Rennes, and these were carried with great pomp out of the carriage and placed on the table too.

Sitting on his mound, Tristan watched all the activity but could not keep his thoughts from wandering to the wagon that looked like a dungeon on wheels. Who else could it be intended for, if not Isolt?

They intended to arrest her at whatever cost, he realised. They obviously had some trick or other ready for her. He could tell from the way the two men had smiled at each other. And why else, now he thought about it, had they arrived here with such a heavy escort of guards, if they did not intend to take her away with them?

He must warn Isolt when she came. She must not cross to the White Moor. He had hidden his horse in a small wood half a mile away, but his sword was concealed just behind him under some dead branches.

Would she even dare to show up? he wondered. A secret hope arose in him that she would fail to appear, and that everyone whose horses had trudged through the mud, and who were now awaiting her arrival, would just have to pack up and go back to where they came from, disappointed. All except him, Tristan, who would find her waiting for him, perhaps in the hut on the beach near Port Saint Marie, and they would sail off together to Ireland.

No sooner had he allowed himself this last thought of holding her in his arms, seeing her white teeth shine as she thrust her head back in laughter, than the timbre of her voice rang like a distant bell in his ears. For an instant he thought he had dropped into a dream. Then, with a jump, he turned to stare down the road along the riverbank. There, in the red light of the sun, he saw two figures riding up towards him.

He could not yet recognise the man riding beside her, but the woman, though he could not distinguish her features, was unmistakably Isolt. Was it the way she sat in the saddle, the way she moved up and down on the horse's back, giving off that feeling of defiance, of boldness, of a willingness to go all the way? Or did he know it was her because he felt suddenly ashamed of having had that moment of weakness when he had seen the wagon with the barred windows?

And now, as she approached the mound where he was sitting, he could feel an aura of determination emanating from her. Behind her confident voice and carefree laughter he sensed something hard and purposeful. He knew instantly that he could not ask her to run away. If she truly loved him it was because, like her, he was not afraid. He would have to go through with whatever her plan was. If he didn't, he would lose her, and that loss would be far deeper than if he were to see her imprisoned in that wagon. For, whatever they did to her, her soul would remain with him; but if he were to let her down now then he would really lose her.

This is Isolt, he thought. This was who she was and only he could understand her, for only he could see what was hiding behind her eyes; even before she had fully awakened to what it was, he had seen it, and it had convinced him that she was the one. Because he had always known that he had come into this world with a mission to fulfil, and now he knew that mission was her.

She too had been waiting for someone, and that someone was him, for together they had to release a force into this world, a power that had been banished from its cities. And it had a name, though Tristan didn't know that name was Eros, or that it had once been a god celebrated by men and women everywhere, but had become just a vagrant spirit haunting the darkness of our deepest forests. Only they, Isolt and him, through their embrace, could bring it back into the light.

It seemed she was being deliberately loud, as if she wanted to draw attention to herself. Her strategy had worked, for he heard somebody shout from the bank of the White Moor. 'It's Isolt and Albert! They have arrived at last!'

'Whoa!' shouted Isolt as she stopped her horse at the edge of the Mal Pas crossing and stared out at the stretch of mud, pitted with holes and pools of water. She shielded her eyes from the glare of the sun.

'I'm certainly not going to ride across that stinking mire of trampled mud,' she said. 'My horse is far too nervous. He will kick it up all around him and I'll be covered in it.' She was wearing a light blue velvet gown, buttoned right up to her neck, and a red cap, at the back of which her hair dropped in a long tress between her shoulders.

'Do you want to be pulled over on a wagon?' Marc's mother shouted from the other bank.

'That sounds like a good idea,' Albert said.

'No. That won't be necessary. I'm coming over!' Isolt shouted back to her mother-in-law. She got down off her horse and handed the reins over to Albert. 'You go on over and take my horse with you. I have found another mount to take me across.'

'But, my lady...' Albert protested.

'Don't argue!' she said. 'I tell you, I have found a better way across.' She turned and waved to Tristan. 'Hey, you there! Get up from your seat and come over here!'

Tristan got up and she made a show of studying him carefully as he made his way over to her. 'You seem strong and sturdy. Your affliction has not yet drained you of your strength. Do you think you could carry me on your back through this mud?'

'With very little trouble indeed,' answered Tristan. His puffed-up face twisted sideways into a grotesque smile.

'But, my lady!' protested Albert.

Isolt turned to him. 'Are you still here?' she said. 'Don't you see that I'll be safer on his back than on that crazy horse? Now go!'

She whipped her hand onto the flank of her horse and, with a loud slap, sent him jumping forward down into the mud, pulling Albert and his own horse down with him.

'Go!' she shouted. 'I will not be far behind you.'

Isolt reached down, grabbed the cloth of her robe on both sides and lifted it. The brown skin of her legs sparkled in the sun.

'Now, bend down and let me climb onto your back,' she said to Tristan.

Tristan pulled up his own robe and folded it into his belt. He bent down, wrapped his arms under the base of her thighs and lifted her onto his back. He straightened himself up and cautiously made his way down from the road into the mud.

There were murmurs, and then whistles, applause, laughter and shouts of encouragement from the other bank. Isolt looked up and saw that a crowd had gathered there, waving at her. She looked down, lifted one of the boots hanging around Tristan's neck and examined it.

'How can a poor beggar such as yourself have such fine footwear?' she asked in a loud voice.

'It is because, my lady, a fine and noble lord, a true gentleman, took pity on me.'

'And he gave you his boots?' she said with mock surprise. 'Well, I see you have not been wasting your time here. I bet you have been begging money off all who have passed your way. Where do you keep your purse?'

'Inside my shirt, my lady,' Tristan replied.

'Ah, well, let's see,' said Isolt, bending forward and reaching down with her arm inside his robe, right down to where his belt was tied around his waist. 'Here we are. I can feel something quite heavy. Let's see what we have?'

She lifted out his purse, opened it and looked inside, shaking the coins around. 'Well, by the looks of things it seems that quite a generous crowd has gathered on the White Moor,' she shouted as she tied up the purse and dropped it back inside his shirt, to the delight of the spectators.

Isabelle turned to her son, her face white with anger. 'She has made us all look like fools! If that's what you wanted, then I hope you are satisfied now.'

Marc looked at his mother but did not answer. He could not

share her anger, her outrage or her shame. He, supposedly king of this patch of land, had no control over anything any more. Isolt had taken it away from him, away from all of them.

It was her anger, her rage, that had taken hold of the reins, and it was she who was steering them to a destination that only her heart could know. And, for the moment, for however long that moment would last, they were all following behind her.

As they reached the bank of the White Moor, Tristan, through the sweat pouring down from his brow, saw the many faces that had gathered around them. He bent down to let Isolt off his back.

It was the Duke de Vitry who took her hand and helped her up onto her feet. 'Queen Isolt, may I be the first to welcome you onto this sacred soil,' he said. 'And may I congratulate you for having landed here without a drop of mud on your clothes and looking as beautiful as ever.'

'Thank you, my lord,' said Isolt. 'It is you who honour this sacred soil and bring back to life its old glory with your presence here today.'

The duke looked at Isolt. A huge smile pushed up the muscles of the cheeks on his broad face, almost causing his eyes to close.

She now saw that Marc was standing beside him, looking weak and tired. She quickly looked away and turned to face Tristan.

'Thank you, my kind fellow, for having carried me safely across the muddy swamp. You'd better be on your way now,' she said.

'Aren't you going to give him some small reward for his effort?' asked the duke.

'Why should I?' replied Isolt. 'The purse in his robe is almost as heavy as I am, filled with coins he has earned by doing no more than sitting on his rear all day. He will not go hungry tonight, nor his family if he has one. But you are right, my lord, I must show him my gratitude, and I will do so with a kiss.'

'Don't forget that he is a leper!' the duke cautioned.

Isolt looked around her and saw that the bishop, his secretary, Santerre and the captain were standing a short distance away from the crowd that had gathered around her, close to the table with the relics.

'Yes, my lord,' she said, raising her voice. 'He is indeed a leper, but I am Isolt, forced to come here onto this sacred soil by accusations of a most vile nature raising doubts about my virtue. I must now clear myself of these accusations by swearing before God and all who wish to hear me that I am innocent of these charges that have been thrown at me, and remain pure of heart. And, if my heart cannot be soiled by these accusations, then how can my body be sullied by a mere kiss?'

Isolt stepped over to face Tristan. He stared at her in disbelief as she raised both hands, placed them on his cheeks, pulled his face to hers and kissed him gently on the lips. As she pulled her hands away from his face, they looked at each other for a brief moment.

Her eyes were dark indeed. But in their darkness shone a light that lit up the world with her fury. What was she doing? Tristan wondered. How could she dare?

He could no longer feel frightened for her. He could see only the beauty of that moment. It toppled everything else that might try to stand in its way. Even his desire for her seemed meaningless right then. She had pushed everything onto another level, as if she had woken up the gods of old, and in that frozen moment they were watching over her. He had a strange conviction that, for all those who stood there with him on the bank of the White Moor that morning, nothing would ever be the same again.

'You had better go now,' she said to him.

Tristan stepped down into the mud and started back across the Mal Pas. Soon he was sitting back on his stump, staring over at the bank where he had carried her a short while before. The crowd had dispersed and returned to their tents, except for the bishop, his secretary and Santerre, who were sitting in the carriage, while the captain and the guards were busy erecting some sort of structure behind the table with the relics.

What was that kiss? Something so quick and gentle. Yet, in that moment, two hearts, two souls had reached out across the walls erected by history as it pushed forward through time, with its artificial laws and barriers to keep men trapped in its furrow. But those two souls had touched and a breach had been created, a tear in the veil that separates this world from the heavens. The stars were no longer sleeping behind the glare of the sun in full daylight, but became instead the blinking eyes of awakening gods.

Tristan had seen this. He had understood it like something whole and solid. He had already felt it the first time he had held her in his arms, and had sensed it even before that, the first time he had looked into her eyes beneath the oak tree.

*

'You have a most remarkable wife!' the Duke de Vitry said to Marc as they sat eating in his tent. 'I have never met, or even heard of, a woman quite like her,' he added, shaking his head as he remembered the events of the morning. 'I hope that kiss she gave the leper did not go unseen by our dear friend the bishop. With that one gesture of pure, exquisite defiance, she has already won over this day to herself. For what weight can be given to all those holy relics gathered out there when compared to that kiss?'

The duke continued to chew his food, his face flushed with his evident admiration for Isolt. Marc, meanwhile, felt something stabbing deeper and deeper into his heart, pushing him further and further down into his own darkness and solitude.

'Don't be nervous, dear friend,' the duke continued. 'We must gather all our strength and stand firmly beside her when she goes through her ordeal today. But you are not eating anything. You must not let go of yourself! It is now more than ever that she needs us.'

Outside, just behind the table, a wooden pulpit had been erected. Two soldiers on either side of it, receiving orders from the captain, lifted their long brass horns and blew. A sharp, plaintive call rang out across the White Moor, over the heads of the crowd already gathering in front of the collection of relics.

'Come!' said the Duke de Vitry to Marc. 'Let us go and fetch Isolt.'

Isolt was waiting for them in Marc's tent, just inside the entrance. To her light blue gown she had added a golden sash around her waist. Little gold coins hung from a chain tied around her brow to keep her hair, now hanging loosely at the sides of her face, from blowing into her eyes.

Isabelle walked out of the tent behind her. She had been watching her daughter-in-law get herself ready without speaking a word, but could hold her tongue no longer.

'Try to act with a little dignity out there when you take the oath,' she said. 'I think you have already covered us with enough mud today. You don't have to soil us any further.'

Isolt looked down at her gown and then at her mother-in-law, whose robe still carried a few stains of mud down by her ankles.

'It's funny,' she replied. 'I think I'm the only one whose clothes haven't been splashed with mud so far.' She took the hands of Marc and Arnaud de Vitry. 'Come on,' she said. 'Let's get this over with.'

Just as they reached the back of the crowd, there came another resounding blast from the two brass horns. The carriage door was flung open and the bishop stepped out; he looked pleased at the size of the crowd that had gathered to bear witness to this solemn occasion. With a faint smile of satisfaction, he walked over and climbed onto his pulpit. When he was comfortably settled there, looking down at the expectant faces, the captain shouted out, 'Would Queen Isolt step forward now, and stand before the holy relics.'

Isolt released her hands from the grip of her two escorts. 'I'll be all right now,' she said to them. She pushed her way through the crowd and came to stand in front of the table.

The bishop's intention, carefully planned with his secretary, had been to look down at her briefly, giving her no more than a quick glance of acknowledgement, before launching into the speech he had prepared. A speech that, in so many words, already condemned her for committing adultery before she was to take the oath proclaiming her innocence. In this way she would be placed on the defensive from the very start. But to his evident surprise the look he gave her turned out to be a much longer one than he had expected.

Maybe all the women from whom he had looked away until then had carried another kind of beauty, the pale beauty of purity and surrender. This was the great temptation that usually sprung off these fair women. For behind their paleness and purity lay an enticement to corruption. This he knew well, and against this he was well guarded. But there was nothing latent in the corruption of the woman who was staring defiantly up at him. It was all too apparent and she did nothing to hide it. It was all there, in the gold chain around her forehead, in the mocking sensuality of her mouth, her brown skin, and the swamp-like liquidity of her black eyes.

But what he was truly not prepared for was her beauty. For that beauty was not just a mask behind which corruption lay, waiting to spring out. No, with her it was the corruption itself that was beautiful, that sprung forth from her face and hit the bishop with its power and its glory, compelling him to understand that it was much older than any of his sermons, that it had been there in the world long before any of his sacred scriptures, long before men had first learnt to speak so that they could invoke their gods to rise up against her. For she *was* that corruption, she herself and not something hiding behind her.

Seeing the bishop's hesitation and sensing her opportunity, Isolt looked away and down at the relics on the table. She picked up a golden cross encrusted with rubies and emeralds and, lifting it high up above her, turned towards the expectant crowd.

'I, Queen Isolt,' she said loudly, 'here in the presence of His Grace the Bishop of Rennes, and before all of you standing here on the sacred ground of the White Moor, who have come here to bear witness to my sermon, do solemnly swear, holding this sacred relic in my hand, and including in my oath all the relics displayed on the table here before you, and all other holy relics spread throughout Christendom, I do solemnly swear that I have let only two men enter between my thighs. The first was my husband, King Marc, who stands here amongst you, and the second was that wretched beggar, who carried me on his back this morning over the mud of the Mal Pas and deposited me here on the White Moor. I have nothing more to say. And may God be my witness that I speak the truth.'

When she had finished speaking there was a huge response from the crowd, a mixture of laughter, cheers and whistles, a sudden outpouring of joy and mockery, which she had aroused from deep within their hearts in the face of the pompous authority and gravity that had been forced onto the occasion.

The bishop, who had watched Isolt take her oath with a fascination that held him speechless and from which he could not break away, was now freed from her ungodly spell by the cheers of the crowd. Regaining his composure, he bent forward and shouted to the guards to blow their horns. He looked over at his secretary, standing beside the captain and Santerre with his hands open to show his dismay.

The brass horns resounded above the clamour rising from the crowd. The bishop gestured impatiently, pointing at the covered wagon parked behind his carriage. His secretary whispered something to the captain, who nodded and called two of the guards. All four walked over to the wagon and disappeared behind it, to where its door was hidden.

When they reappeared, the two guards were escorting a young woman dressed in a white gown with uncombed hair and no shoes on her feet. The men were holding her arms and it was obvious from her face that, with each step she took, she was in pain.

'Marie!' Isolt exclaimed with disbelief as they walked her friend to the table with the display of relics.

The crowd suddenly hushed as everyone caught sight of the young woman, the only noise now a low murmur of voices as Marie stared blankly at them. Her mouth gaped open as if she were lost in some waking dream or, more likely, a nightmare.

'Marie! What have they done to you?' Isolt shouted.

From atop his pulpit, the bishop, clearly not wanting Isolt to steal the attention of the crowd, shouted down at her.

'You were very fast to take your oath and exonerate yourself from the charges we have brought against you,' he began. 'But perhaps now, at the sight of your friend, you will understand that these charges are not to be taken lightly. Your marriage to King Marc was conducted by a priest belonging to the Catholic faith in one of our churches, and your husband's coronation was given the blessing of the Catholic faith, which I myself administered under the auspices of His Grace Pope Innocent III. And the child you carry in your womb, who, if he is a boy, will be heir to the throne of Brittany, will also need our blessing when he is baptised.

'Therefore you must surely see that the oath you take here on the White Moor today is of the utmost importance to us, since the integrity of the Church, of the very laws that govern our faith, is being placed in the balance as a result of your conduct, and the outcome may have the gravest of consequences for us and demand a severe response on our part.

'That is why we have persuaded your friend, whose loyalty to you has put her under great duress, to take an oath here as well, before these holy relics and before God, that what she is about to repeat to us is the truth, word for word.'

*

From his mound on the other side of the Mal Pas, Tristan had been paying close attention to every movement, as well as straining to hear what was being said. He had no trouble following what Isolt said when she took her oath, as she had spoken loudly and the crowd had listened silently as she spoke. He also had no problem hearing what the bishop was saying to her now, as he shouted down at her from his pulpit, but he was no longer listening. As soon as he realised that the young woman in the white gown was Marie, he knew that Isolt had been trapped and that there was surely no escape for her now.

By the time the bishop had finished, Tristan had already spat out the pieces of cloth he had put in his mouth to swell up his face and had thrown off the pair of boots that were hanging around his neck. He had fetched his sword and was trudging through the mud as fast as he could to get onto the White Moor.

'It's Tristan!' someone shouted, and everyone turned to look at the strange figure in a woollen smock, now pulled up and tucked into his belt, wading purposefully through the mud.

'Seize him before he gets over here,' the captain shouted to the line of guards sitting on their horses just at the back of the pulpit.

Tristan brandished the sword high over his head as the mounted guards came charging down the bank of the White Moor towards him.

'Tristan!' Isolt whispered softly, shaking her head. 'What are you doing?'

'I'm sorry, Isolt,' a voice said, as if in answer to her question. She turned around and saw Marie staring at her with tears running down her face.

'It's all right, Marie. It's all my fault,' Isolt said, and turned back to see what would happen to Tristan.

A cloud of wet mud splashed up over the Mal Pas as at least twenty men and horses came crashing down into the swamp in a clamour of kicking and stamping hoofs. It was hard to see clearly what was going on from where Isolt stood. For one thing, the crowd was bobbing up and down and blocking her view. Then, when she did manage to see between their heads, all she could make out was a lot of horses kicking up a lot of mud. There was a lot of shouting too, and shoving, as the men collided with one another as they surrounded Tristan.

Isolt stood with a hand over her mouth, repeating softly to herself, 'Don't hurt him! Please don't hurt him!' Then someone shouted, 'He's knocked him off his horse!' An instant later Tristan came charging out of the melee, in the saddle of one of the guards' horses, kicking his heels into its flank to push it forward towards the bank.

'Tristan!' Isolt shouted as she saw him racing towards her through the mud.

But everybody else saw him, too, including the group of archers stationed on the bank of the White Moor, their bows strung and ready to shoot. And it was an arrow from one of those bows that came racing through the air and landed deep in Tristan's left shoulder, forcing him to let go of the reins of his horse. Moments later, five or six spears were pointing into his neck, throat and chest as the guards caught up and gathered around him.

'Tristan!' Isolt said again, but this time it was just a whisper as she watched him being escorted to the bank of the White Moor, where he was dragged off the stolen horse, his sword was taken from him, his hands were tied together behind his back, and the arrow was pulled roughly out of his shoulder.

While all this was going on, however, there was one man in the crowd who did not content himself with simply standing and waiting to see the outcome of the drama that was unfolding. That man was the Duke de Vitry.

The moment the Pope's guards had gone charging down into the Mal Pas after Tristan, it became all too clear to the duke that Isolt was in trouble. And, even if her behaviour was scandalous and an outrage, he realised that it was this very aspect of her nature that he had glimpsed when they had first met, and that had seduced his heart. Her behaviour today on the White Moor had only intensified this feeling he had for her, which went beyond the reach of his own understanding. And so, seeing that she was in danger, he rushed over to a group of his knights and ordered them to gather their companions. They were to get dressed for battle and to come on their horses, all of them together, and to join him by the pulpit.

The duke rushed back to where Marc and he had been standing. The expression on the king's face was one of disbelief and anger as he watched Tristan down in the Mal Pas, surrounded by the Pope's guards with their long spears. Arnaud de Vitry turned to Marc and shook his shoulder.

'Marc! Listen to me!' he said. 'Go and gather all the knights who are loyal to you and tell them to arm themselves with their swords, to get on their horses and join us by the pulpit.'

Marc looked at him, down at the ground, and then back at the duke. 'Why should I?' he asked.

The duke shook his shoulder again. 'This is no time to act like a spoilt child!' he said urgently. 'She's your wife! Are you going to let them take her away from you?'

'No,' Marc answered. 'But how many times do I have to lose her to get her back?'

Arnaud shook his head in dismay. 'I don't know,' he said. 'But you can be sure that, if they take her away with them now, you will never see her again. Now, gather your men together and join me at the pulpit.'

The bishop looked down as Tristan was brought before him, escorted by four guards, stared at him for a moment and shook his head. The captain, seeing that the bishop was about to speak, shouted over the hum of voices for quiet. The bishop looked around at all the lords, ladies, knights and maidens who had gathered, and lifted his arms.

'I think we have all seen enough horror, outrage and filth here today to last us for a lifetime,' he said. 'This wretched man, whom they call Tristan, was once a proud knight, who fought to defend our faith against the invading barbarians in Constantinople. Look at him now. Look at what this woman, Queen Isolt, has turned him into. A pathetic, masquerading beggar who has dishonoured himself and the whole of our knighthood by his unspeakable, degrading behaviour, pushed by this woman who rewarded him with access to the most intimate parts of her body, as she so graphically admitted to you herself, holding up in her hand one of our most sacred relics as she did so, flaunting her adultery before you all, and before God, as she took her oath. Why else would she do this, if it were not to bring disrepute upon our faith?'

The bishop took a deep breath, as if his heart were swelled by his own rhetoric, and looked at the crowd gathered on the beach of the White Moor as if he were preaching to his congregation.

'Now I want you all to solemnly ask yourselves, as you stand here on this sacred soil, before these holy relics that bear witness to our faith, is not the behaviour of this woman the work of a heretic?'

'I think, Your Grace,' said a voice from the crowd, 'that since Queen Isolt is being put on trial here, it would only be fair that someone be allowed to speak a few words in her defence, if you will permit me?'

The bishop looked down at the man who had pushed his way through the crowd and walked up to stand beside Isolt. It was Arnaud de Vitry. The bishop recognised him immediately as the most powerful man to have come over onto the White Moor for this occasion, and also one of the most influential men in France. But he was not going to let the duke steal Isolt away from him, now that he held her so nicely in his grip.

'I don't see how, in all good faith, one could say anything in her defence after the filthy display of depravity she has subjected us to,' the bishop replied. 'Her adultery is now all too clear. In trying to trick us all while she took her oath, she fully confessed to it. And her intentions were clear. They were to turn into derision our deepest beliefs and the whole of our Christian faith. It is more than clear that this woman is a heretic. She will have a chance to speak in her defence at a proper trial, conducted by a competent body of the clergy in due time. Meanwhile, she is to be made our prisoner, along with her lover Tristan, who will serve as a witness at her trial.'

The bishop was preparing to signal to the captain to have his men take Isolt, Marie and Tristan over to the covered wagon and to lock them away when a movement caught his attention. Turning, he saw at least twenty knights in full armour riding on their horses from where the tents had been pitched, and heading directly towards him.

Arnaud spoke again. 'I still think it would only be fair, since you have already so severely condemned Queen Isolt in our presence, that I should be allowed to say a few words in her defence.'

As he finished, his small battalion of eager young knights, their spirits flapping like sails in the favourable wind that had seen them victorious in the tournament the day before, trotted up and came to a halt behind the crowd. As the bishop contemplated them, neatly grouped together in lines of four, he now saw Marc riding towards them with five knights following behind him.

It did not take the bishop long to calculate that there were now already at least half as many men ready to stand against him as he had brought with him as a persuasive means of enforcing his decisions. This meant that he could no longer keep Isolt, Marie and Tristan locked up without a battle; and even if it turned out in his favour in the end, it would be likely to involve a bloodbath.

'What I said against Queen Isolt was not an outright condemnation,' he said quickly, 'because that can only be done at a proper trial. I am, of course, not referring to her adultery, about which I think there can no longer be any doubt, but to the charge of heresy.

'Now, this charge may not have to be brought against her, if she can prove to us by some gesture or act of speech that she fully supports our determination to fight these heretics that have their breeding ground in the south-west, in the land called the Languedoc.'

'Excuse me, Your Grace...' Isolt began, before the Duke de Vitry grabbed her arm and pulled her towards him, speaking in a low voice loaded with restrained intensity.

'Please don't say any more and let me speak! I beseech you!'

Isolt looked at the duke with surprise. 'All right. But tell me what you're going to say first,' she whispered.

The duke let go of her arm and looked up at the bishop. 'Your Grace, I think it would be useful if I were to spend a moment alone in discussion with Queen Isolt. May we use your carriage for this purpose?'

'If it will help to see us out of this impasse,' the bishop answered, a slight hint of petulance in his voice as he realised that the duke seemed as eager as he was to back down from an armed confrontation.

Arnaud de Vitry took hold of Isolt's arm again, holding it more gently this time, and escorted her over to the carriage. He opened the door and they climbed in. Isolt sat down on the leather seat. After looking around at the silk-lined, padded interior, she smiled at the duke and then caught herself.

'I'm sorry, I shouldn't be smiling,' she said. 'It's just the contrast of this luxurious carriage and the horror of what has been going on outside.'

The duke leant forward and took hold of her hand. 'We must put a stop to it now, before it goes any further,' he said, staring into her deep, dark eyes.

'How can we do that?' Isolt asked.

De Vitry looked carefully at Isolt. There was something about her face, her eyes, some invisible injury that she carried with her that he could feel when she looked at him. It touched him and awakened something in him he could not understand. He knew that this moment he was spending with her in the bishop's carriage was a moment he would never forget.

'I'm going to answer Innocent III's call and join his crusade against the Cathars,' he said.

'You can't do that! You'll be undoing all we have fought for!' Isolt said angrily.

'That's no longer the issue. What's at stake is your life,' the duke replied. 'Your life, and the child you carry inside you, and your daughter's life too, who's waiting for you to return home to her. If I join the Pope's Crusade and take Tristan along with me, as well as all those young knights out there who want nothing more than to prove themselves once again on a battlefield, then the bishop will let you go back to your castle with your husband, where your daughter is waiting for you. If I offer him this, he will accept it. I know that. He will feel he has won the day over to the cause of his faith.'

'But I can't let you do that! I can't let you fight their battle just to save my life,' Isolt protested. 'And what about Tristan!'

'Tristan loves you. He would do anything to save your life.'

'But I still won't let you do it!' she said stubbornly.

'Listen to me,' the duke said. 'It won't be the first time Tristan or I have fought their battles for them. Now, I can't speak for Tristan, but as for myself, fighting is the only thing I am much good at. But the last time I fought on their side, I did not do so out of any deep faith or conviction. What drove me then, as with every other time I raced onto a battlefield, was the fire of ambition, the hunger to forge a reputation for myself. And, in the end, it left me only with an empty feeling in my heart.

'This time, though, it will be different. It is another fire that will drive me onto the battlefield. It is the fire of knowing that you are safely at home with your husband, your daughter and the child you carry in your womb. It is the fire of the spirit I have seen in your eyes, and knowing that I have played a part in keeping it burning there. And knowing that, when we meet again when all this is over, I may look into that fire and know a little part of it belongs to me.'

The carriage door opened and the crowd watched in silence as Isolt and the duke stepped out. They walked over to the pulpit, where the bishop stood looking down at them expectantly. Marie, standing by the table with the relics displayed on it, was still being held by the two guards. She had the same stunned look on her face, her frightened eyes jumping forward from under her brow and staring at nothing in particular. Two more guards were standing on each side of Tristan. There was a big stain of blood on his smock, just under the wound on his left shoulder, but his eyes were burning and alert.

'Well?' the bishop asked.

'I think, Your Grace, that we will be able to come to some kind of arrangement,' Arnaud de Vitry said, looking up at him.

9

THE ISLAND OF SNOW

Marc stood at the window looking down at Isolt and Kore as a small boy joined them to play in the snow. They were on one of the large patches of white that were speckled like islands over the hilly landscape of woodlands and fields. It was early spring and the snow was melting fast, the islands of white shrinking with each passing day. Kore had just turned eight, and Gaba was now almost three years old.

The boy had been conceived at just about the time when Isolt had lost the baby she was carrying in her womb, a week or so after the debacle that took place across the Mal Pas on the White Moor.

Donoalin had insisted on getting married to Marie before departing with the soldiers, knights and noblemen, and a good portion of the women who followed behind them, on their way south to the Languedoc and parts of Aquitaine where the crusade was being fought. Their departure left a feeling of emptiness and silence only interrupted by the odd whisper and murmur of what had once been and was no more. And when Marie had discovered she was pregnant, shortly after his departure, it gave her a new reason to want to go on living.

Gaba was attempting to imitate Kore, who was pushing a snowball on the snow- covered ground. Finding that he couldn't do it, he went over to Kore and placed himself in front of her so that she couldn't roll her own snowball any further. She was trying to coax him to get out of her way, but he just stood staring up at her, stubbornly refusing to move.

Kore called over to Isolt, who was staring at the trees that lined the top of the hill. She seemed momentarily far away. Even though Marc could only see her back, he knew the expression she would have on her face. Her eyes would be looking at something that was invisible to everyone else around her, as if some memory had taken hold of her and dragged her away from the person she'd been only moments before. It had taken her to some other place, perhaps across the Mal Pas onto the White Moor, or to the beach near Port Saint Marie, where she had been that other person, the one he had only watched from a distance, the one he had never held in his arms, had never penetrated, never made love to.

Only she could see that person, from afar now, up there on that hill or through a door in the shadows of another room. The expression on her face would always be the same, one of momentary wonder and mystery, even in her own eyes, as she looked at this double of herself, before shaking herself free and returning to this world.

'What are you looking at?' Marc's mother asked from the bed where she lay, pale and sick, her life force diminishing with each day like the melting snow outside the window.

'At Kore, Mother,' replied Marc. 'Can you believe that she is eight years old? She is out there playing in what's left of the snow, with Gaba and Isolt.'

Isabelle tried to laugh cynically, but the sound that came out of her mouth sounded more like a choked cough.

'That woman thinks the young boy is her own child,' she said, catching her breath.

'It's not because she loves the boy and spends a lot of time with him,' said Marc. 'It's not that she is unaware that he is Marie's son. She's trying to help out. After all, Marie is on her own now that both her parents have died. I think it's quite beautiful the way they share the boy between them.' He continued to stare down at them through the window.

'Yes, and because of the coincidence between that boy's conception and her loss, I think that she feels it's the boy she could have given birth to, who chose to come into the world through another body, where the dark cloud of doubt as to who his father was would not loom over his childhood,' Isabelle said with great pain and effort. She then broke into more laughter, which turned into another cough that was not so easy to restrain.

'It's got nothing to do with that,' Marc said irritably as he turned away from the window. 'She loves the boy because she has helped look after him since his birth, and she is also very close to Marie.'

'That's what you want to see,' his mother said. 'You have only ever seen what you want to see. That's been your problem all along.'

Marc took a few steps across the room and stood looking down at her. There was hardly any flesh left on her bones. Her hair had thinned out and you could see the white skin of her skull beneath it. The beginning of a moustache was growing above her crinkled lips. Her eyes were pale and stared up at him as if from far away.

'What are you complaining about?' he asked her. 'Have I not kept this place going for the past four years, even though everyone has abandoned me? Have I not seen to it that there is wood in the fires every winter, and food on our plates?'

'Yes,' she answered, 'but how have you done this? By selling everything of value in this castle. Soon there will be nothing left that anyone would want to buy. This is typical of how you see only what you want to see. Those who you say have abandoned you have gone to fight and conquer new domains for themselves. They will come back, rich men all of them. But you? What have you done? You have lost a whole kingdom!'

'I have lost nothing!' Marc said indignantly. 'I am still alive, so are you and so is my wife and child. No one has dared challenge my right to rule over this kingdom.'

'There is no kingdom,' his mother retorted. Her voice was weak, but new light had come into her eyes as she spoke. 'And the only reason no one has come here to challenge you, the only reason we can all sleep soundly in our beds, the only reason all our throats have not been slit, is that everyone knows that Isolt has been placed under the Duke de Vitry's protection. That anyone who dares to touch her, or those near to her, will have him to answer to.

'He has won every battle he has fought down there and he will come back even more powerful and richer than he already was. Once settled back here, he will have Isolt as his harlot to play with, and you will have to stand by and watch and pretend you don't see, which you are so good at doing.'

'And you are so good at being bitter and cynical,' Marc said. 'You don't see the beauty and wonder of life any more.'

'You should have seized her the moment she returned after her escapade with Tristan,' replied Isabelle, her voice rasping. 'When she came back here all ruffled and flaunting her disgrace shamelessly for all to see. You should have had her burnt at the stake, right there and then. No one would have blamed you. And you would still have a kingdom to rule over.'

'Yes, and I would also be damned.'

'And what is wrong with that? At least you would be living.

To be alive is to be damned,' his mother said, a last flame flaring up in her eyes before she closed them.

Marc turned away and walked back to the window. Outside, on the island of white, Gaba was picking up snow. Isolt lifted him so that he could place it on top of a giant snowball, while Kore was busy rolling another one on the ground.

As Marc looked down at them, a mixture of warmth and terror hit his heart, like a stone dropping into the still waters of a pond, sending ripples that awakened both joy and sadness as it stirred up the shadows sleeping beneath the water's surface. His mother was right. To be alive was to be damned. He must have somehow always known this, and that was why he had kept himself so carefully away from the real business of living.

When he first met Isolt, his life had taken on a sudden intensity that he had never deemed possible. And then he thought he knew what it was like to be really alive, and everything around him seemed to glow with a new vigour and freshness, as if, like him, the world had awoken from a deep slumber.

However, the true depth of life's nature had not yet revealed itself to him. How deeply its tentacles could encroach into his heart and how far it could drag him into desperation was something he was yet to discover. And that had happened the moment Isolt had fallen in love with Tristan.

Yes, to be alive was to be damned! And didn't he know that now. Yes, his mother was right about that. But what she could no longer see was that to be damned also opened your eyes to something else, to the great beauty of this world.

This beauty had only struck him once he had been forced to face his inadequacy and ineptitude as a human being. It was only when he had been burnt through and through by the paralysing jealousy that overwhelmed him, when he thought about her having lain naked in Tristan's arms, and knew that such moments lived on in her like a ray of sunshine breaking through the dark clouds of a winter's sky. It was only after he had lived through all this pain that the world could sometimes appear to him as unbelievably beautiful. But he knew that he could never participate and celebrate this beauty, could only look at it from the outside, just as he was now looking at his wife down there in the snow, through the glass panes of a window.

That beauty would appear suddenly; it was there in Kore's smile that was so much like her mother's, but he could also see it when he watched Isolt in the morning, in her worn clothes, sitting in front of the mirror and looking at herself with tired eyes as she started to untangle her hair with a comb, or when he thought he had seen himself reflected in her unforgiving eyes. And afterwards, when she had turned and was walking away from him, the movement of her body, the supple swaying of her hips, her elegance in denial of the mess in the courtyard where chickens, ducks and a few goats competed with the pigeons for the leftovers from their table that had been dumped into a trough.

That's what his mother couldn't see, the mystery of it all. That the fact that Isolt could not love him, because he could no longer love her after what she had done, only pushed fate to tighten the noose that tied them together.

And, if his mother could only judge this situation they were caught up in as being miserable and pathetic and would never comprehend why he could be overwhelmed by its beauty, it was because she didn't know that deep down inside him there was still someone who couldn't stop wanting Isolt, and that this desire clung to him like a flame that could not be extinguished, something that so overwhelmed him when he was under its spell that the only way to escape from it was to see the great beauty that lay beyond the pain it was causing him, the beauty of truly feeling alive.

Isolt was helping Kore lift up the snowball she had just rolled and they placed it on top of the first, larger one. She then took

Gaba's hand and, with Kore taking his other hand, they walked towards the castle.

How long can this go on for? Marc wondered. How much longer would the crusade last? How much longer before they came riding home so that he would be confronted with the reality of his situation?'

Most of the castles in the kingdom were now deserted, the ladies having moved south with their children and servants to settle with their husbands into some newly conquered domain. Nordstram was one of the few to have stayed behind. He had taken a good part of Ganelon's land back into his fiefdom once news of the death of Marc's uncle had reached the kingdom. He had been killed on the battlefield, but no one knew what had become of his wife, son and daughter, who had gone down to join him several years ago.

There were a few other castles that were still lived in, but the occupants and sometimes squatters in these places kept very much to themselves, ruling over the fiefdoms and surviving as best they could.

Marc realised his mother was right, of course. He no longer had a kingdom. But, until the crusade was over, he could go on pretending, even if he was only fooling himself.

Everyone knew what was going on. He could see it from the way people looked at him in the markets. That's not to say that there were not people who still treated him with respect. Some were even friendly, but there were all the others who kept their distance, who looked at him with open hostility, contempt or derision. But none of them dared to say anything to him, for they were as uncertain as he was as to what would happen once the crusade was over, and all the lords and knights returned home.

However, from the news that occasionally reached him, nothing seemed to have been solved down there. They were still bogged down in endless battles and sieges. All sorts of alliances were being made and unmade and the advantage passed from one camp to the other without, until now, any decisive effect. And, most important of all, there was still plenty of booty to be stolen and wealth to be pillaged to keep them occupied for many more years, long enough for them to forget the kingdom they had left behind, it would seem. So the crusade could easily go on for a very long time to come, just as it could end tomorrow.

And then there was the problem of how much longer they could go on living off the remaining treasure left in the castle. Once again, his mother was right. One day there would be nothing left to sell. No one paid taxes to him any more, so how could they survive?

Well, that day had not yet come, and they would certainly last out for at least another year, and maybe a few more after that.

Outside the window, down in the pasture, Isolt, Gaba and Kore walked back onto the white island of snow. They brought twigs, fanned-out branches and a few chestnuts with them and proceeded to give arms, eyes and a nose to the snowman. Marc turned suddenly to stare across the room at his mother, feeling a strange silence floating over her bed. He quietly walked over to her and saw her eyes staring up at him, motionless and vacant. The depth of their stillness sent a tremor up his spine.

He bent down and gently took hold of her wrist. He could feel nothing moving under her skin. He stood for a long time staring down at her. To be alive is to be damned, she had said. But what was that force that had pushed those words up through her throat and out of her mouth? Were those words the last cry from the dying flames of that fire that had animated her, that she kept tightly under her control, under lock and key for all those years, accepting that she was damned, not for any deed she may have committed out there in the world, but rather for never having allowed that fire smouldering inside her to set her heart ablaze.

And that's why she had come down so hard on Isolt. It was because his wife had done what his mother had not dared to do. She had let go of the reins and had let that fire inside her burn and take full possession of her life.

This sudden understanding of his mother as she lay dead, and the sudden understanding of Isolt that came with it, brought an unexpected glimpse of something hidden inside him. An understanding that the anger and the rage that would flare up when he thought about Isolt was also aimed at himself for not daring to do what she had done. For she carried the memory of what it was like to be true to herself, and he envied her for that.

The silence in the room was broken by the sporadic shouts and cries of joy rising up from the field outside the window.

*

A few days later, as they sat on the steps leading up to the entrance hall, facing the courtyard where Kore was feeding barley to the chickens and geese, and with the spring sun shining down on them, Marc turned to Isolt and asked her, 'Are you happy?'

'Happy?' she asked, looking back at him.

'Yes, happy.'

Isolt thought for a moment. It was true that, for the past few days, she had felt as though a heavy weight had been lifted off her. She had put this down to the death of her mother-in-law, who had never really liked her. Now that her presence was no longer felt in the castle, Isolt felt a kind of lightness in her heart.

'Yes, Marc. Right now, I'm happy,' she said.

'But not just right now,' Marc said. 'If you look at the whole of your life, you as a person, are you happy?'

As she thought to herself she realised that the lightness she'd felt was not so much due to her mother-in-law's death as to Marc himself. For the last few days he seemed to have lost that heavy disapproval of her that he carried around everywhere with him, and could be felt in everything he said and did to her. But was he now not spoiling it with this question?

'That's silly and you know it,' she said. 'Sometimes I'm happy and sometimes I'm not. Isn't it that way with everyone?'

'Yes,' Marc agreed. 'But that's just on the surface. Underneath there is someone who can absorb the daily vicissitudes of life, and not be so affected by them that he or she must change from moment to moment with them. And that person, over and above these daily changes of humour, is either happy or not.'

'All that may be true,' replied Isolt, 'but I prefer to live from moment to moment. I feel I can handle life that way. I don't want to have to think of someone hiding beneath the surface, who may or may not be happy. What would be the point of it? I prefer to just take life as it comes.'

'You don't want to show this person to me, do you?' Marc said.

Isolt looked at him, surprised, as if he had pushed her into a corner from which she could not escape. She looked away from him for a few moments, but then stared into his eyes. 'Why should I show her to you? You would only disapprove.'

Marc gazed back at her. She was wearing a white scarf tied around her hair at the back of her head. It had dirt marks on it, as did the apron tied around her waist over her blue gown. 'What were you doing this morning?' he asked.

'I was planting carrots and turnips with Marie. The two men who dug your mother's grave ploughed some land for us.'

'You don't have to do that! We can buy what we need at the market!'

'Yes, but for how long? Nobody is going to feed us when we run out of things to sell, so it won't hurt to start planting some of our own food.' Then she smiled at him. 'And anyway, I'm enjoying myself. Isn't that what you want? For me to be happy?'

Marc could see in her eyes that she was aware of how fully she possessed him, and he could also see that this gave her a certain satisfaction.

'Come!' she said as she reached her hand out to him. 'Come closer to me.'

Marc pushed himself right up beside her. Isolt twisted around, brought one of her legs over both of his and sat herself astride him. Her hands had caught hold of his ears and were rubbing them gently. As she did so, she brought her lips down onto his and they kissed. She pulled her head away and looked down at him, the presence behind her eyes now obeying some deep will in the dark chambers of her soul. 'Come upstairs,' she said to him softly.

Kore watched them climb the steps and disappear inside the castle. She stood staring thoughtfully at the steps where they had been sitting, then turned away and threw grain to the geese and ducks again.

*

Tristan walked up and down the field, looking at each fallen body as he went by. Many of their faces were hidden under helmets and, once or twice, he bent down and removed the helmet to look at the face it had been protecting. One of the men was still alive and tried to touch Tristan with his hand, but he moved away and continued his search.

He saw many faces, some whose eyes moved as they watched him walk by, while others stared right through him, at the force that had driven them into this field and had now so easily deserted their body, leaving a look of awe like a departing footprint on their faces.

Flies were gathering around open wounds and there were pools of blood everywhere. Horses stood amongst the bodies, looking bewildered and lost, one or two of them bending their long necks to sniff and prod the corpse of their master.

'Tristan!' a voice called out to him in a broken whisper.

It was Arnaud de Vitry, lying in the grass reddened with the blood that had poured from his back. Someone had rushed him from behind and pierced his armour with a lance before he had been rushed from the front and hit on the head with a ball and chain, knocking him off his horse. He had lost his helmet in the fall and blood ran down over his mouth and chin from his broken nose.

'Arnaud!' Tristan gasped. 'I've been searching for you!'

'Tristan!' he said again as his comrade knelt down beside him. 'You must rush back to Brittany as fast as your horse will carry you.'

'What about you?' Tristan said. 'I can't leave you like this!'

'I am as good as dead,' Arnaud answered. 'But you can still save Isolt if you hurry. You can take my horse with you and ride him when yours gets tired. As soon as they find out that I am dead and news gets back to the Bishop of Rennes, he will have her arrested and burnt at the stake.'

Tristan stared down at him, his bright blue eyes frozen with horror. Arnaud managed a smile. 'You know, Tristan,' he said, 'in the last four years we have become close friends. But how long could our friendship have lasted if, after winning all the battles down here, we had returned together to Brittany? Look at all these dead, who lie here in their hundreds. Many of them joined this crusade to buy back their sins, others to plunder and conquer new land for themselves. But you and I are here because of our love for a woman, a woman called Isolt.'

With great effort, Arnaud lifted his hand in its heavy chain mail gauntlet, and rested it on Tristan's arm.

'God has made his choice,' he said. 'It is up to you now to save her. So don't waste any more time. Be on your way!'

*

Four days after he left Arnaud de Vitry dying on the battlefield near Toulouse, riding night and day almost without sleeping and switching saddles between his horse and Arnaud's, Tristan found himself only a few leagues from the Kingdom of Brittany. He had been following a road that twisted north-west from the city of Rennes, through forests, moorlands and pastures. Now that he was within hours of seeing Isolt once again, he no longer felt tired and his heart was beating with conflicting emotions.

After being away from her for so long, after all the blood, violence and horror of the massacre that was taking place in the south – carnage in which he had played an important part without any real appetite for what he was doing – no victory on a battlefield could fill the hollow of Isolt's absence. After so many nights, so many moons that did not light up her face, so many mornings into which he had awoken to find himself lying alone…

All he wanted, when they met up again, was to take her in his arms and lift her up, to bury his face in her hair, to lose himself in the taste of her lips, to drown in the warmth of her body.

How else could he greet her? What else would be real and honest?

What else would be true?

But he knew that Marc was more than likely to be standing at her side when he saw her next.

So would there be a fight? Would he even have to kill him? He knew that this would be an awful thing to do. Marc was, after all, Kore's father. Would he allow the three of them to leave together? Or would Marc insist on coming with them? And what would it mean if he did?

As Tristan was asking himself these questions, he came upon a shepherd standing by the road watching his flock. He asked him how far away Triaval Castle was. The shepherd answered that, on horseback, he could get there in about as much time as it would take to build a fire and roast one of his sheep on a spit.

The shepherd then burst out laughing and said that was exactly what he'd said to a small battalion of guards, all dressed up in their armour, who had asked him the very same question earlier that morning.

'They didn't seem to appreciate my answer, though. Stuck up lot, they were,' the shepherd said and spat on the ground to show his contempt.

A little further along the road Tristan saw a group of armoured men, tightly gathered together, coming down the hill towards him. At the centre of the group he saw a movement that, for an instant, felt like a rising sun burning through the dark clouds hanging over his heart. As he stared aghast, he realised that it was Isolt's hair bouncing up and down as her horse trotted down the hill.

Tristan dismounted from Arnaud's horse and climbed on to his own. He put his chain mail gauntlets on and removed his sword from its sheath. By the time he was ready the riders had reached the bottom of the dip and were heading up the road towards him.

The guards looked up as they heard the sound of a horse galloping down the hill.

'Pull out your swords!' the man at the front cried out. 'We are being attacked!'

There were only six men, four of whom formed a square, with Isolt and Kore at its centre. Of the other two, one, who must have been their captain, was leading while the other was guarding the rear.

Tristan rushed straight at the captain, but before making contact with him he steered his horse away to his right, transferring the reins from his left hand to the one holding his sword and hooking them onto one of his fingers. He reached down with his left arm, lifted his shield from his saddle and rammed his horse into the guard to the right of the captain, hitting him with his shield, knocking him backwards off his horse, and managed to stab the guard just behind him in the shoulder before pulling away.

Hooking his shield back onto his saddle, Tristan steered his horse around in a half circle. The guard at the back of the convoy had turned his horse around as well and was now charging at Tristan. Tristan pulled on the reins of his horse, which reared up, kicking his front legs in the air and making the charging horse swerve to one side. As the rider tried to steer it back on course and regain his balance, Tristan leant out towards him, holding his own horse's mane with one hand, stretching out the other and stabbing the man in the ribs.

Seeing the evident superiority of his attacker's fighting skills, the captain of the escort snatched Isolt's reins away from her, kicked his horse into a gallop and, pulling Isolt's horse behind him, set off up the hill.

When Tristan saw what was happening, he urged his own horse forward and charged after them. The two remaining guards made no attempt to stop him and did not even try to give chase. As for the captain, when he looked back and saw that Tristan was rapidly gaining ground, he simply let go of the reins of Isolt's horse.

Tristan came to a halt beside her. He looked up the road and saw the captain disappearing over the top of the hill, watched by the shepherd who was still leaning on his staff. In the other direction two of the guards still sat in their saddles, staring up at him, while two others stood by their horses, staring down at the man he had stabbed in the ribs, who was now sprawled out motionless on the road.

Putting his sword in his sheath, Tristan bent down from his saddle to reach for the reins of Isolt's horse and handed them to her.

'Tristan!' she said, and he heard his name resonate like some precious object lost and found again. Seeing how her eyes embraced him as she sat, still clearly shaken, with Kore holding tightly on to her, it was all too clear how much she had missed him. Her eyes held on to him as if he filled a great absence, and that was all he needed to know.

'Can you follow me?' he asked.

She nodded. He steered his horse out onto the moor and kicked it into a slow gallop. Isolt followed, with Kore holding on to her waist. At the top of the hill, standing beside the shepherd, Arnaud de Vitry's horse watched them ride away.

*

Marc got off his horse and tied it to the wall outside Market Town, and stood gazing over at the ramparts. It had become something of a ritual to pause and stare at the tall, arched doorway leading into town, to try to visualise Isolt's face when, nearly eight years ago, standing close to where he now stood, she had hesitated and looked at the man she had only met that morning, and said to him with a self-mocking smile, 'All right then, take me to your fortress.'

Marc sighed and felt the same bittersweet twinge he felt each time he remembered that moment.

It was never hard to spot the red tent in the crowded square, for apart from the church it was the most imposing structure there on market day. As he approached, he saw Salma standing amongst the pots, pans, clay jars and other kitchen utensils on display, along with mirrors and small tables, waiting for a customer to bargain for one of them.

Salma was a handsome, dark-haired woman of about Marc's age, with vivid blue eyes that were all the more striking because of the fact she could not speak. When she saw Marc, her mouth curled into a faint smile.

'Is he inside?' Marc asked.

Salma nodded and Marc walked into the tent, where Forsin sat on a raised chair behind a small table. He was surrounded on one side by more pots and pans of a finer craftsmanship, and, on the other, by dresses, robes, belts, boots and silver tableware, neatly gathered on several tables.

'I'll never understand how you two manage to carry all this junk around from one place to another,' Marc said.

'It's hard work,' replied Forsin. 'But then, I'm not surprised you don't understand, as it's something you've not yet experienced.'

'Is that what you're doing right now?'

'I'm having a well-deserved rest. With your permission, of course,' said Forsin.

'I bet she does all the loading and unloading and you give out the instructions!'

'No, that's not exactly how it happens,' said Forsin. 'But you'll never find that out for yourself because you're still asleep in your bed when we're unpacking, and you never stay long enough to help us when we're ready to pack up and go. So you'll just have to take my word for it, my friend.'

Marc said nothing and just stood for a moment looking at all the articles on display.

'By the way,' Forsin said, 'I only heard about your mother this morning. You could have sent someone round to tell me.'

'No one could find you. Where were you hiding?'

'In Rennes.'

'Well, Gauvin spent four days looking for you,' said Marc. 'At least, that's what he said. Personally, I think he just went to Port Saint Marie and got drunk. I don't think he could face watching my mother being dropped into a dark hole. I think everything he fought for, for so many years, was being dumped into that hole along with her body, and he didn't want to have to stand there and watch it happen at this late hour in his life.'

'Well, I would have come, but to be honest I'm glad I wasn't there,' replied Forsin. 'She never could forgive me for leaving the castle.'

'She wasn't very good at letting go of a grudge. That's true.' Marc sighed. 'But with someone like my father for a husband, and me for a son, she didn't have much to rejoice about in life. The only good thing that happened to her was my brother, and he had to go and get himself killed. So, God bless her soul.'

'Good Lord! We are happy today, aren't we?' Forsin exclaimed.

'You don't know me any more, Forsin. I'm at my happiest when I'm in this kind of mood.'

'How can your wife put up with you?'

'I don't think she can, most of the time.'

'What are you trying to do to her?' said Forsin. 'Turn her into someone like your mother?'

He had not intended it as a serious question, but he realised as he heard himself speaking how serious it was. He saw the shock in Marc's eyes, and realised that something tender and vulnerable inside his friend had been jolted.

The tension was broken when Marc suddenly smiled. 'And what about you?' he asked. 'How are you getting along with Salma?'

Forsin's eyes lit up.

'She is a jewel,' he replied. 'A gift sent down by the gods and placed on the sorry path of my life so that, while still living in this world, I can get a foretaste of heaven.'

Outside the tent, voices could be heard.

'How much for that chair?' somebody was asking. And then the same voice: 'What! Three crowns! That's far too much.'

There was another, longer pause, and then the voice spoke again. 'It belonged to the castle? Is that what you're trying to tell me? But it's still too expensive. I'll give you two and a half and that's my final offer.' Another pause and then, 'All right, three crowns for the chair and the small mirror.'

Forsin was sitting behind the table with a big smile on his face.

'What an absolute gem that woman is. No one can resist those eyes. What's more, the fact that she can't talk back seems to intimidate most people.'

'I can see that you have become a rich man in more ways than one.' Marc smiled.

'Oh, don't use that milky voice to flatter me. I know what's coming. So, what is it you want to sell today?'

'My mother's necklace.'

'Already?' said Forsin in surprise. 'You've only just buried her!'

'I looked after her to the very end,' replied Marc. 'I was there when she let out her final breath. Do you want to know what her last words were?' He thought he saw a slight look of fear in Forsin's eyes. As he didn't answer right away, Marc continued. 'Well, I'm going to tell you anyway. She said, "To live is to be damned." Then she closed her eyes and quietly passed away.'

'Sometimes you frighten me,' Forsin said.

'Why?' Marc asked. 'That's what she said. I'm not making it up. So, what are you going to offer me for her necklace?'

'I can't afford to buy that off you,' said Forsin, looking uncomfortable.

'Then just give me what you can afford,' Marc said. 'You know it's worth a lot and that you won't have any trouble selling it. And don't call your wife in here. I don't want to start bargaining with her eyes. I do enough of that at home with Isolt. So just give me what you can for it.'

Forsin smiled.

'All right, you old rascal,' he replied. 'Show it to me. I want to make sure you haven't removed any jewels already.'

As he rode back to the castle, Marc felt pleased with himself. He had enough money in his purse to see them through summer and still have something left to help stock up for winter.

Isolt would be pleased, even though she wouldn't show it.

There would be barley to feed the goats and the chickens, which meant there would be a plentiful supply of cheese, milk, eggs and meat for the table. They could also buy sacks of flour so that Brangien could continue baking bread every week, and they could hire a few people from the town to help bring in wood for the stoves.

All this would help to keep things working. Life would go on, and the daily effort to keep things as they were would bring a certain satisfaction to Isolt. He could see it sometimes in her eyes. He could see how her friendship with Marie had grown, how having to share in this daily struggle had brought them closer together. He could also see how her attachment to Kore, as well as to Gaba, made her spend time every day making sure there was gaiety and happiness in their lives as well. She was so good at doing all this.

But he also knew that it was the uncertainty of their future that kept her tied to this life they were living. The fact that it was only a temporary solution, one that could not go on for ever, kept her from sinking into despair and stopped her heart from spreading its wings and flying away from him.

He noticed that the drawbridge was down. It had long become their custom to leave it open during the day, even though there were no guards to keep watch any more, except for Gauvin, who had a problem with one of his knees and was walking with a cane.

As Marc crossed the moat and entered the courtyard, he gave a quick glance up at the bedroom window. Something seemed wrong. There were no goats wandering around and the few ducks that were there quacked loudly and scampered away as he rode in.

When he reached the stable, he got off his horse, and it was then that he noticed the other horses in the stalls, which should have been empty. He let go of the reins and took a closer look. The moment he stepped over the threshold he felt the sharp sting of two swords pricking him in the ribs from both sides of the doorway.

'Stay right where you are!' a voice commanded.

Marc froze and, from the corners of his eyes, could see the silhouettes of the two men who were pressing the swords against him.

'What do you want?' he asked.

A third man walked up towards him from the shadows at the back of the stable.

'Are you Marc, King of Brittany?' he asked.

Marc shrugged. 'If that's how you want to address me, then yes, I am.'

'Perhaps you would like to step out into the courtyard, where we can see each other a bit better,' the man suggested.

In the light outside, Marc recognised one of the Bishop of Rennes' guards. The other two followed behind him.

'Now, perhaps you will tell me what this is all about?' asked Marc indignantly. 'What is the meaning of invading my castle like this?'

'We are acting under orders given to us by the Bishop of Rennes,' the third man said.

'And what exactly are those orders?' Marc demanded.

'To escort you, your wife, Isolt, and your daughter to Rennes.'

'And where are my wife and daughter?' Marc asked, trying to keep his voice even.

'They are already on their way to Rennes.'

'For what purpose?'

'I am not able to tell you that,' the man said. 'All I am permitted to say is that, if you cooperate with His Grace, no harm will come to you or your daughter.'

'What about my wife?' Marc asked in a sudden rage.

'I cannot answer that question,' the man said.

Marc felt his legs weaken and made a great effort to hold himself straight.

'But he has no right to arrest Isolt!' he shouted. 'That would be a betrayal of the agreement that was reached between him and Arnaud de Vitry on the White Moor four years ago. And you know that for a fact. You may even have been there when that agreement was reached, for I'm sure I recognise you.'

The man facing Marc had a strong, handsome face. But now, as he smiled, revealing the gaps between his teeth, his jaw tightened, showing something bestial that had been hiding behind his good looks.

'The winds of fortune are not constant,' he said. 'They can change direction at any moment, and I'm afraid that's what's happened. Your neighbour, the Duke de Vitry, could testify to this sad fact if only he were still alive to do so.'

Marc noticed his horse standing behind him, a little to his right. He stretched his arm out and took hold of its reins, for no reason other than an urgent need to have something to hold on to.

The two guards raised their swords and pointed them at his ribs again. 'What are you doing?' the man with the ugly smile asked.

'We might as well start off right away,' Marc said, hardly aware of the words that had left his mouth.

One of the guards went to fetch their horses from the stable, while the other walked over to the steps leading down into the kitchen. He shouted something and another man appeared at the top of the steps.

'What was he doing in the kitchen?' Marc asked angrily, realising how futile his indignation sounded as it echoed back to him.

'He was sitting with the old man, the women and the child,' the man answered.

'Oh, Gauvin!' Marc said, suddenly remembering the four of them. 'I need to give him something.'

'What?' the man asked.

'Some money,' Marc said. 'They will need it.'

'I'll take the money,' the man said with the same ugly smile.

'Look,' Marc said, 'in view of the fact that His Grace would welcome my cooperation, I think it would be better if you let me give Gauvin the money he needs for the upkeep of the castle. Otherwise, I will have to explain to His Grace the reason why I refuse to cooperate.'

The man turned to the guard. 'Go to the kitchen and call the old man out,' he commanded.

When Gauvin reached the top of the steps he stopped to catch his breath and, with squinting eyes, he stared across the courtyard. Then, helped by his cane, he slowly made his way over to them. Marc lifted the strap of his shoulder bag over his head and bent down. 'Here, take this,' he said to Gauvin. 'It's got some coins that will keep you all fed for a while. Give it to Brangien to look after and tell her not to spend it all at once. I don't know when I will be back. And take good care of Marie and the boy.'

Gauvin stared up at him. Marc saw something unmovable in the old man's faded grey eyes that he had seen there, staring back at him, ever since he was a little boy. 'You look after yourself,' Gauvin said. 'Don't worry about us.'

As Marc rode over the drawbridge towards the dark menace that had been hanging over their lives for the last four years, he knew that it was finally over, that this dream of an independent kingdom founded on its own principles and rules, grown, in turn, out of the ferocity and daring of his ancestors, had finally run aground with him at its helm.

PART 2

10

OGRIN

It was early in the morning. The merchants had just set up their stands and put their merchandise on display in the market square in the town of Rennes. Ogrin stood for a while in front of a stand covered with linen sheets. He rubbed some of the cloth between his index finger and thumb, then, lifting one end of a sheet up, he stretched it out between his hands, giving it little jerks to see how tightly it was woven. A man selling knives from a stand further down the square was staring at him, as if wondering who was this foreigner who had wandered in, acting like a lord while wearing clothes more suited to a peasant or brigand. And then suddenly this dark-skinned, bald-headed figure looked up and stared right at him as if reading his thoughts. The merchant tried to stare him down but soon felt dizzy, as if caught in a spell, as he looked at the face gazing back at him with frowning eyebrows, the motion of his nostrils sending ripples down into his moustache that seemed to mimic the movement of the cloth he held between his hands. This behaviour was so outrageously strange that the knife seller could not stop himself from bursting into laughter, as if he had become a child again. But it was fear that made him regain his composure. For he realised that this was no ordinary man, and this frightened him, especially as he was now walking over towards his stall. Without saying anything, Ogrin stood staring down at the display of knives, daggers and small axes.

'Can I help you?' the knife merchant nervously asked.

Ogrin had fished out a coin from his pouch and now bent over, picked up a dagger from the stand and reached towards the man with his coin.

'Here, take this for the dagger,' he said.

The man reached over and took the coin. 'What?' he exclaimed, looking into his hand. 'Just one crown for my best dagger?'

'I'll take this dagger back to my country and then I'll make you a rich man,' Ogrin said. 'I'll come back with several donkeys and buy many daggers for a good price, then you'll be a rich man. You'll see.' Ogrin put his hand back in his pouch, pulled out a gold coin and held it up between his fingers so the man could see it. 'There will be many more of these for you if you give me a good price for this dagger now,' he said.

'But where is it you come from?' the merchant asked.

'From the Orient,' Ogrin said. 'There are countless rich people there.' He dropped the gold coin back into his pouch, tucked the knife into his belt, then looked up at the stallholder one last time.

'I'll make you a rich man.'

Ogrin turned and walked away across the square.

'But wait a minute...' the man said, though only half-heartedly for there was something about the way this stranger had looked at him, his glare reaching something inside him that had made him feel strangely ashamed and unwilling to bargain.

Down the long narrow street there were many shops and workshops. Ogrin took his time. He was enjoying the sounds and the smells. People were sweeping in front of their doors. Horses and carts were parked in front of shops, goods were being unloaded.

He could hear laughter coming from an open doorway. He stepped inside. The room had many tables crowded with people drinking ale and eating salted meat or sardines before starting their day's work. He searched through the shadows for the silhouette that he knew would be sitting alone. It did not take him long to see the towering figure, whose dark outline was drawn under the light falling from a torch on the wall. Ogrin walked over, took the dagger from his belt and placed it on the table. The big man looked at the dagger and then up at Ogrin.

'What's that?' he asked.

'It's a gift for you,' Ogrin replied.

'I told you, I want money,' the big man said.

Ogrin sat down on the chair opposite him and fished a finger into the pouch tied to his belt. He pulled out the gold coin he had already showed to the merchant and held it up once again between his thumb and his forefinger. The big man looked at it as the flames from the torch danced off its surface into his eyes, setting them alight.

*

Marc heard the scraping of the bolts being pushed back, then the sound of the key as it turned in the lock. The door was pushed open and a man walked into his cell. Behind him, the big face of his jailer, Gabo, peered in from the corridor.

'I'll come and fetch you in an hour's time,' Gabo said to the man, then pulled the door shut and locked it again without another word.

For a moment, the man just stood staring at Marc, who was sitting on his bed at the far end of his cell beneath the small barred window high up on the wall.

'Who are you?' Marc asked finally.

'They call me Ogrin, the traveller,' the man said. 'My real name is unpronounceable for people around here.'

'And to what do I owe the honour of your visit?'

'Well, let's just say that your story is not unfamiliar to me,' Ogrin replied.

'Do I know you?' Marc asked.

'No, you don't,' Ogrin answered. 'But I know a little about you. As a young man, I was initiated into the science of astrology. If you are well versed in this science and you know which planet was moving through which constellation at the moment of a person's birth, then you already know quite a lot about him.'

'And you've been given that information about me?' said Marc.

'Sometimes you don't need to be given that information,' replied Ogrin. 'Sometimes, the planet in the constellation under which a person was born is written in the expression on his face.'

When the man had walked through the door, Marc had caught a glimpse of his dark eyes and had been struck by their intensity as the torch held by Gabo shone light onto his face. He had also been drawn to the intelligence that seemed to resonate in the timbre of this man's voice. The only person Marc had talked to in the last two years was Gabo, and with Gabo everything was either black or white, this way or that. There was nothing in between, no shades of grey. In contrast, the sound of this man's voice, so filled with nuance, was like the trickle of a cool stream on a hot day.

'I'm sorry I can offer you no other place to sit than beside me on this bed,' Marc said.

'That's all right. I'm quite happy to stand for the moment,' replied Ogrin.

'And so you would have me believe that you can tell, from the expression on my face, what planet I was born under?' Marc asked.

'Yes, absolutely.'

'And I suppose this planet will determine what sort of character I have?'

Ogrin looked at him for a moment. 'It has a lot to do with the kind of humour that will predominate in that character of yours,' he said. 'Let me put this in a different way, so that you will understand it a little better.

'At the time of your birth, the stars and the planets were disposed in a certain way in the heavens. Now, there are many possible ways of reading the particular configuration belonging to the time and place of your birth, but the one I favour is to relate a story to every possible configuration associated with our coming into this world. And so, to each person that is born, there belongs a story written up there in the heavens. What that story means to the person to whose birth it is attached, what he makes of it, the power it will have over his life, will depend on many other influences.

'Now, all these other influences are far too numerous to take into account, but the story attached to each person's time and place of birth can be seen by a trained eye. The ease with which he carries that story, how lightly or how heavily it weighs upon his life, can also be seen in the expression on his face. In the look in his eyes, in the way he stands or sits, in the manner he goes about his daily chores. All this, of course, also points to the nature of his inherited character.'

'So you are telling me that you can see the story that is attached to my birth?' Marc asked.

'In its broad lines, yes,' Ogrin answered. 'As a matter of fact, with you it is obvious, for it weighs heavily on your shoulders.'

'And are you going to tell me my story?' Marc could not hide his interest and a certain excitement at the sudden presence of this mysterious man in his cell.

'If I do, I shall expect something in return from you,' Ogrin said.

'I can't possibly think of what I could give you in return,' Marc replied. 'I have nothing of my own any more. I have lost everything: my wife, my daughter, all my belongings. I have even lost a whole kingdom. But if you think that there is, besides all this, still something I can give you, then I will gladly do so if only you will tell me the story that you say weighs so heavily on my shoulders.'

'It may not mean much to you when you hear it,' Ogrin said. 'But you must think of it as a mirror that reflects back to you the one element of eternity that accompanies you during your short passage through this world.'

'So what use is this story to me? You seem to be implying that it should be held above all other influences,' Marc said.

'Well, you are not entirely wrong to think that,' replied Ogrin, 'because the story that attaches itself to you at birth is the only thing about you that is bigger than you. All the other influences that have shaped you fit you perfectly, for you have taken from them only as much as you can absorb from them. But this story cannot be absorbed by you, and in the end it is you who will be absorbed by the story. And even if this is painful for you, it still has a grandeur that can liberate you from the numbing grind of your daily struggles.

'Now, do you still want to hear the story that is attached to your birth?'

Marc felt a moment of hesitation and doubt as he looked into the dark, glaring eyes of this strange intruder into his cell.

'Who are you?' he asked.

Ogrin ignored the question.

'Do you want to hear the story or not?' he asked.

Marc thought about it for a moment before replying. 'Yes, of course I do.'

'Well, in its broadest outline, as it is depicted up there in the heavens at night, it is just three stars grouped together in the shape of a triangle.'

'Is that all?' Marc asked, disappointed.

'No, that is not all. These three stars, representing the three angles of a triangle, are three different forces, or quantities, that are depicted in a set of cards.'

'What sort of cards?' Marc asked.

'They are small, rectangular flat plates, twenty-two in all, each one carrying a different image painted on it. These cards are carried by a tribe of travellers in the East who trace their origin all the way back to ancient Egypt, and who use these cards mostly to predict the future. But, in the right hands, they can also be used to determine the hidden fate that is influencing a person. The invisible forces that are informing his life. So, do you want to know more about the three cards belonging to the triangle attached to your birth?'

'Yes, I do,' Marc answered with renewed enthusiasm.

'Well, the first card that represents an active force is called The City of God. The image painted on this card depicts a walled city built in the middle of a forest. The city is showered with light falling down on it from a hole in the sky, whereas the forest surrounding it has heavy dark clouds floating above it.'

Ogrin paused for a moment to stare down at Marc, who had an eager but bewildered look on his face.

'The second card,' he said, 'which now represents a passive force was once called The Wolf and the image painted on this card originally depicted a creature with a wolf's head and man's body wearing a shirt, trousers and boots as it wandered across a field, chased by a dog that had torn a piece out of its trousers. But this representation can be found on only a few ancient cards because the card that now occupies the same place in the Tarot today is no longer called The Wolf but has been renamed The Fool and depicts a real man walking through the same field, no longer chased but is accompanied by his dog, who follows obediently beside him. And the third card representing a third force—'

'When you say that the second card now represents a passive force, are you suggesting that this was not always the case?' Marc interrupted.

Ogrin looked at Marc and hesitated, as if he had not expected this question.

'Yes,' he said. 'In ancient times The Wolf was an active force and The City of God a passive force, though there is no ancient version of the latter that has survived to bear witness to this assertion. We don't know what this card could have been called back then. You have to understand that these three forces that exist in all the various phenomena that can be found in this world also exist inside you as the three functions that make up your being: the mind, the body and the heart, which, in your case, are depicted on the three cards belonging to the Tarot as The City of God, The Fool and The World.'

'But you said that there are twenty-two of these cards...' Marc pointed out.

'Yes,' Ogrin replied, 'but the forces that make up our being are always the mind, the heart and the instincts. But each one of these three forces can be depicted by any one of those twenty-two cards.'

'How?' Marc asked.

'Well, depending on which cards represent these three forces in a given individual, you may get a glimpse of the story that is attached to his life, of its potential destiny. These three forces – the positive, the negative and the neutralising – represent, each one of them, one of the three functions that make up our being. They are at play with each other, conspiring and battling with each other, rotating around and around each other throughout the whole of the cosmos, and can get trapped in their excessive ardour and then congeal into a repetitive pattern that, as a constellation, occupies a determined space up there in the heavens.

'And it is one of these permanent patterns, the one that is the most active at the time and place of our birth, that will act like a seal stamped on our heart.'

Ogrin stared down at his boots, which reflected the light of the sun that was suddenly shining through the window high up on the wall facing him. 'So this seal that is sleeping inside us must be awakened into a myth that carries within it the seed of our true individuality. The measure of who we really are. Unfortunately, this rarely happens these days due to this City of God which has now imprisoned us within its walls by gathering us all under the influence of a single myth.'

'If I understand you properly, what is the difference between these myths that act like a seal stamped on our lives, at the time and place of our birth, and this single myth that holds us all under its influence that we now call The City of God?' Marc asked.

'Before the advent of The City of God, these myths served as maps illustrating the various roads that the spirit could follow once it had descended into our flesh, so that it could acquire the necessary ingredients to become a being in its own right and not be immediately swallowed into this vortex, this fire that is devouring itself and that we have named life. Whereas the myth inside The City of God that has gathered us all under its wing has coaxed us further and further away from our real nature so that it may be bent into serving its own ends.

'But don't get me wrong. It would be an even greater mistake to allow our lives to be absorbed into one of these myths without holding on to that accidental element that caused our parents to lie together at a given time and place, which resulted in our being born into this world. For this accidental element is what draws the heroes and heroines of our myths to come down here and incarnate themselves into our mortal flesh. It also allows a small margin of movement into the rigid, repetitive pattern into which the lives of these gods have been congealed. And it is through this small margin of movement that the tragedy depicted in these myths can be transferred into our lives and give us a quick glance of the fire that burns inside these gods without ever consuming them. But I did not really come here to talk about this.'

'So why are you here?'

'I want to tell you a story,' Ogrin replied.

'What story?' Marc asked wearily.

'Just a story,' Ogrin replied and, after a moment's silence, added, 'Neither of us have anywhere to go right now, so why don't you just listen?'

'Okay, so tell me a story,' Marc said, still disappointed that Ogrin had not told him more about The Wolf.

Ogrin slowly paced up and down between the walls of Marc's cell as he talked.

'It has to do with a beautiful young girl, only down here in the world her beauty was taken away from her. It happened on the island called Cyprus, and her name was Melissa.

'My father, who was an astrologer, was employed by a wealthy merchant who owned a fleet of ships that carried merchandise from the East to Venice, Rome, Genoa and Marseille.'

'I still don't know why you're telling me all this,' Marc protested.

'Well,' replied Ogrin, 'as you have no pressing business awaiting your attention, or anywhere to go, I was hoping that you might indulge me for a while and listen. If you do, you may understand a little better some of the events that have taken place in your own life. So, pray let me continue.

'So, this merchant, whose name was Carules, had a large family and the palace we lived in was magnificent, with gardens, courtyards, fountains and innumerable rooms. Paphos, where the merchant had built his palace, was a very busy port, with many lords and knights on their way to, or coming back from, Jerusalem. These lords and knights were often invited to the palace, where great banquets were held in their honour by Carules, always eager to find new outlets for the merchandise transported on his ships.

'Now, one of the servants attached to the palace was a girl of twenty or so, who was called Melissa. Her father was a shepherd who tended one of Carules' herds of goats up in the hills behind Paphos.

'Every day she would descend to the port with two donkeys loaded with jars of milk for the palace. As she walked through the busy streets, there would always be a group of men calling out and joking with her. They would ask her if she had found a husband yet, adding that she should make a detour down by the harbour to see if there was not a young knight freshly off a ship who might want to carry her home with him.

'Melissa obviously had a good nature, for these remarks would simply make her laugh, along with the men. Sometimes she would even pull a face at them in good humour and start walking with an exaggerated roll of the hips in mockery of a woman showing off her curves, causing more laughter as she continued down the road followed by her two donkeys. This mimicry was all the funnier because Melissa had a natural limp caused by one of her legs being shorter than the other. Nor could she answer the men back because her voice was hoarse, and the words she spoke were almost incomprehensible, to the point that the men would joke that only her two donkeys could understand what she said. This was due to her deformed mouth and a nose flattened out of shape above it, under her big blue eyes and golden curly hair.

'As for me, I was what you would call a dour, withdrawn young man. I was not unpleasant to look at, perhaps even handsome if I could have lost some of my corpulence, for I weighed far too much for someone of my age.

'When I was a child, my mother left the island and never returned. I think my father made life impossible for her in the end. It seems that he had bought her in the slave market in Alexandria and, now that he had landed this important position as Carules' personal astrologer, he felt she did not fit in at the palace and was more of an embarrassment to him than anything else.

'I often wondered why she did not take me with her when she ran away, but I suppose she must have felt that her future was uncertain, having no place to go; and that, in the palace, I would be looked after and not lack for anything, except a miserable mother who was constantly being humiliated by her husband. That is when I became withdrawn and shunned the company of other children my age. I also started having dreams about events that had not yet happened. But she was right to think that I would be well cared for in the palace.

'When my father became aware of this talent of mine, as he put it, he started to exploit it to enhance his own reputation as an astrologer. I was not allowed to talk about these dreams to anyone else, which cut me off even further from other children and prevented me from having any friends. I made up for this by hanging around in the palace kitchen and developed a taste for good food, of which there was no shortage there. All the palace cooks liked me and would feed me plates of something they had just prepared and wait for me to voice my appreciation.

'The first time I saw Melissa was in the street in Paphos. She was still a child, but a few years older than me. All the daily activity in the street seemed to be suspended as she walked by, with the two donkeys following behind her. Even then, people seemed to feel the need to shout at her, but the meaning of the words I did not understand.

'It was only when she got close enough and I saw her face that I realised what all the fuss was about. She was some kind of monster. A few years later, someone explained to me that her father had fornicated with one of his goats and that she was the result of such an abomination. Then, one morning, as I was having breakfast in the kitchen eating bread, boiled quince and cheese, I heard a noise outside in the courtyard that sounded like someone was being strangled. A moment later, Melissa walked in through the door. I immediately thought that the donkeys must be outside in the courtyard and that they had produced this strange sound, but then, as she pulled at the shirt of one of the cooks, the same sound came out from between her lips.

'The cook, who was carefully cutting up a piece of meat, said, "Yes, Melissa, I'm coming." He sighed and then, looking over at me, added, "When she arrives with her milk, she thinks it's the most important event of the day. You just watch how she fusses when we bring in the jars and what a scandal she'll cause if we spill any of the milk. The whole town could be on fire, but this would still be the main event of the day."

'For a moment,' continued Ogrin, 'as he was talking, Melissa's eyes looked into mine, and I saw a proud, humorous glint in their bright blue gaze. After that, I hardly ever saw her. I made a point of avoiding the kitchen at the time of day when she would deliver her father's milk. She both frightened and disgusted me. Was I not also a freak, with my strange dreams transporting me into the future? But the wounds and scars I carried inside me made me withdrawn and taciturn. Whereas she carried all her scars on her face, on her crooked, limping body, in the roar of her voice, and yet she was joyful and outgoing. I concluded, like almost everyone else, that she was an idiot and I did not want to get any closer to her for fear of finding out that perhaps she was not.

'As time went by, Melissa grew into a young woman. She still came down from the hills every morning, delivering the milk that was carried by the two donkeys that followed behind her. The only thing that changed was that people no longer shouted obscure names at her, but instead the men cracked lewd jokes about her finding herself a husband.

'As for me, I was now officially my father's assistant. He had initiated me into the mystery of reading the stars and the planets and in interpreting their movements. The more I learnt, the more I could see that there was some strange wisdom hidden behind this occult science, but that it was not to be found in the way it was being practised by my father.

'But even though I knew this, I was not about to search for this wisdom on my own. My real dream was to join up with one of the troops of Crusaders that were still passing through Paphos on their way to Jerusalem. But I knew nothing of the art of handling a sword and I could expect no support from my father if I were to try to become a soldier. I think I was strongly influenced by the fact that all the pretty girls in Paphos only had eyes for these knights and warriors who were passing through our port, and I longed for some of their attention as well. But life in the palace was too comfortable and easy. All I had to do was to play my father's game and I was assured of a full belly and a soft bed to sleep in. And was there any better place to dream of being a knight than in a soft bed with a full belly?

'Around that time, I began seeing Melissa again. This came about because, as my father's assistant, I now had my place every evening at Carules' table, where he dined with his family, friends and close associates. At times when these dinners included visiting gentry from abroad, as often happened, Melissa would be included amongst the servants who carried the food in from the kitchen and served at the table.

'Even though, on such occasions, she had learnt to pull the reins on her wild nature, combed her hair and wore a clean blouse and skirt, and even managed to straighten out her body so that she would barely limp at all, her face still came as a shock to many of the guests as they looked up at her when she bent over to place a plate of food in front of them.

'I once heard Carules tell my father that he liked to observe his guests' reaction to her. He said that a man who reacted to her naturally would be much harder to manipulate than someone who was visibly shaken when he first set eyes on her, and this made my father laugh. I suppose that Carules was only joking, but at the time I took what I had overheard seriously.

'Poor Melissa, I thought, when I heard this. She would never share any of the profit her master might squeeze out of his guests thanks to her face. All she might get out of them was their disgust, embarrassment or guilt-ridden pity. But then I had it in for both Carules and my father. I did not like the way they were using each other, and I did not like myself for having been too cowardly to resist being drawn into their game.

'I did not like Melissa, either. I did not want to have to feel pity or admiration, or whatever else it was I was resisting when I thought of her. I wished she had stayed up there in the hills with her father. I realised suddenly that my own reactions to her were far from natural and I felt deeply embarrassed about this, for that placed me in the category of people who could easily be manipulated, according to Carules.

'It was at the banquet that followed the conversation I had overheard between Carules and my father that something happened that was to change the whole course of my life dramatically.'

Ogrin paused for a moment to take a drink from his flask. When he was ready, he continued.

'Melissa had walked into the dining room and was serving

a plate of food to someone at the far side of the table, when the guest sitting next to me, a young knight who had come in the company of a French lord, leant towards me and asked me discreetly, "Does our host not pay his servants properly?" I replied that I had no reason to think otherwise. The knight then looked at Melissa and said, "Well, he certainly doesn't choose them from amongst the prettiest girls on the island."

'I looked at him. There didn't seem to be any malicious intent behind what he had said. He was just trying to strike up a friendly conversation, so I shrugged and laughed.

'And then, a while later, there she was leaning over me, placing a plate of food on the table before me. I thought to myself angrily, well, I'm not one of the guests whose reaction has to be scrutinised and was determined not to look up at her, or acknowledge her presence in any other way, for fear that Carules or my father might be looking at me.

'Just as I was having this thought, for the very first time I noticed her hand as she placed the plate down on the table. It was a fine, woman's hand, and it struck me as being quite beautiful. Suddenly, I had a moment of doubt. Had I made a mistake? Was it somebody else standing behind me?

'Then, as I looked up at her, I felt myself suddenly held motionless in the glare of her blue eyes that illuminated her whole face and stilled it in an aura of great beauty that I could not turn away from. And yet, some part of me wanted to look away; the part that could still see her deformed features. But that other part of me, there, was caught in the aura of her beauty that shone through her deformity and pulled me into it all at once, as if into an extraordinary battle that was being waged between two opposite, elementary forces that I could feel both inside me and sense out there in the dining hall.'

Ogrin stared at the barred window high up on the wall behind Marc's bed.

'I was a young man then, and I thought I had no choice but to follow the path that was mapped out for me by my father and Carules, in conformity with the needs and demands that were driving our world. But suddenly, in the spell of that moment, I saw that there was another life I could live, shining on me through her eyes, fraught with difficulty and danger, but touching something unexplored in me... this ability to find her beautiful that transcended the conventional laws that had been instilled into me. It was like discovering that I had wings and was no longer bound to the earth, but could be carried by the winds into the sky.'

Ogrin walked over to the bed and sat down beside Marc.

'*This*,' he continued, 'was the moment in my life when "my story" written in small letters and "MY STORY" written in capital letters came face to face with each other.'

He paused again and whipped one of his large hands over the top of his bald head, which he then shook from side to side.

'You see, the truth about Melissa was that she had fallen off a cliff when she was a very young girl while tending her father's goats up in the hills behind their house. And what I saw, when I turned round and looked up at her and she smiled at me, was that other Melissa, the one that should have been, had she not fallen off that cliff and broken all her bones.'

Ogrin laughed quietly to himself for a moment.

'I was now in a state of total confusion, because I could see that she was the one who had wings, that she had been able to hold on to that other Melissa, the one she should have been had she not had that accident. That she had been able to hold on to that other Melissa against all of us, against the whole town that would have her be otherwise; this poor, deformed cripple. Without knowing what I was doing, I stood up, took a step towards her and reached for her hand. I stood, holding on to her, and stared into her eyes. I couldn't speak.

'I realised that people must be looking at us now, but I didn't care because something much more important had just happened. I could feel the pulse of her heart beating in her hand as I held on to it, and all I could think of, or feel, as she stood there smiling at me, was what a remarkable person she was. How different from anyone I had ever met before!'

'And what did you do?' Marc asked.

'I fell hopelessly in love with her,' Ogrin replied. 'I became someone else. The person who had been hiding inside me now emerged and took over my whole being. This palace, with its fountains and well-kept gardens, its shining corridors with tiled floors, its kitchen where delicious meals were being prepared, was suddenly a dark dungeon from which she had delivered me.

'Do you understand what I am saying? I was in love!' Ogrin shouted.

'So what did you do?' Marc persisted.

'I married her.'

'And is she still your wife?'

'No,' said Ogrin. 'This happened a long time ago – over twenty-five years, at least. No, we were only together for a little over a year, but it was the happiest time of my life.'

'What became of her?' said Marc.

'Shortly after we married she became pregnant. Unfortunately, she did not live to see her own child, for she died giving birth to her.'

Marc stared at Ogrin and noticed how dark his skin was.

'The baby she brought into the world was a little girl,' continued Ogrin. 'At Melissa's funeral, apart from myself and the baby in my arms, there was only the old shepherd, a handful of people from the village in the hills and one of the cooks from Carules' palace. My father didn't come. He didn't want to see or hear of me again after I married Melissa.'

'Was the baby girl's name Isolt?' Marc asked impulsively, but Ogrin ignored his question.

'I made a big mistake,' he said, 'one which will haunt me until I die. It happened not long after Melissa was buried. I was still very young and suddenly on my own, apart from Melissa's father, who was old and dying. I couldn't face staying up in the hills with him. My heart was on fire with pain. I wanted to run as far away as I could from those hills, so I went with the baby in my arms to see Carules, asked him for some money and told him that he would never see me or the child again after that. He looked at the child in my arms with a certain fascination. He said that she was very beautiful. That's all he said to me, but he gave me the money.

'That evening I embarked with the baby and one of Carules' goats on a ship that was sailing to Rome. During the day, I entertained the sailors, who watched as I held my daughter under the goat and she suckled milk directly from its udder.

'When we arrived in Rome, I took the baby and the goat to a convent just outside the town. I asked the nun in charge of the place to take care of my daughter and gave her the money Carules had given to me. I explained the circumstances which had brought me to the convent and told her that, as soon as I was able, I would return, take back my daughter and pay them whatever money I owed them.'

'Had you already named her Isolt?' Marc asked.

'No, it was the nun, who was originally from Ireland, who suggested calling her by that name. I couldn't bear to think of giving her a name myself. I was abandoning her. I couldn't even look into her eyes. How could I have chosen a name for her?'

This last question seemed to be hovering somewhere in the shadows filling the dark corners of the cell as they sat staring at each other, until Ogrin sighed and said, 'You see, for a whole year I had lived as if in a state of grace. The whole world seemed to have changed. I had been given a new vision of life. The simplest things, be it the surrounding landscape or just the daily activities that made up our lives, all seemed to be bathed in an extraordinary beauty. And this beauty was her lost beauty that she was able to project into the world now. I felt free, as if I had been released from myself, from the palace, from Carules and my father.

'But after Melissa's death I realised that this was because I had been able to see everything through her eyes. And now that she was dead, the old demons had returned and that other vision of the world took possession of me again.'

Ogrin stared at Marc. 'That's why I abandoned Isolt in that convent. I didn't feel strong enough to carry her with me. I felt that the only way I could save myself was to be alone with my pain. I felt that if I stayed with that pain, without turning away from it, without letting any distraction steer my attention away from it, maybe then I could find my way back to that state of grace I had experienced when we were together.'

Ogrin closed his eyes, as if he was remembering something. 'It was this amazing confidence, calling to her from the myth buried in her heart, urging her to follow that road, its road, even if she had to follow its winding path on her own. This was the secret of her immense courage and strength.'

'So why was Isolt running away from you when I first met her?' Marc asked.

Ogrin sighed and wiped his hand over his face. 'When I went back to take her out of the convent, sixteen years later, we spent our first six months together working the markets in Italy. I had brought over a boatload of carpets and silk from Constantinople, most of which we managed to sell by the end of that time, and then we boarded a boat and sailed to Cyprus. I wanted to show her the little house up in the hills where she was born. I thought that, maybe, if she touched the stones of that house, and saw those hills, it might have helped her to understand my pain and why I had to abandon her.

'The evening after our arrival, the villagers came up to the house and brought food and a lot of wine. There was also music and dancing. I had not been back since I'd left with her a few weeks after her birth and the villagers wanted to celebrate our return. Of course, a lot of us got drunk. I don't know really what happened. It was already late and I must have said something that upset her.'

Ogrin sat in silence for a moment and then shrugged.

'I don't know what it was. I must have talked to her roughly or said something out of place. Anyway, she got upset and ran up the hill into the night and I ran after her. I wanted to apologise and bring her back, but she had a good head start and, by some extraordinary irony of fate, she fell from the very same cliff where her mother had fallen when she was a child. Luckily, it was not in exactly the same place. Not as high up and not as steep, and she was not mutilated and scarred for life like her mother. She got away with just a few scratches and a few bruises, but she wasn't the same after that. She seemed to have been affected in her mind and had somehow convinced herself that I had pushed her.

'She wouldn't talk to me after the accident. She eventually fled back to Italy with two sacks full of silk shawls and my horse. She sold the shawls in the markets as she travelled up through Italy and then France, right up into Brittany, where she met you.'

'You never told me about the third card, the one you said was attached to our hearts,' Marc said, not wanting Ogrin to stop talking.

'This card, the third card, representing a neutral force, a reconciling force, is named The World,' Ogrin said. 'The image painted on this card is of a naked woman with a shawl thrown over her shoulders. It falls over her body with one of its extremities covering her thigh. She is framed within a flowering wreath, and by the way her arms are thrown out at her sides, and one of her legs is lifted off the ground, she is obviously dancing.'

'Did you say that a shawl was thrown over her shoulders?' Marc exclaimed.

'Yes,' Ogrin replied. 'A shawl. She is the reconciling force brought into being by the clash between the active and the passive forces battling inside us, and can become the animating spirit that awakens the myth that was given to you at the time and place of your birth.'

11

INNOCENT III

'Hey, look at those bastards!' the coachman said to his companion.

On a mound to their left, three wolves stood over a carcass, its torn, open belly gaping up at the frozen early morning sky.

'They say it's been a hard winter when one wolf eats another,' the coachman said.

'Yes, well it's spring now and that's more likely a deer,' his companion retorted.

'I tell you it's a wolf!' the coachman insisted. 'Look at its leg. That's a paw sticking up there. It's not a hoof.'

Two of the wolves had their faces buried inside the belly of the carcass. The third one, meanwhile, stood watching the wagon and the mounted guards pass by as it chewed on a long piece of intestine that hung from its mouth.

'What awful creatures!' the coachman's companion said.

In the closed wooden cabin, with only a small barred opening at the front through which he could see a patch of sky and hear their conversation, Marc sat on the floor, his ankles chained together.

It was only a week since Ogrin had visited him in his cell. Now, after having spent the last two years imprisoned within the same four walls, he was travelling across France, on his way to Rome to meet the Pope, His Grace Innocent III.

The Bishop of Rennes was not pleased. He couldn't understand how Marc had managed to smuggle a letter out of his prison and get it delivered to the Pope in Rome. 'You'd better have something very important to tell him, or you will have embarrassed all of us here, which will not work in your favour,' he had told Marc, his mean, pinched face threatening all kinds of discomforts waiting for him upon his return.

But Marc did not worry about that. Nor that the bumpy road sorely shook his body, he was hungry and thirsty and his head was aching. None of this mattered. After two years he was moving forward again; and, despite the pain it was causing him, it felt good. He could feel his heart pumping blood into his veins. It was as if, for the last twenty-four months, it had stopped doing so, or was beating at such a slow rate that it was hardly noticeable. He was alive again and, though it frightened him, he could feel an inner warmth, as if, despite the cold outside, there was a hot wind blowing inside him.

It was her. It was the memory of her breath when, holding her close against him, she whispered his name.

*

It was several months before Marc and the escorting convoy arrived in Rome. The following day, Marc was standing upon a shining marble floor with a new pair of sandals on his feet and a clean set of clothes.

The room was quite barren, with high windows, white walls, a heavy wooden pulpit at one end and a crucifix on the wall behind it. The man sitting at the pulpit was staring down at him, but said nothing. Marc was surprised to see him dressed in just a simple white robe. He was wearing none of the artefacts that would have confirmed his rank as the ruling authority overseeing the whole of Christendom, except for a gold ring with his seal.

'Are you not going to speak?' the Pope asked finally. 'It was you who asked for this interview and I have gone to some expense to bring you here. Are you now going to remain silent?'

'For the last two years I have been shut away in a cell,' Marc replied. 'Apart from the occasional conversation with the prison guard, I have spent most of that time sitting on my own in the dark.'

'That is not necessarily a bad thing,' the Pope interrupted. 'It must have provided you with plenty of time to meditate on your plight.'

'Yes, it has indeed,' Marc answered. 'But finding myself suddenly in the raw light of this room, I have some trouble loosening my tongue.'

'You must have noticed that there are many others behind that door waiting for an audience, so you must make an effort to speak,' the Pope said.

Marc could detect a certain sympathy in his voice, which took him by surprise. Perhaps it was not sympathy, perhaps it was just curiosity, but it had a human slant that went beyond the purely cold and calculating. And this was only the first of many surprises, for now Innocent III turned to the two guards standing at either side of him and waved them away.

'Perhaps you'd better both go and wait outside,' he said to them.

'But, Your Grace...' one of the guards protested.

'Don't question my orders!' the Pope retorted and the guards left the room, closing the door behind them, shutting out once again the murmur of voices in the anteroom.

'Every morning there are hundreds of people waiting for an audience with me,' Innocent said to Marc. 'Each one a troubled soul with a problem they would like me to solve for them. It may be a disobedient wife, or a drunken husband, or an inconsiderate neighbour. Sometimes it is just advice they want, sometimes it is material help, sometimes it is faith that they want from me. What I tell them all is to search in their hearts for faith, for that is where it resides, and it is through faith that they shall receive help.

'And then, when the morning is over, I take time to rest, pray and feed my body, for in the afternoon I must give my attention to the one single soul that includes all the individuals I see in the morning, and the many more spread throughout the whole of Christendom. I am talking about the soul of our Church, which also has its troubles and needs our help.

'Now, before you tell me why you are here, let me ask you something. To what time of day do you think the matter you wish to discuss with me belongs? In the morning, or the afternoon?'

Marc stared down at the marble slabs under his feet. He was momentarily frozen into a stunned silence once again. The man looking down at him from the pulpit was not only human, but of a high intelligence. He seemed to have anticipated the purpose of Marc's visit, and was very clearly warning him that, if he wished to plead for clemency for Isolt and himself, his arguments would have to reach beyond their own self-interest and serve the larger interest of the Church in its present conflict with the heretics in Aquitaine. Otherwise, if he could not show clearly that what he was requesting was to the advantage of the Church, first and foremost, then he would simply be sent back to his cell to search in his heart for faith.

'I think what I wish to discuss with you belongs to the afternoon,' Marc said finally.

'Well then,' Innocent III replied, 'I will ask one of our guards to take you on a tour around the presbytery. You may also pray in our church if you wish. Then, when the morning is over, you may go to the refectory and have some food, after which we shall meet up again in the afternoon.'

Marc, escorted by the guard, walked through a pretty garden with several fountains and large cypress trees. He did not say much to his companion. He was worried about what he was going to say to the Pope. How he was going to persuade him that it would be in the Church's best interests to save Isolt from the bloodstained hands of Simon de Montfort and his besieging army. So much depended on this that he could feel the overwhelming pressure of responsibility weighing down on him, and even caught himself wanting to blame Ogrin for pushing him into this mess.

'Would you like to visit our church now?' the guard asked.

'Yes!' Marc answered, having only vaguely registered the question that was put to him. And so he found himself heading towards the imposing church towering before him. It was not until they were halfway down the aisle that Marc, still only vaguely aware of where he was, noticed an opening to his left. It led into a shrine that seemed to be cut into the wall. Something in there had caught his attention and he took hold of the arm of his companion and signalled to him that he wanted to go inside.

There were many candles on several trays covering a table that had been placed against the far wall. Above the table, quivering in the light sent up from the candles, was a large fresco. Its central figure was a woman standing in front of a tree. The two lower branches of this tree fanned out on both sides of the woman so that she seemed to be holding them up with her outstretched arms. She had golden hair and big, turquoise eyes. She wore a gown of red and gold. On the two branches at her sides, just where her hands seemed to be holding them up, sat two girls, both of whom had black hair and dark eyes and wore blue gowns. The girl sitting on the woman's right was looking down at her pensively, whereas the girl sitting on her left was looking away. She seemed anxious, with the fingers of one hand touching her chin.

Marc stood staring up at the image, bewildered and unable to look away. Suddenly the resounding, deep clang of a bell shook the stone floor under his feet and made the many small flames on the table flutter all at once. The tree in the fresco moved, as if blown by the wind, and Marc stared at it, aghast. As he did so he heard a voice that seemed to come to him through the echo of the bell and bounce off the walls of the church. Only now did he look again and notice that there was a face staring down at him through the clouds painted at the very top of the fresco, and it seemed that it was this face that was talking to him, now in a soft whisper.

'You have placed me,' it began, 'in the images depicted in your church windows and in the figure nailed to a cross, in the paintings, frescoes and other treasures that adorn this place of worship and all others like it. But have you ever been able to recognise me in the pain and suffering outside of their walls? Because, if you can travel deep enough and far enough into the suffering you will find there, you should then be able to see me there as well, and if you can do that, then you will have changed this devouring fire we call life into a God. And this God, and him alone, I will recognise as my son.

'He has drifted too far away from me and I am unable to recognise him. But you, Marc, who have been placed on the threshold of his soul, you have turned away from his cry for help by refusing to live out your destiny.'

As they made their way back to the main entrance door, Marc felt his heart swell, and his life fill with significance.

They sat in the refectory, each with a bowl of soup, Marc relishing the taste of every spoonful he brought to his mouth. He talked at length with the guard, whose name was Vincent, asking him about the church and the fresco. Vincent didn't seem to know too much about the painting, except that it was very old. But Marc went on talking to him, asking him about his life, why he became a guard and where he was from, all the time biting into a piece of bread and drinking from his glass of wine mixed with water.

He felt ecstatic, as if hit by some kind of spell. A state of grace that had fallen down on him from heaven, even though he didn't understand the meaning of what had been said to him in the church.

'Ah, wine!' he cried. 'What an extraordinary gift God made to men when He inspired them to turn grapes into wine.'

And what a fine refectory they were sitting in, with so many devout men from all over Christendom sharing a meal together! The guard was looking at Marc with a mixture of surprise and curiosity.

'Do you know, Vincent, what it is like to be free?' asked Marc. 'To be sitting here, sharing a meal with you, and not to know where I'll be later on this evening, or what bed I'll be sleeping in tonight? And yet it is not just the four walls of my cell that I have been released from. For something far deeper, I feel, is letting go of me as well.'

*

Innocent III was sitting behind a large desk, his arms folded in front of him. Behind him, two windows looked out onto the cloister and its gardens.

'You look rested,' the Pope said. 'Did you have a chance to visit our church and pray there?'

'We did enter the church, but I'm afraid all my attention was taken up by a fresco on one of its walls,' Marc answered.

'Ah, you mean *The Jerusalem Bride*,' the Pope exclaimed with approval. 'Is it not beautiful?'

'Yes, beautiful and powerful all at once,' said Marc.

'It was created by a Byzantine artist several hundred years ago,' Innocent explained. 'The bride standing before the tree is an allegorical representation of our Church, which is married to Jesus Christ our Lord, who stares down at her from the heavens at the very top of the fresco. The tree symbolises the growth upwards of our faith from the soil, under which the Patriarchs are buried. It reaches up to heaven from where our Lord descended. And she, the Jerusalem Bride, is the fruit of that tree.'

'And what about the two girls sitting on the branches on either side of her?' asked Marc. 'Why is the one to her right looking down at her, and why is the one to her left looking away from her?'

'You have indeed studied the picture carefully,' the Pope said with evident approval and surprise.

'I could not take my eyes away from it,' Marc said. 'It took no less than the bell ringing in the tower to awaken me from the spell it seemed to have cast on me.'

'The young girl sitting on the branch to the right of the bride is the heart of all Christian souls. She is looking down at the glory of her Church, shown here as the Jerusalem Bride. The girl sitting on the branch to her left represents the Synagogue, unable to look at the truth.'

'Oh!' said Marc, before he could stop himself.

'You seem surprised.'

'Well, Your Grace, I must confess that, in my ignorance, I had not thought of it in that way.'

'And in what way did you think of it, then?' asked the Pope.

'What struck me,' explained Marc, 'was that the whole painting seemed to be reaching upwards towards God, or Jesus, who is depicted looking down from the very top of the fresco, as you have already said, Your Grace. But the image is strangely cut off from the rest of the picture, for even the tree cannot reach that far up. And the young woman standing before the trunk with her arms reaching out at her sides, mimicking the two lower branches of the tree, seems to be divided with regard to this ascension. For one side of her, illustrated by the girl sitting on the branch to her right, seems to be looking at her in awe, thus following this movement upwards, whereas another side of her, the left side, illustrated by the girl sitting on the branch to her left, is turning her head away from the woman in the centre and seems to be rejecting this ascension.' Marc paused for a moment, then found the confidence to carry on.

'What I mean is that it never occurred to me that these two different attitudes represented, on the one hand, the heart and soul of Christianity, and, on the other hand, the Synagogue. I saw the whole mosaic rather as an illustration of the division in the human heart when it looks at God in the heavens above. For, although such a sight seems to lift the heart up towards something of great splendour and beauty high above this world, when it tries to express what it sees up there, down here in the world, all the beauty and splendour seems to change into something harsh, cruel and narrow.

'I think a good illustration of this would be the campaign that Simon de Montfort is fighting against the heretics in the south-west of France. The main claim of these heretics would seem to be that this world of flesh and matter, in which our spirit is imprisoned, was created by a false God, or even the Devil according to some, and is in its essence evil.

'Now Simon de Montfort, in an effort to convince the people of the land where this heresy is flourishing that the world is not evil but good, and the creation of the only true real God who is in his essence also good, is burning these heretics by the thousands, spilling the blood of men and women alike and despoiling their country to drive home his point. I do not question his sincerity, but cannot help wondering if there is not a deep contradiction in his actions that are carried out in the name of God?'

When Marc finished, he saw that the Pope was sitting very still behind his desk. The crucifix, high up on the wall behind him, seemed to be looking down at the room as if from far away, with resigned acceptance, compared to the intensity in the eyes staring at him from behind the desk.

The muffled, sporadic sounds from beyond the windows, from the cloister or from the gardens, only added to the tension as Marc waited for the Pope to speak.

And then he remembered something he had read, a long time ago, that had puzzled him as he had never been able to decipher its true meaning. He realised that what had so captured him in the fresco was the discreet reference it seemed to be making to those very same words he had read, and that now made them comprehensible to him.

'Is this contradiction not illustrated by some words written by St Augustine?' Marc asked.

'Which words?' the Pope enquired.

'These words, Your Grace. "That is why the science of the creature, which is in itself in the evening, was in God in the morning. Because the creature is seen more clearly in God than in itself."'

'When we find ourselves in a church,' continued Marc, 'as I was this morning, staring at a beautiful illustration of our faith depicted in this fresco, we may very briefly be able to see ourselves in God, and our hearts may be opened to the beauty of his message that seems, at that moment, to be present everywhere in the fabric of this world he has created for us.

'But when we walk out of the church we are assailed by the evening light, where we only see ourselves in ourselves, and everything we do seems to be in contradiction to what we were able to see inside the church.

'Is it not this contradiction that the fresco is pointing to, beyond the message of faith that is so clearly depicted in it as well? Is the girl sitting on the branch, to the right of the Jerusalem Bride, not bathed in the morning light as she stares down at the bride? And is the girl sitting to her left not lost in the evening light, as she looks away from the bride, at what is going on in the world beyond the church?'

His Grace Innocent III sighed. 'What is it you want from me?'

'I want to save my wife and daughter,' Marc replied.

The Pope gazed at him for a while, then sighed again.

'I must confess,' he replied, 'that I thought you were just a poor buffoon led astray by a pretty wife, but I see that you have far more depth than I imagined. But, tell me one thing: don't you think your wife has chosen her fate?'

'She accepted her life with me in the end and had no intention of leaving me,' said Marc. 'If the Bishop of Rennes had not attempted to arrest her, she would still be in Brittany at my side.'

'It was unfortunate that the Bishop of Rennes went back on his word and tried to apprehend her,' replied Innocent. 'He did this without consulting me, I might add. But your wife's effrontery, her attempt to ridicule his authority publicly on the White Moor and make nonsense of all that we hold as most sacred was too much of a provocation. Though I don't approve of what he did, I understand the forces that pushed him to do it.

'However, if I understand you rightly, you are saying that your wife now finds herself in the besieged town of Penn against her best intentions. Are you suggesting that she would be willing to come back to you and live at your side once more, were she given the opportunity to do so?'

'I am certain that she would. She would put her daughter's life before any other consideration. I know that.'

'Then we must act in haste,' the Pope said. 'I fear there may not be much time left. If you are really convinced that you can persuade her to come back here with you, I will provide you with a letter giving you full authority to carry out this mission.'

'She will need your word in writing,' replied Marc, trying to hold back the euphoria he felt from his voice, 'stating that you will not arrest her once she has been delivered from Penn. That she will be free to live her life with me as before.'

'She will have that,' the Pope answered. 'The only thing I ask of her is that she confess to me, or any of my bishops, thus showing her will to reinsert herself into the Christian faith. If she does this, then you will be free to return to France and start a new life together.'

'There is one more thing,' Marc said. 'It is possible that she will not leave without Tristan.'

The Pope thought for a moment before replying.

'If Tristan, like Isolt, is willing to come here to Rome and confess to one of my bishops and give his word as a knight that he will only use his sword in defence of the Christian faith from then onwards, then he will have my word in writing that no harm will be done to him. But he must first surrender his sword upon leaving Penn.'

'I think that if Isolt asks him to, and if he sees that he can save her by doing this, there can be no doubt that he will comply with your demands,' said Marc.

'You are probably right,' the Pope said. 'Judging by his behaviour so far, he seems willing to make any sacrifice for her. He used to be an honest, valiant young knight, whose prowess during the last crusade became legendary. But your wife seems to have turned him around and made him betray every single one of the values he had sworn to uphold.

'That is why I insist that he shows some kind of repentance for his recent behaviour by confessing to a bishop here in Rome.

Troubadours have written songs about your wife and this man, extolling their adulterous behaviour, and it is time to put a stop to it. They have caused enough harm already. The only reason I am willing to help you save your wife is because I think it is better for us to have her and Tristan come here to Rome and be seen to repent for their past folly than to have them die in Penn and become martyrs.

'There is also the fact that you have sufficiently impressed me to make me think that you may succeed in accomplishing this mission. But do not make the error of thinking that I will forgive you if you fail.

'As for Simon de Montfort, don't think that he won't try to put obstacles in your path. He will stop at nothing to win the war and will not tolerate anyone standing in his way. He believes that the more ruthless he is with his enemies, the more this will sap their resolve to go on fighting.'

Innocent paused for a moment, looking at Marc. 'I fully agree with you,' he continued, 'that there is a contradiction between the strategy he is using and the spiritual message he is supposed to be defending, but I also know that if this heresy is not crushed it will spread, for the Cathars are offering an easy answer to the harsh world we are living in. They would have us take flight from our responsibilities, claiming that this world is the creation of a false God or the Devil.

'It is not hard to see that, if we let them have their way, they would soon drag the whole of Christendom into a state of chaos and barbarity. So I cannot afford to wholly condemn de Montfort and his methods. When I was first chosen to become the guide and counsellor of my fellow bishops in how to best serve our Lord Jesus Christ, through the ministry of our many churches, I thought I would receive clear counsel through prayer for all the difficult decisions I'd have to make. But, as you can see, all is not clear, even after prayer, even when sitting on this high throne,

and what seems the best way forward can only seem to be that
way through a glass, darkly.

'The morning light that St Augustine speaks of shines down
on us through the images in the stained-glass windows of our
church and the celebration of Mass that is performed there. But,
apart from the Saints, the rest of us must wander through the
obscurity of the evening light once we have left the confines of
our church.'

*

It took more than a week to ride up through Italy, and then
several more days of twisting and winding through the hills
of Provence before they descended towards the coast, west of
Marseille. From there, they crossed through the sandy meadows
and marshlands of the Rhone estuary.

The man commanding the twenty guards escorting Marc was
Captain Roberto Narrizano. The Pope had briefed the captain
on the purpose of their mission and had made it clear that, once
they reached Penn, he was to follow Marc's instructions and not
take orders from Simon de Montfort. Although the captain had
nodded his head in acknowledgement and agreement, Marc
could see that he was not altogether happy with what he was
hearing.

It seemed the five days they had spent travelling together
had done nothing to reassure the captain about the man riding
at his side, who was rumoured to have spent the last two years
in a prison in France and to be on his way back there purely to
rescue his wife and her lover from a besieged city in the heart of
Languedoc. From their conversations together, the captain had
concluded that this man was quite oblivious to the possibility of
any obstacles or dangers crossing their path during this mission.
The only thing that seemed to be occupying his thoughts was

the anticipated joy of meeting up with his wife and daughter again. Did he really think that Tristan would stand by and let him take his wife back? This mysterious, legendary knight, who had caused such devastation on the battlefields around Jerusalem – did Marc really believe that such a man would just step aside like a gentle lamb and let him climb back into his wife's bed? The captain could see nothing ahead of him on this journey but trouble.

12

THE CITY OF GOD

He was lying on a beach outside a village, Les Saintes Maries de la Mer. It was a strange place, a small gathering of fishermen's huts built around an enormous high- walled church with an imposing flat bell tower. They had stopped there for the night because there was a stream with clean fresh water, there had been a good catch of fish brought in by the villagers, and they had been able to buy a good portion of it from them. Enough to feed the twenty guards, Captain Roberto and him.

They had grilled the fish over a fire outside the village, down across the salt marsh, on the beach by the sea. After they had all eaten, they unsaddled their horses and Captain Roberto and the guards lay with their blankets on a dry patch of earth above the beach, close to where their horses were grazing. But Marc had fallen asleep on the sand and it was there that he had a dream in which he was standing on a pier with Ogrin, listening to a discourse he was giving about an intervention that took place in The City of God.

'And what did it involve?' Marc asked.

'They cast all the wolves they had not managed to tame out of the city and only kept those that they could transform into dogs.'

'Who did this?' Marc asked.

'The philosophers and theologians whose influence shaped the city,' Ogrin answered.

He could not remember the full content of the conversation, but the general feeling he remembered from the dream was of being given a precious map, drawn on parchment, that depicted a road, a path, that would lead him out of the darkness that had overtaken his life. But this map was very complicated, had many intertwining paths drawn on it, and before Ogrin had been able to finish his explanation Marc had lost his temper; he could still feel the pain in his chest from this sudden outburst of anger. Ogrin had tried to calm him with a rose that he had picked out of one of the many pockets sewn into his robe. The sun had already sunk down behind the horizon and there was very little light left in the sky. Only portions of Ogrin's face were visible, a few islands of reflected light moving through the shadows of dusk, but the flattened rose that he held in his hand was truly luminous.

'What is it?' Marc asked.

'It will bring you luck on this mission. It was given to Isolt in one of the towns in Italy where we were selling carpets. We had packed everything up and were sitting on the terrace of an inn, when suddenly a young man came charging across the street, jumped over the barrier, handed her this rose and then ran away. He was magnificent, but Isolt was not impressed. She wanted to leave the rose on the table when we left. I protested, saying that the rose was beautiful, and she agreed, but added that it was given to her by the wrong person. "What makes you say that?" I asked. She answered that the person who should have given her that rose should have been me.

'So I picked it up off the table and put it in the pocket of this robe. I had already understood that the apparition of this young man was a vision of something that was to come, something that would turn her life upside-down, as if he was really a spirit who had come to test her, to see if she was ready for this upheaval. But the fact that she did not pick up the rose showed that it was too early, that she was not yet ready to carry this myth that was waiting to take hold of her. I realised that she had become too attached to me. She needed to have a life of her own before this fate could take it away from her.'

'What fate?' Marc asked.

'You already know,' Ogrin answered.

'No, I don't,' Marc replied. 'I can't recognise spirits. I don't have this gift, so tell me what she wasn't ready for.'

'She was not yet ready to be confronted by another wolf. That means, by a man who, when he looked at her, could perceive her directly with his heart. She was not ready for that. Her myth was still deeply asleep inside her.'

'And was it still too early when she met me, then?' Marc asked.

'Yes,' Ogrin answered. 'You could say it was too early. She needed to be a woman first. She needed to have something she could sacrifice. And anyway, you were the wrong person. You had another role to play in the myth. You were serving the wrong god, the one who reigned in The City of God, and she was looking for someone to take her out of there and lead her into the wilderness.'

'But that's not my God!' Marc protested angrily.

'Of course it is!' Ogrin insisted. 'Don't you see that you have been tamed and trained to serve its needs, that you have become a dog?'

'What needs?' Marc asked. 'Where have I served a single one of its needs?'

'When you tried to tame Isolt. When you tried to keep her in a cage like a canary.'

'That's not true. I was not serving any other needs than my own. And I never tried to shut her in a cage. I loved her, and naturally I wanted her for myself.'

'But you have no self!' Ogrin exclaimed. 'You only think you have a self. But that imaginary person who answers to the name Marc is an illusion concocted for you by The City of God, so that it can bend your will to better serve its needs. It is an imposter standing in for something that is buried deep inside your heart, that has yet to be awakened.'

Marc stared at Ogrin, half aware that this conversation was really only a dream. But when a cloud moved away from the moon, it appeared in the sky like a lantern lighting up Ogrin's face. His dark eyes stared back at Marc and melted his awareness of being in a dream away again.

'So the sudden apparition of this young man is an impersonation of The Wolf depicted on the Tarot card, and could be said to be an omen, a premonition of the descent of this myth carrying all three of your destinies – yours, Tristan's and Isolt's – into this world,' Ogrin said.

'Well, I certainly could have done without it having to descend here,' Marc said angrily, though also half in jest, as a weak attempt to make light of his fate.

'You see,' Ogrin said, his voice now blending into the night as if it were falling from up there where the moon was staring down at them, 'in your case, Marc, like most people today you are quite happy to live your life using your instincts and your mind to see you through your daily routine, through the joys and the tribulations that greet you along the road you are travelling that begins with childhood and ends with old age, if you are lucky. But somewhere along the way you chanced to meet Isolt…'

Ogrin fell silent. He was just a dark shadow again as they stood on the pier, listening to the water breaking against the wooden pilings beneath them.

'So aren't you going to finish?' Marc asked.

'Well, when you looked at her you felt her beauty moving inside your chest, and this prompted you to throw that shawl over her shoulders, which moved something inside her as well. It was something warm and pleasant, like a premonition of the life you were to spend together during those years when you were living in the fortress before your father's death. But it didn't reach into the centre of her being, it didn't reach the myth containing her sacrifice that was sleeping there, waiting to be awakened.

'You couldn't do that. Only Tristan could reach far enough into her to make her abandon all her comforts and run away with him.'

'I can't accept that!' Marc shouted, and then, his voice dropping to a near whisper, he added, 'I just can't live with that.' Now sounding like a child, he asked, 'What am I supposed to do?'

There was a long silence, after which Ogrin asked him, 'What is your deepest desire right now?'

'Her!' Marc replied. 'I can't see anything beyond her. She is The World, as you have pointed out, she is the woman dancing naked inside a wreath. She is both inside me and outside me. She is the air I breathe and I can't break away from her because I can't see anything beyond her.'

'I'm afraid that the only thing left for you to do is to find your heart out there in the wilderness and help fulfil its desires. But to help it do this, you must first become a wolf again, and you must find her and take her into that forest.'

13

THE HEART OF DARKNESS

'So you are the king without a kingdom?' Simon de Montfort said as he looked up from the letter he had snatched out of Marc's hand only moments before. 'Would she not be better off staying here rather than going off with you? After all, where would you take her, now that you have lost your kingdom?'

'Quite so,' Marc replied. 'I have no plans to take her anywhere beyond Rome, where she will confess her sins and beg for God's mercy in the presence of His Grace Innocent III. That should be clear from what is stated in the letter.'

De Montfort, who had glanced down at the letter as Marc was speaking, looked back at Marc and, with an arrogant sweep of his neck that pushed his chest forward, shouted, 'Well, I too am acting on the Pope's orders, and I am fighting a war here! That also should be clear. I don't know if you noticed the man hanging from a tree as you arrived... He was the lord of this castle. I left him hanging there so that anyone passing this way should have no doubts about how we treat our enemies. This is the kind of war we are fighting, and these are the kinds of methods that work down here. I have put my life at risk too many times and seen too many good men die in this crusade to believe that anything aside from the most ruthless determination to crush these people can bring victory to our cause.

'So I propose to ignore this letter of yours, for I know that if His Grace were here to witness how hard and at what cost we have fought to wrench back every inch of this land, to place it back under God's rule, he would understand that this is not the time or place to show mercy.'

'I know, my lord,' replied Marc, 'and I quite agree that this may be true down here, where the war is being fought on the battlefield. And I am sure that there is no one who would question your determination or doubt the sincerity of your devotion to your faith.'

He paused to look around the room. A fire was burning in the hearth, around which a group of men and women were either standing or sitting in chairs. On a table behind him were trays of roasted meats, jars of wine, bread and cakes. The guards who had escorted him had eagerly taken up de Montfort's invitation to help themselves to what food and drink they desired.

'But, my lord,' Marc went on, 'you cannot ignore that there is another war being fought by His Grace Innocent III and the many missionaries he has sent throughout Europe to preach and defend the purpose of his crusade, and to raise funds and recruit men to help you here on the battlefield. It would be a great support to his cause if Isolt were to come to Rome, publicly repent and ask for God's forgiveness. This would indeed be a great thing, for Isolt is known to everyone. Songs praising her name, her beauty and devotion to love are sung in courts throughout France and beyond.'

De Montfort glared at Marc again, but this time there was a glint of surprise in his piercing eyes. 'I see,' he said. 'Then perhaps I'd better help you after all. Please excuse me for a moment. I must go and fetch someone. I will be back in a little while. Why don't you take the opportunity to eat some of the food on the table? You must be hungry.'

He turned and left the room with the same sweep and thrust of his body that seemed to cut through any possible objection to anything he did or decided. On his way out he tapped the shoulder of one of the men standing by the fire and gestured for him to follow.

Marc picked up a piece of roasted meat, bit into it and poured himself some wine to wash it down. The tension of the situation had somewhat tightened his stomach and he was not hungry.

Captain Roberto walked over to him. 'Is everything all right?' he asked.

'I don't know,' Marc said. 'We shall have to wait and see.' He noticed that one of the men by the fireplace had said something and that all but one of the women had got up from their chairs and were leaving the room. The guards were still chatting and eating heartily around the table, but the party of Simon de Montfort's companions grouped around the fireplace was silent.

Marc thought he heard a cry. The sound seemed distant and was immediately swallowed by the voices and laughter coming from the table. He heard the sound again, and once more it was lost among the noise in the room. But by the third time it had grown louder and was unmistakably the sound of a man crying. At first Marc could not make any sense of it. But as the room fell silent he could hear the words that came tumbling out in a rapid avalanche between the man's shrieks.

'I have done nothing wrong! Please, before God, I have done nothing wrong!'

A man was pushed in through the door. His hair was long, fair and curly, he wore a coarse sackcloth smock and his hands were tied behind his back. The young man who had followed Simon de Montfort out of the room was standing behind him and holding him by the hair. Following them came de Montfort himself, dragging another man by the arm. He shouted something to him and let go of his arm. Then he looked over at Marc.

'Isolt might be a little reluctant to follow you out of her hiding hole, so I'm going to help her make up her mind. Get him on his knees!' he bellowed above the sobbing pleas for mercy. The man holding the prisoner from behind kicked the back of his legs and forced him down onto his knees. De Montfort moved to the side of the kneeling man and drew his sword. The captive still seemed to want to say something, but nothing more than an animal-like howl came from his mouth. The sword came down, sure and precise, scraping over the front of the man's face like a kitchen knife cleaning a cutting-board. When it had finished its journey downwards, it had cut off the man's nose and most of his lips.

The only woman left in the room screamed and lifted her hands to her face. There was no more sound from the kneeling man. With blood oozing from the gash in his face and his body shaking, he simply stared up with eyes wide open.

Marc felt he was losing control of his own body, as if it wanted to start shaking as well.

'Don't let go of him!' Simon de Montfort shouted.

As Marc watched him poke his sword into the already mutilated face, stabbing the kneeling man in both his eyes, his own vision became blurred. It seemed as though a violent gale had blown into the room and that everyone was holding on to something for support – some to the table, others to the walls, others still to the mantelpiece over the hearth.

Marc felt somehow relieved that the man no longer had eyes with which to stare at them. In their place were two small holes with flesh hanging out of them and blood running down, like two streams joining the river flowing out of the gash between them. There was nothing human in the face any more. Marc felt his body relax and a strange calm settle over him, even though the storm still seemed to be raging in the room.

He could see Captain Roberto looking over at him as if awaiting instructions of some sort, but Marc made no sign or gesture and said nothing. He just stood still, for this was the best thing to do, he realised – just stand very still.

It was Simon de Montfort's turn to look at Marc and, when their eyes met, something strange happened. It was as if Marc were looking at the same eyes that had glared into the room only moments before, staring out of the mutilated face of the kneeling man, as if they were lost in the same darkness, in the same void.

The man without a face was pulled up onto his feet by de Montfort's men, gripping him under both arms, his legs shaking wildly and his feet dancing lightly on the floor, trampling the blood that had gushed out of his wounded face.

'Sit him on a donkey!' Simon de Montfort yelled into the face of the man he had dragged into the room. 'Take him up to the gates of Penn and tell them that this is a little present for them from me. And, as for you, if I don't see you back here in the morning with the donkey, you know what will be awaiting you when I catch up with you.'

The mutilated man was marched out of the room, and two women from the kitchen came and mopped up the blood. No one was touching the food any more. When de Montfort saw this, he walked over to the table, grabbed a chicken leg, bit into it and poured himself some wine.

'Come on!' he said to the Pope's guards. 'Don't let a little thing like that spoil your appetite! I know you must all be hungry, so come and eat the food we've laid out for you! Don't offend me!'

The gale had ceased. Hands were reaching across the table to pick up pieces of food and to pour wine. De Montfort was talking cheerfully to the guards and calling over to his own men, still gathered around the fireplace, to come to the table and join the party. There was much laughter, and pleasantries were exchanged between the two groups, and Marc watched in admiration at how this big man, no longer young but still powerful, could carry all the other men in the room with him. How, moments before, he had plunged them into a scene of such horror that it seemed that their souls were clinging to the walls and furniture of the room as they looked on, with disbelief, and how he now had them all laughing and drinking at his side as if nothing had happened. But Marc had seen that look in his eyes and knew where his real abode was, and it belonged alongside the blind terror of the man he had just mutilated, not with the cheerful crowd now eating and drinking around the table.

Every now and then de Montfort would look over at Marc and see him watching him, then quickly glance away as if he suspected that Marc had seen something more about him than he wished to reveal.

'Do you think you'll be ready to go up there tomorrow and bring Isolt back with you?' The voice was soft and conciliatory, but Marc could not see the expression on Simon de Montfort's face. The fire in the hearth had gone leaving only two candles at the far end of the room still burning, and they did not throw enough light to show whether or not there was a slight glimmer of irony in his eyes as he spoke.

The two men had sat themselves by the fireplace and were facing each other across the darkness. Simon had insisted that Marc stay for a while, so that they could get to know each other after everyone else had retired to their beds.

'Are you all right?' Simon asked, as Marc had remained silent.

'Yes, I'm all right,' Marc answered. 'I'm just a bit confused. Why did you mutilate and blind that man?'

'Because he was a traitor. He tried to get a message through to Raymond VI, the Count of Toulouse. Had that message not been intercepted, it would have caused a lot of harm. He betrayed his Church and he betrayed God.'

'When there is no mercy to be found anywhere, is that too not a betrayal of God?' Marc knew that Simon must be looking at him, even though he could see no more of his eyes than a dark shadow.

'Is that how you tried holding on to your kingdom?' he asked scornfully. 'By being merciful to everyone?'

'You make a lot of my losing my kingdom,' Marc said. 'But, to tell you the truth, it was the best thing that could have happened to me.'

There was another silence and then Simon spoke. 'And losing Isolt? Was that a good thing too?'

Marc did not answer and, after a long interval, Simon spoke again. 'You won't answer me?'

'Who is to say that I've lost her?' Marc asked.

Simon let out a loud laugh. 'Of course you've lost her!' he barked. 'As you've already told me, her love for Tristan is sung in every court in France by now. Yet you still hang on to the belief that you might win her back one day! Even if you manage to take her with you to Rome, you know very well that she will only have followed you because the alternative awaiting her is death, whether by starvation or one of our swords, or even on a bonfire.'

Simon paused for a moment to give Marc time to absorb this fact. 'And you lecture me about mercy!' he continued, sighing. 'Well, let me tell you something. If you want to set an example and show some mercy, then let her stay up there in Penn and die beside the man she really loves. That's what would be best for them, to die holding on to their love for each other. For such passion cannot last for long in this world. So be merciful and let them die while their hearts are still on fire.'

Marc felt hot flames of horror blow into him and set fire to his own heart.

'You are forgetting that Isolt and I have a daughter trapped up there with the rest of them,' he said.

'Is she really your daughter?' Simon sneered.

'Yes!' Marc answered, trying to hold back his anger.

'Then go up there tomorrow and rescue your daughter. Isolt would be relieved to hand her over to you. And then you can leave Tristan and Isolt to live out their fate together.'

'That would not meet with the commitment I have made to Innocent III,' Marc objected, immediately uncomfortably aware that he was ducking the challenge Simon had thrown into his path. He knew he was being dishonest in pretending that he could be bound by a commitment he had made, even to the highest representative of God down here in the world, when it was all too clear to him that he would be prepared to break that commitment if this would bring Isolt back into his arms. He felt ashamed that he had to resort to this kind of deceit and could find no argument of his own, or anything from his heart to fight back with.

'What do you care?' Simon answered. 'You can tell him that Isolt refused to come with you to Rome. And he would not dare condemn you for saving your daughter.'

'The Pope wishes that the people of Penn should surrender their town without any lives being taken,' replied Marc, 'and for Isolt to come back to Rome with me and confess her error. This might also put a stop to the terrible rumours of the butchery being perpetrated down here that have reached the ears of many people, including the rich merchants that are helping to finance this crusade.

'The Pope fully realises that his war is far from over and will need the further backing of these merchants if it is to be fought through to a final victory. That is why he must put a stop to these sordid rumours, otherwise this crusade will be thought of as simply a barbaric attempt to invade these people's land and plunder its riches, and not as a Christian attempt to win them back to their faith.'

Simon did not seem to catch the irony. As Marc looked at the dim outline of his silhouette, he began to see darker patches in the round shape of his head from where two eyes must have been staring back at him.

'These people you are talking about, these rich merchants, these dukes and lords, what do they know?' Simon asked. 'They have no understanding of God. They have been spoon-fed all sorts of comforting stories, pleasing images and thoughts to soothe their troubled hearts, and that's all. Fear God and obey his commandments, and once you die you will join him in paradise, where everything will be given to you. That's all they want to hear – fairy tales with a happy ending.

'But I went all the way to Jerusalem to fight for God, to defend his name against all those savage barbarians who would erase it from the land where he first revealed himself to mankind. And what do you think God showed me when I was there? He took me into a desert where, all around me, for as far as the eye could see, there was only emptiness, where nothing grew and no sign of life was to be seen. There were no trees, no plants, no animals, nothing alive, just bare, scorched earth and rocks.

'And as I stood there looking all around me, I heard God's voice whisper to me, and as he spoke, images from far away in the past drifted before my eyes. He told me that, once upon a time, there had been people living there, villages and towns and ploughed fields and forests full of game to hunt, rivers full of fish. And the people who lived there had parents and children of their own, and their children also had children, and they all swam in the rivers and hunted in the forests and tasted the bread made from the produce of the fields.

'And yet, of all those people who lived there, who loved and battled and fought for a decent life, who sang and danced and rejoiced to celebrate their victories, and who cried and lamented their losses, not one of them, God said, was left to tell any of this. Not one of their names has been remembered. They were all wiped out by his armies and there is nothing left of who they were or of what they did, apart from a bit of dust maybe, blown up during a sandstorm. That is all that remains.

"'And why did this happen?" God went on to ask. "It is because they worshipped another God than me. A false God, for I am the only true God, and only those amongst you who worship me and follow my laws and commandments will be remembered. For, if you do this, far into the future, long after your death, anyone who lives by these laws and commandments which you, yourself, were bound to, will bring you back to life through their deeds and gestures.

"'For I am the great devouring fire, and only those amongst you who live by my laws and obey my commandments will escape being annihilated in the flames of this raging fire."'

'That was the voice of God that spoke to me out there in the desert,' Simon said proudly, 'speaking the same words that were spoken to the patriarchs who laid the foundations on which our Church was built, and on which our whole Christian dogma has been erected.

'And I carried those words with me back to France and based my whole life on them. And I was happy, I felt blessed, full of faith and enthusiasm, and wanted to give my whole life over to God. I wasn't interested any more in enlarging my fiefdoms, in acquiring more riches and honours. None of that mattered; all I wanted now was to serve God.'

There was a long silence. Marc could think of nothing to say, and then he heard Simon de Montfort take a deep breath, as if he was about to awaken a painful memory.

'And then, several years later, I returned to the Holy Land to fight Saladin and his great army, to try and stop him from reconquering Jerusalem, from occupying that sacred soil and subjecting it to his foreign customs and blasphemy.

'I was riding one day, at the head of a small garrison of knights, through a village, and saw a noisy procession of people heading down the road in our direction. They came to a stop as they reached the village square. We had stopped our horses there as well and now watched as they lined up in two rows facing each other across the square. A few baskets filled with stones had been placed in front of them.

'A cloud of silence hung over the square, and then, suddenly, there she was, dragged out of a small alley by two men and thrown into the blinding glare of the sun. She fell down but sprang back to her feet and rushed towards the alley but was caught by the men, who threw her back into the square where she fell to the ground again. As she tried to rise I caught a glimpse of her dark eyes staring up at me pleadingly. But before she could get up a flurry of stones were thrown at her and knocked her, face down, into the dirt.

'In that moment when she looked up at me, I saw that she was small and frail and very beautiful. And I knew that there could be only one reason she had been dragged into that square, which was that she had committed adultery. But what can you tell about a person, a complete stranger, in a split instant, when all you can catch of her is, perhaps, just a glimpse of yourself, as if she had managed to drag you down there with her for an instant?

'Before I realised what I was doing, I had already managed to kick my horse forward into the square and was now sitting in my saddle, staring down at her as she lay flat out on the ground.

'No one dared throw a stone in her direction now. I called to my garrison to come over and join me and told one of my knights to dismount, pick her up and hand her to me. I rode out of the village, holding her against me with one arm, and soon life came back into her own arms that she then wrapped around me as she twisted herself into my lap with her hands clinging to my shirt and her face buried in my collar. Her scalp had been cut open and streaks of blood had coagulated in her black hair. The stink of open flesh blended with the scent of perfumed oil and filled my heart with both desire and despair. I could feel her pulsating body as I stared, transfixed, at the city of Jerusalem perched up on the hill far ahead of us.

'That night, I made love to her with an unstoppable passion, and she responded with the unleashed gratitude of someone whose life had been given back to her.'

A long silence filled the room once again. Simon de Montfort seemed to be trapped in the memory of an event that had tarnished the landscape of his life.

'Why am I telling you all this?' he finally said. 'Perhaps because I feel some kind of fraternity between us, as if, despite the huge difference of character that differentiates us, we share something similar.

'I will never forget that girl. I will never forgive myself for what I did to her. In that one night of total abandon, I lost everything.'

There was another long moment during which Marc could think of nothing he could say to Simon that would deliver either of them from the silence and darkness of that room.

Finally, it was Simon who spoke again. 'I know what it is that we share. We have both fallen from grace.'

*

It was a beautiful morning. The sky was a deep blue with white clouds slanting across it like ghostly vessels on a calm sea. The ramparts of Penn could be seen perched on the top of the hill across the river. As Marc stared up at them, a cold wind pushed against his back even while the sun shone down on his face.

'Are you sure about what you are doing?' Simon de Montfort asked.

'I have never been less sure of anything I've undertaken,' replied Marc. 'But it's not going to stop me from going up there.'

'Then go,' Simon said, 'and may you achieve what you came here to accomplish.'

'I will try.' Marc walked through the archway towards the stables, where the boy was waiting with his horse.

'Are you taking no escort?' Simon asked as he followed behind him.

'I'll stand a better chance alone,' Marc replied. 'Captain Roberto and his men will wait for me here, if that is all right with you?'

'Why shouldn't it be? We are all fighting for the same cause, are we not?' Simon said sardonically. He stood watching as Marc settled into his saddle.

'You will never win her back,' he added. 'Whatever she agrees to. You know that, don't you?'

'I don't want to win her back,' replied Marc. 'I just want to bring her and Kore down from there alive.'

'And Tristan?'

'Yes, and Tristan, if it has to be that way.'

'And what will your daughter think of you later,' asked Simon, 'knowing that you accepted having that man in her mother's arms?'

'She will be alive. Whatever she thinks of me, she will be alive to have those thoughts.' Marc kicked his heels into the horse's flanks, set off across the courtyard and disappeared through its main gateway, away from the flaring glare of Simon's eyes. He was wearing a shirt and trousers and a pair of boots, all provided for him by Innocent III, along with a belt and shoulder bag with the Pope's letter inside.

As he trotted along the dusty road that followed the Olt river for a couple of miles to the bridge, he heard a horse galloping up behind him. One of Simon de Montfort's lieutenants had been instructed to escort Marc through the encampments of soldiers surrounding the town. But once he had crossed through the lines of the encircling army – over twenty thousand men – the man pulled up and Marc continued on his own. He was no longer riding his horse, but instead had transferred onto a mule, on the pretext that his horse would most likely be slaughtered and eaten by the starving citizens of Penn as soon as he passed through the town's gates.

The officers who explained this to him seemed surprisingly cheerful and there was generally a light-hearted atmosphere throughout the camp. The men were clearly relieved to see that winter had reached its end, and were looking forward to the fast-approaching day when they would be given orders to take Penn by storm.

So it was that Marc found himself alone on his mule, climbing the rocky road that circled up the hill. He was holding a pole with a white flag flapping at its extremity, staring down at the valley stretching out below him. He noticed that the fields, which should have been ploughed and sown with crops, were overgrown with weeds and thistles. Further up the river, as he had been making his way towards the castle, he had been struck by the beauty of the fields, all covered with a transparent green carpet of freshly sprouted wheat.

But now, the sight of these unploughed fields brought in a sudden cloud of loneliness and doubt, and Simon's voice echoed back to him, repeating the words he had spoken just before showing him to his room the previous night.

'Why don't you just leave her alone, so that she can die in Tristan's arms?'

Had he any right to go up there and ask her to come away with him? Why was he riding up this road, towards the high ramparts of the town perched on the top of this hill, wanting to insinuate himself back into the life of a woman he had sorely let down and had been unable to make happy in any real, lasting way?

He felt exhausted. He had spent the whole night tossing and turning in his bed, battling with strange dreams brought on by the events of the evening. And it was now as if he was seeing himself for the first time just as he was, this pathetic creature sitting on a mule, holding a white cloth at the end of a pole instead of a spear. Had he been overtaken by a desire not to run away from himself any more? He felt humbled by the thought that this was who he really was, and yet for a brief instant he also felt strong, whole, full of courage, the courage to face himself for once.

But, before he could fully catch hold of that moment, it had already vanished.

And now he was going to be confronted with Isolt, and he knew he would need all the strength he had left to persuade her to come out of that town and down the hill with him.

Most of all, he knew that he couldn't afford to entertain any doubts about this mission if he wanted to carry it through. So he pushed Simon's question, unanswered, back into the night from where it had emerged, telling himself that it didn't belong to this day, with its bright sun and cool breeze blowing white clouds cheerfully across the sky above him.

'Hey, stranger! Identify yourself. What is your business here?'

The voice was coming from the tower by the main gate leading into the town, which now loomed close overhead.

'I am Marc, the husband of Isolt. I have come to talk with her!' Marc shouted back. There was no reply from the tower. Marc continued upwards on his mule and covered the hundred or so paces to the town walls. When he reached them, he stopped before the high, arched doorway that locked away the world hiding behind it. A voice shouted once again from the tower, asked him to dismount and take a few paces away from the gate so that he could be seen in the full light of the morning sun. As Marc stood blinking in the bright glare, he could feel himself being watched from one of the loopholes in the tower. After what seemed like a very long time, as if an endless conversation was taking place behind those walls, there was at last the creaking sound of wood and metal as the great doors began to part, creating an opening just wide enough for Marc and his mule to pass through.

He found himself face to face with a group of about twenty men armed with swords and shields. They were not wearing armour, and their clothes were tattered. Their hair was long and uncombed and most of their faces were hidden by beards. Their eyes stared at him with great intensity, as if they were standing on the roof of a burning tower ready to jump off.

She wove her way to the front of the crowd of staring faces. Her hair was brushed back and fell in a braid between her shoulders. Her dress was worn and he noticed a tear under one of her arms. She looked very thin, but her eyes were the same eyes that, out of all the eyes in this world, had once made him feel that he really mattered.

'What are you doing here?' she asked.

'I have come with a letter from the Pope.'

'A letter?' she said with mock indifference. 'And to whom is that letter addressed?'

'To you.'

'To me?' she exclaimed with a flash of surprise.

'Yes, to you,' replied Marc. 'He would like you to read it carefully and to consider what he has to propose to you.'

There was a long silence, during which Isolt looked at him and Marc looked back at her. He was trying hard not to desire her. Trying hard not to fall into that river and be swept away in its current, in the flow that was rushing towards her embrace, as if all the mysteries and unanswered questions in his life, all its longings and disappointments, its deepest fears and highest hopes, could all be drowned by the contact of her body, in the pure pleasure of holding her in his arms, of feeling her breath rising from her ribs, brushing like a hot wind over his face and invading his nostrils as he filled her with his desire.

'I thought you were locked away in prison,' she said finally. 'By what twist of fate are you now the Pope's messenger?' For all those men with their swords held in their hands lined up behind her she was like a tiger, her sharp claws well in evidence.

'Wouldn't it be possible to talk to you in some quieter place?' asked Marc. 'I have so much to explain. If you could listen to me and read the Pope's letter, you would realise how important this is, not only for you but for all the people in Penn.'

'Why can't you explain it to me here, in front of my friends, if it concerns the people of Penn as you claim?'

It is true, Marc thought to himself. She was as irresistible as Ogrin had predicted she would be. What he felt for her right then could not be spoken. It could only be shrieked or hollered, like a wild animal bellowing in the night.

'Look, I'm not asking for much,' he heard himself say. 'Just a little bit of your time in private conversation. Then you can send me on my way if it doesn't interest you. Don't you think you owe me that?'

Isolt stared at him for a moment. Then she turned around and walked over to the man she had been standing beside; only now did Marc realise this was Tristan. The two men on either side also joined in the conversation. Finally, Isolt left them and came over to Marc.

'All right,' she said. 'Come with us and we will take you somewhere where we can talk, just you and me.'

Surrounded by the armed party, with Isolt at his side,

he climbed up a long, narrow alley. Most towns had a strong stink rising from their streets, Marc knew, but this town smelt different. It was less harsh, less pungent, less offensive, as if something had been washed out of it. Perhaps it was the stench of sweating souls battling to cling on to life that made the smell of other towns so offensive. But here, in Penn, they had already given up hope and were only waiting for death. That was it, Marc thought. It is death, slowly approaching and gathering like a cloud over the town that has already thrown a veil over the sharp edges of life.

'How is Kore?' he asked.

'She is fine and well,' Isolt answered. 'There are other girls of her age here to keep her company. Luckily, she does not seem to realise the gravity of our situation.'

'Is she getting enough to eat?'

'Yes, there is still plenty of food,' she replied.

Marc knew this could not be true, for they were all very thin. Even Tristan seemed to have lost the broadness of his shoulders, as if hunger had melted them away.

They stopped in front of a house. Isolt told Marc to follow her and, with Tristan and the other men waiting outside in the street, they entered, climbed to the top floor and walked into a room that was empty apart from four heavy chests. There were two openings in the wall where there once must have been windows. 'You can sit on one of the chests,' Isolt said. 'I'm afraid it's been a hard winter and all the chairs have been used as firewood to cook our food and keep us from freezing. Even the windows have been pulled out, making this room uninhabitable, so we filled these chests with all the books we could save from the fire, hoping we wouldn't need to burn them. Now, go on, sit down here and give me the letter.'

Marc pulled the rolled-up parchment from his bag and handed it over. She took it, sat down, examined it and saw that the seal had been broken. 'Has Simon de Montfort read this already?' she asked.

'Yes,' Marc replied. 'I had to show it to him, otherwise he wouldn't have let me come up here.'

Isolt unrolled the parchment and began to read. He looked at her hands as she held the letter, watching as she pinched it between her fingers and her thumbs. For a brief instant he imagined those same hands pressing against Tristan's naked body as he made love to her, and a flood of outrage filled his heart. He hated her for this, yet he knew Ogrin was right when he'd said that this feeling of betrayal went far back into his life, way before he had even met her. He could not remember when it had started. It just seemed to have always been there, hovering at the periphery of his existence.

And it seemed quite reasonable to believe that this feeling of betrayal had something to do with the time and place of his birth. Did Ogrin not say that the time and place of our birth was like a mood hanging over our lives, pervading our thoughts and activities, which would remain that way unless, one day, it should be awakened into a destiny?

And was this not what had happened when he had met her, and when she had then met Tristan? Had that vague feeling of betrayal not moved from the periphery of his existence to its very core? Had not its glare set fire to his life? And she, because she had placed it at its centre, was she not the pivotal point around which everything in his life was turning?

When she finished reading the parchment, she went back and examined certain passages again. Then, finally, she looked up at Marc.

'I'm sorry, but what he's asking me to do is impossible. I can't abandon everybody here just to save my own skin.'

'But he's not asking you to do that!' Marc protested.

'He says that Tristan and I will be saved if we confess and

repent of our sins and, of course, Kore will be saved as well. But as for the inhabitants of Penn, he says only that he hopes our gesture will lead them to surrender peacefully and that clemency may be shown to them as well. He is deliberately vague about this and gives no guarantee for their safety.'

'He is only trying not to offend Simon de Montfort by not seeming to be imposing his rule on the direction the campaign takes down here,' replied Marc. 'But he clearly states that he wishes...'

'Simon de Montfort is not going to pay any attention to what he wishes,' Isolt interrupted. 'Did you see what he did to that poor man he sent up here on a donkey?'

'Yes, I'm afraid I was a witness to that.'

'And you still think I should leave these people to that kind of fate, while I go and confess in Rome?'

'What good will it do them if you needlessly die at their side?' Marc replied.

'No good at all,' she said. 'But you have not shared your life with these people for the last six months. You have not laughed with them, day after day, to chase away the cold in your bones and the pain of not having filled your stomach with enough food. There is only one well in this town. The other two are outside the town walls and too dangerous to get to, if you don't want to be shot down by de Montfort's archers. So we were always thirsty as well. If a week went by without any rain, we all began to worry because we knew that the well could dry up and it would be over for us. And yet, through all this, not one child in the town was ever treated by any of the inhabitants as if it were not their own, and wherever that child may have been, if he or she happened to be very thirsty at that time, there would always be a cup of water to quench their thirst.

'Now, do you think I'm going to abandon these people after what we have been through together? Do you think I'm going to walk out of here and leave them behind?'

As Marc looked at her, her eyes shining, her hair pulled tightly away from her face, her lips slightly parted showing the slight gap between her two front teeth, he saw that nothing, no amount of deprivation, could tarnish her special kind of beauty. It was a beauty that stuck to her, like something from outside this cruel world, in defiance of its hard, ruthless brutality.

'All right!' Marc said. 'I'll get de Montfort to write a letter. In it he will give his word that no reprisals shall be brought against the people of Penn if they surrender their town peacefully to him.'

Isolt looked at Marc with a puzzled frown on her face. 'You think you could do that?' she asked.

'Yes,' Marc said. 'I think I can.'

Isolt shook her head. 'Even if you could, what meaning would it have? A man like Simon de Montfort would never feel bound by any promise he made, even if it were written down in a letter.'

'Yes he would!' Marc cried. 'He can't win this war down here without the Pope's blessing. He needs him, both financially and morally. I have been escorted here by twenty of the Pope's guards and by the captain in charge of them. I will make sure that he is a witness to this letter. With the Pope's captain as a witness, Simon de Montfort would not dare go back on his word.'

Isolt looked at him again with the same puzzled frown. 'Why have you really come here?' she asked.

'Why do you think?'

Isolt shook her head. She seemed to be staring right through Marc, as if all she could see were the empty walls of the room.

'Can't you understand?' she asked. 'Can't you imagine how hard it is? This mad rush forward into the world with all its delights and wonders, all its agony and pain, tossing you up and down as if you were on a galloping horse. Because all the attitudes and opinions you felt so sure about are no longer there to hold on to when you suddenly realise that all this is coming to an end, that your journey is over.'

Isolt lifted her arms, holding the palms of her hands wide open, exposing them to the bare emptiness of the room. 'I have never done what I really wanted to do. Tristan made me see that. I was always just following rules laid down by other people, first by the nuns and then by my father, or whoever he really was.'

Isolt hesitated, as if she was reluctant to say what followed. 'Of course, during the short spell when we were working the markets together in Italy, my father taught me a lot, but he never taught me how to think for myself. It was Tristan who taught me that.

'And now, through circumstances beyond our control, we are here, prisoners in this town awaiting our fate, and the one thing I have had to confront by myself is the inevitability of death, how you can either run away and try to escape from it, or how you can stand and face it with a peaceful heart when it confronts you. For this is the fate awaiting us at this moment up here.

'And yet, to me, it now seems that I have reached the top of the mountain. That, at last, I can sit straight in my saddle, because the end of my life is standing right before me and I can accept it.'

She shook her head again. There were tears in her eyes. 'Why have you come here, Marc? Why do you want to take this away from me?'

She brought her hands up to her face and Marc noticed how her body was shaking as she sobbed silently into her open palms. He watched aghast, not knowing what to do or say.

'Isolt!' he finally said, but she did not answer. 'Isolt, listen to me. I don't want to take anything away from you. Once you have confessed in Rome, you can go away with Tristan and take Kore with you if that's what you want. I will not try to hold on to you.

That's not what I want to do. I want you to be happy. As long as I know that you and Kore are alive and well, that's all I need. I don't want anything else.

'So at least let me try! Let me go back to Simon de Montfort and get that letter from him. All you have to do is persuade the citizens of Penn to accept his terms for their surrender, which I will bring back with me by tomorrow. We can do this together, you and I.'

As Marc looked at her he felt lost and bewildered. She remained bent forward with her face buried in her hands, one foot sticking out from under her long dress, and he realised that she had not been wearing any shoes. This seemed to make things even worse, to throw a dark cloud over his already troubled heart.

He also noticed that she had dropped the letter written by the Pope, which was now lying on the floor by her foot. He bent forward to pick it up, rolled it, opened his shoulder bag and was about to drop it in there when he noticed something dimly glowing at the bottom of the bag. He reached down and felt something soft.

Marc's heart jumped as he stared at the red rose he held in his hand, its petals folded together as if it had been sleeping in the darkness at the bottom of his bag. This was undoubtedly the same flower that Ogrin had handed him in his dream, and the thought of this was so overwhelming that Marc could feel his hand shaking and had to rest the rose on his thigh and then place both his hands on his knees to steady himself.

Isolt's hands fell away from her face as she straightened up her back, and, sitting upright on the wooden trunk, stared straight into Marc's eyes. 'Say something to me Marc, say something real and I will follow you.'

'What do you want me to say?' Marc asked, realising how pathetic that sounded.

'It doesn't matter what you say as long as it comes from you. As long as it is real.'

Although he could hear his voice pronouncing the words he spoke, Marc could not be sure if he was still in the room with Isolt or if he had fallen back into the dream in which Ogrin had handed him the flower.

'You know, Isolt, when I was shut away in that dungeon I had time to think about the moments we spent together, the good times and the bad times. But the moment I would go back to over and over again was that moment when you told me you were in love with Tristan. Even though I could feel that something had gone wrong between us and was prepared to hear what you had to say, after I saw you standing up against Tristan in the moonlit courtyard, whispering to him, when you actually said it it still came as an enormous shock, something I could never have been prepared to hear.

'And yet it was the most fateful moment in my life, as if everything I had ever lived was a preparation leading me up to this. As if I had come into the world to live this moment. And I realised in the loneliness of my cell, listening to the whispers of the passing seasons riding on the breeze that would blow through the bars of the small window high up on the wall; I realised that this moment you had brought me to was the only moment that still cried out in me, that could still awaken me from my sleep, that was still alive, as if all my other moments had died and dissolved into the silence of my cell.'

Marc sighed, managed a wry half smile, stood and walked away from the love of his life.

*

When Marc arrived back at the castle that afternoon, he found Simon de Montfort with a group of men in the courtyard. They were all in armour and watching two men sparring in a mock battle. They looked at him with amusement as he dismounted from his mule.

'Ah! Our emissary has returned!' Simon said jokingly. 'I see he has changed his mount.'

One of the men said something that Marc did not understand and they all laughed.

'Come over here and tell us the results of your negotiation,' Simon called out.

As Marc walked over, he realised that he was fighting back a feeling of shame and embarrassment, and this made him angry. He remembered Ogrin's advice that he must try to feel sympathy for Simon when dealing with him.

'Hello, Simon,' he said. 'Perhaps I should wait until you have finished your combat practice and talk to you then?'

'Oh no! Let us hear of their response to that letter. We are all impatient to find out,' Simon said with the same forced good humour.

'Well, they agree to surrender,' Marc said. He saw something flare up in Simon's eyes, only to be instantly pushed aside and replaced with a smile as he turned to his friends.

'You see! What did I tell you? This man is a real master when it comes to striking a bargain. He offers them a horse and they give him a mule in return.' Simon looked back at Marc. 'They will surrender whether they agree to or not,' he said angrily. 'They have no other choice. It is just a matter of time.'

'I am no expert in these matters,' Marc said, 'but it seems to me that they have the means and the determination to fight this thing out to the very end, if they have to.'

'And on what do you base this evaluation?' Simon asked.

'They still have food to last for quite some time and their well has plenty of water in it. And they have faith in their leaders,' Marc replied.

'And who might those leaders be?'

'You know very well,' Marc replied. 'Tristan and Isolt.'

'And Isolt?' Simon asked with mock surprise.

'Yes,' Marc answered. 'Perhaps I should have mentioned her name first, for she is the one everybody seems to trust and turn to for guidance. She is the one who convinced everyone that they should surrender peacefully on condition that you agreed that no reprisals would be exacted on any one of them.'

'And when did I agree to that?' Simon asked, raising his eyebrows to emphasise his astonishment.

'You haven't yet,' Marc said. 'I am simply giving you the terms they have set for a peaceful surrender of the town. There are only a dozen or so members of the Cathar clergy among them. The rest are simply followers of the faith or sympathisers who would rather hang on to their lives and give up their faith than die in the flames of a bonfire. But, if they must die at your hands anyway, then they would rather die fighting.'

'And what of Tristan?' Simon asked. 'Has he agreed to surrender his sword, follow you to Rome and see Isolt return to your bed?'

'Yes, he has.'

'Then what kind of man is he?' replied Simon in bemusement. 'This great warrior, whose prowess on the battlefield is sung by troubadours all across this land? And it is not only his talent with the sword that they praise in their songs, but they also sing of his other skill, the one he put to full use when he conquered Isolt's heart. And you are telling me he is now willing to surrender both his sword and Isolt without putting up a fight, as if he were a gentle lamb? Well, I don't believe you!'

'It is true, nonetheless,' said Marc. 'I have his seal, at the bottom of the written terms for the surrender of the town, right here to prove it.'

'And who gave him a signet?' Simon exclaimed. 'The Duke de Foix, I suppose! It was his reward for ambushing and slaughtering three hundred good Christians who were coming to join forces with me. Well, if what you say now is true, then I no longer consider Tristan to be a man. No creature is worthy to be called a man who is willing to toss aside all that he has valued and fought for, just for the saving of his own hide. That is not the behaviour of a real man, whatever his origins. If he cannot hold on to his convictions in the face of death, then he is no better than an animal.

'And why should I accept his seal as proof of anything? A monkey with a ring can put his seal on a parchment, but would anyone lend it any value? And if he has agreed to your terms, then in my eyes he is no better than a monkey, and is certainly not a real man.'

Marc looked at Simon and saw that his eyes were shining brightly. He knew from the events of the previous night that this could signal a sudden and imminent act of violence and decided to back off for the moment.

'Perhaps we should talk about this at a more appropriate time,' said Marc. 'I don't want to interrupt your practice any longer. Perhaps you will accord me a few moments later on, so that I can explain matters to you more fully?'

'There is nothing more to explain,' Simon shouted as Marc walked away. 'If they want to surrender then let them surrender, and I shall deal with them as I see fit to. I will not negotiate the surrender of a town with a woman, nor will I with someone whose behaviour falls short of what you would expect from a real man.

'So you can go back there and tell them that I accept their surrender. But if they have anything they want to negotiate with me, let them send somebody other than Tristan or Isolt to do so.'

Marc did not even answer. He went over to his mule, took hold of its reins and walked it over to the stables.

'What happened to your horse, sire?' the stable boy asked.

'He's being looked after in the encampment,' replied Marc. 'I'll get him back tomorrow.' Then, looking beyond the drawbridge, he saw two men juggling with wooden pins in a field where a number of caravans were parked.

'Who are those men?' he asked.

'They are part of a troupe of troubadours and acrobats who are going to perform at the castle tonight,' the boy replied.

'Is this in honour of some special occasion?'

'All I've been told is that Simon de Montfort is welcoming many important guests tonight for a feast.'

Marc walked over to the drawbridge, leant against one of the supporting pillars of the doorway and watched the two men as they tossed the pins to each other. There were six pins in all, and they had to keep throwing and catching them to keep them flying through the air.

Simon has decided on a delaying tactic, Marc thought. He has already managed to make a fool out of me, by arranging to deprive me of my horse and having me ride on that mule, but this is only the beginning. He must have many more tricks hidden up his sleeve that he is waiting to play on me.

A dark cloud, which he could feel creeping up on him, was already weakening his resolve. The wave of inspiration that had come to his rescue when Isolt had asked him to tell her something real had returned to its hiding place and now left him once again in the company of his confusion and despair.

Marc turned away from the two jugglers and walked back across the courtyard. He needed to sit down somewhere quiet to think things through. As he passed the group of knights, who were continuing their combat practice with Simon, he decided to ignore them and headed towards the far wall, where a gateway led into the terraced garden overlooking the river.

He found a bench by some bushes and sat there, warming himself in the afternoon sun. He still didn't understand what had come over him to make him say the things that he had said to Isolt up there in the town of Penn.

It seemed to him that he had been lifted up into another reality, one that did not belong to the world he had now returned to down here in the valley where those words would sound pathetic, grotesque even. Yet, in the context of the besieged town on the mountain, where this other reality had attached itself to the lives of the people held prisoner up there, those words had a power, were held together by an unshakeable certainty, a beauty even.

As he sat on this bench down here in the valley he was caught up in another reality, the one represented by the card that symbolised one of the three forces that made up our being and that had taken over our world down here, the card that Ogrin had named The City of God.

Marc leant forward with his face buried in his hands, feeling tired and lost and no longer knowing what he could do to change Simon's mind. From some distance away he heard the sound of laughter. He tried to regain his composure, for he could now see three women walking down the path that followed the wall along the edge of the terrace. They were coming in his direction.

As they approached, Marc thought he recognised two of the ladies as members of the group gathered around the fireplace in the castle last night. But he did not recognise the figure walking between them.

She was older than the other two, though her hair, woven into a braid, was still black. So, too, were her eyes, in contrast to her pale face, which carried the lines of her age.

'Good evening, sire,' she said. 'I am Alix de Momerancy, Simon's wife. My companions tell me that you are Marc, King of Brittany.'

Marc stood, bowed, and took a deep breath before replying.

'I was indeed, my lady. Though I'm afraid it would be more appropriate to call me "The king without a kingdom" now, to quote your husband.'

'Did he really say that?' she asked, feigning surprise.

'He was only speaking the truth,' Marc answered.

'Well, that is one of his qualities,' she replied, 'though he can, at times, be quite blunt and lacking in delicacy.' The two women at her side smiled and giggled discreetly.

This lady pleasantly surprised Marc. He liked her warmth, her friendliness and the way her eyes seemed to hide a deep intelligence behind their customary cheerfulness.

'I must say, my lady, that I am surprised to find you here at your husband's side on this rugged campaign.'

'This land is full of contrasts,' she replied with a smile. 'It may be harsh, rugged and brutal for the men who have to do the fighting, but there is another side to it that is far gentler, far sweeter and more delicate than anything you would find up in the north. Just take a look at this garden. Have you ever seen anything that is so soft on the senses, so quietly beautiful? Is there anything to compare with it around Paris or in Normandy, or even in your own Brittany?'

Marc let his eyes move around the garden. Behind him, jutting out from the wall, was a slanting roof supported by stone arches. People must have once sat there taking shelter from the hot summer sun, or from the rain, but now the benches appeared old and forgotten. A gnarled vine climbed up one of the arches and spread out along the edge of the roof, with only one or two of its grape-like flowers hanging down from the top of the arches like purple bells lost in a jungle of green leaves. The few remaining bushes planted along the pathway had blossomed into flower and were busy with the flights of butterflies and bees. Beneath the terrace wall, the Olt river flowed down along the valley, shaded by tall trees. A clear, almost mocking whistle echoed across the river and, from the top of one of the trees, a bright yellow bird flew over the fields and towards the encampment of the besieging army. Marc looked towards the hill, at the top of which could be seen the ramparts of Penn, and thought again of the room with the gutted windows where Isolt had asked him to say something real to her.

He looked back at the garden, slightly puzzled by Alix de Momerancy's enthusiasm for a beauty that seemed to have deserted this place, probably through neglect due to the ravages of the past six years.

And then he thought of Melissa, Isolt's mother. He thought about how Ogrin, through seeing her hands, had been confronted suddenly with the beauty that had been stolen away from her by that terrible accident when, still a little girl, she had fallen off the cliff.

And, in a flash, he realised this was what must have happened to this woman now standing before him. She must have seen something in this garden that was unaffected by all that neglect, which still carried a fragment of the garden's lost beauty. A butterfly resting on the flower of one of the remaining bushes, perhaps.

Marc felt her hand come to rest on his forearm. There was amusement and kindness in her eyes. 'Don't be put off by my husband's harshness and brutality,' she said. 'I can tell you one thing. He likes you. I think he sees that you understand him and feels that, just maybe, you can help him find his way back home.'

With this final enigmatic sentence she gave a slight squeeze to his arm and then walked away, her two companions at her side.

A short while later, Marc was walking back across the now deserted courtyard, out through the archway towards the caravans in the field. The two jugglers were no longer there, but a man with bushy white hair and a prominent belly under his brown velvet vest was standing in the door of one of the caravans.

'Good day, sir,' Marc said to him. 'Are you one of the artists who will entertain us tonight?'

'Yes, my friend,' the man answered. 'My name is Jean Latour. I am a musician, poet and performer of tricks by trade. Are you a member of Lord Simon de Montfort's household?'

'No,' replied Marc. 'I am just a visitor. However, I would very much like to perform a little trick of my own tonight. But I would need your cooperation.'

The man looked at Marc dubiously.

'Of course I would like to oblige,' he said, 'but I have heard that Simon de Montfort has a quick temper. I would not wish to be involved in anything that might cause offence to him.'

'You are quite right about his quick temper,' Marc answered. 'But you must also have heard that he is a good sport and not at all averse to a little amusement, even at his own expense. But rest assured, what I wish to do would in no way be offensive. I simply wish, in some form of disguise, to appear to be a member of your troupe and to offer, once you have finished your performance, my services as a fortune teller and thus read the palm of Madame Alix de Momerancy, Simon de Montfort's wife. I simply wish, in this way, to cause some amusement and also to use this occasion to flatter her husband. As you can see, it would all be quite harmless.'

The man in the doorway was still hesitating. It was not the first time he'd been asked by the host of such an occasion, or one of its guests, to include one of their poems in the repertoire of songs to be sung or, even worse, to have to accompany the host or a guest on the lute while they sang one of their songs themselves. As embarrassing as these impromptu performances could turn out to be, Jean Latour also knew from experience that they also had the potential to cause great amusement to the friends and family of the performer who, deeply flattered by his own prowess, would show his appreciation with a generous tip afterwards.

'Of course I would like to help,' he said, 'but in order to carry off something like this effectively you need a good disguise. For if you are recognised then the whole purpose of your endeavour will be defeated before you even get started.'

'Of course, and that's precisely where I thought you might be able to help me,' Marc said.

Latour rubbed his chin with his thumb and forefinger and looked at Marc thoughtfully. 'Well, if I were to shave and powder your face, dress you in women's clothes and give you a healthy bosom under your dress, I think we could make you unrecognisable, even to your closest friends. Then, of course, I would have to show you how to raise your voice to a higher pitch without dropping it as you speak. And, of course, all the time I'm going to spend doing this I should really be using to practise my own performance.'

'Rest assured that I will reward you generously for your trouble,' Marc insisted. 'And I suppose you must be a follower of the Catholic faith, otherwise you would not be entertaining the host of this castle. Is that not so?'

'It is most certainly so!' Latour said, straightening his back and making the sign of the Cross to prove it.

'Well then,' Marc said, 'I have been sent here by His Grace Pope Innocent III, on a special mission, accompanied by twenty of his guards, and I will not forget your name when I report back to His Grace. He will hear about Jean Latour and of how he helped me flatter Simon de Montfort so that he would lend a sympathetic ear to the cause I have come to defend.'

The man's eyes opened wide. 'Is that really so? You're not pulling my leg?'

'Of course not,' Marc answered. 'You may ask anyone belonging to the castle if there is not here, at this present time, a messenger sent by the Pope, accompanied by twenty of his guards.'

'And you would really mention my name to His Grace?'

'Yes, of course, if you help me,' Marc answered.

'Then you could have found no better man than Jean Latour to help you out. I will dress you up in a perfect disguise.'

*

Later that evening the guests assembled in the great hall, their plates filled with roast boar and venison and their cups with wine. Simon de Montfort, who was sitting with Alix at his side at the top of the U-shaped table that stretched along three of the walls, searched in vain amongst his guests for Marc.

'Where is that devil?' he said aloud to himself.

'Who?' Alix asked, having overheard him.

'Marc.'

'Oh, you mean King Marc of Brittany?'

'Yes!' said Simon irritably. 'Where the hell has he gone to? He can't have gone back up to Penn already.'

Simon called over to Captain Roberto. 'Hey, Roberto! Have you seen Marc at all?'

'No, my lord, not recently,' replied the captain. 'I only caught a glimpse of him on his return from Penn this afternoon.'

'Then where the devil has he got to?' Simon asked once again.

'Don't worry,' his wife said. 'He can't be far away. He simply has other things to worry about and is not in the mood for feasting.'

'Then he's a fool!' Simon muttered as he stuck his fork into a piece of meat.

Sitting to his right were the Count of Lacausade and his wife. The count now rose from his chair and tapped on a silver cup to gain everyone's attention. When most of the faces in the hall had turned expectantly in his direction, he began to address them.

'My lords and ladies, please excuse me for interrupting your conversation, but I think it is time we raise our cups and drink to the health and good fortune of our host, Simon de Montfort.'

There was a murmur of approval from the guests as they smiled politely in Simon's direction.

'I first met Simon in Jerusalem, where he had come to fight the Muslim heathens for possession of that most holy of cities, which had just been reconquered by our enemy. So this is not the first time that this man, sitting among us today, has put his life at risk in defence of the Christian cause. When Simon returned from Jerusalem, had he been an ordinary man he could well have chosen to spend the rest of his days honourably tending his quite considerable estates in the North of France, and occupied himself with the welfare of his family.

'But Simon is no ordinary man, and when His Grace Pope Innocent III called for help to put a stop to the increasing abomination of heretic ceremonials and growing congregations that were spreading like a plague down here in this beautiful country of ours, Simon was among the first to pick up his sword and rush to our rescue.

'And so, my dear Simon, in raising our cups to you, let this gesture express our gratitude for all you have done for us, and also our unflinching support for the cause you are defending here. To your good health, Simon de Montfort!'

There was loud banging on the table and hearty cheers as everyone lifted their cups and swallowed some wine.

It was Simon de Montfort's turn now to stand up. He waited for the clamour to die down so he could speak. 'Thank you all very much,' he said loudly. 'How touching it is to see you raising your cups to toast this most Holy Crusade we are fighting here. I am fully aware that the battles we have fought have been harsh and cruel, but I am also aware that, in fighting such an evil as these heresies, there is a danger that in the intense heat of battle some of the values that characterise the faith that we are so fervently defending may be neglected. I speak of the friendship and of the brotherhood of all the many people who are united under this faith. So, let us tonight rejoice together in each other's company and strengthen this friendship that comes from sharing a common faith, which is being so severely challenged in these hard times.'

As de Montfort sat down to more applause and more banging on the table, he signalled to a footman at the rear of the hall, who disappeared through a side doorway. Moments later, Jean Latour walked through the same doorway and into the hall, strumming a sweet melody on his lute. A young, barefoot woman accompanied him with a tambourine, which she clapped against her hand in rhythm to the tune while jumping and kicking out her legs in a dance.

Marc stood in an alcove where a circular stairway climbed up into a tower, watching the bustle of valets and kitchen girls rushing to and fro with platters on their way between the kitchen and the dining hall. The two acrobats and jugglers were also standing chatting, listening with one ear to Jean Latour's voice as he sang so that they would know when he was about to finish and be ready to make their entrance.

Marc was breathing heavily and he could feel his heart pounding inside his chest, which was strapped with padding to create the effect of a woman's bosom under his dress. When the young woman had tried to make up his face with white powder, Jean Latour had looked at him, studied the result of her endeavours and finally shook his head.

'It won't do,' he had said, and had gone over to an old chest in his caravan and fished out a white mask that, he told Marc, had been used by the nobility of a castle near Limoges to play a game they called charades. The delicate shape of its face, as well as its extreme pallor, gave it a strongly feminine aspect and, with a shawl covering his head and falling down over his shoulders, no one could tell that he was not a woman.

But what on earth was he doing all dressed up, waiting to walk out into the dining hall and pass himself off as a fortune teller? It was all completely crazy! What had got into him? It was all because of Alix de Momerancy and the last words she had spoken in the gardens overlooking the river before she took leave of him. These words had made a deep impression on him and had finally convinced him that he could do just what she had said: help him to find his way back home...

After all, wasn't this what he most wanted for himself? To find his way back home. To find his way back to those first years he and Isolt had spent together, when she had seemed to be in love with him, when he had married her and become the father of her child. Those first years, when he was still under the spell of her sudden, miraculous appearance into his life, a life in which he seemed to be walking through a dream.

And, if he so longed to find his way back there, shouldn't he be the one to also help Simon find his way back to where he wished to be? To that time when, still a young knight, he had thought of himself as embodying the prime values of virtue and courage as he set off on the crusade to reconquer Jerusalem.

So there he was, dressed up in the most absurd costume he could ever imagine wearing, about to walk out in front of a crowd of strangers and, most likely, make a total fool of himself as he tried, through the pretence of reading Simon's wife's palm, to somehow reawaken her husband into that state of grace.

Finally, after waiting for what seemed like an hour inside his absurd costume while the jugglers and acrobats took turns rushing in and out of the dining hall, to punctuate Latour's songs and poems with their tricks and exploits, he heard the minstrel announce in a loud pompous voice: 'My lords and ladies, before taking leave of you, we have one final treat for your pleasure and entertainment. Her name is Princess Nefertiti. She comes from far away in Egypt, where she was taught the ancient art of reading a person's fortune from the way the lines are disposed on the palms of his or her palm.

'As is the tradition of the mystic East, she will perform this reading with her face hidden behind a mask and with her hands clothed in gloves to shield herself from any personal contact. This will allow her to concentrate all her attention and feelings on the lines of the hand. And so, my lords and ladies, I give you now... Princess Nefertiti!'

'What kind of silly superstitious nonsense are we going to witness now?' Simon asked his wife.

'Wait and see, my lord,' she said. 'It might be quite entertaining.'

As Marc walked into the dining hall, through the holes in his mask he could see a long row of faces on both sides of him, all looking his way, and all at once he remembered an incident that had happened when he was a little boy. He had put on one of his cousin's dresses and had gone down to the kitchen, where the valets and the cooks were having their meal, and they had all stared at him.

A man from the town, who had delivered salt to the castle, was sitting eating with the rest of them. 'Oh, aren't we a pretty little girl?' he had said, and what until then had been just a silly prank instantly became the source of deep embarrassment. It was as if, for the first time, he was setting his own limits, as if an inner voice was telling him he should not cross that line again.

And yet here he was, thirty years later, on the other side of that line. This time, however, there was no inner voice to hold him back, so he took a few brave steps forward and curtsied three times to include all the onlookers. He then walked over to a group of young knights, who were whispering mockingly to each other as they watched him. He reached over, took the hand of the youngest-looking one and pulled it towards him, but the young knight resisted and tried to pull his hand loose.

'Don't be afraid, my lord, I'm not going to bite it,' Marc said in a high-pitched voice. 'I only want to have a look at your lines.'

The knight's companions laughed and urged him on, goading him to let the woman read his palm. Marc pulled the hand to him once again and turned its palm up so he could examine it. He then pushed it away and let go, shaking his head.

'No, it's not the hand I'm looking for,' he said. There was a loud 'Ahh' of disappointment as he walked away from the knight and up along the table. Marc was relieved that the tone of his voice had not sounded too unnatural.

A man offered him his hand as he passed, but as he was sitting next to a priest with a mean look of disapproval on his face, Marc ignored him. Then, as if suddenly seeing the person he was searching for, he hastened his step and headed up to the far end of the hall, where Simon de Montfort was sitting. He stopped in front of Alix de Momerancy and stretched his hand out to her.

'My lady, may I look at your hand?'

'But of course, Princess,' she answered, stretching out her hand so Marc could take it in his. 'I offer it to you with pleasure if you will read my fortune.'

'This is the hand I was looking for!' Marc exclaimed as he examined it. 'A hand whose lines are drawn as if they were mapping out the path of the constellations through the sky. A hand with a true destiny written on it.'

Alix de Momerancy laughed.

'I sense that I am being somewhat flattered right now,' she said.

'Not at all,' Marc protested. 'I am only voicing what I see in your hand. There is a great destiny written there that raises it far above an ordinary hand.'

'So let us hear what that destiny consists of,' Alix requested, and Marc could see a soft, gentle amusement in her eyes that made him feel reassured, as if the strangeness of this invented creature he was impersonating was familiar to, or accepted by, at least one person in this great hall of staring faces. This sense of acceptance enabled him to let go of his embarrassment.

'So, let me tell you a story that, I think, will reflect that destiny back to you in a way that will allow you to recognise yourself in it. It is about a lady who lived in a castle with a magical garden that had, at one time, been so beautiful that no one could ever look at it and have any doubts that the world was of a divine nature, even if their lives were beset with pain and sorrow. For, from that moment onwards, that pain and sorrow would affect only their bodies while their hearts would forever remain lost in the memory of that garden.

'Now, at one time, long ago, everybody knew of this garden and would pay it a visit, as it was at that time open to all the people of the land. But gradually, because of neglect, because of wars and invasions and changing attitudes, it seemed that the people lost the ability to see the beauty of the garden.

'And so, for the greatest number of them, their lives seemed to be nothing but pain, sorrow and misery. Because of this, a heresy began to spread amongst the people of that land, which claimed that the God who had created this world was a false God, and it was even suggested by some that he might be the Devil.

'Well, the lady who lived in the castle had, in fact, come there with her husband, a noble knight who had been sent to this land to wipe out the heresy that was spreading like a plague there. As for the garden in the castle, its magical nature and its supposed great beauty had long been forgotten.

'And so, when the newly arrived lady first stepped through its gate and stood as if thunderstruck by the beautiful sight before her, she was the first person in many hundreds of years to have been affected by it in this way. But the problem was that no one else could see this beauty, even when she tried to draw other people's attention to it. Even her husband, who was a noble and honest man, could not see it when she brought him there and tried to open his eyes to what stood before her...'

'Isn't it time, Princess, that we discovered who is hiding behind that mask?' broke in Simon de Montfort, who for some time had been looking at him with growing curiosity. 'So why don't you take it off?'

'If I were to do so, my lord, I could no longer go on reading your wife's palm,' Marc answered, still holding Alix de Momerancy's upturned hand.

'Well, I think that might be quite a good idea,' replied Simon, 'since your voice is jumping up and down from high to low as if you were no longer sure if you are a princess or a prince. So why don't you just let go of my wife's hand and remove your mask? It will be far more amusing for everyone here to see who is really hiding behind that mask than to have to go on listening to your dreary story. After all, we have come here tonight to amuse ourselves.'

'Well then, my lord,' Marc said in desperation, 'perhaps you will permit me to ask your wife if it is also her wish that I stop reading her hand and remove my mask?'

'By all means,' Simon answered, but Marc did not get the chance to raise his question because Alix de Momerancy, gently releasing her hand from Marc's hold on it, spoke immediately.

'I'm afraid I quite agree with my husband,' she said. 'We are here tonight to have fun. And since you are wearing a mask that is used in the game of charades, I suggest my husband asks you a series of questions about yourself, other than directly asking you who you are, of course. To these questions – no more than five, let us say – you must answer either yes or no. And if no one can guess your identity after that, then you can go on reading my hand. What do you think of that, my lord?' she asked, turning to her husband.

'That sounds like it could be very amusing, my lady. But, of course, we would have to be assured that the answers the Princess gives to my questions are truthful. So why doesn't she take some kind of oath to reassure us?' Simon suggested.

Everything is lost, Marc thought in a panic. He knows who I am. And he is going to make full use of this game of charades to ask me some very awkward questions. That's why he wants me to take an oath, because he wants to hold me to the truth and use these five questions to make an utter fool out of me.

'Are you going to take that oath, Princess?' Simon urged.

'Yes, of course, my lord,' Marc replied. 'Very well then, I hereby swear, and may God be my witness, that I, Princess Nef...'

'No, no,' Simon interrupted. 'The whole point is that we don't know if you are Princess Nefertiti or not. So if you take an oath using her name and it turns out you are not Princess Nefertiti, you will not be held by that oath. So, just refer to yourself as "I who stand behind this mask" and so on.'

'All right,' Marc said, feeling drops of sweat pouring from behind his mask, down along his neck and into his dress. 'I, who stand behind this mask, do solemnly swear before God that all my answers to your questions will be the truth.'

'Very good, now we can start.' Simon rubbed his chin. 'My first question is quite simple and you shouldn't have too much trouble answering it. Are you a man or a woman?'

'A man,' Marc answered.

There was a loud uproar of claps and whistles from all the guests, many of whom had surely guessed that this grotesque effigy of a woman standing amongst them must surely be a man.

Hearing 'her' confirm what they already suspected somehow turned the seriousness of the palmistry into pure comedy; they laughed freely in expression of their relief.

Simon waited patiently for them to quieten down. Marc was looking at him through the slits in his mask and could see the cruel smile on his face. He is going to use Isolt to humiliate me, he thought. This was not so very hard to foresee, but what was really surprising was the feeling that rose up from his chest along with this thought. It was a feeling of hope, of release, though he couldn't understand why.

When silence fell, Simon spoke again. 'My second question is, are you married?'

'Yes,' Marc answered and already knew what would come next.

'My third question is, has your wife shared a bed and given herself to a man other than yourself since you have been married?'

Loud cheers and whistles resounded through the dining hall. Marc felt something flare up inside him. At first he thought it was the flush of blood before an eruption of anger. But when he closed his eyes to catch hold of himself, to his amazement he saw the image of Isolt standing on the White Moor with a holy relic lifted high above her head.

'You're not answering me, Princess,' Simon said in a mocking voice, provoking a further outburst of laughter from his guests.

'The answer is no,' Marc said when, at last, the laughter died down.

'No?' Simon repeated. 'Is that really your answer?'

'That is correct. My answer to your question is no,' Marc replied.

'Then you are a liar!' Simon said. 'And all I have to do is tear that mask off your face to prove it.'

There was silence in the hall now as Marc took a step towards Simon de Montfort, removed his glove, leant forward and laid his right hand on the table before him.

'If I am a liar, then you may cut my hand off right here and now. But are you willing to take a wager yourself on whether I speak the truth or not?'

Simon looked at the masked face leaning defiantly over him and for a moment could not hide his surprise. This was the first time since he had taken command of the crusade that anyone had dared challenge him so audaciously other than on the battlefield. Could this really be Marc, the man who had swooned when he had seen him mutilate that traitor the night before? Was this the same man who was now offering his hand to be chopped off should he be shown to be a liar?

For a moment, Simon thought he was losing his hold on reality. He looked up at the masked face leaning across the table, taunting him with its painted, empty smile. Then he looked at all the other faces in the hall, all now looking his way, equally shocked and surprised as he was, and suddenly realised that he had just been challenged to a form of duel. The realisation brought him back onto firm ground.

'Yes, of course I accept the challenge of a wager,' he said loudly. 'Did I not call you a liar?'

'And, if I prove to you that I am not a liar, will you for once show some Christian charity and not take any reprisals or punish, in any way, the inhabitants of Penn when they surrender their town to you tomorrow?'

Simon felt a surge of rage as he stared at the expectant faces of his guests, all waiting for his answer. This buffoon dressed as a woman and hiding behind a mask, crouching down with his hand splayed out on the table, was definitely Marc. Even his voice was now betraying him. But what was his game? What was he trying to achieve? Was he trying to expose his host as a brutal thug by having him cut off his hand in front of all his guests? Or was he foolishly risking his hand on the assumption that his opponent would not dare carry this wager through in front of all those people he was trying to win over as allies?

Of course, the simple solution would be to snatch off his mask right now before agreeing to his terms and expose him as a pathetic liar. But that would be to behave like a poor sport. And besides, he couldn't help feeling a certain admiration for him. He had felt, from the first time he saw him, that he was no ordinary man. And Marc's behaviour right now was only proving him right, which flattered him, for he liked to think that he rarely misjudged a man.

'All right then, I accept your terms,' Simon said finally. 'If you can prove you have not lied, I shall take no reprisals on the inhabitants of Penn when they surrender their town to me tomorrow.'

Marc removed his hand from the table, straightened himself up, untied the shawl from around his head, unstrapped the mask and removed it from his face. As he stood there in a woman's dress, with a bulging chest and with white powder covering his face, the tension and expectation in the hall was released and the guests, feeling the effects of the wine once again, burst into a loud roar of laughter. Simon joined in with them but Marc just stood there with a vague amused smile.

'Well!' Simon said when the laughter had died down. 'Just look at who our exotic princess turns out to be – none other than Marc, the one-time King of Brittany, certainly the most famous cuckold in the whole of France, whose wife's amorous adventures in the arms of Tristan have been sung in practically every court from north to south. And yet he is willing to risk losing a hand in defence of his wife's virtue. How very noble of you, my dear Marc!'

'I was willing to lose my hand if I had lied to you,' Marc answered.

'And what was my question?' Simon asked.

'You asked me if my wife had shared a bed and given her favours to another man since the time of our wedding,' Marc said.

'And has she?' Simon asked.

'No.'

'So you maintain the same answer, even though everyone here knows full well that your wife, Isolt, is at Tristan's side right here, in the town of Penn, which my army has surrounded for the last six months. What are you trying to say? That they don't sleep in the same bed?'

'No,' Marc replied. 'I'm sure they share the same bed.'

'So you want us to believe that, though they share the same bed, your wife's virtue remains intact?'

'I never said that,' Marc said.

'Then how can you not be a liar?' Simon asked in mock desperation, exploiting the moment to its fullest.

'May I ask you a question?' Marc enquired.

'Yes, by all means.'

'Did you not repeat to me several times this afternoon that you did not consider Tristan to be a man?'

'Yes,' Simon said, laughing. 'But I was referring to his lack of courage, not his capabilities in bed.'

'For whatever reason, did you not insist that you did not consider Tristan to be a man, and for that reason refuse to accept the treaty with his seal on it?' Marc asked.

'Yes, but the circumstances...' Simon began, and then hesitated for a moment, searching for the right words to finish his sentence.

'If your answer is yes,' replied Marc, 'then is it not reasonable that, in answer to your question as to whether my wife has slept with another man, I should use as a reference your own interpretation of who is and who is not a man?'

Simon was looking up at him with a vague smile on his face. His eyes were locked into a state of quiet contemplation. Then he replied, in a loud enough voice that all the guests could hear him.

'Well done, Marc. You have just won your wager. So come, sit down and drink with us that we may enjoy your company, for tomorrow is going to be a big day.'

14

THE REPRISAL

She was standing by the window, brushing her daughter's hair. Both their heads turned and looked at him as he entered the room. Kore stood up. She was still a child, but not for very much longer, Marc realised. You could see the beginnings of womanhood in the growing assurance of her posture and in the way she looked at him. Her hair was long and of a reddish colour. Marc got the distinct feeling that he was an intruder into an intimacy in which he no longer had any place, and almost forgot the letter he was carrying in his shoulder bag.

'Marc,' Isolt said, 'come over and say hello to your daughter.'

Marc walked over to the window, bent down and kissed Kore rather awkwardly.

'Hello, Kore,' he said.

'Hello,' she answered, almost swallowing the words as she spoke.

'You both seem embarrassed,' Isolt said with a laugh. 'It's only normal after such a long time. Why don't you sit down, Marc? Kore, make sure you have gathered all the things you want to take with you.' When their daughter had left the room, Isolt sat down opposite Marc and stared at him for a moment.

'So, is it true you dressed up as a woman last night?'

'How did you find out?' Marc asked with surprise.

'One of Simon de Montfort's men came up to the gate and shouted it to the guards early this morning. He said you tricked de Montfort into signing an agreement for a peaceful surrender.'

'He agreed to do so in front of at least a hundred people,' replied Marc. 'So I don't think he can possibly go back on his word, which he's given in the letter I have brought.'

'Let me see it,' Isolt requested.

Marc took the letter out of his bag and handed it over. While she was reading he did not allow any memories or sense of longing to rise up and trouble his heart, but simply sat up straight in his chair proudly awaiting her reaction.

When she had finished reading, Isolt rolled up the parchment and handed it back to Marc.

'You'd better hold on to this,' she said.

'Well?' Marc asked. 'What do you think?'

Isolt took a deep breath and looked into Marc's eyes. 'We're putting ourselves in your hands, Marc. You are going to be responsible for the lives of all the people of this town. Do you think you are up to this?'

Marc sat for a while, still and silent, frozen by an overwhelming feeling inside him. He could hear shouts and hurried steps in the alleyway below and saw big white clouds move across the blue morning sky. He felt sure that whatever happened now could not be avoided. It had to be this way.

'Yes, I feel up to it,' he answered.

*

An hour or so later, the heavy wooden doors built into the ramparts of Penn were opened and Marc, riding his horse, was the first to leave the besieged town. As he slowly made his way down the winding road into the valley, Tristan, Isolt and Kore followed barefoot immediately behind him. And behind them all the noblemen, knights and soldiers – well over a thousand of them, all unarmed, barefoot and wearing no armour – marched in rows of three or four. At the tail end of this long procession came the women and children.

In the town they had left behind them, a mountain of weapons, of swords, spears and shields, of bows and arrows, helmets, steel gloves, chain mail shirts and other pieces of armour, was piled up in front of the church.

As Marc had walked past this mound earlier on, he had noticed a book lying open at the bottom of the pile. He had stopped to pick it up. To his amazement, he discovered that it was a Latin copy of *The City of God* by St Augustine.

Far below in the valley, Simon's men, dressed in armour, were lined up in a field awaiting their arrival. There seemed to be several thousand, of whom nearly half were knights on horseback; the rest, lined up behind them, were foot soldiers. Marc could see their flags displaying the Christian Cross – red on gold, blue on white – flapping in the stream of a new rule, a new order that had come to impose its ways on this land.

Why had he closed the book and dropped it into his bag? He remembered St Augustine's question. 'Can you really love or are you just in love with love?' Maybe the impulse that had prompted him to pick up that book was driven by St Augustine's spirit, to remind him that this question still remained unanswered.

When Marc reached the bottom of the hill, he looked at the long line of knights sitting on their horses. And there, halfway down the field, a lonely figure sat in front of them. It was Simon de Montfort. At the far end of the field there was another, much smaller group of horsemen, lined up in a row that ran perpendicular to Simon's army. Captain Roberto and the Pope's guards.

Marc left the road and led the long line of people across the field, past the row of knights, bringing his horse to a stop when he reached the point where Simon was waiting for him.

'The people of Penn have come down to surrender their town to you,' Marc said. 'They are all unarmed and their weapons are stacked in front of the church.'

'Well done, Marc. Let me compliment you on accomplishing your mission here,' Simon said in a friendly, conciliatory tone of voice. 'You may take Isolt and Kore over to the Vatican guards. I have given them two extra horses for the journey and you may depart for Rome with them whenever you feel ready. I have arranged with Captain Roberto to leave two of his guards behind to bear witness that the surrender of the town proceeds on the terms I have agreed to.'

'We will need an extra horse,' Marc said.

'Why?' Simon enquired. 'Excuse me asking, but we are fighting a war down here and we are not overly supplied with horses at the moment.'

Marc felt as if de Montfort was playing some kind of game with him, but he decided to respond quite innocently. 'It's going to be a long journey. It will be very uncomfortable for Kore if she has to share a horse with her mother all that way,' he said.

'But I've supplied you with two horses,' replied Simon.

'You're forgetting about Tristan,' Marc said.

'No, I'm not. He stays here,' Simon replied and gave a small signal with his hand. As if the whole thing had been rehearsed, twenty knights now moved forward and, with lightning speed, surrounded Isolt, Kore and Tristan. The three huddled together as spears pointed down on them from all sides. Marc felt a sudden rush of desperation invade his heart.

'In his letter, His Grace requests that Tristan comes with us to Rome,' he insisted.

'His Grace Innocent III,' replied Simon, tension rising in his voice, 'does not know that Tristan is directly responsible for the slaughter of three hundred valiant soldiers who were ambushed on their way to join me in our battle to capture this land. If he knew about that, I think he would be as keen as I am to see him punished for his crime.'

'Should we not let His Grace decide about that?' Marc answered.

'No, I'll decide. I'm in charge here.'

'If you will not pay any heed to the Pope's instructions in this letter, then at least you should honour the agreement that followed our wager last night!' Marc shouted.

'I do, and I shall continue to honour it,' Simon replied. 'You need not worry about that.'

'Then you know very well that Tristan has been a resident of Penn just as much as the other men and women who follow behind him. And you have given your word in writing that no reprisals would be taken on any one of them if they were to surrender the town to you.'

'Any man, woman or child; I think it is clearly written in the agreement I signed,' Simon replied, a cruel smile growing on his face. 'It is written that I would not take any reprisals on any man, woman or child who resided in Penn. And, though I would certainly not contest that Tristan has been residing in Penn, I think we both agreed last night, and you were even willing to risk losing your hand on the grounds of this affirmation, that Tristan was not worthy to be considered a man. And, as he is neither a woman nor any longer a child, I don't think he is covered by the agreement I signed.'

As he spoke, three knights dismounted and took hold of Tristan, forcing his arms behind his back and binding his wrists together with a leather strap. The sharp spears pointing at both Kore and Isolt prevented him from offering any resistance.

Marc sat helplessly on his horse and watched, realising how easily he had been tricked. As he stared blankly at Simon, searching for something to say, a voice suddenly whispered in his ear and awoke him from his stupor.

'Leave The City of God behind you.'

'Then cut off my hand!' Marc shouted at him, showing his open palm with outstretched fingers. 'For we all know that Tristan is as much a man as any one of us.'

Simon smiled triumphantly. 'You don't really want me to do that,' he replied. 'If I did, I would no longer be bound by the signed agreement I gave you, for it would mean you had lost your wager. Is that not so?'

'Yes, I have lost my wager! For we all know that Tristan is a man!' Marc repeated, his eyes wild. 'So cut off my hand!'

'It's too late, Marc. You set the terms of this agreement and you can't go back on them now.' Dismounting from his horse, he removed his sword from its sheath. 'Now you have a choice,' he continued. 'You can either take Isolt and Kore over to the Vatican guards and be on your way, or you can stay and watch as I chop off Tristan's head. It will be quick, and he will not suffer, but I rather think you should spare your daughter the pain of such a sight at her tender age.'

De Montfort pushed his way through to Tristan, grabbed him by the hair, and told the two knights to let go of him and hold on to Isolt and Kore instead. He then dragged Tristan forward into the field where all could see him.

'I'm giving you a second chance to die like a man,' said Simon. 'If you stand and take your punishment like a man, I will not harm Isolt or Kore as agreed. So don't force me to break my word.'

Marc jumped off his horse and rushed up to them.

'My hand!' he shouted. 'Take off my hand first. I implore you, Simon. Before God, both you and I know I was lying last night.' He placed himself between Simon, and Tristan, whose bowed head was held tightly in the other man's grip. 'We have been playing a game with each other,' Marc said. 'We have been trying to outwit each other, and you have certainly proved to be the smarter. But as we now stand before God, and in his presence, can either of us say that we don't believe Tristan to be a man? I certainly can't. So here, before God, if you are going to take any reprisals, it is my hand you must cut off first.'

Simon stared at Marc, his eyes glaring as if from some unknown distance.

'So you want to place yourself before God?' he said. 'Is that where you want to place your life now, not hiding behind signed letters and treaties but out here in the open, exposed to God's judgement? Very well then, take my sword.'

'What for?' Marc asked, as Simon pushed the handle of his sword against his chest. 'Just take it.'

'I don't want your sword,' replied Marc. 'I have no use for weapons.'

'And yet you want us to stand before God, to act in the full light of his presence! Take my sword and use it on Tristan!'

'Whatever for?' Marc exclaimed.

'Because he has dishonoured you. He has stolen your wife away from you. In doing so, he has broken one of God's commandments,' Simon shouted.

'That's between him and God. It's not for me to punish him,' Marc said.

'He has stolen your wife! He has dirtied your house! And, as well as you, it is also God he has offended,' Simon said. 'Do you think you can stand here, having called on God to take notice of you and do nothing now to wash this sin from his eyes?'

As he spoke, eyes glaring at him, Marc realised that whoever it was staring out from deep within their depths was not only beyond Marc's reach but also beyond Simon's own. It was some other creature neither of them knew.

'If you believe that,' Simon went on, 'then I will have to kill you and Tristan, your wife and then your daughter so that she does not suffer the cruelty of being alone and an orphan in this world. For I, too, now stand in the glare of God's sight and, just like you, my actions are no longer my own.

'So take my sword, Marc, and do what he asks of you. He may then spare me the pain of having to spill any more blood with my own hands today.'

'Very well, I will have your sword.' Marc stood for a moment with the weapon in his hand. So this is what it is like to be outside in the wilderness beyond the City's walls, he thought. He looked up and saw the white clouds, and felt the cold wind that was pushing them across the blue sky brush against his face. He looked around at the hills that locked in this valley and saw all the eyes that were staring at him, and he remembered the voice that had spoken to him through the clanging sound of bells in that church he had visited in Rome. It was telling him that he wouldn't find God in the images and treasures that were gathered there to honour him, but rather in the suffering and pain outside its walls.

'Marc!' someone shouted. 'Don't let him do this to us!'

Through the shifting bodies of the horses and armour-clad knights, Marc saw Isolt's face staring out at him. He was instantly transported to the moment when he had first set eyes on her in the marketplace, when she had looked up at him as he stood on the church porch.

It was the same face, but somewhere in the lapse of time that separated their life together as man and wife, in Brittany, from this shared moment below the town of Penn, those eyes had

313

acquired something new. It struck him like an arrow shot into his belly that her eyes were staring at him from some newfound depth, the depth of her love for Tristan. It struck him so hard that he froze for a moment, searching for something that would belie this ungodly truth that seemed to rob him of everything they had lived together.

The horses around her were moving backwards and forwards, blocking her out of his vision before reappearing. And then a gap was created that gave him a full view of her as she knelt hugging her daughter in the grass and dirt.

She was staring into a void she had created that was now filling up with her pain. It made her seem older, but it could not rob her face of its beauty. And it was this that touched Marc's heart. It was the thought that her beauty would not surrender to the horror of that moment, and this recognition seemed suddenly like some sacred fact that could stop the world from caving in on itself.

'Lie him down, face to the ground, with his right arm stretched out and hold him there,' Marc said to Simon.

'For God's sake, Marc, what are you doing?' Isolt cried out, but her voice now seemed far away.

'Godfrey and Siprian! Come and give me a hand!' Simon called out and two more knights dismounted from their horses and helped him push Tristan down onto his stomach and untie his hands.

Simon was pinning Tristan's outstretched arm on the grass. With his face buried into the ground, Tristan did not seem to offer any resistance as the three men held him down with the weight of their bodies.

'All right, Marc, get to it,' Simon said.

'No, Marc – don't!' Isolt's voice cried out.

But Marc did not hear either of them. He had just remembered something. He knelt down, placed Simon's sword on the ground, opened up his shoulder bag and pulled out the leather-bound book that he had seen lying on the cobbled pavement in the square as they were leaving Penn.

'What on earth are you doing?' Simon shouted.

Marc said nothing, but simply leant forward and placed the book under Tristan's wrist. He picked up the sword and, still with one knee on the ground, positioned himself at a right angle to Tristan's outstretched arm. Then he lifted the sword high over his head, holding it with both hands.

'Don't move,' Marc whispered before he thrust downwards with all his might. Through the blinding glare reflected from the descending blade, Marc heard someone calling out his name. It was Isolt. And then came the dull thud of the blade coming to a halt on the book under Tristan's wrist.

The first thing Marc saw was the blood that had splashed onto Simon's armour. Then the hand, with crinkled fingers, no longer attached to Tristan's arm, lying in the grass by the bloodstained book.

Simon stood up and the two knights holding Tristan down did likewise, leaving him on the ground gripping what was left of his sliced wrist, trying to stop the blood from flowing out of it. Isolt was shouting, screaming and fighting to break loose from the knight who was holding her. Many of the inhabitants of Penn were running across the field towards the road that led back up to their town.

'What are you waiting for?' said de Montfort to the knights lined up behind him. 'Go after them! And let go of the woman and the girl!'

Isolt came running over and screamed as she saw Tristan writhing on the ground, holding his severed wrist. She pulled the shawl off her shoulders, knelt down and wrapped it as tightly as she could around his upper arm. Tristan looked up at her with disbelieving eyes, his face twisted with pain.

'Don't worry, I'm going to stop the bleeding,' she said and ran over to a clump of plants with thick, spongy leaves.

Simon mounted his horse and rode over to where Marc was standing. 'Get him out of here,' he ordered. 'I don't want to see any of you hanging around here any more. You, him, Isolt and the girl. And take your escort with you.'

Marc looked behind him and saw the Vatican guards approaching.

'You know, Marc, you may thank me one day,' said Simon. Then, kicking the flank of his horse, he galloped off to join the rest of his men, who were rounding up the fleeing citizens as they ran back towards the walls surrounding their town at the top of the hill, behind which, for the last six months, they had found some measure of peace and shelter from the chaos and violence that was ravaging the world around them.

15

INTO THE FOREST

They had lifted him onto his horse, which Captain Roberto held by its reins as he rode alongside him, Isolt and Kore flanking him on the other side. He held the bunched-up leaves that Isolt had picked in his left hand, and was pressing them against his open wound, but blood was still dripping out of the gash where the sword had sliced through his wrist. When they saw a farm, they stopped and the captain found a piece of wood in the yard. He retied the shawl around Tristan's arm and used the wood to tighten it, twisting it around like a tourniquet, which stopped the flow of blood.

After that, they had ridden on immersed in a deep silence, as if driven by a single purpose: to create as much distance as possible between themselves and that field they had left behind them before having to stop again.

But now, in the gentle light that filtered down through the leaves and rained down on them like shining drops of hope in the dim underworld of the forest they were crossing, they seemed far enough away from the horror to begin to piece it together with words.

'I don't think I have ever felt so helpless!' Roberto was saying to Isolt. 'This whole mission has been so very strange, right from the start. No details were given to us other than our instructions to assist Marc in whatever way might be needed to carry out this mission. And he certainly didn't seem to have any plan as to how he was going to achieve it.' The captain shook his head. 'I certainly didn't expect to see him dressed up as a woman last night,' he continued. 'By then, I'd given up trying to follow what was going on. As for what just happened, I simply didn't know what to do. Simon de Montfort has such an unpredictable and violent nature, and Marc's way of proceeding is so unusual. When I saw him kneeling down over Tristan with a sword held up over his head, I didn't know if he was bluffing...'

The captain paused and seemed to be wrestling with himself for a moment. He let out a great sob as his whole upper body shook and tears ran down his cheeks.

'I'm sorry!' he said. 'All we could do was sit and watch. Never before have I felt so deeply that I have failed in my duty.'

Tristan, hunched over his horse, began to cough and asked for water. It was the first time he had spoken since losing his hand. Isolt took the cap off her flask, leant over, held it up to his lips and tilted it so he could drink. When he had finished she leant over and dabbed his chin with her sleeve.

'You must not reproach yourself, Captain,' Tristan said. 'Some things are meant to happen. They are written somewhere up in the sky. Hidden away from us, for it is better we don't know about them until they happen. And it was written that I should one day lose the right hand that had served me so well in the past. No one can be blamed for this.'

Marc was riding a good fifty paces behind them and yet he could hear every word that was spoken, even though Tristan's voice had been barely louder than a whisper. In ordinary circumstances he would have thought this very strange, but

Marc felt he was no longer living in the realm of ordinary circumstances. It was as if, once he had thrust the sword down onto Tristan's wrist and chopped off his hand, he had also cut through the moorings that bound him to the world, for everything was now hanging on something he had to know. Was the fact that her beauty was stronger than the horror of that moment they had just lived, down there in the valley below Penn, was this truth the ultimate message lying at the heart of nature? Was this the ultimate aim of life in all its forms, to create beauty?

'This seems a good place to stop,' Isolt said. 'I don't think Tristan can stay on his horse any longer. He must get some sleep. Besides, I see some comfrey leaves over there and can put a fresh dressing on his wound.'

'Then we will stop here for the night,' Captain Roberto said, shouting orders to his men to stop and unload their horses. He did not look back to check with Marc before giving his orders. It was as if he, too, had noticed Marc's absence and decided to take charge from here onwards. But none of this mattered to Marc.

They had reached a place where the path they had been following joined up with a small river. The trees growing here were enormous, spread far apart from each other, and yet their long branches reached out and touched, forming a high ceiling over the forest floor.

'I must confess, I don't remember coming through here on our way over,' the captain said as he looked up at the web of spiralling branches high above him. With Isolt he helped Tristan off his horse and, supporting him on either side, they walked him over to one of the trees and sat him down so that his back could rest against its trunk.

The packs were unloaded from the horses and when their saddles had been removed they went down to the river and drank. A rope was tied between trees so they could be tied up there for the night. Some of the men were gathering wood from the forest floor to build a fire.

Isolt went down to the riverbank and came back with freshly picked comfrey leaves, which she placed on Tristan's lap. She gently pulled his hand away from the stump of his right arm and examined the wound. Tristan, who was resting his head against the trunk, turned away so as not to see. Isolt seemed satisfied that the comfrey had dried the wound enough to stop it from bleeding, so she untwisted the tourniquet around his upper arm and used the shawl to hold the fresh leaves against his wound. She tied its two ends together into a knot and then looped a belt borrowed from Captain Roberto over Tristan's head and used it to hold the arm against his chest.

When she had finished, Tristan looked up at her. His face was pale and the look in his eyes seemed to come from far away. He had lost a lot of blood and was very weak, but he still managed to smile at her.

'Ah, you poor man!' she said softly. 'Of all of us, you are the one who least deserves this.'

He lifted his left hand up and caressed her cheek with the back of his fingers. 'I'll be all right. I've got you,' he said.

Kneeling opposite him, Isolt leant forward, placed her hands on his shoulders and pressed her forehead against his. 'Tristan!' she said. It was an exclamation of hope and love, but one she had spoken no louder than a whisper.

Kore stood by watching them. 'Is he really going to be all right?' she asked.

'Yes, of course, my darling,' Isolt answered. 'But he is in a lot of pain right now.'

'He's very brave,' said Kore.

'Yes, very brave,' Isolt agreed.

Kore turned her head, looked behind her and quickly turned away again. Isolt noticed this and twisted around to look fiercely at Marc, still sitting on his horse some distance away and staring down at them.

Bread, cheese and salted meat were handed out to everyone, and there was wine in a large goatskin flask. Night had fallen, the fire had been lit and they sat eating. The light from the flames moved shadows over their faces. Hungry faces, most of them, eager to enjoy whatever gratification life could offer them as a distraction from its harshness. To Marc they seemed like lost children, abandoned in this cruel world. And there, apart from these men, was Isolt, sitting under the tree with Kore and Tristan beside her.

What is her secret? Why does she stand out from the rest of them? Marc wondered. Because she is the force that brought us all into this forest. That force called love, Amor, that was sleeping inside her and Tristan, has awakened and we are all following in its wake as it leads us to this place. That same force that filled me with strength as she stared at me in the valley below Penn, that guided my hand holding Simon de Montfort's sword as it cut through Tristan's wrist and that she then gathered back inside her when it was all over, leaving me standing there wondering what I had done.

It was her. She has led us all here.

Awaking from these thoughts, Marc saw Captain Roberto staring up at him. The fire was dying out and most of the men had already found a place to stretch out for the night.

Marc laughed and got down from his horse with a smile and a shake of the head. The captain looked at his silhouette as it became just a vague shadow moving in the darkness. It was his turn to shake his head, but there was no smile on his face.

For several hours the following morning they rode along the path that followed the small river. Every now and then, Roberto would look up in the hope of catching a glimpse of the sky, but the long branches still stretched into each other, even across the banks of the river, only allowing light to filter down and illuminate dimly the world that lay below the high ceiling of leaves, but offering no glimpse of what was above it.

'It's strange, I really don't remember any of this at all,' the captain said finally. 'I really do not recall coming through here on our way out. And yet I don't see where we could have strayed off our path. Everything seemed perfectly familiar until we entered this forest.'

Tristan, whose resilience and powers of recovery were quite extraordinary, was now sitting up on his horse with his right arm in a sling, firmly holding the reins in his left hand. 'I should not worry, Captain,' he said. 'As long as we follow this river downstream, it will necessarily feed into a larger river at some point. And where there is a large river there are always villages and farms not far away.'

By early afternoon, everyone was hungry and tired. When they stopped for a midday rest, Captain Roberto told them that there was enough bread, ham and cheese for just one more meal. He admitted that neither he nor anyone else in the party knew where they were or how long it would take them to pass through the forest. In view of this, he said, it would be better if they all abstained from eating any food until they stopped for the night, and just contented themselves for now with drinking water mixed with a little wine.

As the horses were tied up there was a noticeable atmosphere of unease. The men were talking to each other in low voices, but once they had finished drinking they seemed less interested in expressing their discontent and mumbled suspicions than in just lying back and resting their weary bodies. Soon everyone had found themselves a comfortable place to lie down, closed their eyes and let their thoughts drift off into the eerie silence of the forest.

Everyone, that is, except Marc, who was once again still sitting on his horse. He had not even bothered to drink. Perhaps he too felt thirsty, hungry and tired, but it did not seem to matter to him. At least, not enough for him to climb down from his saddle.

He had watched Isolt drink from her flask, shared with Tristan and Kore, and had looked on as they walked over to a tree. Isolt had insisted that she be the one who sat and leant back against its trunk, while Tristan lay down with his head resting in her lap. Kore sat at her side and leant her head back against her mother's shoulder as Isolt closed her eyes. Marc just sat on his horse and watched her. He watched the slow rising and falling of her chest as Tristan, with his ear and cheek resting against her stomach, and Kore with her head now leaning down on one of her breasts, were rocked by the slow rhythm of her breath. And at that moment he could not fight back a feeling of admiration for her.

When Captain Roberto clapped his hands and shouted that it was time for everyone to get back on their horses, the men lazily stretched and slowly got up and went over to untie their mounts. As the captain walked past Marc he did not even look up at him, but Marc could see him shaking his head.

Tristan opened his eyes and saw Isolt looking down at him. He reached up with his left hand and caressed her face, then turned over, pushed himself up onto his knees and rose to his feet. Isolt gently stroked Kore's forehead and told her that it was time to get back on their horses.

'Already!' Kore protested, making a painful grimace. Then they too stood up and all three walked over to where the horses were tied up. Not once did they look up at Marc, sitting in his saddle and watching them.

All afternoon they rode along the river, past tall trunks that sprouted up like pillars, supporting a high vault of foliage that blotted out the sky and imprisoned them in a dim half-light where time seemed to stand still. It came almost as a relief when the light began to fade, the oncoming night absorbed the surrounding trees into the darkness and they found a place to stop for the night, unpacked their horses, and sat around a fire to eat.

All except Marc, of course, who was still on his horse, just beyond the periphery of the light cast by the flames. No one seemed to even notice him any more. Tristan, Isolt and Kore were clearly avoiding looking at him and the guards were preoccupied with other matters. The captain must have decided that there was no point in trying to reason with him, so was leaving him alone as well.

'That's the last of the food,' Roberto said. 'I can only hope that His Grace includes us in his prayers tonight so that God may help us find our way out of this forest.'

'I would not be surprised to find there is someone amongst us who is using other powers, ungodly powers, to prevent us from doing so.' The voice came from one of the guards, his face was moving in and out of the shadows unleashed by the dancing flames on the fire.

'What are you insinuating?' said his captain. 'Are you saying that someone has called upon the Devil to keep us trapped here? What nonsense! We are all God-fearing men and need not fear the Devil.'

'Does it not, though, seem strange how quickly Tristan's wound has healed?' the voice enquired. 'How, only a day later, he is sitting on his horse, as strong and healthy as any one of us, without any fever or any sign of what he suffered just a day ago, except for the absence of a hand at the end of his right arm? Do you not find that strange?'

'And what should make you think that this is not God's miracle, but rather the work of the Devil?' Roberto asked.

'The fact that we have been wandering for the last two days through this dark forest without knowing where we are or where we are going, as if it had just suddenly sprung up around us, called out of the ground by some magic spell. I mean, has anyone heard a bird call out or sing? Has anyone seen a deer or a rabbit or a squirrel, even?'

There were mumbles of agreement from other soldiers around the fire.

'This is rubbish!' the captain said. 'I think we are all very tired and that you are letting your imagination run away with you.'

'I say she is not just a mere heretic. She is some sort of witch. She has made a pact with the Devil, and he has cast a spell on all of us. He has caused this forest to spring up around us and we are doomed to wander around in here until we are too weak from hunger to go any further, at which point she, Tristan and the girl will go back and join up with the rest of those lost souls.'

'Who is to say that it is not the Devil speaking to us right now, through your own mouth?' Marc asked, jumping down from his horse. All eyes looked at him with surprise.

'Why should the Devil's words come out of the mouth of a devout Christian?' the voice asked. 'A churchgoer, a man who celebrates Mass every Sunday?'

Marc stood staring across the flames at the face of the man who had spoken out against Isolt. He probably had a wife and children waiting for him back in Rome, didn't want to die in this forest without ever seeing them again and had simply spoken out of panic.

'I don't question that you are all of those things,' said Marc, 'but you are also frightened right now and you are letting doubt and fear spoil your judgement. For what advantage could the heretics gain if Tristan were to join up with them again, now that he has lost his right hand? And as for you, where do you think you are taking us with these accusations? Do you want us to punish Isolt for having supposedly cast a spell on us? Don't you think that harming Isolt would only serve the Cathars' cause? Instead of losing her back to Christianity, as is now the case, they would hail her as a martyr. Is that what you want? Is this what you are trying to draw us into with your accusations?'

The man lowered his eyes. 'Perhaps you are right,' he said. 'Perhaps we are just tired. May God give us peace in our sleep tonight and help us find our way out of this forest tomorrow.'

'Yes, we must all get some sleep now,' Roberto agreed. 'Tomorrow, I'm sure, we will find our way out of here.'

The men rose and walked past Marc without a word. Silently, they fetched their saddles to rest their heads and, covered by the horses' blankets, fall asleep. Only the captain hesitated for a moment, as if he were about to say something, but then he seemed to catch himself and continued about his business.

*

Somewhere in the shadows of the night, when everyone had settled down, Marc could hear Kore talking to her mother. At moments her voice was just a low hum, which would then drop into a whisper and, after a while, rise again into a hum. When Isolt answered, her voice was barely distinguishable from the soft whistle of the fire and the coughs and muffled sound of shifting hoofs from the horses.

And then he couldn't hear them any more, their conversation absorbed by the night, by the gentle breathing of all the bodies lying asleep close by them. For only he was awake, still standing and gazing into the fire. He had been thinking all day about Isolt. Had he really seen something supernatural, like a revelation reaching into him through her eyes, as he had stood with a sword in his hand down there in the field below Penn?

Marc felt a hand squeeze his arm from behind and, with a start, he turned. In the dimness of the night, he could only just recognise Isolt. The fire had nearly burnt itself out. Over the red-hot cinders, a single flame would flutter back to life and die away again.

'Come with me!' she whispered. 'You must find a place to lie down and get some sleep. But first you must tie up your horse.'

Pulling him by the arm, she led him over to his horse. But Marc did not take hold of the reins and just stood facing her. She led it over to where the other horses were tied up. Marc followed behind her.

'You cannot give up now,' she said, unstrapping the saddle. 'You've taken us this far. You persuaded us to follow you and it has cost Tristan his right hand, though he does not blame you, for he knows as well as you that it was the only way out of there for him. But you cannot give up now. You must hold on to yourself. And to do that, you need to sleep.'

She pulled the heavy saddle off the horse.

'Here, take this and find yourself a place to lie down.' She shoved it against his chest to break the unease, for although they were just faint shadows she could feel his gaze piercing through the darkness.

Marc took hold of the saddle and dropped it on the ground. 'This is as good a place as any,' he said. 'I have grown to like the company of horses since I no longer have my wife lying by my side.'

'You know as well as I do that such talk can lead nowhere,' Isolt said in a low voice.

'You are quite right,' Marc said. 'But let me ask you a very important question.'

'Wouldn't it be better if we were both to sleep now and save our strength for tomorrow?' she said gently.

'It would be better if I ask you this question now, and for you to give me an honest answer. That would be best. I would not be asking it just for my own satisfaction, but also because your answer – if it is honest, if you do not hold back the truth – may be our only chance of ever getting out of this forest.'

'What are you talking about?' Isolt asked, keeping her voice to a whisper.

'You know as well as I do that we are trapped here,' Marc said. 'I don't pretend to know the exact nature of what is holding us here, but I think that man was right when he suggested it was some kind of spell. Now I can't explain why, but I have a strong feeling that this spell is working through us or, more specifically, through my feelings for you. So, if you answer this question I want to ask you, if you are completely honest with me, I think the spell would then be broken.'

Marc didn't really know if he believed what he was saying, but he did know that he had her there standing close up to him, so close that he could feel her breath on his face as she whispered to him. He knew that when she walked away, she would lie down beside Tristan and fall asleep at his side. He couldn't bear the thought of the pain and anger this would cause him. So he wanted to provoke her. He wanted her to be cruel and brutal with him so that he could feel justified in his pain and anger, for he didn't know what to feel any more.

'Are you going to ask me the question, then?' Isolt reluctantly enquired.

'Only if you promise to be absolutely honest and not to try and spare my feelings,' Marc insisted.

'Yes, yes, I promise!'

'All right then,' he replied. 'My question is really quite simple. I know that I haven't always done right by you. I let you down badly and I didn't listen to you when I should have, and I dragged you into living a life you never wanted. I should have stood up to my mother and not accepted the crown of Brittany. It didn't belong on my head. You knew that, and I didn't listen to you. But, suppose I had made none of these mistakes. Suppose I had always supported you, had done my very best never to neglect you, always to stand up for you. Would you still have been drawn to Tristan? Would you still have fallen in love with him? Would you have resisted running away with him, or could you still not have deprived yourself of those nights you spent in his arms?'

Their silhouettes were dark shadows that rocked in the night like anchored vessels.

'What I am really asking you,' continued Marc, 'is, if I had done right by you, if I had followed you down your road, if we had gone to Ireland together, could Tristan still have walked into your heart and pushed me aside the way he did?'

There was a moment's silence. Then Isolt spoke and, though her voice was just a whisper, it seemed to Marc that she spat out each word as if it were a red-hot cinder.

'As a young girl growing up in a convent, I had watched all those young nuns who had given up their lives to Jesus. For most of them, it was a difficult sacrifice that had been imposed on them, but there were one or two who had real fervour in their abandonment. I recognised that same fervour as something that could burn in me as well, but I knew that I could never sacrifice my life to some dead image nailed on a cross. It was clear that I could only do it for someone who was made of flesh and blood, who was alive and breathing, just like me.

'But I had no idea how dangerous and out of control things could get once you let go of yourself and let your passion drive you outside the walls that keep you tightly sequestered within the limits of conduct condoned by our Church. It happened to me once I left the convent and nearly drove me to my death.

'And then I met you, Marc. You threw that shawl over my shoulders and that gesture touched me, and I immediately felt I needed someone like you. I was alone and frightened in a foreign land, and I felt I'd be safe with you, that you would look after me after all I'd been through after leaving the convent. But, as the years went by, I began to feel that something was missing from my life. I thought of those few nuns back in the convent who seemed to have found real devotion, and one especially, Anna Maria, who was penetrated by something that had opened her up, that made her seem fearless and full of grace.

'I wished I could be like her, I wished I could have felt that kind of love for everything I did, the way she did. And, despite the fact that what happened to me once I left the convent was such a disaster, as the years went by, living with you, watching our daughter grow up, I began to feel uncomfortable, as if I had closed myself to something that was buried inside me that should have been mine, that was waiting to be discovered and was wasting away inside me because of my lack of courage, and I began to resent you for confining me to this life we were living. And then, with the death of your father and you wanting to take over the kingdom and sit on its throne, I felt that this would further chain me down to living this life that didn't really belong to me.'

She stopped for a moment to regain her calm, as if she had reawakened old emotions that were choking her and that found an echo in one or two of the horses that started coughing and stamping their hoofs. Then, when silence had taken possession of the forest again, she continued. 'And so, when Tristan appeared out of nowhere and asked me if it was really my ambition to become queen, something that no one in my entourage, you included, would ever have dared question, I knew that he was the one who could open up my heart and help me climb towards the light that could illuminate my life as it had illuminated the life of Sister Anna Maria, with the only difference that she received that light from her devotion to God, and that I would receive it by giving myself, body and soul, to life, through Tristan.'

Once again they stood staring at the dim outline of each other's silhouettes. They could hear a horse sneezing and shaking its neck, and the faint sound of someone snoring near the extinguished fire.

'Thank you for being honest with me,' Marc said, trying to mask the crushed feeling in his heart.

'I haven't finished!' said Isolt.

'What do you mean?' Marc asked, searching through the darkness for the outline of her face.

'That's not enough to break the spell, if there really is one holding us prisoner in this forest.'

'Why not?' he asked.

'Because I don't think you ever realised how hard it was for me to come back to you. When I rode back over the moor towards the castle, with Kore sitting behind me, it was as if I was whipping myself to keep on course and not to turn around and rush back into his arms. I felt I was doing myself great harm coming back to you, that I was betraying something fundamental in my soul, that I was being a coward, again. I hated you for this because I felt you had made me become that way, that your weakness in facing up to life had somehow contaminated me. And that night, after I arrived back and felt your hands grope for me when we were in bed, I pushed you away because I couldn't bear feeling you touch me, as if all you wanted was to drag me into your weakness and away from life, away from the truth, from what I had been living with Tristan.'

'So why did you come back?' Marc asked.

For a moment, as if he had been overcome by the tiredness he had been fighting back, Marc felt himself fall away from where they stood, from the forest and its big trees, and for an instant he found himself on the shore of an ocean. It was a hot, windless night and he was listening to the wash of a wave slowly pulling away into the darkness, eagerly waiting for it to come rolling back and wet the sand between the rocks, like a great tongue stretching over the shore. He was awoken by her soft whisper.

'I had to,' she said. 'I was obeying a force I couldn't really understand. But I also made a promise to myself that I would return to Tristan if I couldn't think of a reason to stay that held the slightest ray of hope for you and me. A reason that had a real spark of light in it, other than the purely practical and convenient.'

'You must have found something, since you ended up staying,' Marc said.

'It was like a voice,' she replied. 'A vague thought or a wish hovering in the background of my confusion and despair, which said that if, when I returned to the castle, you could have found the necessary force to still love me after all those nights spent in Tristan's arms, if you could have found that force in yourself, just like I had to dig inside myself to find the force to bring myself back to you, then it would have been as if you were showing me some undiscovered part of yourself that would allow us to start all over again.'

Marc was amazed, for it was now Isolt who was showing him some undiscovered part of herself, and though this was heart-warming and beautiful it also filled him with pain because this unknown part of her nature had evidently been revealed to her in Tristan's arms.

'I'd watch you,' she said, 'try and guess what you were thinking, what was going on in your heart. But you would never say anything real to me. When you were happy and joyful it never seemed real either, maybe because you were never able to include me in your happiness. The only thing that was real was your anger and misery.

'Even when we were living together after what happened on the White Moor, when we were forced together by circumstances beyond our control, when all the veils had been dropped between us, I still thought there was a real chance for us if only you could have brought yourself to love me as I was then, fully revealed to you without anything hidden away any more, stripped of all pretence. Can't you see that, if only you could have done that, we could have been happy together, despite everything... But even when you made love to me you were angry. Maybe there was love hidden away somewhere in that anger, but you could never bring it forward and show it to me. I kept waiting for you to do something, but you never seemed able to break through that barrier you had built up against me...'

Her voice trailed off and silence filled the night. There was no horse coughing or even anyone snoring. Just silence.

'It's a shame,' she said, and with these last words she left him standing in the dark, listening as she walked away from him, her footsteps disappearing like whispers into the night.

16

THE VALEDICTION

The following morning, as they stood stretching and rubbing their eyes, the saddles and ruffled blankets on the forest floor, the fallen leaves and the water rustling over the rocks in the river all seemed trapped in the half-light that filtered down through the intertwining branches and carpet of leaves above them.

It was Captain Roberto who, after looking around him and up over his head, shouted out with forced enthusiasm, 'Come on, all of you! Saddle your horses and let's get an early start. Let's see if we can't find our way out of here.'

Marc still had the echo of Isolt's voice ringing in his ears. He wondered how he was ever going to forget what she had said. He saw her walking towards her horse holding her saddle in one hand and her blanket in the other, her body pulling sideways against the weight of the saddle as she walked. With her untied hair falling down in long curls along the sides of her face and her big black eyes, it hurt to look at her, so he turned his eyes away and continued pulling on the strap of his own saddle.

'Are you all right?'

Marc turned around and found her standing next to him.

She looked at him, hesitant. 'Our conversation took an unexpected turn last night,' she said, 'and I forgot my main intention, which was to thank you for stepping in and defending me against the man who was calling me a witch. Things could have taken a very nasty turn if you hadn't intervened.'

'That's all right,' Marc said. 'Think nothing of it.'

'Do you really think the spell has been broken?' Isolt asked with an embarrassed laugh. Marc was about to answer when Kore called out to her mother and she turned to help her.

'I don't like it!' the captain said. 'There's no let up from this cover. It seems to go on forever. There is not the slightest breach between the trees to let in any real light that might give us some hope of finding our way out of here. I really don't understand what's going on.'

'We just have to keep following the river downstream,' Tristan said. 'It has to lead out of here in the end, and at least we know we are not going around in circles.'

'You are quite right,' said Roberto. 'I'm just a little worried about the morale of my men. We have no food left, there's nothing here to hunt, and there's nothing growing on the ground for the horses to feed on.'

'At least we have a plentiful supply of water,' Tristan said.

'I admire your composure. It is quite remarkable, given what you have had to suffer. You have certainly lived up to the reputation that precedes you.'

Tristan laughed. 'I am as eager as everyone else to get out of this forest and see the sky again,' he replied. 'But our stomachs are not yet aching with hunger yet, and our horses are still able to carry us forwards, so the only real danger that seems to be threatening us right now is our own thoughts and suspicions. That's why I'm trying to look on the bright side, so as not to fall into that trap.'

'You are, indeed, an extraordinary man!' Captain Roberto exclaimed. 'The one bright light in this dark maze we're trapped in.'

Marc paid little attention to what they were saying. He had caught a few words of their conversation here and there, but his thoughts and his heart were still immersed in the total blackness of the previous night.

And there she was once again, riding on her horse in front of him, beside the man who had set fire to her heart, a fire whose flames had burnt down all the resistance behind which this other Isolt had been hiding. The man who had revealed her to herself and, most extraordinary of all, the man with whom she had escaped into the night, not returning until two weeks later, coming back to the castle in great pain and clinging to the faint hope that if Marc could love her as she now was, as she had been revealed to herself, then maybe they could still have a meaningful life together.

But how could she have expected me to do this? Marc wondered, as he felt all the weariness of the last few days pour into him and carry him into a dream, not even realising that he had closed his eyes and was slouching forward, his body rocking gently with the swaying of his horse.

Ogrin was speaking to him again, just as he had on the pier outside Les Saintes Maries de la Mer. 'A wolf will always be true to his nature, whereas a dog has sold his inner being to The City of God. He has lost sight of the overriding myth he belongs to and is no longer in touch with the living spirit inside him.

'You see, the wolf is your instincts before The City of God went to work on them. He has not sold himself to the hand that feeds him because, contrary to what the philosophers would have you believe, what drives him is not an instinct to survive or to perpetuate his kind; no, the overriding aim driving him is much broader. It is connected to the survival of his world, for the seasons to continue succeeding each other, for the moon to continue to grow and diminish in the sky, for the sun to rise every morning, for there to be deer in the meadows and fish in the streams and wild geese in the sky. This is what is driving him, because he understands that this world cannot hold itself together without our sacrifice. That this is the only thing that is keeping it alive.'

'What sacrifice are you talking about?' Marc asked.

'Well, let's consider Isolt for a moment,' Ogrin said. 'Her passion for Tristan was so powerful that she was willing to sacrifice everything she had acquired: her husband, her social rank, her comfort, her life. She was willing to risk losing all that for the sake of love when she gave herself to Tristan, when she fell into his embrace.

'But at some point, when she was lost in the bliss of this embrace, she had a vision, a profound vision such as has rarely been given throughout the ages.'

'What vision?' Marc asked.

'She must have seen,' Ogrin replied, 'as her own body was released from all the hesitations and scruples that tethered it to this City of God, that this body was driven by a force that stretched beyond her own fulfilment to the joy and passion that emanates out of life in its entirety, and that the movement of her body was no longer in response to Tristan's passion but felt as if she was now in this god's arms, that carried her in his dance, spinning her around and around in celebration of his victory over death. And, in this moment of insight, she saw through him, through this god, into his myth. She saw that he was trapped in this world, in its cycle of life and death, having to eat himself and reproduce himself in order to keep alive. That's his sacrifice.

'And that's why she had to break away from Tristan and return to her life with you, Marc.'

'But why?' Marc asked.

'Because Tristan had taken her too close to this god, and this frightened her. She didn't want to be consumed by its flames. And she was a mother and had a child to think about. But she couldn't forget those flames either. They were there somewhere inside her, calling to her. She needed your help, Marc! But you were too stupid, too weak, too much of a child yourself to understand.'

His muscular brow like a dark cloud carrying a storm that was about to erupt, Ogrin stared at Marc. But suddenly his expression changed, as if the storm had blown over.

'If you could have loved her,' he said more gently, 'right then, just as she was when she came back to you, if you could have reached far enough down inside yourself and found the courage to do that, you could have brought a new light into her eyes. A light that comes from a flame burning at the heart of this fire she was so afraid of. A fire within this fire, one that burns without consuming you. Only you could have done this, Marc. But to do so you would have had to step into that fire yourself, as she had done. You could have done this by loving her when she returned from her adventure with Tristan. This would have been your fire, the doorway into this myth that all three of you were enacting down here in this world. Your doorway... The one that would have taken you into this devouring fire, all the way to that other doorway leading to the flame that shines at its heart as it burns without consuming you. Only you could have done this, and she would have followed you there.'

*

'Ah. At last!' Captain Roberto exclaimed.

They approached in stunned silence as the light grew brighter and gained ground on the darkness, until finally the forest opened out onto the ridge of a plateau that dropped steeply into a valley with a broad river flowing out towards the Mediterranean, far below them to the right.

And then they were all lined up along the ridge, their eyes blinking in the bright glare of the sun. For a while they just stared down into the valley in disbelief, speechless, stunned to find themselves delivered from the eerie half-light that had haunted them for the last two days. Finally, Tristan pointed to a cluster of houses and fortifications on a hill further along the coast.

'There seems to be a fair-sized town over there,' he said. 'I suggest we go and have a look.'

'I hope it's not a Cathar stronghold,' the captain said.

'It can't be,' Tristan replied. 'All the coastal towns were captured two years ago.'

'Then let's go and see if we can purchase some food and wine,' Roberto exclaimed, unable to suppress his joy.

They filed down the slope into the valley, following a stream that cascaded down towards the river. Marc felt dizzy in the bright light of the sun. He was trying to remember what had happened to him just before the captain had shouted and he had seen the light ahead leading out of the forest. It was as if he had felt a light shining inside him before they all saw the light shining ahead of them, but it seemed to have been lost in the general joy of the moment.

He looked back longingly at the forest they were leaving behind them. Nothing about it seemed unusual from here. The trees that had appeared so huge now seemed quite normal in size. As he turned away he saw that Isolt too was looking behind her, and it was not her beauty that struck him but something about her that was less striking but which moved into him awkwardly and took hold of his heart.

*

There was much laughter and the conversation amongst the men was joyful as they ate roasted chicken and drank wine on the sandy grassland south of the town of Béziers on the shore of the Mediterranean Sea, where they had stopped to graze their horses and feed their own hungry stomachs.

While the guards were gathered around a fire, Roberto, Tristan, Isolt and Kore were sitting under a tree away from the rowdy crowd. Also sitting apart, but on the other side of the fire, was Marc. He had eaten a few pieces of chicken and drunk some wine and was just sitting, staring out at the sea glistening in the distance beyond the long stretch of sandy grassland.

'So, are you going to tell me?' Isolt asked. She was kneeling beside him with a mug of wine in her hand.

'Tell you what?' he replied.

'If you still think we are under a spell, or if our conversation last night helped dispel it?'

Marc didn't like her making light of their conversation in the darkness of the forest. He had heard her laughing with her companions under the tree, and her happiness in their company irritated him in spite of himself.

'Perhaps we should ask Ogrin what he thinks,' he said. 'He seems to know a lot about these things.'

There was horror and disbelief in Isolt's eyes.

'Ogrin!' She repeated the name as if she were in a dream.

'Yes, Ogrin. Or, if you prefer, your father.'

'But how do you know his name?' she asked.

'He told me himself.'

Isolt stared down at her lap. 'What else did he tell you?' she asked without looking up.

'A lot of things. He told me about your mother, about Cyprus, about your birth.'

Isolt looked at him as if he had no right to possess that kind of knowledge about her.

'You like to keep people tucked away in little boxes – "I'll give this much of myself to this one, and that much more to that one." Isn't that so?' Marc asked.

'That's not true, Marc. I've given you much more than you deserved.'

Marc could see the anger in her eyes, and the hurt. And, maybe because of the wine she had been drinking, he felt she was close to tears. He looked around him. The guards were still laughing and joking between mouthfuls of chicken and wine around the fire. Tristan was talking to Roberto under the tree, Kore listening to them and throwing occasional looks over at her mother and her estranged father. Marc stood up.

'Why don't we go for a walk down towards the sea?' he said.

'Why not?' Isolt stood up as well. She seemed to hesitate for a moment. 'I'll just take my mug back and tell Tristan I'm going for a walk.' Marc watched as she said a few words to Tristan, and then as Kore grabbed hold of her dress. Isolt talked with her for a moment and Kore reluctantly let go. Isolt walked back towards him.

As they started together down towards the sea, Marc asked, 'Does Tristan mind you going off with me?'

'No, of course not,' Isolt replied. 'After we have both confessed in Rome, he knows that you and I are supposed to live together under the same roof. He also knows that you and I will have to come to some kind of arrangement about him.'

'Do you want to talk about that now?' Marc asked.

'No, we can do that at some later date,' Isolt replied. 'What I want you to tell me is how you met my father.'

'He paid me a visit when I was in prison.'

'What?' Isolt exclaimed.

'It seems that, for all these years, he was never that far away from you.'

'I just don't understand!' she said, her eyes caught between an expression of horror and bewilderment.

'Nor do I,' Marc replied. 'All I know is that he knows all about us. About you and me, the kind of life we led, and about Tristan and you. He knew that I was in prison and he knew that you and Tristan were holed up in Penn, which Simon de Montfort had besieged. In fact, you could say that he was the initiator of this mission to salvage you from there.'

'So it wasn't your idea?' Isolt asked.

'No. When he came to see me in my cell I had lost all hope of ever seeing you again. It was your father who convinced me that I could save you from certain death at de Montfort's hands.'

'And what does he hope to get out of this?'

'You're his daughter,' Marc replied. 'He obviously wants you to live and not to die.'

'If that is so, then why did he try to kill me?' Isolt asked scornfully.

'That's what you told me the first day we met,' Marc said. 'But your father doesn't tell the same story as you do.'

'I bet he doesn't,' she replied angrily. 'What has he told you, then?'

'He said he took you on a trip to Cyprus to show you the island where you were born. He said that, one day, you all went on a picnic up in the hills behind Paphos, where your grandfather had lived with your mother. The villagers had killed a lamb and brought it up to your grandfather's old house and had roasted it there on the salt marsh. He said that everyone had drunk a lot of wine as they ate, and that he had drunk more than anyone else, due to the emotion of finding himself up there in front of the old broken-down house where he had lived with your mother.'

'I know about the old house. I was there. I saw it! Just tell me what he said happened there!' Isolt said, her eyes wide open with anger.

'He said that he didn't remember too clearly, but that at some point he must have said something to you that offended you, for you sprang to your feet and started running up the hill, and that he chased after you to apologise for whatever he had said. That, quite extraordinarily, in your eagerness to get away from him, you accidentally fell off the same ledge your mother had fallen from when she was a little girl. Only, unlike your mother, you survived with only a sprained ankle and light cuts and bruises.'

'And you believed him?'

'He seemed to be sincere when he told me that story.'

'So you believed him rather than me,' Isolt said sharply.

'Well, I did think that, being young and impressionable, you could have fallen off the ledge while trying to escape from him. And, after the shock of the fall, you might have convinced yourself that he actually pushed you.'

'Thank you for your trust and support!' she said.

'So, what is your version of the story?' Marc asked.

Isolt didn't answer. She just kept on walking, staring straight ahead. Marc wondered what her father could have done to her to cause her never to talk about him. Why had Marc not been allowed to even mention his name during all the time they had shared together? Why had it been so important to her to exclude him from the part of her life that she had shared with her father?

She seemed to have reverted to the fragile, explosive young girl who had come to live with him in the fortress above the cliffs in Brittany all those years ago.

'You know, Isolt,' he continued, 'I now understand there was a part of you that you always kept hidden from me, and that this was the most important part of you, something wonderful and powerful, but it was attached to a deep wound you were carrying when we first met and you never told me about it.'

Isolt looked at Marc, her pupils wide, like a startled wild cat ready to fend off an attack. They had stopped walking, for they had reached the end of the long stretch of sand and grass, where the land fell suddenly onto a small strip of beach that sloped down into the sea.

She said nothing but simply shrugged, laughed and bent down to remove her boots. She lifted her dress, jumped down onto the beach and ran until her feet splashed in the water. She let out a scream and turned towards Marc.

'It's very cold!'

Small waves broke over her calves. She now had a big smile on her face and her eyes glistened in the early afternoon sun.

'The convent where I grew up was very close to the sea,' she said as he caught up with her, 'and whenever we had a chance, which was not often, some of the young nuns would escape and go for a walk along the shore. I'd go with them and loved getting my feet wet and feeling my toes sink into the sand. Such a small thing as that made me feel alive, as if I'd broken free from the stuffy, suffocating silence of the convent.' She turned away from him and stared out at the infinite space stretching out before her.

Marc sat down on the bank and watched her. After a while, Isolt turned around again and, as Marc stared at her, standing there with her feet in the water, with the vast horizon far behind her, absorbing the story she had just told him, as her voice ran away from her towards that distant silence it was as if the space that separated them as he sat there listening to her would always be there, that this was how it was now, and that he had to accept it this way. But he could not do that. He could not accept she would always love this other life inside her, from which he was excluded. His heart could not stretch that far, even if he wanted it to. She was asking him to do the impossible, but did he not also want the impossible from her, wanting her to turn against herself and reject that part of her life she had shared with Tristan?

Isolt walked out of the water and came to sit down next to him.

'Wow!' she exclaimed. 'I'm glad we came down here.'

'You don't like stuffy atmospheres, do you?' Marc said.

'No, I don't,' she said. 'But if you are referring to you and me, you're wrong. I enjoyed a lot of the time we spent together, especially in the beginning, when we lived in the fortress up on the cliffs.'

'We could go and live there again,' Marc said.

'Yes,' she said, 'but there would be three of us, plus Kore. And one of us would be too many in the end. I know that.'

There was a moment's silence.

'And who would that be?' asked Marc.

Isolt turned and looked at him with sadness in her eyes.

'It would probably end up being you.'

It was silly to have asked the question when he already knew the answer. They had been through all that last night. But he was not going to let it stop there. He was not going to let all the years they had spent together end in the way she had just described. He was not going to accept that. Not after what she had revealed to him the previous night. He knew there was another possible ending for them.

'You don't have to worry about this because none of it is going to happen,' he said suddenly.

'What are you talking about?'

'You are not going to Rome. You are not going to confess to the Pope and you are not coming back with me to Brittany. You, Kore and Tristan are going to sail with your father to the East and start a new life over there.'

'What on earth are you saying?' Isolt asked. 'Have you gone mad?'

'We are going to meet your father in a few days outside a small town called Les Saintes Marie de la Mer. He will be waiting for us there. I think he just wants to take a last look at you. He has rented a ship and is sailing back to Constantinople with some merchandise, and you are going to get on that boat with him. You, Kore and Tristan – all three of you.'

'Is this what you have just decided? Or did you work this out with my father beforehand?' Isolt asked.

'This is what I've just decided,' said Marc, 'though I wonder now if this was not his intention all along.'

'Well, it's not really important whose idea it was, because I'm not going to get into that boat either way,' Isolt said with a sudden look of fear in her eyes.

'Yes, you are going to get into that boat. Don't you see? This is the only chance for you and Tristan to be together, and for Kore to grow up with two happy people looking after her.'

'I'm not getting into a boat with my father!' Isolt said. 'I'm not going anywhere near him. You can't make me do that, so don't even try.'

Marc wondered, once again, what Ogrin could have said or done to her to cause such a violent reaction.

'Anyway,' she said, 'I don't know why we are even talking about this since it could never happen, even if I agreed to it. Captain Roberto would never let us get away with such a stupid plan.'

'Don't worry about Roberto. I will be able to persuade him. His admiration for Tristan has no limits, and that already puts him halfway on our side. It will only take a little bit of persuasion to win over the other half, you'll see.'

'I don't care who you persuade,' she replied. 'You are not going to persuade me!'

Isolt stood up and started walking purposefully back across the sandy grassland towards the fire where Kore, Tristan and the others seemed to be getting ready to leave.

Marc caught up with her.

'I'm not going in that boat with my father!' Isolt insisted.

'You'll see. You talk to Tristan – he'll tell you. It's the only way to put an end to this mess. He'll tell you.' Marc wondered if he was really going to be able to see this through.

*

They had been riding for several hours along the beach, following the endless line that stretched before them. Long ago in the mythical past, it had marked the place where the land had become separated from the sea so that creatures could crawl out of the sea onto dry land and prosper there, and the heavens would then be visible to them.

What's wrong with her? Marc wondered. What does she want? She wants you to love her as she is, but you can't; you can't accept this side of her. The side that can exist apart from you, that can enjoy herself with somebody else, that can let that person into parts of herself she has never explored with you. You can't give her that. And yet she wants you to. But that is unfair, he told himself. That is selfish and inconsiderate.

No, he replied to himself, that is her, Isolt, the person she wants you to love. But you're not strong enough and you don't understand that if you could include all of her in your love you would be doing the thing you complain she has not done with you. You would be exploring those parts of her you say she has excluded you from. You do not understand that, when she wanted you to love her just as she was, she was trying to open those doors for you.

*

Once again Marc realised he had fallen asleep on his horse. When he awoke the sun had vanished, leaving a faint pink glow hovering over the horizon behind him. The guards had dismounted and were busy gathering wood for a fire. He stopped and sat in his saddle for a moment.

Tristan, Isolt and Kore were standing in a tight circle, locked together in discussion. When Marc saw them, he was overcome by a terrible feeling that went further than sadness or loneliness, an overwhelming sense of guilt as if he must sever a sacred bond. This would be more than just a personal loss for him because he was going to throw away his most precious dream, the dream of two souls finding each other amongst all the chaos and murderous brutality that had taken possession of this world. The dream of an island far away from all this. The dream of a lost paradise. And she, who embodied all this, had given herself to somebody else and he was going to have to let go of her... A dream that did not belong only to him but to the whole of this aching world.

Was it this dream that had held him together, and were the walls of The City of God now crumbling? Was he at last drifting away into its surrounding wilderness?

And this last question, much to his surprise, awakened a faint feeling of hope that he could feel growing inside him.

They had brought with them a goatskin flask of wine and several loaves of bread that they shared out between them once the fire had been lit. When night had fallen and they were finishing off the wine, the man who had spoken out the night before stood up and spoke again.

'Can I have your attention, please!' he said loudly. 'I wish to apologise for having lost hold of myself last night and wrongly accusing Queen Isolt of casting a spell on us. I deeply regret my behaviour and hope, my lady, that you will bear no grudge against me, and so would like to propose a toast to your good health and future happiness.' He lifted his cup. 'To Queen Isolt, to her beauty and courage! May God bless her! Long live our lady!' There were cheers from all the men as they raised their own cups. When the noise had subsided, Isolt stood up.

'Thank you,' she said. 'I accept the gentleman's apology. Everything that was said in the dark night of that forest should be forgotten now that we have found our way back to this open sky, where the moon is rising to watch over us. So I drink to the good health of all of you!' There were more cheers as Isolt sat down.

But I will never forget what was said in that dark night of the forest, Marc thought as he watched her laughing at Tristan's side.

It was now Captain Roberto's turn to stand up and speak.

'Since there is still a little wine left in my cup,' he began, 'I would like to use it to toast a very brave man, whose audacity and skill with a sword has no equal on the battlefield. He has now become legendary wherever he sets foot, even in faraway places where he has not yet been! But his courage in the face of the cruellest adversity that could befall a man is, in my opinion, even more astonishing. And it is this courage, which I have been witness to, that I would like to toast now.

'For the past few days, as we drifted through that dark forest without being sure of ever finding our way out, Tristan was riding at my side, having to endure the pain caused by the loss of his hand, the hand that had served him so well on so many battlefields. Yet, never was there a more cheerful companion, even as things went from bad to worse as we wandered, lost in that haunted place. When he should have been the most distraught of all of us, he was the most hopeful and showed the most fortitude.

'So, let us raise our cups, drink to his health and praise his courage!'

Tristan rose to his feet. He looked around him with a wry smile that stood in strange contrast to the intensity shining out of his eyes. 'It seems,' he said, 'that I'm going to have to learn to do with my left hand all the things I once did with my right. So, let me start with something simple, like lifting this cup to toast in return all of you who made this long journey to come to our rescue at Penn. You managed to get all of us out of there in one piece, all, that is, except one miserable hand, which Simon de Montfort can add to his trophy chest. And why not, if that makes him happy? As for me, I'm happy to be alive, and I have you all to thank for that!'

There were more cheers and whistles from the men as Tristan sat down. Then a strange silence fell over the group of travellers gathered around the fire, as if an angel were flying overhead, or as if they had been moved by his words to become more pensive and think about their own lives.

It was their captain who broke the silence. 'It is getting late,' Roberto said. 'I think we should get some sleep. Our journey is not yet over and tomorrow will be another long day.'

*

The following morning, Marc was fixing his saddle when, out of the corner of his eye, he saw Isolt walking over to her horse. He turned to look at her.

'What are you looking at?' she asked.

'At you,' Marc answered. No sooner had he spoken than he felt a longing enter into his stare and looked away again.

'And so?' Isolt enquired with a smile on her face.

'And so, how are you this morning?' Marc asked. 'Did you have a good sleep?'

'Yes, I slept well,' Isolt replied, still smiling at him.

'They say sleep brings good counsel,' Marc said.

Isolt stopped smiling and came over to him.

'I talked to Tristan last night, if that's what you want to know,' she said in a low voice.

'And what did he have to say?'

'He seems to agree with you.'

'And what about you?' Marc asked. He could feel his heart beating fast inside his chest. Did he secretly hope that she would still unequivocally reject his plan?

'You already know how I feel,' she said.

'And so?'

'Do what you want,' she said. 'Just don't involve me.'

She turned to go and pick up her saddle, then stopped and looked at him again.

'What?' asked Marc.

'Nothing,' she said. 'I'm not telling you anything.'

A short while afterwards, as they set off down the shoreline once again, Marc moved up alongside Roberto, who was riding beside Tristan, Isolt and Kore.

'I found what you said about Tristan very true,' Marc said to the captain. 'But the things you said got me thinking. I must confess that I could not sleep, troubled as I was by these thoughts.'

'I'm very sorry to hear that,' the captain said drily. 'It was not my intention.'

'Oh, I don't mean to blame you in any way for what you said,' replied Marc. 'I am, in fact, very grateful that you spoke out in praise of Tristan, for it made me think about what I have done to him, and about what kind of future awaits him now. You must understand that when I cut off his hand I did so only because I thought it would save his head from suffering the same fate. I thought that this was the only way to save his life. But now, after having heard you talk, I wonder what kind of life it is that I have saved for him.'

'Yes,' replied the captain bitterly. 'I only wish you had let me in on the details of how you planned to proceed. If we had worked together, maybe we could have prevented this outcome.'

'It was my mistake,' said Marc, 'and I take full responsibility for it. But that does not help Tristan, who will now be at the mercy of any knight or brigand who wishes to challenge him to a duel. And there are many who will wish to do so, just for the pleasure of humiliating a man who, once upon a time, no one in the whole of Christendom would have dared challenge.'

'But that is a horrible prospect!' Roberto protested. 'How can we stop this from happening?'

'And the worst of it is that Tristan is bound to take up their challenge. And with a sword in his left hand and no shield to protect him, he will end up being cut to pieces by some scoundrel who, in ordinary circumstances, would be unworthy to polish his boots.'

'We cannot allow this to happen!' the captain said, overwhelmed with outrage at the thought.

'We are not going to,' Marc said. 'Not if we work together this time.'

'But how can we prevent it?'

Marc paused for a moment, and saw that Isolt had taken hold of Tristan's forearm and was holding it tightly, as if to stop him from speaking. She noticed that Marc was looking at her, and the glance she threw back at him seemed a mixture of hostility and surrender.

'There is a merchant I met once or twice in Brittany who has a boat moored in Les Saintes Marie de la Mer,' Marc said. 'I happened to recognise him on our way over here and talked to him briefly that evening when we set up camp there...'

'I never noticed him,' Roberto interrupted.

'I think you must have all fallen asleep by the time he came over to our camp,' Marc explained. 'I know this must sound like a very strange coincidence to you, this man being there just at the very time we were passing through, but to say it happened any other way would be to tell a lie. In fact, I think now, in view of what happened to Tristan, that this man being there must have something to do with God's providence.

'Anyway, this merchant told me that he had delivered a shipment of silk to a merchant in Genoa. He would be spending a couple of weeks there while waiting for a delivery of flax that he was going to take back in his boat with him to sell in the East.

'I think we can easily persuade this man to take Tristan, Isolt and Kore with him. Isolt's father lives somewhere out in the East. He is a very rich man and will reward this merchant generously if he accepts. I think Tristan would be safe there, for he would benefit from the protection of a rich man's household.'

'But it was my understanding that we were to take Tristan and Isolt back to Rome,' the captain protested.

'That was part of my mission, but what is it going to look like now? Both Tristan and Isolt were supposed to come with us on their own initiative, moved by a desire to confess their sins and reintegrate themselves into the Christian faith. But, with Tristan's hand freshly cut off, it will seem like he has been forced into doing so. I think His Grace will understand and agree that it was better to let them both discreetly disappear out of sight. After all, the other part of our mission was to negotiate a peaceful surrender of the town of Penn with no reprisals, and, with Tristan and Isolt safely out of the way, I think we can say that this has been achieved.'

'I do wish I had been given more information,' Roberto repeated. 'It is hard to make a decision when you are not in full possession of all the facts.'

'The facts are pretty clear right now,' Marc said. 'If we take Tristan back to Rome, he will be placed under my protection once he has confessed to the Pope. But the truth is, I have no kingdom left in Brittany. I have no means of offering him any protection and we know what that would mean for him. So it's up to us to act now and follow our consciences, if we have enough courage to do so. For whatever we decide now we are going to have to live with for the rest of our lives.'

The captain sat on his horse with his head bent forward, his brow pushed down over his eyes in deep concentration.

'So what do you say, Captain?' Marc asked. His companion remained silent.

Marc took a deep breath and swallowed his pride. 'Tristan and my wife are deeply in love,' he continued. 'Everybody knows that. This is their only chance to live a decent life together. I know that I can explain this to Innocent III and that he will understand. After all, his main concern was not to have their love confused with, and assimilated into, the Cathar heresy and used as a symbol of nobility and high aspirations, which would have happened had they been slaughtered during the capture of Penn, or burnt at the stake afterwards. But the rumour of their having sailed off to the East will put a stop to all that. So, do you agree, Captain?'

Roberto straightened himself up in his saddle and looked directly at Marc.

'It seems we have no choice,' he replied. 'We have to get him onto that boat.' He turned to Tristan. 'Is this also what you wish?'

Tristan looked at Isolt, then turned back to the captain.

'Yes. I think that this would be the best outcome for everyone, all things considered.'

'Then this is what we shall do!' Captain Roberto said enthusiastically.

'I really do appreciate this,' Tristan said, catching Marc's eye as he spoke. Marc nodded back to him. Isolt didn't say anything but stared straight ahead at the shoreline stretching into the distance.

There was another pair of eyes staring at Marc, though. They belonged to Kore. When he saw her looking at him, he was for a brief instant caught in their interrogation. Who are you? she seemed to be asking through the black glare of her pupils. And, at that precise moment, he realised he had no answer to give her because he did not know himself.

*

By the middle of the day they had stopped, eaten and rested for a while, and were back on their horses, following the coastline, making their way along endless beaches. They rode on through pine forests, across salt marshes and along more stretches of beach, where the hoofs of their horses splashed in the wash of incoming waves.

As the evening approached, Isolt manoeuvred herself so that she was riding at Marc's side. Kore was sitting behind Tristan some distance ahead of them, while Captain Roberto was still further up the beach alongside one of his men.

'What's wrong with you?' she asked. 'You've been looking miserable all day, and yet you've managed to manipulate things so that you're going to get me out of your life once and for all. Why aren't you happy?'

'I don't think I can ever be happy again. The only time I was really happy was when we lived together on the moor.'

Isolt laughed. 'I did warn you then that I could only bring trouble into your life!'

Marc said nothing. It had been a beautiful clear day. The sun was setting and a carpet of red light covered the sea behind them. The sand, the riders, their horses and the pine trees further up the shore were all drowned in the pink evening light.

17

THE HOUSE IN THE HILLS

Marc felt a hand shaking his shoulder and opened his eyes. He recognised Isolt's face looking down at him through the veil of the moonlit night. She brought a finger up and touched her lips, then signalled to him to follow her. All the others were asleep, their bodies just shadows on the sandy grassland. Beyond them, further from the shore, were the row of horses stretched out like a line of ghosts.

As he followed Isolt down towards the sea he could not help feeling apprehensive. When they reached the water's edge she stopped, waited for him to come close to her and then took hold of his hand. Leaning up to him, she whispered into his ear.

'Don't ask any questions, just follow me.'

Marc looked at her eyes glowing in the moonlight and felt the warm grip of her hand. He took a step forward to move right up against her, but she raised her hand, placed it over his lips and gently pushed him away.

'No,' she said. 'Follow me.'

They walked for at least half an hour, their hurried steps

accompanied by the rhythmic sound of waves breaking gently onto the shore. All that time she said nothing, just held firmly to his hand until, finally, as if she felt she'd gone far enough, she stopped, let go of his hand, took a few steps away and stood in the wash of the waves, facing him.

'When Ogrin came to fetch me out of the convent,' she began, 'it was the nuns who told me that my father had come to take me away with him. But, once we were alone together, he said that he was not really my father, that my father was waiting for me in Constantinople, and that he was a friend of his who had come to Italy with a shipload of carpets and silk that he intended to sell in the markets of its wealthy towns.

'It was early spring. He told me that, by summer's end, he would be ready to go back home and that, if I was willing to help him out in the markets, he would take me back to Constantinople with him, where I could be with my father.'

Isolt sat down on the sand, just out of the reach of the waves. 'Sit down next to me,' she said.

He could now see her face close up to him, bathing in the soft light of the moon, and it seemed that the whole world had fallen into a deep sleep, drowned in a gentle state of forgetfulness brought on by the night. But not her eyes. They were burning with harsh memories, alive, awake and shining with the inner light of past events that could find no rest in her soul.

'I don't know if you can imagine what a change this brought about in my life. I mean, suddenly finding myself in the big, wide world outside that convent, the world I had dreamt about all those years I'd spent growing up, trapped between those walls. And now I was out there, working the markets with him.

'It was terrifying to see all those faces staring at me as I unrolled carpets and unfolded shawls, wearing a silk dress, a gold chain around my waist and with my hair tied back so that everyone could see my golden earrings. But then I saw how Ogrin never lost control of a situation, however large the crowd was. He could pick out, from amongst all those people, the one person who was really interested in buying a carpet. He would draw the crowd's attention away from me to that person by flattering his pride and his vanity, until he had no choice but to empty the contents of his purse into Ogrin's hands and walk away proudly with one of his carpets.'

Isolt paused for a moment, picked up a handful of sand and let it filter out through her fingers back onto the beach.

'He was the first person who ever told me I was beautiful,' she continued. 'I always thought that my dark skin and my dark eyes made me unattractive, but he convinced me that I was very special. He bought me the gold chain and the earrings and had several silk dresses made for me. He even adjusted some of them himself so that they fitted me perfectly.

'He taught me how to move and hold myself so that people could see my beauty. He told me that, up until then, I had done my best to hide it from everyone but that now it was time to let everyone see this beauty, and to make full use of it, because he had silk and carpets to sell, and it would help us sell them.

'I just couldn't believe what was happening to me, how my life had suddenly changed, how everything was so different all of a sudden, so exciting, and how happy I was. It was all thanks to him. At first, I just felt incredibly grateful. But then, as the weeks went by, I began to feel something growing inside me. It was strange. I think it started one morning in a market square as we were unpacking our wagon and placing the silks and the carpets on display. I was watching his hands, noticing how precise each of his gestures were, as he unfolded the shawls and arranged them on a table. It was a pleasure to look at him and it gave me a warm feeling in my chest. Then I'd get that feeling over and over again, when he'd look me in the eyes, when he'd say certain things to me, when he'd smile.'

Isolt picked up more sand and let it trickle through her fingers again.

'I was falling in love with him,' she said finally. 'One time, I was on my knees, bent over the stack of carpets with my face buried in my hands. My whole body was shaking with laughter at first, but then the laughter changed into tears and my chest heaved loud sobs, up through my throat, and I began to cry hysterically. Ogrin bent down and knelt beside me. I felt his hand stroke my head as he talked to me. He said he was sorry, that I should not pay attention to him when he got into one of his moods. That he meant no harm when he made fun of me, that sometimes he just couldn't stop himself. He said I should look the other way and wait for it to pass. He told me that it didn't mean anything, that one day he would explain it all to me.'

As Isolt told her story she had been looking out to sea, at the silver glow of the moon reflecting on the water. When she turned to look at him, Marc could see the same glow shining in her eyes.

'But that was not why I was crying, really,' she went on. 'It was because I loved him. I loved the way his hand was stroking my head, I loved his smell when I moved close to him, I loved his voice, I loved the things he said. I loved the way he would sometimes look into my eyes, as if he could see so much more of me than I was able to see myself.

'That's why I was crying, because I wanted him to do more than just stroke my head, and that frightened me. I knew nothing about what went on between a man and a woman when they lay together in bed. The only act of physical love I had witnessed was on the beach outside the convent in Rome. We had escaped for a walk one evening, and two young nuns who had been chasing and splashing one another along the shore were trying to push each other down onto the ground, when suddenly their lips came together and their arms wrapped around each other. It seemed to me, then, that they were trying to break through the outer crust of words, manners and rituals – which was all our lives consisted of inside the convent – to reach the much deeper, unspoken mystery of what drew one person to another, of what made them want to fuse into each other.

'And if that person already pleases your eyes, if her voice soothes your heart and you like what she does and what she says, then tasting her with your tongue is like putting her seal somewhere inside you and carrying it like a deeper memory that cannot be erased because it has imprinted itself in your flesh.'

Isolt looked up at the moon. The bright ball of light above her seemed only a pale reflection of what was now burning like a great fire in her soul.

'I think he knew all along what was going on,' she said. 'I had the strange sensation that he could read my thoughts. Often, I'd be sitting or standing staring into empty space and he'd say something that had a direct connection to what I was thinking. So he had to know what was going on in my heart.'

'So what happened?' Marc asked.

Isolt looked down at the waves breaking onto the shore, pushing white froth up onto the sand, just a little below her feet. She sighed. 'When summer was over, he told me that we were going to sail out to an island called Cyprus, where we would spend a few days before continuing our journey to Constantinople.

'When we reached the island, we moored our ship in the harbour of a town called Paphos. The first place he showed me in that town was a big palace in the middle of a beautiful walled-in garden. As we stared in at it through the bars of its gates, he told me that this was where he had spent his childhood. "Your parents must have been very rich and powerful," I said. He laughed and told me that his family did not own the palace, but that his father had worked there once. Then, all at once, he took hold of my shoulders and said, "Come, I'm going to take you somewhere far more interesting than this pretentious palace." We walked for over an hour, climbing through vineyards at first. Then, further up, we reached the pastures where sheep and goats grazed, watched by a young boy or girl. Then we reached a village, where an old man recognised Ogrin and called out his name. Soon a crowd of people had gathered around us and there was a lot of lively talk and excitement.

'At one point Ogrin pointed at me, said something and they all stared at me with wide-open eyes, nodded their heads and mumbled to each other. When I asked Ogrin what they were saying, he answered that they were overcome with how beautiful I was. He then told me that he had once lived up here for a while when he was a young man.

'When he had finished talking to the villagers, he told me that he was going to take me to the house where I was born, further up the hill, but that first he wanted to show me another place.

'So we left the village and walked up and along the edge of a steep drop that descended precipitously towards a dried-out riverbed. There was something foreboding and uncomfortable about the path we were following that went beyond the danger of the drop. It had something to do with the way the villagers had stared at me, and the fact that he was suddenly going to show me the house where I was born, here on this island.

'I had tried to ask him about my father on several occasions, but he had always been vague in his answers and had quickly steered the conversation onto another subject. I had the feeling that he was now taking me somewhere to make some unpleasant revelation to me. After walking for about an hour along this narrow path, we reached its summit and sat down to admire the view. Far below us we could see Paphos and the harbour where our ship was moored, and beyond it the sea.

There was a strong wind blowing patches of white froth off the top of the waves.

'Ogrin began talking to me. He told me about Melissa, a shepherdess who had slipped off this very ledge as a young child and had broken many of her bones against the boulders in the riverbed. He told me how he had fallen in love with her when she was a young woman, had married her and lived up here in the hills with her until she'd died giving birth to their child.'

Isolt stopped talking and looked at Marc for a moment.

'I was gazing at the sea when he was telling me all this,' she continued. 'On a windy day, the shepherds in those hills say there are white sheep on the sea. As I listened to him, I felt that the dream that was holding me together was being blown away with those white sheep and would vanish along with them over the horizon.

'He finished his story by saying that the baby girl's name was Isolt and that he had brought me up onto this cliff so that Melissa's spirit might see what a beautiful woman I had turned into. When I heard this, I buried my face in my hands and began to sob uncontrollably.

'When he saw that I was crying, he placed his hand on my shoulder, apologised and said that he'd wanted to have time for us to get to know each other before he told me that he was my father, so that I would not judge him right away for having abandoned me in the convent when I was just a baby.

'I don't know if he was telling me the truth or not. I'll never know why he did what he did. Perhaps his intention was a lot more sinister than he'd led me to believe. I don't know. I felt deeply humiliated and crushed. Yet, when I listened to him, I couldn't help but feel sorry for him, for this should have been a happy moment, but it wasn't.'

Isolt paused for a moment and stared out at the night clouds floating over the sea. There was a slight chill in the air now and Marc thought he saw her shiver, and then she went on.

'Before this happened, when we were travelling through Italy, we would mostly spend the night in an inn and we would share the same room. He would let me have the bed and would sleep on the carpet with a blanket and a pillow. As we lay waiting to fall asleep, after he had blown out the candle, it seemed to me that the silence in the room was weighed down by our unavowed desire for each other.

'He would sometimes treat me like a little girl because he knew it annoyed me, and yet I could see in his eyes the same glare when he looked at me as I could see in the eyes of the men who stared at me in the markets. I was waiting for him to do something about it, but of course he didn't. The reason for this, I thought, was that he was a friend of my father and did not want to dishonour that friendship by behaving indecently towards his daughter. And this reserve on his part only made my love for him grow deeper. But it was not the love of a daughter for her father, but the love of a woman for a man.

'And now he had decided to put a stop to it by telling me the truth. Perhaps it was a last desperate attempt to save his soul from eternal damnation. Once again, I don't know. All I knew was that my own soul was already in the hands of the Devil. As far as I was concerned, it was already too late. The kind of love I felt for him had grown and sunk its roots deep into me by then, and you could not just tear it out and put something else in its place without causing great damage.'

'What did you do?' asked Marc, suddenly uncomfortable about what was about to follow.

'That night there was a feast,' she said, staring up at the moon, as if she wished to place the events she was about to describe as far away from her as she could. 'It seemed like the whole village had moved up to the meadow in front of the broken-down house where I was born. They brought food and drink with them and built a fire to roast the meat, around which we all sat, ate and drank.

'And then some of the men picked up their instruments, and once they had warmed up they broke into a fast tempo, and people stood up in a circle linked together by the shoulders, their legs kicking outwards as they moved around the fire. They danced like this to several different melodies, urged on by the clapping, the laughter and the whistles and jeers from the women and older men who sat watching them. And then finally, when the musicians took a break and the laughter lessened and they had all drunk more, a young girl got up and some of the musicians picked up their instruments again to accompany her song.

'She had a beautiful clear voice that resounded into the night as the dancing flames of the fire and the half moon shining down on her lit up her face. Her song released me from my sadness, from the chains that Ogrin's confession had fastened around my heart, and I suddenly stood up too and, as if I were no longer bound inside my body, I watched myself walk over to where he was sitting. I don't know what came over me but I was dancing suddenly, watching my body perform the steps of the courtly dance that a nun who came from an aristocratic family had taught me in one of our secret escapades from the convent.

'All eyes were on me now as I mimicked the gestures of a young aristocratic lady being courted by her suitor. But it was to Ogrin sitting there staring up at me that I was addressing these moves. When the music stopped, when the song was over, I stood staring down at him. I could hear the whistles and the laughter, coming mostly from the men who had been dancing around the fire, and he just looked up at me, his face as still as the moon shining down on him.

'I turned away from him and started walking towards the old broken-down house, the silhouette of which was outlined in the night by the moon. I stepped in through the open doorway. It was dark inside but, at the far end of the room, the roof had caved in and the light of the half moon shone in through a gaping hole. I could see a stone sink against the wall in the shadows, and an old wooden bed. That's where my mother must have died, I thought, and where, in that last moment of her life, I had broken through into this world.

'I walked over some broken tiles, stepped over a fallen beam, and reached the far wall. I leant my back against it, looked up at the sky, at the moon, and then closed my eyes.'

Isolt fell silent. She buried her face in her hands for a moment. 'I don't think I can go on with this.'

'Of course you can,' Marc said. 'You can't stop now.'

'Well, there I was with my back against the wall, waiting for him to step through the doorway. The musicians had just started playing again when I saw his shadow. He was no more than a dark silhouette hesitating in the doorway, but I knew it was him. I knew he wanted me as much as I wanted him.

'I don't know how I had that kind of lucidity, but it was there, like a bright light shining in the dark, absorbing my soul. A light without warmth, like the glow of the moon falling onto my face from the hole in the roof. I wanted the warmth of his body. I wanted to feel the torment of his love.

'He stood there without moving for a while, perhaps absorbed by the memories hiding in the shadows of that room. Then, as if he had just noticed me, he called my name. He started crossing the room, over to the wall where I was leaning. When he stood facing me, I lifted up my hand and gently caressed his cheek. He took hold of my hand, held it there against his face and rubbed the fingers of his other hand over my lips. "Isolt!" he whispered.

'I took a step forward, my body pressed against him. I wrapped my arm around his back, my lips touched his mouth, my tongue moistened his lips and I tasted the wine that lingered on his teeth. I felt myself drown in the pleasure of that moment and thought that I would live forever in that night, in its cold light, in the fire it sent racing through my limbs.

'He shouted out and pushed me violently away from him. My back hit the wall behind me. He looked at me with his fierce, piercing eyes, then spat on the floor and rubbed his mouth with his hand. "It's wrong!" he said. "Don't you see that it's wrong? Did they teach you nothing in that convent?"

'I was staring at him, finding it hard to breathe, partly because of the shock of my back hitting the wall, and partly because I felt I had been pushed into a world where there was no air to breathe, just empty space and, around that empty space, a great big fire.

'I must have got past him somehow. I must have walked out through the doorway into the meadow. I have a vague memory of seeing the fire again and of people dancing, and then it was just the night and the cold light of the moon as I ran up the hill. I think, once or twice, I turned around and saw his dark silhouette following me and then everything became a blank...'

'I fell off that cliff,' she said after a while. 'The same one my mother fell from. By some miracle I didn't really hurt myself, but I managed to convince myself that he had pushed me. I can see that more clearly now. I suppose he was only running after me because he wanted to talk to me, but I didn't want to hear his voice, or ever look at him again...'

They sat in silence for a while, listening to the rise and fall of the surf.

'So, are you happy?' Isolt asked after a long silence.

'Happy is hardly the word,' replied Marc.

She had removed the last veil behind which she had been hiding for all these years and, in the cold light of the moon, he realised that what she had told him a few nights ago in the darkness of the forest was true. He had never possessed her. She had always managed to keep herself at a safe distance from him, despite him being the father of her child, despite being her husband. She had never let him overwhelm her. She had never fully let go of herself in his arms. She was saving this privilege for someone else, for Tristan, for she knew that he would show up one day. Whereas he, Marc, knew that he had been totally possessed by her, that he had lost himself in her eyes, in her smile, in her arms, her smell, her voice, her breath, in her body.

Just as she had been possessed by her father, by what he had taught her, by the complicity that had slowly developed between them as they played the markets throughout Italy that summer, entertaining the crowds that would gather around them, creating laughter as they rolled out their carpets for display. Yes, she had been possessed by this man and wanted to lose herself in him, but she could not because he was her father.

And it was in the aftermath of that terrible night in the hills in Cyprus that she met me! Marc thought. She must have known from the start that she could never really lose herself in someone like me. She must have known this in her dreams, just as she must have known that, one day, someone more like her father would walk into her life.

And that someone had turned out to be Tristan.

Had he not seen that same complicity between them when, dressed up as a leper, Tristan carried her on his back across the Mal Pas? Were she and Tristan not playing to the crowd, just as she had done before with her father in the markets?

So this was it. This was the naked truth he had been running away from for so long. This was what he could not face.

'Marc!' Isolt's voice broke the silence that had settled between them. 'Come and sit closer to me.'

18

HECTOR'S SONG

Some of the guards were sitting under a tree at the top of the beach, while the others had accompanied Captain Roberto to the village to purchase supplies. The boat that was to sail to the East was tied to the wooden pier. Half a dozen men were carrying sacks of flax down the beach and dumping them into the boat, where Tristan and another man were packing them tightly together.

Children stood with their feet in the water, watching the activity. They laughed and shouted at the men and occasionally pushed and splashed each other as they squabbled amongst themselves.

Kore was standing a little distance apart, watching them.

'Tristan has not yet accepted the loss of his hand,' Ogrin said.

'What makes you say that?' Isolt asked. She was sitting on the sand next to Marc and her father.

'He feels the need to prove that he still can be of some use,' Ogrin answered.

'I think it is all the more to his credit that he has not given up,' Isolt said aggressively. Both she and her father seemed tense. But Ogrin especially was not himself. At first, Marc thought that it must be because her father was eager to sail away from this place, taking the three of them with him and leaving Marc behind. But he was the one who had suggested that they sit on the beach and wait while the hired men packed the boat.

No, he realised; what was really bothering Ogrin was Isolt.

'He knows,' Marc said to himself, and he too felt the tension, the ripples of her body shaking inside him, testing his resolve. How was he going to let her go? How was he going to stand on that pier and just wave to her as the boat sailed away from this beach? Ogrin could see the echo of this question stirring up those ripples in Marc's eyes.

Marc could still smell her body, the scent of the love they had made together lingering inside him; he could feel it sticking to him, mixed with sweat and sand and the salt of the sea as she spoke.

Yet, last night, he had felt he could accept anything. He had felt strong, felt that he had been lifted to a place where he had become another person. They had been honest with each other last night; neither of them hiding anything from the other any longer. And this had brought them closer together. But the moment was gone when he woke up in the morning. He was trapped once again in time, by the forthcoming departure of the ship that would take her away from him. He had woken up alone; she had gone to lie beside Tristan when they had crept back to the encampment. How was he going to let go of her? How was he going to say goodbye to her now?

'I quite agree,' Ogrin was saying to Isolt, 'and it is to his credit that he hasn't given up. But there are far better ways he can be of use. In fact, I have great plans for him, once you are comfortably settled in Constantinople.'

'And what would these plans be?' Isolt asked.

Ogrin let out a deep breath before replying. 'I have done some trading in Egypt and Arabia,' he said, 'and have seen what fine horses they have down there. I also know that Tristan knows a lot about horses, since he has been riding them for most of his life. I would be very interested in returning, especially to Arabia, to purchase some of their finest specimens and ship them back to Italy, where I'm sure they would sell for a handsome price. But to do this, I would need Tristan's help.'

'I'm sure he could be a great help if you could persuade him to go there with you,' replied Isolt. 'But that may not be so easy. All he seems to talk about right now is how, in a year's time, he will be as able with a sword in his left hand as he once was when he held it in his right hand.'

'That's because he has not yet understood that he can use his skills in other places than on a battlefield,' Ogrin said.

'He has been a soldier for so long. He has no equal on a battlefield. How can that kind of skill be used to choose a horse?' Isolt asked.

Ogrin sighed. 'When you are engaged in a physical battle with another man, the more you are able to sense and understand about that man, whether he is stupid or very cunning, frightened or fearless, bold or cautious, the better are your chances of defeating him. And, on top of that, when that man you are fighting is sitting on a horse, the more you are able to sense in the same way about his horse, the more you will have increased your chances of victory over him.'

'I don't see how,' Isolt said.

'Because sometimes, in the heat of battle, a man may lose his sense of initiative and, without knowing it, find himself following the impulses of his horse.'

Ogrin burst out laughing. Isolt just stared at him without saying anything, and then twisted around to look at Tristan.

She still loves him, Marc thought.

370

Three of the men who had been carrying the sacks were now standing on the pier looking down into the boat. They seemed to be deep in discussion, probably on how to best place the sacks, of which there were still a considerable number up on the beach.

Seeing the pain in Marc's face, Ogrin asked him, 'What about you, Marc? Are you planning to return to Brittany?'

The question caused a strange feeling in Marc's heart. It was as if he could see himself sitting on that beach, looking at the boat that was going to sail away with the woman who, the night before, had shaken any possible reproach, any resistance to who she was, to what she had done, out of his soul like a storm ridding a tree of its overripe fruit, but he could not reconcile this feeling with the knowledge that he was about to lose her forever once she stepped into that boat.

'Your problem is that you don't realise that you are not just the person witnessing these events but in a larger sense you are part of the fire through which they are able to manifest themselves,' Ogrin said. 'If you could understand this then you would not see yourself as such a victim all the time.'

Marc was anxiously watching the activity in the boat.

'Did you ever question why Tristan suddenly appeared in your lives? Not the visible sequence of events that brought him into the forest in Brittany where you first met him. I'm asking you about the initial impulse that pushed him into finding you both. Do you know what that was?' Ogrin asked.

'No,' Marc answered despairingly.

'It was the kiss that happened in that old broken-down house up in the hills behind Paphos. I'm sure my daughter must have told you about that kiss by now.'

'Not willingly,' Isolt retorted. 'He had to coax that out of me, for it has been a curse on my life.'

'You should not say that, because that kiss gave birth to Tristan. That kiss was the cause of it all. It was that kiss that brought this myth down here to be re-enacted once more in our world, so that, through your flesh, the spirit could continue entering into matter. It is that spirit that is moving through each of our lives.'

'But what for?' Isolt asked, aghast.

'To be able to understand why we have first to lift our lives onto a higher level,' Ogrin said.

'What level?' Isolt asked.

'The level of life exemplified by the myths.'

Marc's face turned red with exasperation and anger. 'The way you tell it, you make this kiss sound very pretty, beautiful and poetic even. In your eyes maybe, but not in mine! Quite to the contrary: from my point of view that kiss and the so-called myth it called down into this world has brought nothing but pain and ugliness into my life!'

Ogrin shook his head despairingly. 'Do you remember, that night after the duel, when you woke up back at the castle and found yourself alone? Do you remember that moment when you walked over to your bedroom window and saw her down there in the courtyard, lit up by the moon as she stood facing Tristan, right up against him? Do you remember your disbelief, how you were stricken with panic, how your mind was drowning in a sea of horror as you felt your world collapse inside you, your body paralysed with pain as you watched her slowly raising and dropping her hands to emphasise her love for him, so close together that their bodies were nearly touching?'

'How do you know all this?' Isolt asked in disbelief, yet unable to hide her admiration for her father.

'This is not your problem,' Ogrin answered. Looking back at Marc, he asked: 'What was life trying to do to you, bringing you to that window so that you could watch them confessing their love for one another? Life in its entirety, in all its multiple forms taken as a single entity, a being, a god. What was this god doing bringing you to that window so you could watch them?'

Unable to answer, Marc turned away to watch the children on the shoreline who had formed a circle holding each other's hands and were screaming with delight and laughing as they splashed each other. A boy broke free from the circle and walked over to Kore, who was standing, her feet in the water, looking at them. He took hold of her hand and led her over to the circle where, after initial hesitation, she was soon laughing and splashing with the others.

'Life had called you over there so you could take part in its banquet', Ogrin said. 'This god was offering you a seat at his table so that you could stare at your destiny right then, at the person you really are. That person that she was betraying down there in the courtyard.'

Isolt looked at her father. She seemed for a moment to be shaking, as if she were about to lose control of herself, but the beauty and the pride in her face didn't let this happen. She just coughed, cleared her throat and stared back at her father.

'That kiss happened because you lied to me,' she said without taking her eyes off him.

'And it was that kiss that brought Tristan into your life,' Ogrin replied, holding her gaze.

'I don't see how,' Isolt said.

Ogrin continued looking at her and it was as if she could feel the weight of his stare penetrating into her chest.

'Try to understand that everything in this world is caught up in this struggle between two opposing forces, one of which is pushing us further and further away from where we come from, and another that is pulling us back into the mystery out of which we emerged into this world. All myths are an attempt to resolve this struggle, so that on the battlefield the sight of clashing bodies may be turned into a dance, a celebration of life, so that we may discover how close we are in our pain, in our tragedy, to this celebration, to this dance.

'Do you remember when I explained to you how all myths took shape in the vortex caused by the storms blowing up there in the heavens, where the three basic impulses, the affirming, the denying and the reconciling, fashion all things into what they are in this world, as they twirl around and around each other in a frantic dance? Do you remember this?'

Marc did not answer.

'You should not have run away from what you saw in the courtyard as you stood by your bedroom window staring down at them. You should have stayed and faced what was happening down there.'

'Why should I have stayed and faced it?' Marc asked.

'Because if you had done that, you could have seen who you really are, and finally stepped into the myth belonging to the time and the place of your birth. But you could not face the pain that this moment would cost you. It's a shame, because if you could have faced the pain of walking into that fire instead of running away from it, you would have been taking a step towards inhabiting this myth, which is what your heart wants you to do. But you have never listened to your heart.'

'My heart wants Isolt,' Marc said.

'No!' Ogrin retorted. 'It's your body backed up by your mind that wants her. Your heart wants something much bigger and harder to achieve than keeping Isolt imprisoned in your castle.'

'And what would that be?'

Ogrin looked over at the children laughing by the shoreline, then at the boat moored beside the pier and beyond at the horizon where the sea melted into the sky.

'Only an overwhelming sense of the beauty of their two bodies under the moonlight and your own reflection in the glass of the window through which you were watching them

374

coming together in your heart could have done this. Only some emotion inside you that would have lifted you into a higher state of being could have intervened to keep you there, to stop you from running away.

'She had reached a part of herself that she had kept hidden inside after that terrible mistake she made in the broken-down house up in the hills behind Paphos when she tried to seduce me, her father, before she met you. And gave herself to you, because you seemed safe, someone who would keep her from opening those doors ever again.'

Ogrin stopped for a moment, then said with regret, 'But things didn't turn out that way.'

'Why?' Marc asked.

'Because you didn't give them a chance to do so, because you panicked and ran away from that window, because you weren't brave enough to step out of yourself and see the beauty of that moment which could have opened your heart so that its desires, carried by that sense of beauty, could have become the desires of your mind.'

Isolt was looking at Marc as he listened to her father, and she saw that he seemed to have the same glow in his eyes that had struck her when she first met him, selling her shawls in the market square in Brittany. That glow had long since disappeared and she had forgotten all about it. But now, as she looked at him, she felt a sudden sadness.

'Why don't you leave him alone?' she said to her father. 'It's hard enough for him to have to be separated from his daughter, so why don't you just leave him be?'

'I'm trying to prevent him from sinking back into that state of despair he carries with him. I'm trying to help him. Don't you see?' Ogrin answered.

'Yes,' Isolt said, 'but all this talk about myth and destiny must be confusing him, because it is certainly confusing me.'

'There is nothing confusing about myths,' Ogrin replied. 'Myths are what can save you from all the confusion that has poisoned our world since the advent of The City of God.'

'Myths are tragic and paint a very sad picture of life,' Isolt said.

'No, myths are a celebration of life, of the sacrifice it demands from us if we really want to be alive and possess a soul. That's the tragedy that is celebrated in all the great myths, the beauty and magnificence of possessing a soul that can only be bought with suffering and pain. This is the real meaning of tragedy.

'This is the truth you have to carry inside you because, without this truth, nothing you say or do will make any real sense. And this truth must come to you through your heart to carry any real weight and not be just speculation elaborated in your mind.'

A faint burst of laughter drifted over the sand. Ogrin rose quickly to his feet and looked towards the village.

'Ah! At last,' he exclaimed. 'I had better go and see if Tristan is ready to leave. That Roberto fellow is on his way back and I don't want to hang around here any longer.'

As Ogrin turned and started walking to the pier, Marc looked towards the village. In the distance he could see Captain Roberto and some of the guards crossing the meadow and heading in their direction.

Down in the boat, it was clear that Tristan had also noticed that the Vatican guards were on their way back. He turned towards the beach and shouted to Kore, who was still playing in the water with the other children. Isolt stood up and grabbed Marc's hand, then stood facing him and looking straight into his eyes so that she blotted out everything else that was happening around them.

'Come with us, Marc! Come with me! I don't think I will be able to stand it if you don't.'

Kore was running up the beach. 'Mama!' she shouted as she came closer. 'Tristan says we have to get into the boat.' She stopped by her mother and looked at the two hands that were locked together.

'Mama!' she repeated with emphasis, taking hold of Isolt's other hand and pulling it. 'Mama, come!' she said.

Marc felt the tension in her hand relax as Isolt slowly pulled it away from him. He felt the rub of her skin as it slipped through his grip. She was watching him closely. He looked away and saw that Kore was also staring at him. It was the wide-open stare of a child about to become a woman. There was wonder and curiosity in her eyes.

He looked back at Isolt.

'I don't want to get onto that boat without you,' she said.

'You won't be alone. You will have Tristan at your side.'

'What good will that do? I know Tristan. He is his own man and I love him for that. But he won't stand between me and my father.'

'And I would?' Marc asked.

She did not answer.

The voices of the men on their way across the salt marsh grew louder. And then those voices were drowned out by the clang of a bell. Far away in the distance Marc could see the bells swinging at the top of the flat tower that reached up out of the village like a giant hand pointing to the heavens. Perhaps they were ringing in celebration of a wedding, he thought, which carried him back to the delights of her body. And now she seemed to be promising more of that to come his way if he stepped into that boat with her!

'Are you going to just stand there or are you getting into the boat with us?' she asked.

He held on to her, aware of her extraordinary beauty as she stood with the blue glow of the sea behind her, and her beauty drifted into him and brought with it its unbearable pain, the paralysing pain that had penetrated too far into him, and he was unable to let go of her now. But through the corner of his eye he could see Kore looking at him and was touched by some deep recognition, as if he had suddenly awakened to the full weight of the fact that she was his daughter, and into the urgency of that moment the thought arose in his mind that he had never had the chance to show her any part of himself that was real and straightforward.

So he let go of her mother's hand…

For a moment Isolt just stared down at it, shaking her head slightly, and then she looked up at him and smiled. And, without saying anything, she turned away from him as if she was performing a pirouette in a courtly dance. She pulled Kore by the arm and walked towards the pier with their daughter tripping behind her, turning several times to stare back at him with bewildered eyes.

The bells kept on ringing, their notes sometimes clashing into each other in their rush towards the sea. He could not help admiring her strength, the way she had pirouetted away from him with a smile, not needing words, not seeking comfort in them, as he watched her now, moving further and further away.

Before stepping up onto the pier, she stopped and looked back at him, turned around, lifted her hand and touched her lips, as Kore gave him a timid wave.

Tristan climbed out of the boat and went over to meet Captain Roberto, placing his hand on the captain's shoulder as they talked. Isolt and Kore had stepped up onto the pier and were now walking over to join them. The captain bent over Kore and said a few words to her. She listened and nodded once or twice, but her eyes were focused straight ahead of her. Marc could not tell if she was watching the children playing in the water or if she was looking at him.

The captain kissed her, then Isolt took hold of Kore's hand. With Tristan at her side, they walked over to the boat, where Ogrin was sitting waiting for them. They climbed aboard and joined him.

A man on the pier untied the ropes as Marc watched, spellbound. Two men were pushing the boat away from the pier with long poles. A rusty red sail was hoisted up the mast and immediately caught the wind, blowing down from the north and still carrying the sound of the bells, whose echo he could feel in his chest. The sail swelled, pulling the boat away from the pier and out to sea. Marc's heart swelled like the sail on the mast.

'This can't be,' he said to himself.

He was still standing on the beach staring out to sea when Captain Roberto and the guards began to round up the horses and pack them with supplies they had purchased in the village. The boat was now barely visible as it moved south-eastwards over the great expanse of water. It was no more than a dot moving in and out of the haze caused by the bright midday sun. Finally, it vanished into the glare and did not reappear.

'Isolt!' Marc whispered.

19

AMOR FATI

When Marc returned to Rome, he found himself again, early one afternoon, standing before Innocent III as he sat behind his desk in his private quarters scrutinising him.

Marc had told him everything, held nothing back, made no attempt to excuse his actions or justify his behaviour, and taken full responsibility for everything that had happened both in Aquitaine and on the beach outside Les Saintes Marie de la Mer. The only thing he left out of his account was the night he spent in Isolt's arms.

When he had finished his story, after a long silence the Pope finally spoke. 'Before you set off on this mission, I judged you to be an intelligent human being with a strong conscience,' he said. 'I had my doubts about you at first, but you impressed me with your unorthodox interpretation of the fresco in our church, and by the awareness you expressed of the painful innate contradiction that lay behind the concept of launching a crusade against the Cathars.

'But it seems I was wrong. I can see now quite clearly that

you are just a fool. Perhaps I was touched by your concern for the well-being of your wife and child, by the fact that you were blindly clinging to your loyalty towards your wife despite her outrageous behaviour. Perhaps this is what really impressed me, against my better judgement, though it is hard and painful for me to admit.

'Because of you this mission has been a total waste of time, effort and expense. You have told me nothing positive that could remotely justify the endeavour you persuaded me to support with my blessing. What have you to say? Have you not at least learnt something from this disaster?'

Marc hesitated for a moment. He felt trapped between the barren walls of the room, which offered his eyes no paintings, no images to awaken his imagination.

'I am sure,' he said finally, 'that if it is even considered worthy of mention in the annals recounting the crusade, mounted by lords and knights from so many different lands, to eradicate the heresy and protect the purity and sanctity of our faith, this expedition of ours will be just a minor incident in the telling of this great story. But was it really a waste of time?'

Marc took a deep breath and then continued with profound conviction. 'I could have got into that boat and sailed away with them. But something told me that she didn't really want me to, that in some strange way what she really wanted was for me to show her who I was right then.

'But as I looked at her I could see a fire, and it pained me that this fire was there in her eyes and not in mine, for she had done what I had been unable to do. She had given her life, her breath, her flesh, to the desire she carried in her heart.'

The Pope stared at him with eyes that betrayed nothing of what he was feeling, as though, if he really wanted to hear what Marc had to say, he had to place himself outside the wall surrounding the dogma, the parables, the proverbs and the gospels on which his faith had placed a throne for him to sit on.

And strangely enough it seemed he did want to hear him out, as if the tale Marc had to tell might bring some fresh air into his city.

'Go on, finish what you have started,' Innocent said.

Marc took a step forward into the room as if to get closer to what he was trying to remember.

'There were bells ringing in the village and there was a dog barking at some children who were playing with their feet in the water, down by the shore. And suddenly all I wanted was the truth. The truth I was running away from, the truth I thought I didn't want to hear until this moment when something shifted inside me and I realised that this truth was what my heart had been searching for all along.

'The truth which said that I had never managed to ignite a passion in her heart, the passion she had felt for her father, who she was running away from when we met, the passion that she could not transfer onto me but that was reawakened when she met Tristan.

'I had suspected this for a long time, since that moment when, after her love affair, she returned to the castle and reappeared in our bedroom to resume her life at my side. I suppose I'd seen this in her eyes on odd occasions when her pupils would dart away from me like rabbits disappearing into their warren. But I can see now it was me, my refusal to face the truth, my fear that it would annihilate me, that chased those rabbits away.

'And now, suddenly, as I held on to her fingers while we stood staring at each other on that beach, the promise of her body, of her warmth, of her laughter, stood in contrast to the humiliation I would have to suffer over and over again if I boarded that boat with her. And so I let go of her hand.'

Marc and Innocent III stared at each other for a moment until the Pope let out a sigh. 'So what? Do you think that you have saved your soul by letting go of her? But what about the commitment you made to bring her back to Rome? What about the commitment I made when I was ordained to sit on the throne of the Church of Rome to give my life up to the defence of the integrity of our faith, which she has slandered with her outrageous behaviour? What have you got to say about that?'

When Marc did not answer, he added, in a softer voice, 'Tell me how saving your soul helps the bigger picture of our Church's interest?'

Marc thought about this for a moment. 'As I looked at her I could feel that something was changing inside me, as if her beauty was escaping from my eyes and moving to some other place, leaving her looking quite ordinary now as she stood on that beach, and no sooner had I questioned where that beauty had escaped to than I realised I was standing in another world where I could see through my heart, and I finally understood that it was out of that ordinariness that her beauty had grown, and that it was the soil that had nourished her defiance and audacity, that had set fire to her face, when I first looked at her in the market square in Brittany.

'All this came to me in a flash as I opened my hand to let go of her, and I had an overwhelming feeling of awe as I watched her walk away from me, as if I was witnessing the waters of the Red Sea being parted so that she, accompanied by our daughter, could join the man she really loved and sail together to their own Jerusalem hidden somewhere behind the horizon.

'And if there was any moment in my life that I would want to live over and over again it would be that moment when I watched her walk away from me, for she was repeating what she had already done when she ran away with Tristan. But this time my heart was able to rid this moment of all its tragedy and pain and fill it with awe and amazement, the awe and amazement of being.'

There was a long silence. Marc could sense a quiet battle going on behind the eyes that were appraising him, and then, as he had done once before, when Marc had been brought before him for the first time, the Pope surprised him.

'Go!' he shouted. 'Get out of here! Don't say another word and never let me see or hear of you again or you will be sorry, very sorry! Now just go!'

20

THE KINGDOM

When I walked out into the square outside the Pope's palace, I was stopped momentarily by the glare of the mid-afternoon sun. I seemed suddenly lost in a sea of moving shadows. And then, as I managed to focus properly, I could see the people, swerving around each other, coming from all directions on their way across the square. Most of them seemed to have somewhere to go and they all seemed to be guided by some kind of objective, which, for better or worse, would carry them through the day.

But where was I going? I wondered, in a sudden state of panic. All I could feel inside me was emptiness and apprehension as I watched all those faces. What was I going to do? How was I going to survive?

And then I saw her face! Our eyes met, and then she turned away, for she too seemed to know where she was going, and she continued in that direction.

She was wearing a golden shawl over her hair and a red silk dress like the one she wore in the market square in Brittany on that first day.

I watched the golden shawl bobbing up and down through the crowd as she walked away from me and saw her disappear down a narrow lane at the far end of the square. I was once again in a daze and unable to move.

And then, suddenly, I was rushing after her, dodging my way through the people. I couldn't believe it! How was this possible? Could they have reached Rome before us, and had they stopped here for supplies before continuing to Constantinople?

I reached the narrow lane. It was dark and deserted. All the houses, on both sides, were backed against it. There were no windows, no doors, no balconies. And then I saw her, just a shadow moving far ahead of me. I began to run.

At some point, as I got close to her, she turned and saw me running after her and started to run as well, but I was faster than her and managed to catch up and tap her on the shoulder.

'Isolt!' I shouted.

It was a joyful cry and she must have heard the happiness in my voice.

She stopped and looked at me, and at that moment I was caught between the joy and anticipation, burning like a fire inside me, of looking once again into her eyes, and the heart-wrenching disappointment of seeing that it wasn't really her.

But the shock provoked by these two events, about to collide together, was something that illuminated me from inside. I smiled at her.

'Who are you?' the girl asked, reassured, if still a bit frightened.

'I am Marc, a king on his way back home to his kingdom,' I said.

'And where is this kingdom?' she asked.

I realised then that my kingdom was in that instant when I saw that she was not Isolt, before my disappointment could reach into me. That became my kingdom.

I was about to answer when I heard the clapping sound of a pigeon's wings, looked up and saw it fly off the roof above us, and through the glare of the sun I thought I saw a burning twig held in its beak. Perhaps she thought I was answering her question when I pointed to that pigeon escaping into the sky, and she laughed. And the sound of her laughter brought back something Isolt said to me many years ago. 'If you can make a woman laugh you already have one foot through the door leading to her heart.'

Acknowledgements

I wish to thank with all my heart…

My mother Oona O'Neill Chaplin for passing onto me her love of literature

My children Christian, Tim, Dolores, Carmen, Kathleen, Tracy, and George

My grandchildren Junaiy, James, Lily, Akilles, Uma, Jayden, Helio, Shania, Alma, Liam, Eden, Orlando and anymore still to enter this world

My sisters Geraldine and Victoria for their generosity when my health was at stake

My daughter Dolores and Stany Coppet for keeping me alive in Toulouse

Ashim Bhalla for all the time and energy invested in giving this story a chance to make it out into the world

Françoise Betaudier and Jorge Mendy Montagne for helping me in the tumultuous transition from typewriter to computer

Tew Bunnag, my brother-in-arms, for the shared journeys into other realms

Henrik Hirsch for telling me "Michael you've got to put yourself on the page" – Henrik, I finally did it

Gideon Jaglom for the many long walks through London at night

Alphonse Rivier for pointing me to Denis de Rougemont's *Love and the West*

James Thackera for making me realise that film scripts are not literature (at least not the ones I wrote)

Gottfried Wagner for saying of his great grandfather's *Tristan und Isolde* – "I wish he'd written more operas like that one"

Gerald Martin for the beautiful endorsement of my writing

Copy Editor Ian Howe for improving the text without changing my voice

Patrice Chaplin, Patricia Scanlan and Michael Soussan for all the advice and editorial work

Michael Arditti for reading my manuscript and for the encouragement

Michael John Carson for supporting the publication of this book

Chloe May, Fern Bushnell, Daniel Burchmore, Editor Hannah McCall, Proofreader Lauren Stenning, Cover Designer Chelsea Taylor and everyone in The Book Guild production team

Fiona Marsh for recommending the novel to The Book Guild and MIDAS for the book PR campaign

The Literary Consultancy, Cassandra Clarke and Paul Cooper for the invaluable feedback on my manuscript

George Gurdjieff for opening up a whole new vista on life

And to The Troubadours who sang the songs of Tristan & Isolde.